Princess

RAVEN
THE PIRATE PRINCESS

Year Three: Monsters of the Deep

Chapter Five: A New Heading

Written By: Jeremy Whitley

Pencils By: Telênia Albuquerque

Inks By: Pocket Owl

Colors By: Lexillo

Lettered By: Alex Scherkenbach

Edited By: Nicole D'Andria

Cover By: Telênia Albuquerque

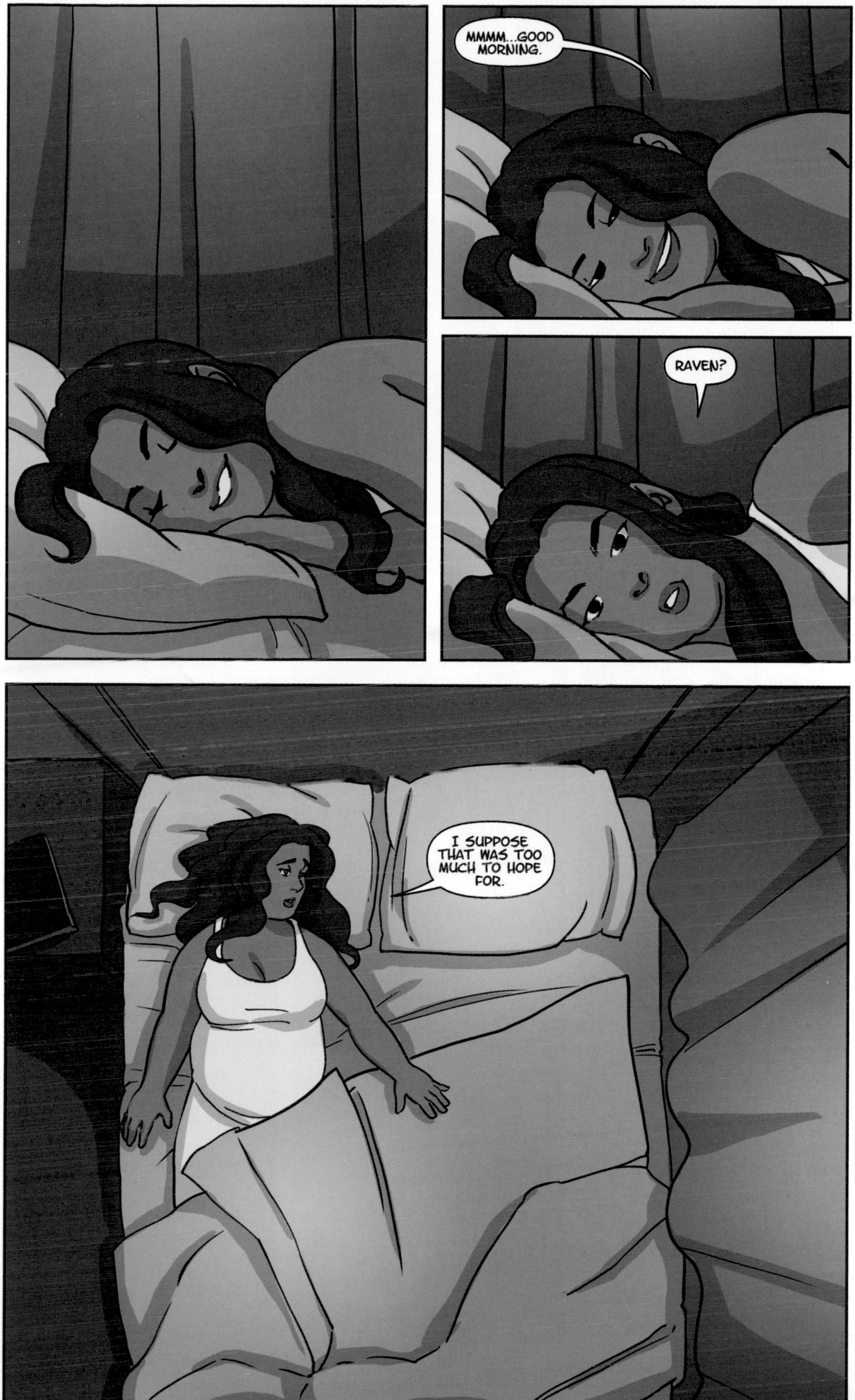
MMMM...GOOD MORNING.
RAVEN?
I SUPPOSE THAT WAS TOO MUCH TO HOPE FOR.

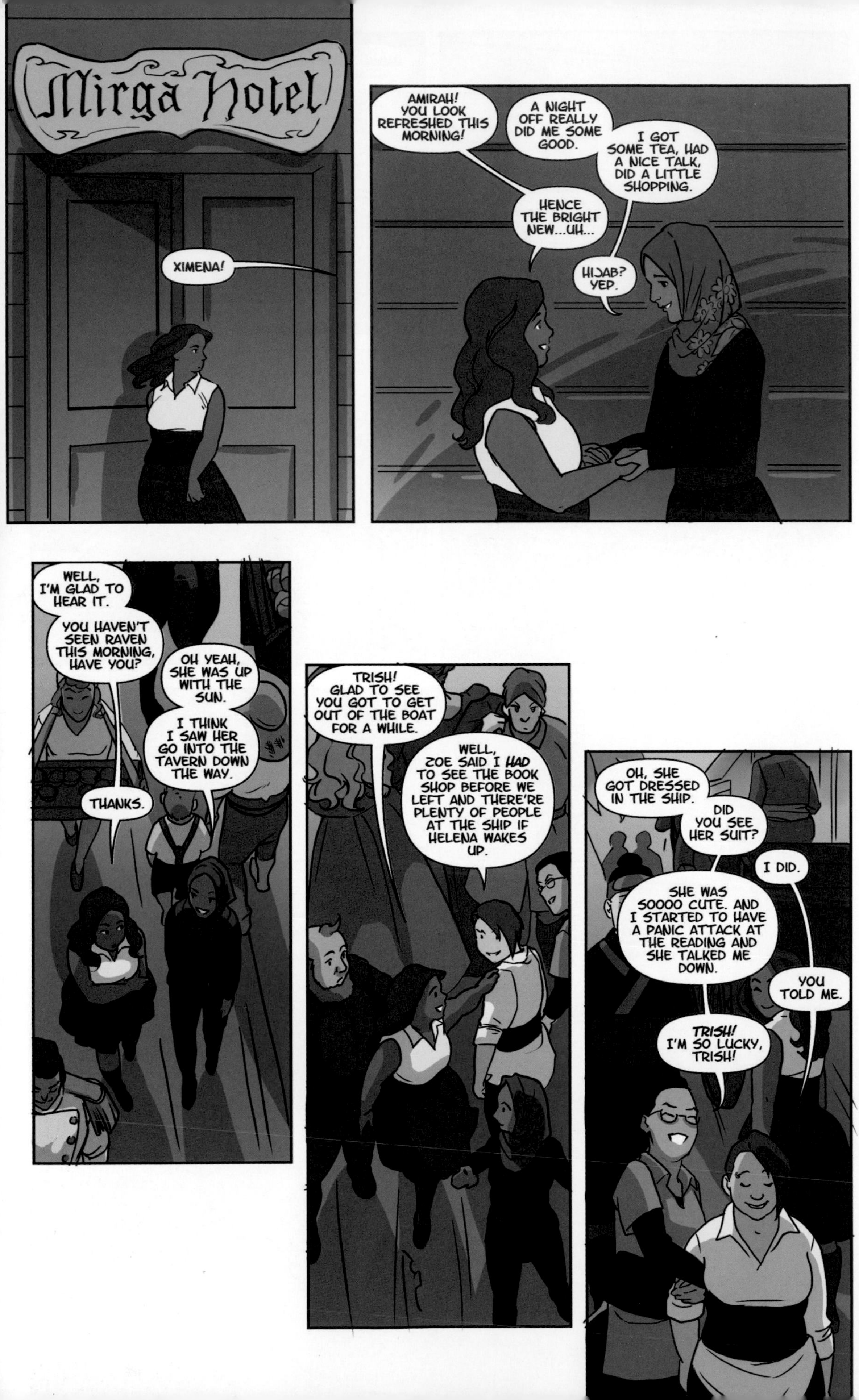
Mirga Hotel
XIMENA!
AMIRAH! YOU LOOK REFRESHED THIS MORNING!
A NIGHT OFF REALLY DID ME SOME GOOD.
I GOT SOME TEA, HAD A NICE TALK, DID A LITTLE SHOPPING.
HENCE THE BRIGHT NEW...UH...
HIJAB? YEP.
WELL, I'M GLAD TO HEAR IT.
YOU HAVEN'T SEEN RAVEN THIS MORNING, HAVE YOU?
OH YEAH, SHE WAS UP WITH THE SUN.
I THINK I SAW HER GO INTO THE TAVERN DOWN THE WAY.
THANKS.
TRISH! GLAD TO SEE YOU GOT TO GET OUT OF THE BOAT FOR A WHILE.
WELL, ZOE SAID I *HAD* TO SEE THE BOOK SHOP BEFORE WE LEFT AND THERE'RE PLENTY OF PEOPLE AT THE SHIP IF HELENA WAKES UP.
OH, SHE GOT DRESSED IN THE SHIP.
DID YOU SEE HER SUIT?
I DID.
SHE WAS SOOOO CUTE. AND I STARTED TO HAVE A PANIC ATTACK AT THE READING AND SHE TALKED ME DOWN.
YOU TOLD ME.
TRISH! I'M SO LUCKY, TRISH!

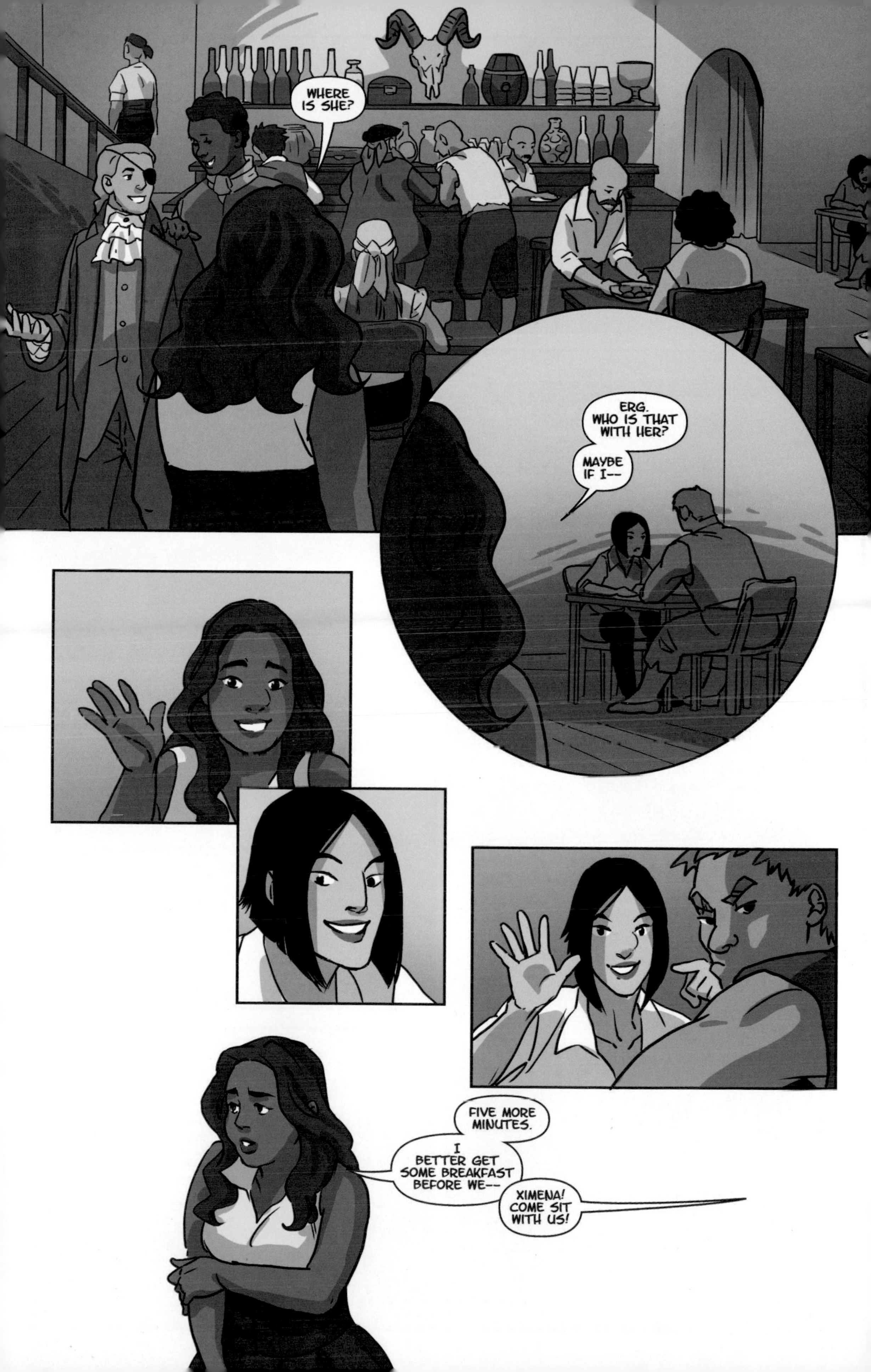
WHERE IS SHE?
ERG. WHO IS THAT WITH HER?
MAYBE IF I--
FIVE MORE MINUTES.
I BETTER GET SOME BREAKFAST BEFORE WE--
XIMENA! COME SIT WITH US!

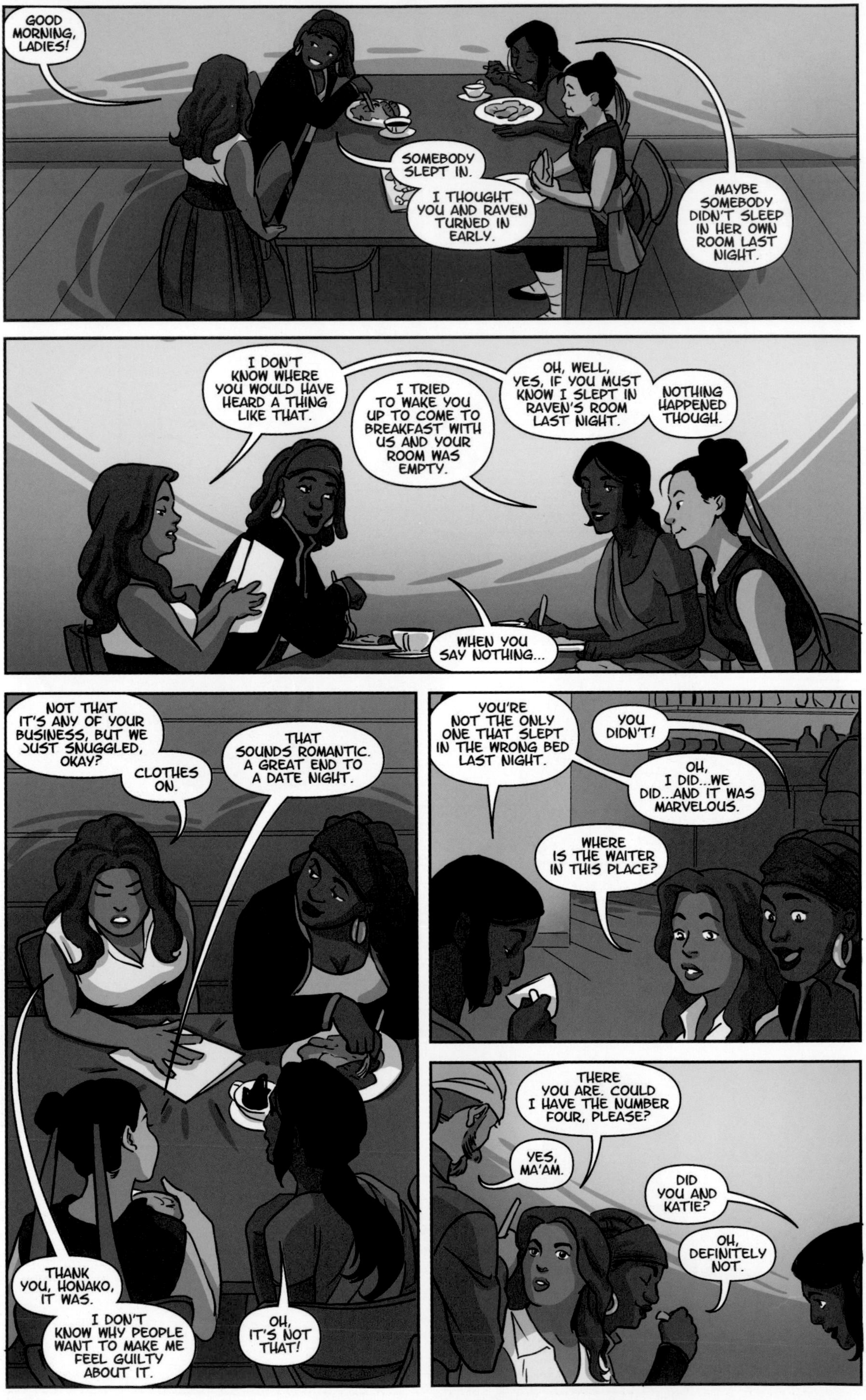
GOOD MORNING, LADIES!
SOMEBODY SLEPT IN.
I THOUGHT YOU AND RAVEN TURNED IN EARLY.
MAYBE SOMEBODY DIDN'T SLEEP IN HER OWN ROOM LAST NIGHT.
I DON'T KNOW WHERE YOU WOULD HAVE HEARD A THING LIKE THAT.
I TRIED TO WAKE YOU UP TO COME TO BREAKFAST WITH US AND YOUR ROOM WAS EMPTY.
OH, WELL, YES, IF YOU MUST KNOW I SLEPT IN RAVEN'S ROOM LAST NIGHT.
NOTHING HAPPENED THOUGH.
WHEN YOU SAY NOTHING...
NOT THAT IT'S ANY OF YOUR BUSINESS, BUT WE JUST SNUGGLED, OKAY?
CLOTHES ON.
THAT SOUNDS ROMANTIC. A GREAT END TO A DATE NIGHT.
THANK YOU, HONAKO, IT WAS.
I DON'T KNOW WHY PEOPLE WANT TO MAKE ME FEEL GUILTY ABOUT IT.
OH, IT'S NOT THAT!
YOU'RE NOT THE ONLY ONE THAT SLEPT IN THE WRONG BED LAST NIGHT.
YOU DIDN'T!
OH, I DID...WE DID...AND IT WAS MARVELOUS.
WHERE IS THE WAITER IN THIS PLACE?
THERE YOU ARE. COULD I HAVE THE NUMBER FOUR, PLEASE?
YES, MA'AM.
DID YOU AND KATIE?
OH, DEFINITELY NOT.

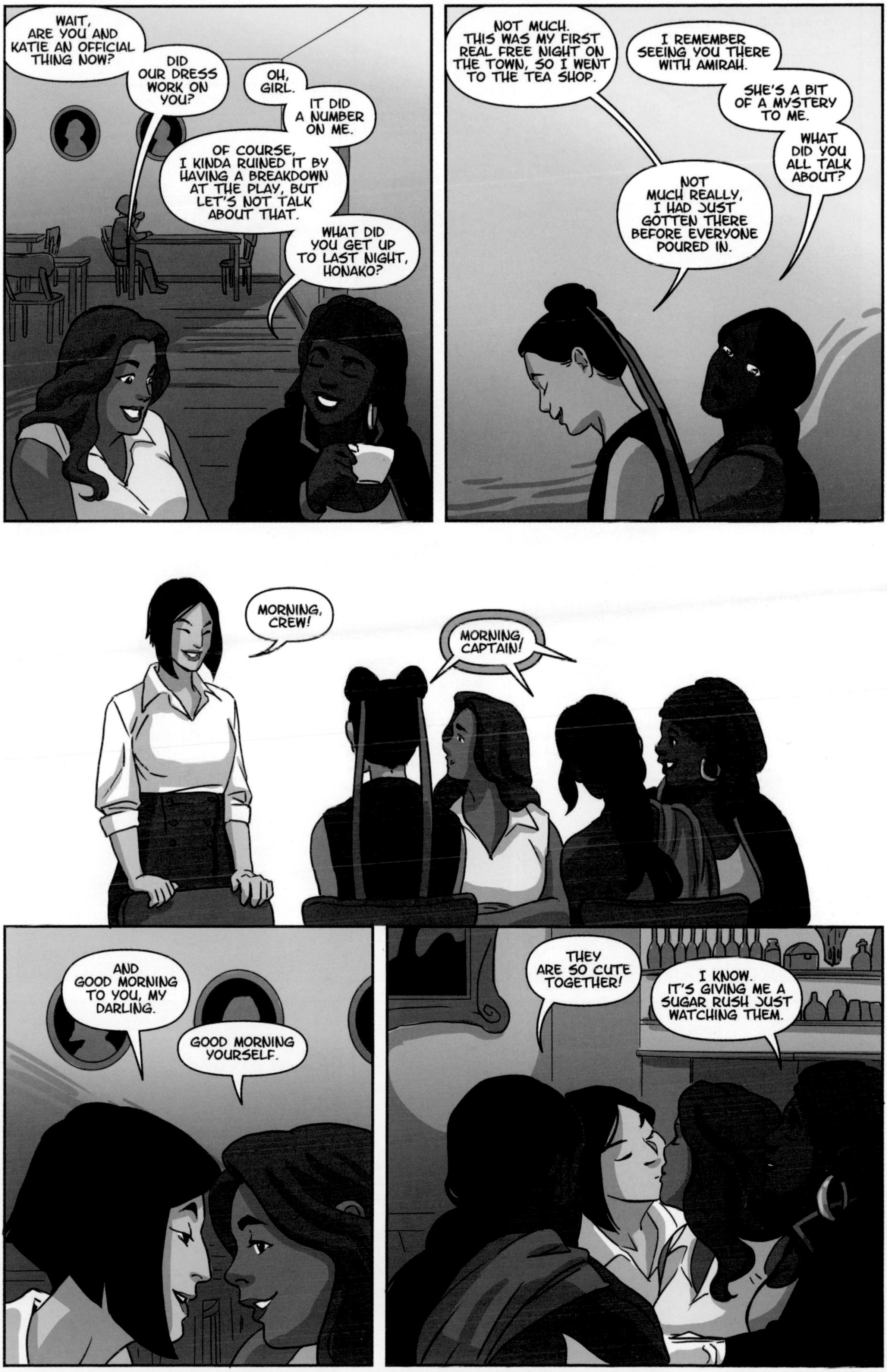

WAIT, ARE YOU AND KATIE AN OFFICIAL THING NOW?
DID OUR DRESS WORK ON YOU?
OH, GIRL.
IT DID A NUMBER ON ME.
OF COURSE, I KINDA RUINED IT BY HAVING A BREAKDOWN AT THE PLAY, BUT LET'S NOT TALK ABOUT THAT.
WHAT DID YOU GET UP TO LAST NIGHT, HONAKO?
NOT MUCH. THIS WAS MY FIRST REAL FREE NIGHT ON THE TOWN, SO I WENT TO THE TEA SHOP.
I REMEMBER SEEING YOU THERE WITH AMIRAH.
SHE'S A BIT OF A MYSTERY TO ME.
WHAT DID YOU ALL TALK ABOUT?
NOT MUCH REALLY, I HAD JUST GOTTEN THERE BEFORE EVERYONE POURED IN.
MORNING, CREW!
MORNING, CAPTAIN!
AND GOOD MORNING TO YOU, MY DARLING.
GOOD MORNING YOURSELF.
THEY ARE SO CUTE TOGETHER!
I KNOW. IT'S GIVING ME A SUGAR RUSH JUST WATCHING THEM.

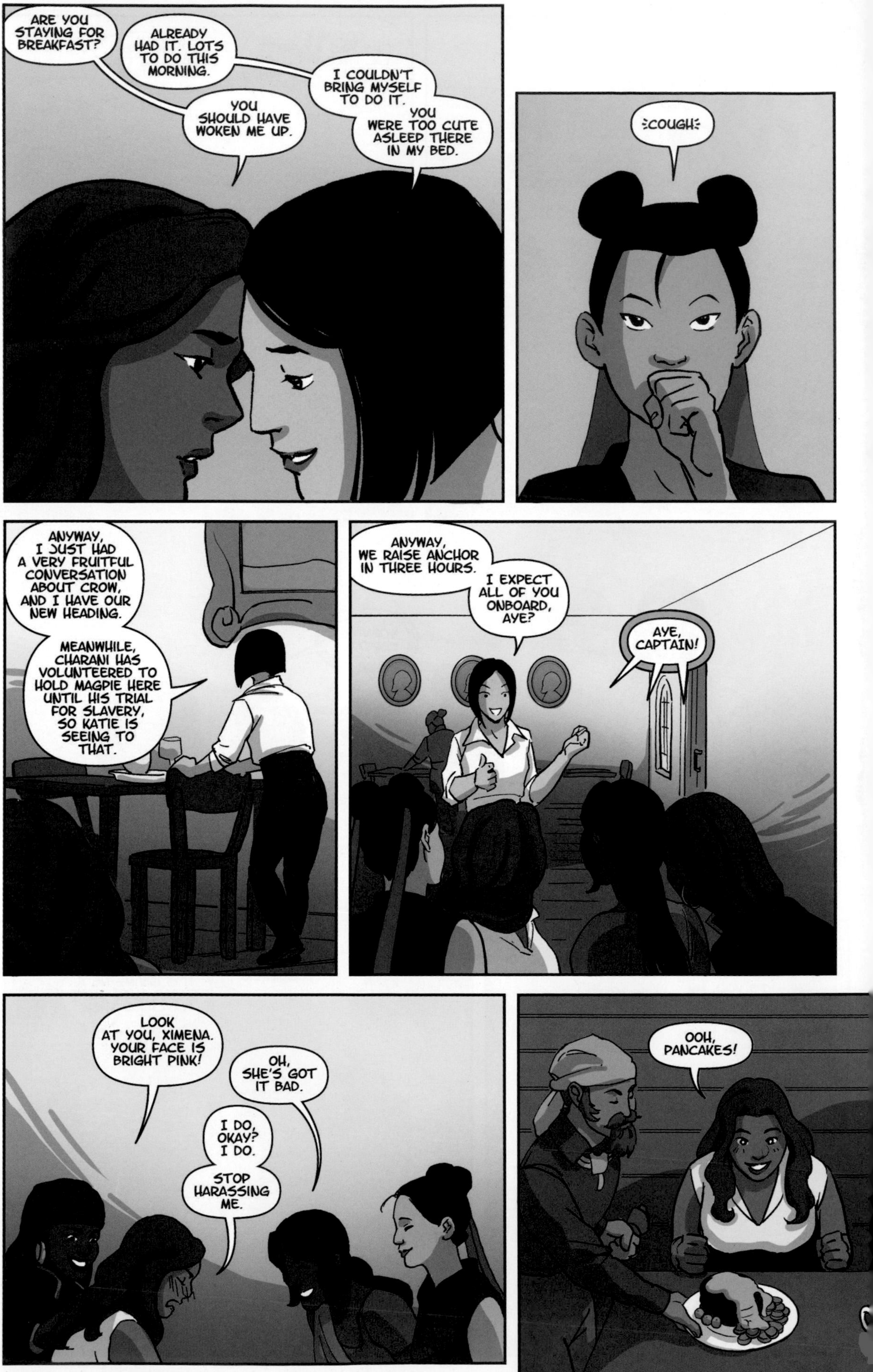
ARE YOU STAYING FOR BREAKFAST?
ALREADY HAD IT. LOTS TO DO THIS MORNING.
YOU SHOULD HAVE WOKEN ME UP.
I COULDN'T BRING MYSELF TO DO IT.
YOU WERE TOO CUTE ASLEEP THERE IN MY BED.
COUGH
ANYWAY, I JUST HAD A VERY FRUITFUL CONVERSATION ABOUT CROW, AND I HAVE OUR NEW HEADING.
MEANWHILE, CHARANI HAS VOLUNTEERED TO HOLD MAGPIE HERE UNTIL HIS TRIAL FOR SLAVERY, SO KATIE IS SEEING TO THAT.
ANYWAY, WE RAISE ANCHOR IN THREE HOURS.
I EXPECT ALL OF YOU ONBOARD, AYE?
AYE, CAPTAIN!
LOOK AT YOU, XIMENA. YOUR FACE IS BRIGHT PINK!
OH, SHE'S GOT IT BAD.
I DO, OKAY? I DO.
STOP HARASSING ME.
OOH, PANCAKES!

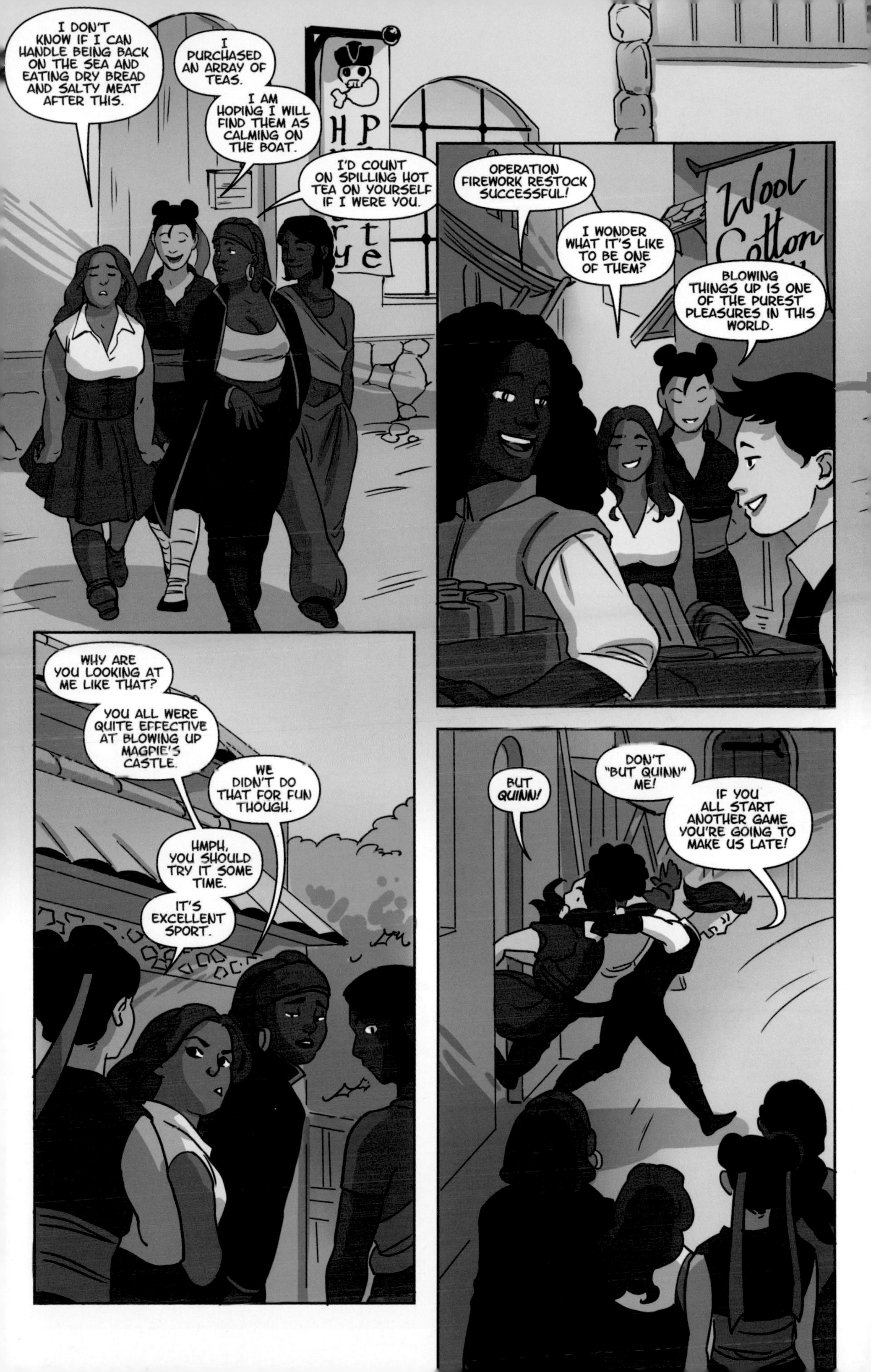
I DON'T KNOW IF I CAN HANDLE BEING BACK ON THE SEA AND EATING DRY BREAD AND SALTY MEAT AFTER THIS.
I PURCHASED AN ARRAY OF TEAS.
I AM HOPING I WILL FIND THEM AS CALMING ON THE BOAT.
I'D COUNT ON SPILLING HOT TEA ON YOURSELF IF I WERE YOU.
OPERATION FIREWORK RESTOCK SUCCESSFUL!
I WONDER WHAT IT'S LIKE TO BE ONE OF THEM?
BLOWING THINGS UP IS ONE OF THE PUREST PLEASURES IN THIS WORLD.
Wool
Cotton
WHY ARE YOU LOOKING AT ME LIKE THAT?
YOU ALL WERE QUITE EFFECTIVE AT BLOWING UP MAGPIE'S CASTLE.
WE DIDN'T DO THAT FOR FUN THOUGH.
HMPH, YOU SHOULD TRY IT SOME TIME.
IT'S EXCELLENT SPORT.
BUT QUINN!
DON'T "BUT QUINN" ME!
IF YOU ALL START ANOTHER GAME YOU'RE GOING TO MAKE US LATE!

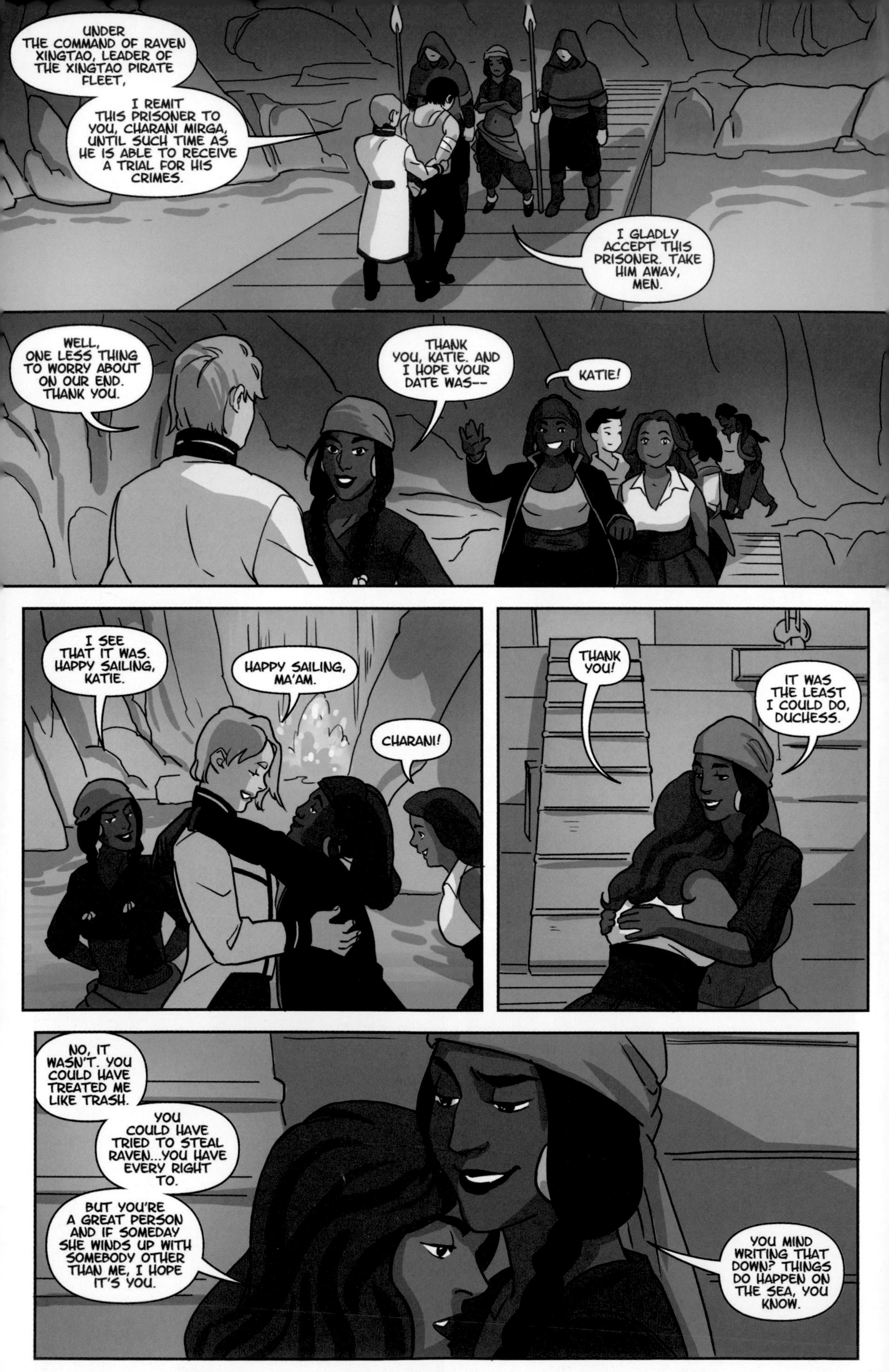
UNDER THE COMMAND OF RAVEN XINGTAO, LEADER OF THE XINGTAO PIRATE FLEET,
I REMIT THIS PRISONER TO YOU, CHARANI MIRGA, UNTIL SUCH TIME AS HE IS ABLE TO RECEIVE A TRIAL FOR HIS CRIMES.
I GLADLY ACCEPT THIS PRISONER. TAKE HIM AWAY, MEN.
WELL, ONE LESS THING TO WORRY ABOUT ON OUR END. THANK YOU.
THANK YOU, KATIE. AND I HOPE YOUR DATE WAS--
KATIE!
I SEE THAT IT WAS. HAPPY SAILING, KATIE.
HAPPY SAILING, MA'AM.
CHARANI!
THANK YOU!
IT WAS THE LEAST I COULD DO, DUCHESS.
NO, IT WASN'T. YOU COULD HAVE TREATED ME LIKE TRASH.
YOU COULD HAVE TRIED TO STEAL RAVEN...YOU HAVE EVERY RIGHT TO.
BUT YOU'RE A GREAT PERSON AND IF SOMEDAY SHE WINDS UP WITH SOMEBODY OTHER THAN ME, I HOPE IT'S YOU.
YOU MIND WRITING THAT DOWN? THINGS DO HAPPEN ON THE SEA, YOU KNOW.

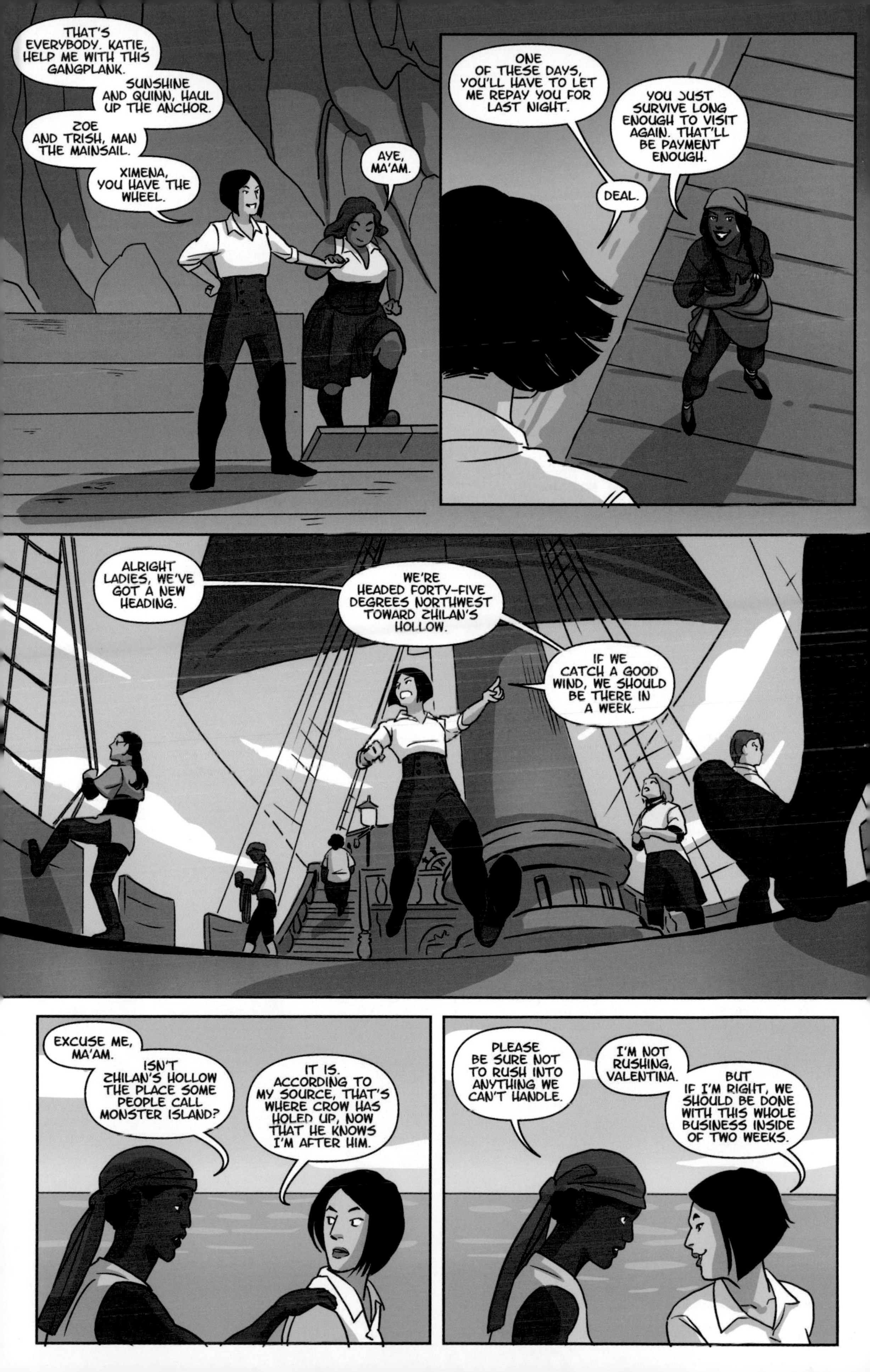
THAT'S EVERYBODY. KATIE, HELP ME WITH THIS GANGPLANK.
SUNSHINE AND QUINN, HAUL UP THE ANCHOR.
ZOE AND TRISH, MAN THE MAINSAIL.
XIMENA, YOU HAVE THE WHEEL.
AYE, MA'AM.
ONE OF THESE DAYS, YOU'LL HAVE TO LET ME REPAY YOU FOR LAST NIGHT.
YOU JUST SURVIVE LONG ENOUGH TO VISIT AGAIN. THAT'LL BE PAYMENT ENOUGH.
DEAL.
ALRIGHT LADIES, WE'VE GOT A NEW HEADING.
WE'RE HEADED FORTY-FIVE DEGREES NORTHWEST TOWARD ZHILAN'S HOLLOW.
IF WE CATCH A GOOD WIND, WE SHOULD BE THERE IN A WEEK.
EXCUSE ME, MA'AM.
ISN'T ZHILAN'S HOLLOW THE PLACE SOME PEOPLE CALL MONSTER ISLAND?
IT IS. ACCORDING TO MY SOURCE, THAT'S WHERE CROW HAS HOLED UP, NOW THAT HE KNOWS I'M AFTER HIM.
PLEASE BE SURE NOT TO RUSH INTO ANYTHING WE CAN'T HANDLE.
I'M NOT RUSHING, VALENTINA.
BUT IF I'M RIGHT, WE SHOULD BE DONE WITH THIS WHOLE BUSINESS INSIDE OF TWO WEEKS.

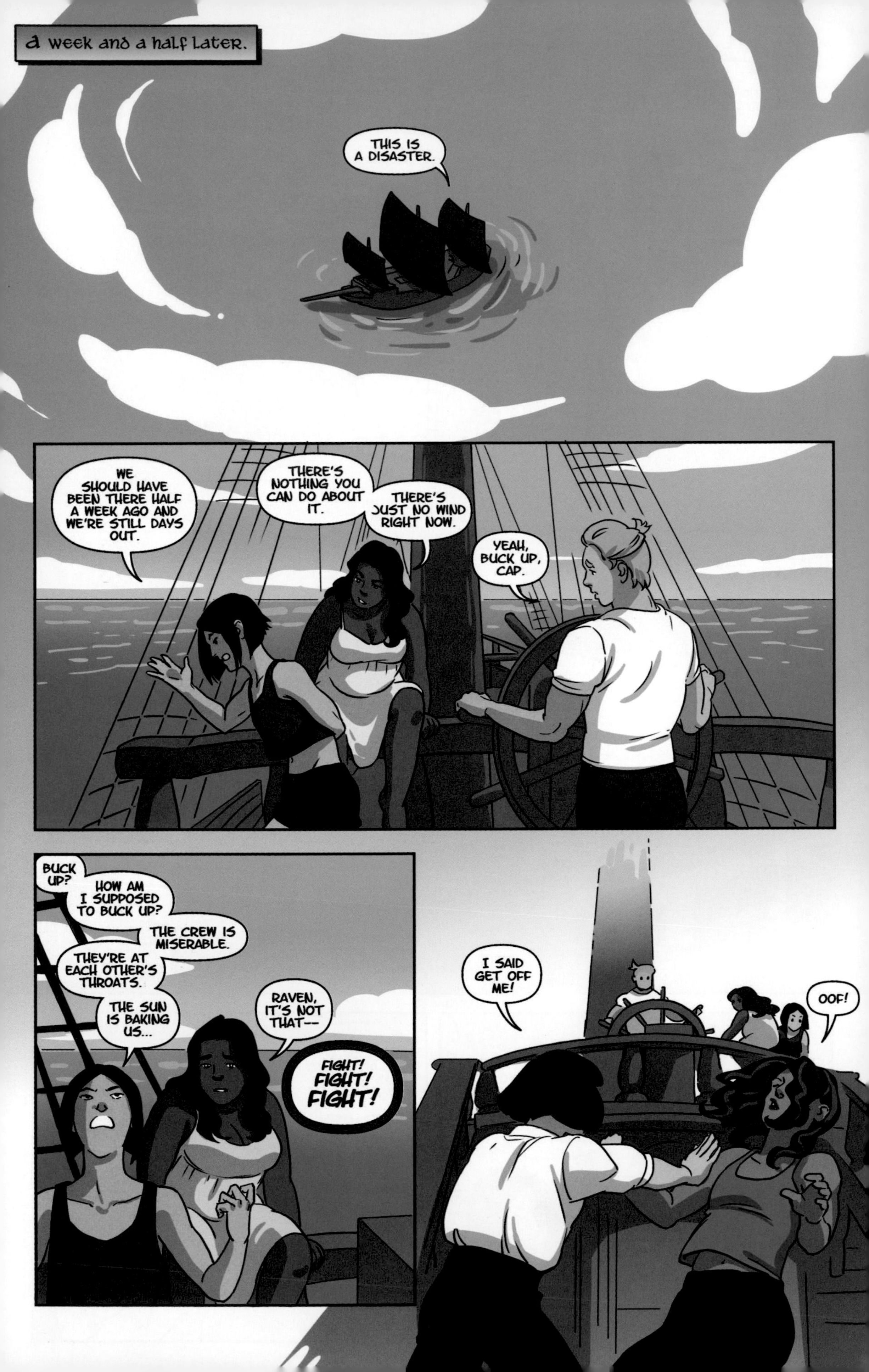
A WEEK AND A HALF LATER.
THIS IS A DISASTER.
WE SHOULD HAVE BEEN THERE HALF A WEEK AGO AND WE'RE STILL DAYS OUT.
THERE'S NOTHING YOU CAN DO ABOUT IT.
THERE'S JUST NO WIND RIGHT NOW.
YEAH, BUCK UP, CAP.
BUCK UP?
HOW AM I SUPPOSED TO BUCK UP?
THE CREW IS MISERABLE.
THEY'RE AT EACH OTHER'S THROATS.
THE SUN IS BAKING US...
RAVEN, IT'S NOT THAT--
FIGHT! FIGHT! FIGHT!
I SAID GET OFF ME!
OOF!

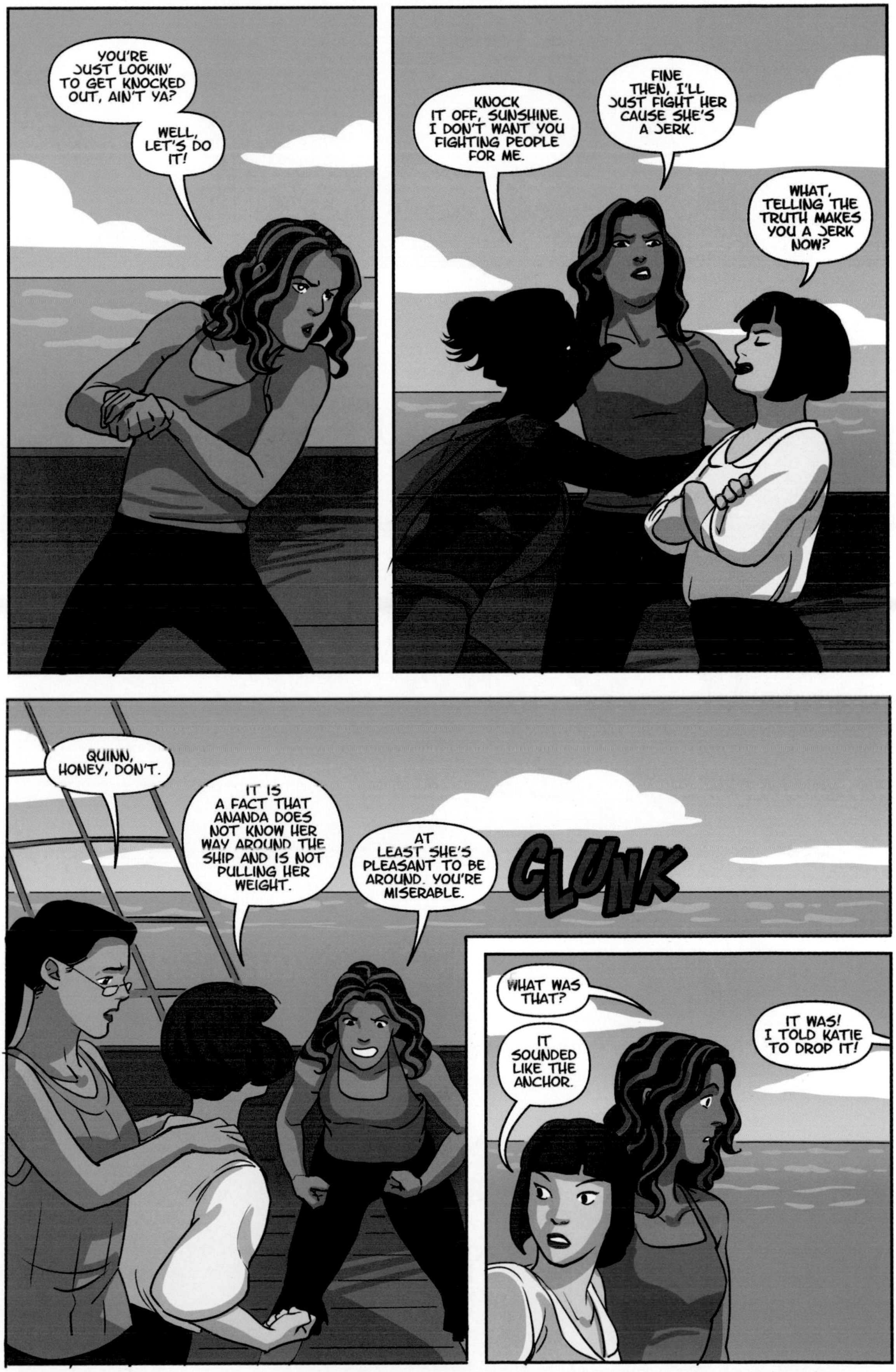
YOU'RE JUST LOOKIN' TO GET KNOCKED OUT, AIN'T YA?
WELL, LET'S DO IT!
KNOCK IT OFF, SUNSHINE. I DON'T WANT YOU FIGHTING PEOPLE FOR ME.
FINE THEN, I'LL JUST FIGHT HER CAUSE SHE'S A JERK.
WHAT, TELLING THE TRUTH MAKES YOU A JERK NOW?
QUINN, HONEY, DON'T.
IT IS A FACT THAT ANANDA DOES NOT KNOW HER WAY AROUND THE SHIP AND IS NOT PULLING HER WEIGHT.
AT LEAST SHE'S PLEASANT TO BE AROUND. YOU'RE MISERABLE.
CLUNK
WHAT WAS THAT?
IT SOUNDED LIKE THE ANCHOR.
IT WAS! I TOLD KATIE TO DROP IT!

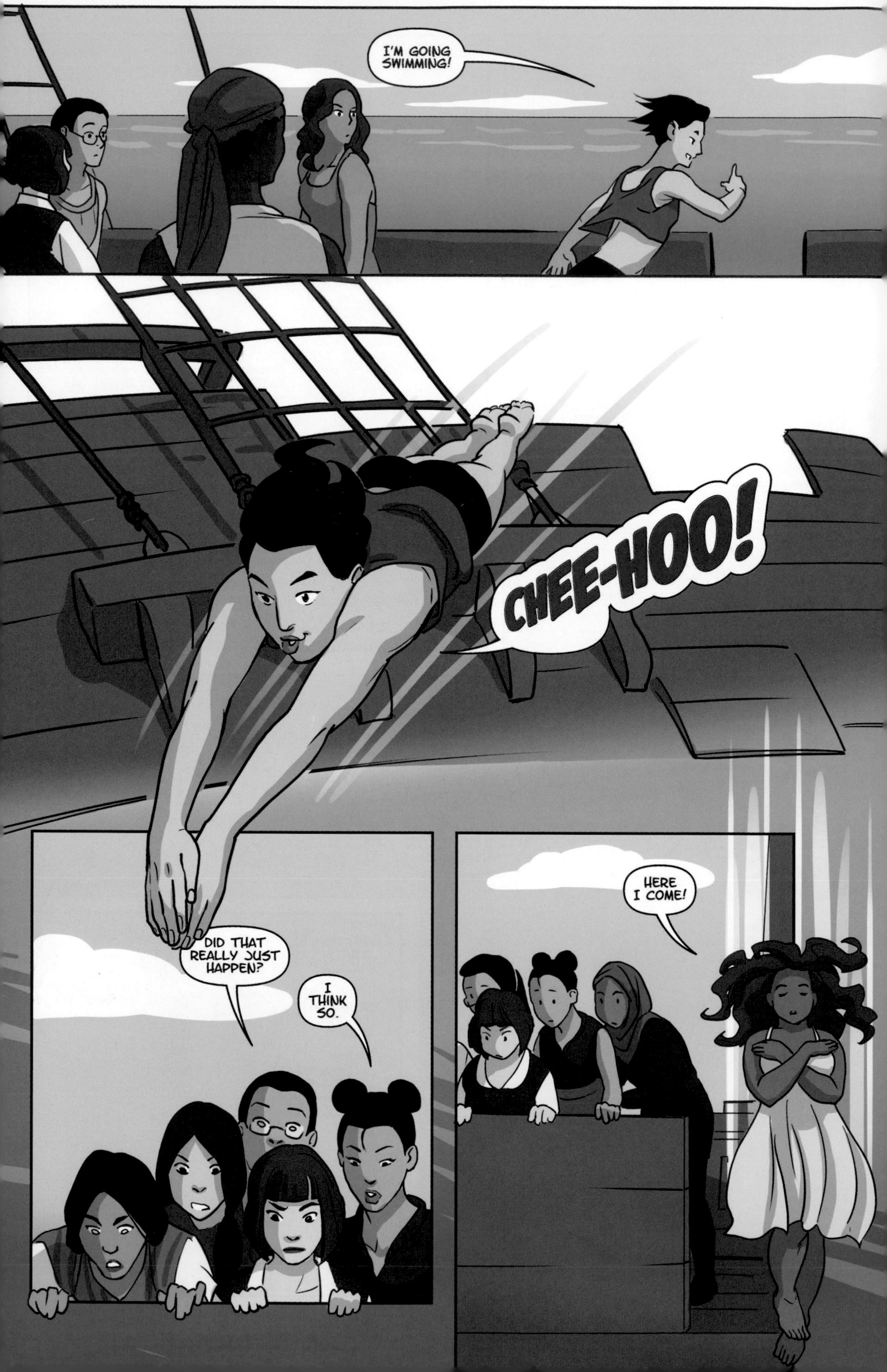
I'M GOING SWIMMING!
CHEE-HOO!
DID THAT REALLY JUST HAPPEN?
I THINK SO.
HERE I COME!

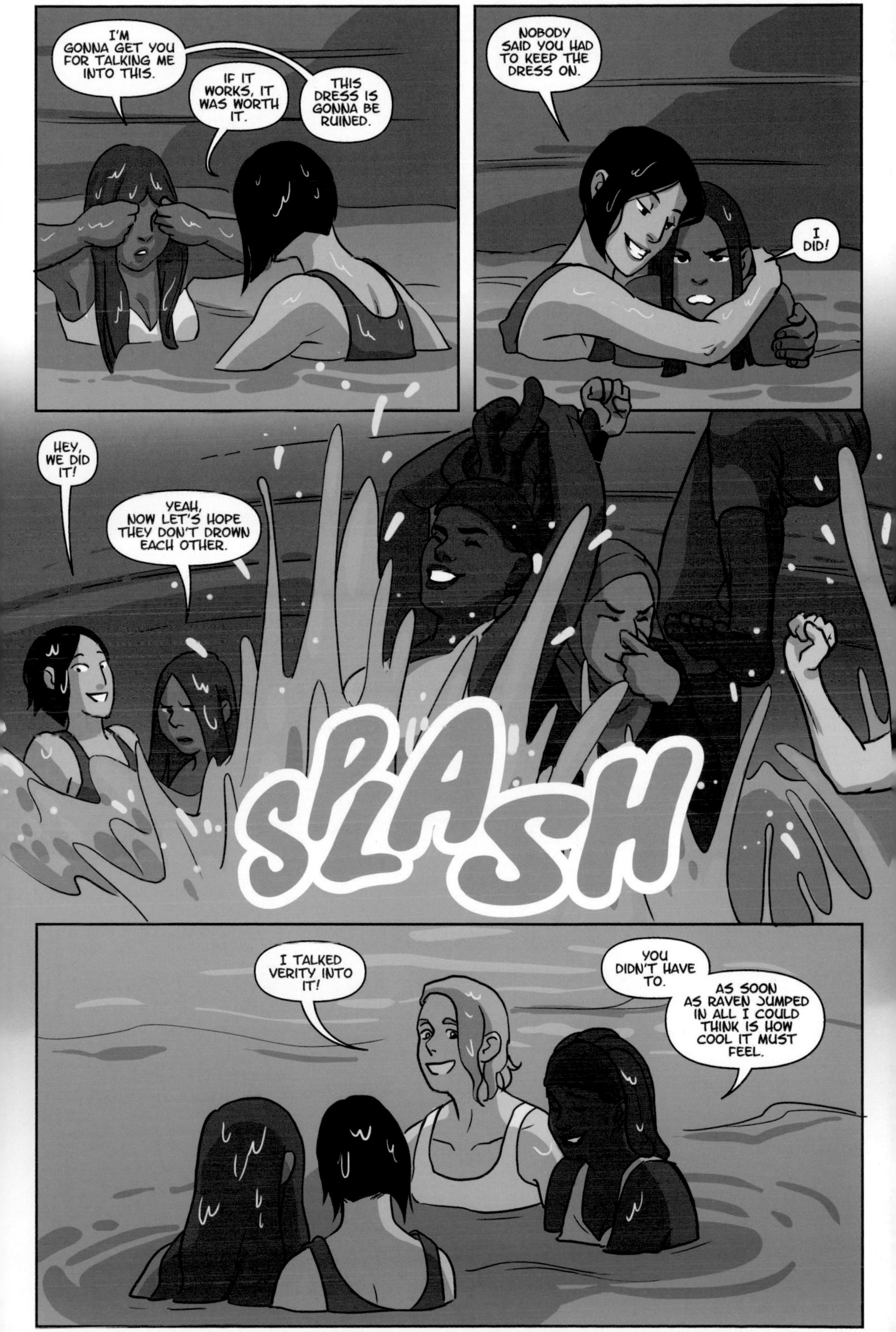

I'M GONNA GET YOU FOR TALKING ME INTO THIS.
IF IT WORKS, IT WAS WORTH IT.
THIS DRESS IS GONNA BE RUINED.
NOBODY SAID YOU HAD TO KEEP THE DRESS ON.
I DID!
HEY, WE DID IT!
YEAH, NOW LET'S HOPE THEY DON'T DROWN EACH OTHER.
SPLASH
I TALKED VERITY INTO IT!
YOU DIDN'T HAVE TO.
AS SOON AS RAVEN JUMPED IN ALL I COULD THINK IS HOW COOL IT MUST FEEL.

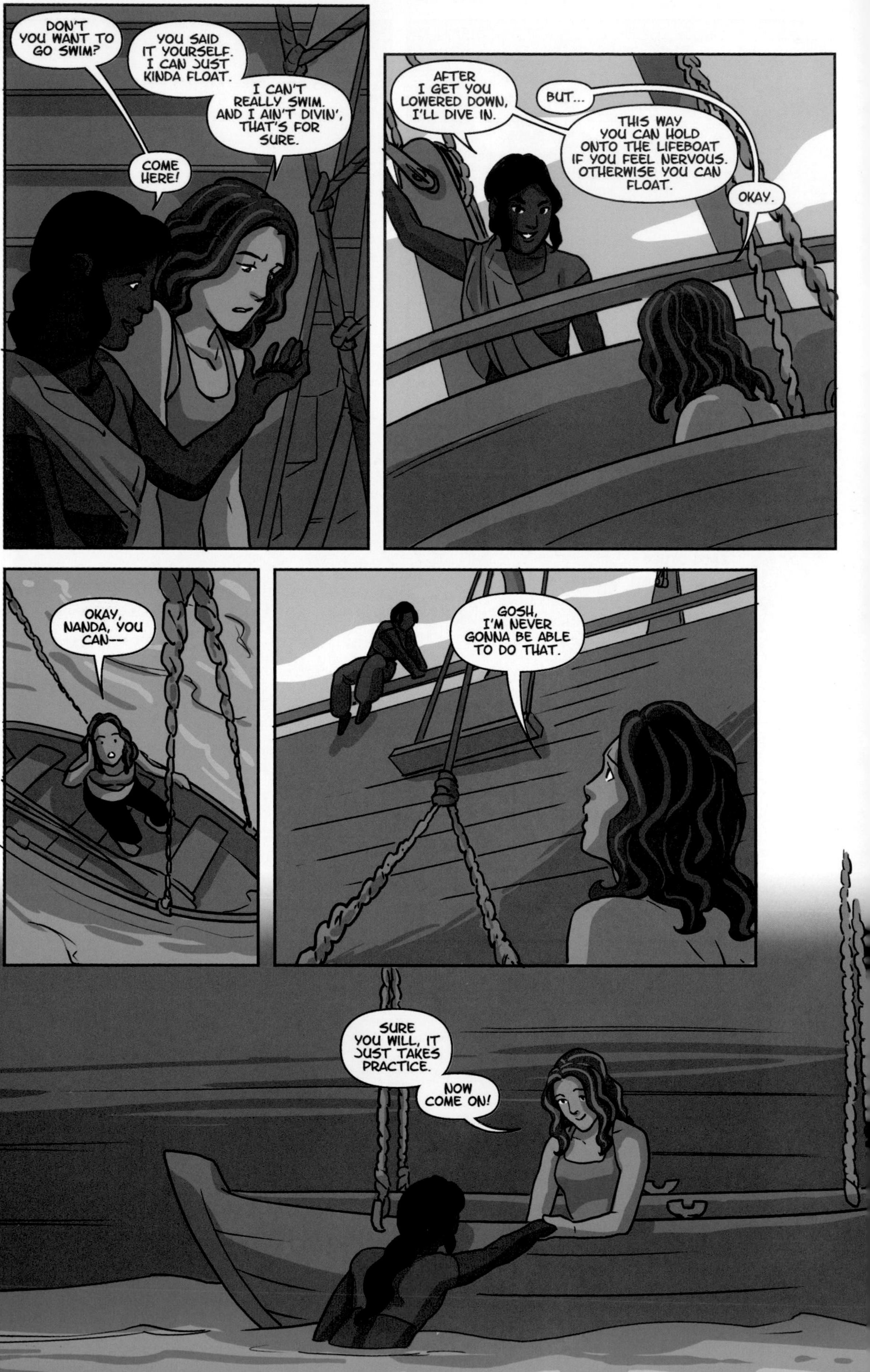
DON'T YOU WANT TO GO SWIM?
YOU SAID IT YOURSELF. I CAN JUST KINDA FLOAT.
I CAN'T REALLY SWIM. AND I AIN'T DIVIN', THAT'S FOR SURE.
COME HERE!
AFTER I GET YOU LOWERED DOWN, I'LL DIVE IN.
BUT...
THIS WAY YOU CAN HOLD ONTO THE LIFEBOAT IF YOU FEEL NERVOUS. OTHERWISE YOU CAN FLOAT.
OKAY.
OKAY, NANDA, YOU CAN--
GOSH, I'M NEVER GONNA BE ABLE TO DO THAT.
SURE YOU WILL, IT JUST TAKES PRACTICE.
NOW COME ON!

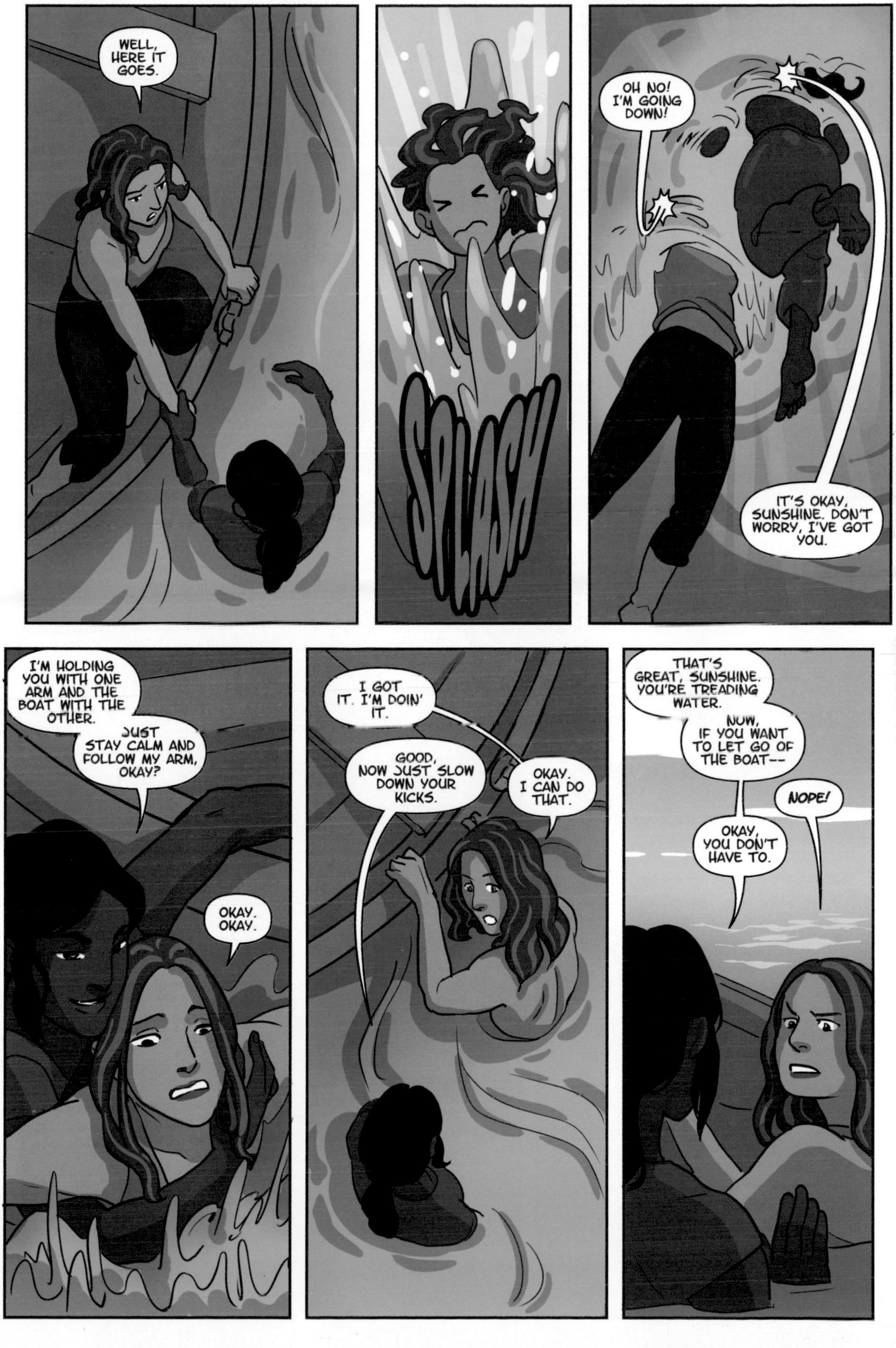
WELL, HERE IT GOES.
SPLASH
OH NO! I'M GOING DOWN!
IT'S OKAY, SUNSHINE. DON'T WORRY, I'VE GOT YOU.
I'M HOLDING YOU WITH ONE ARM AND THE BOAT WITH THE OTHER.
JUST STAY CALM AND FOLLOW MY ARM, OKAY?
OKAY. OKAY.
I GOT IT. I'M DOIN' IT.
GOOD, NOW JUST SLOW DOWN YOUR KICKS.
OKAY. I CAN DO THAT.
THAT'S GREAT, SUNSHINE. YOU'RE TREADING WATER.
NOW, IF YOU WANT TO LET GO OF THE BOAT--
NOPE!
OKAY, YOU DON'T HAVE TO.

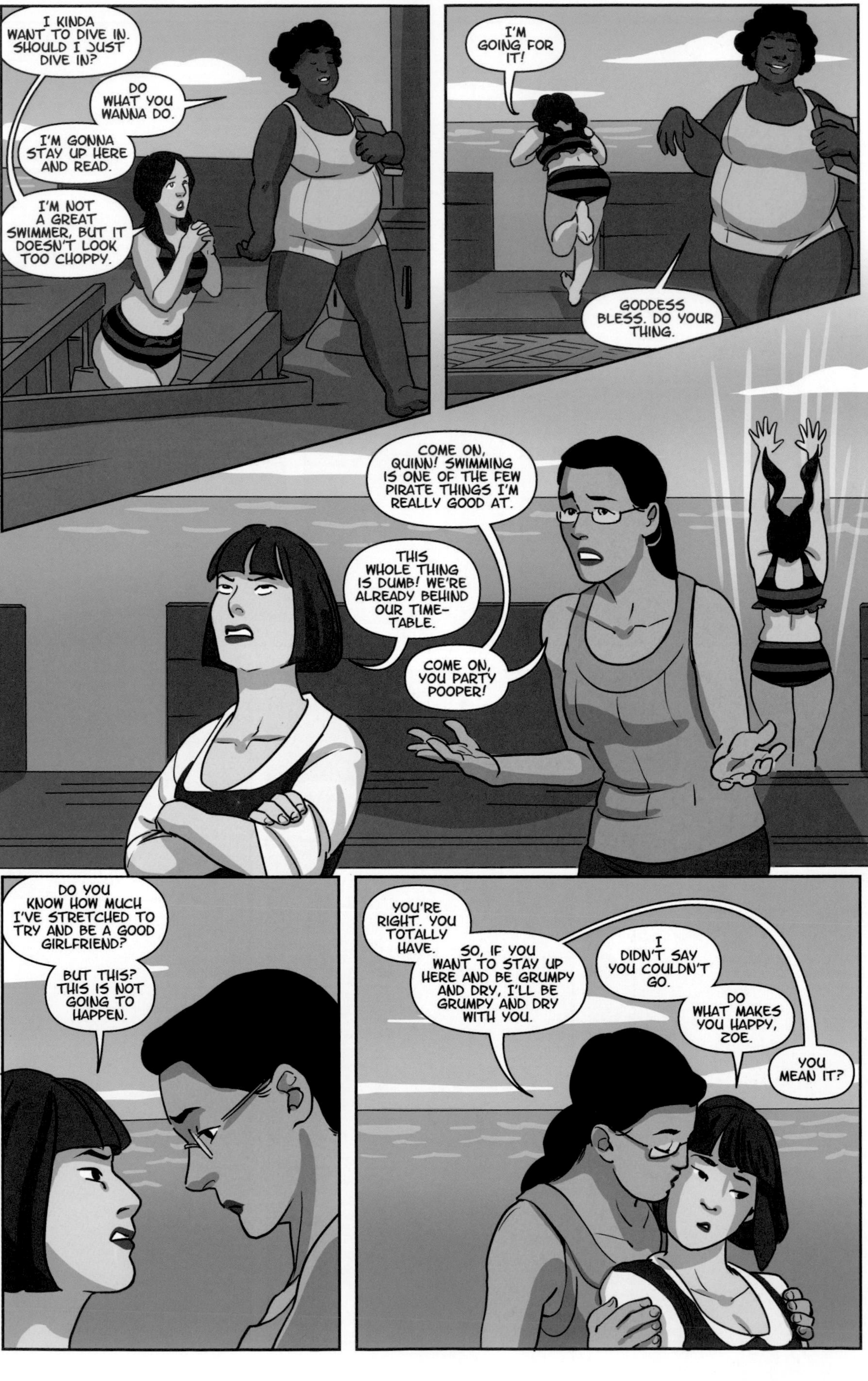
I KINDA WANT TO DIVE IN. SHOULD I JUST DIVE IN?
DO WHAT YOU WANNA DO.
I'M GONNA STAY UP HERE AND READ.
I'M NOT A GREAT SWIMMER, BUT IT DOESN'T LOOK TOO CHOPPY.
I'M GOING FOR IT!
GODDESS BLESS. DO YOUR THING.
COME ON, QUINN! SWIMMING IS ONE OF THE FEW PIRATE THINGS I'M REALLY GOOD AT.
THIS WHOLE THING IS DUMB! WE'RE ALREADY BEHIND OUR TIME-TABLE.
COME ON, YOU PARTY POOPER!
DO YOU KNOW HOW MUCH I'VE STRETCHED TO TRY AND BE A GOOD GIRLFRIEND?
BUT THIS? THIS IS NOT GOING TO HAPPEN.
YOU'RE RIGHT. YOU TOTALLY HAVE.
SO, IF YOU WANT TO STAY UP HERE AND BE GRUMPY AND DRY, I'LL BE GRUMPY AND DRY WITH YOU.
I DIDN'T SAY YOU COULDN'T GO.
DO WHAT MAKES YOU HAPPY, ZOE.
YOU MEAN IT?

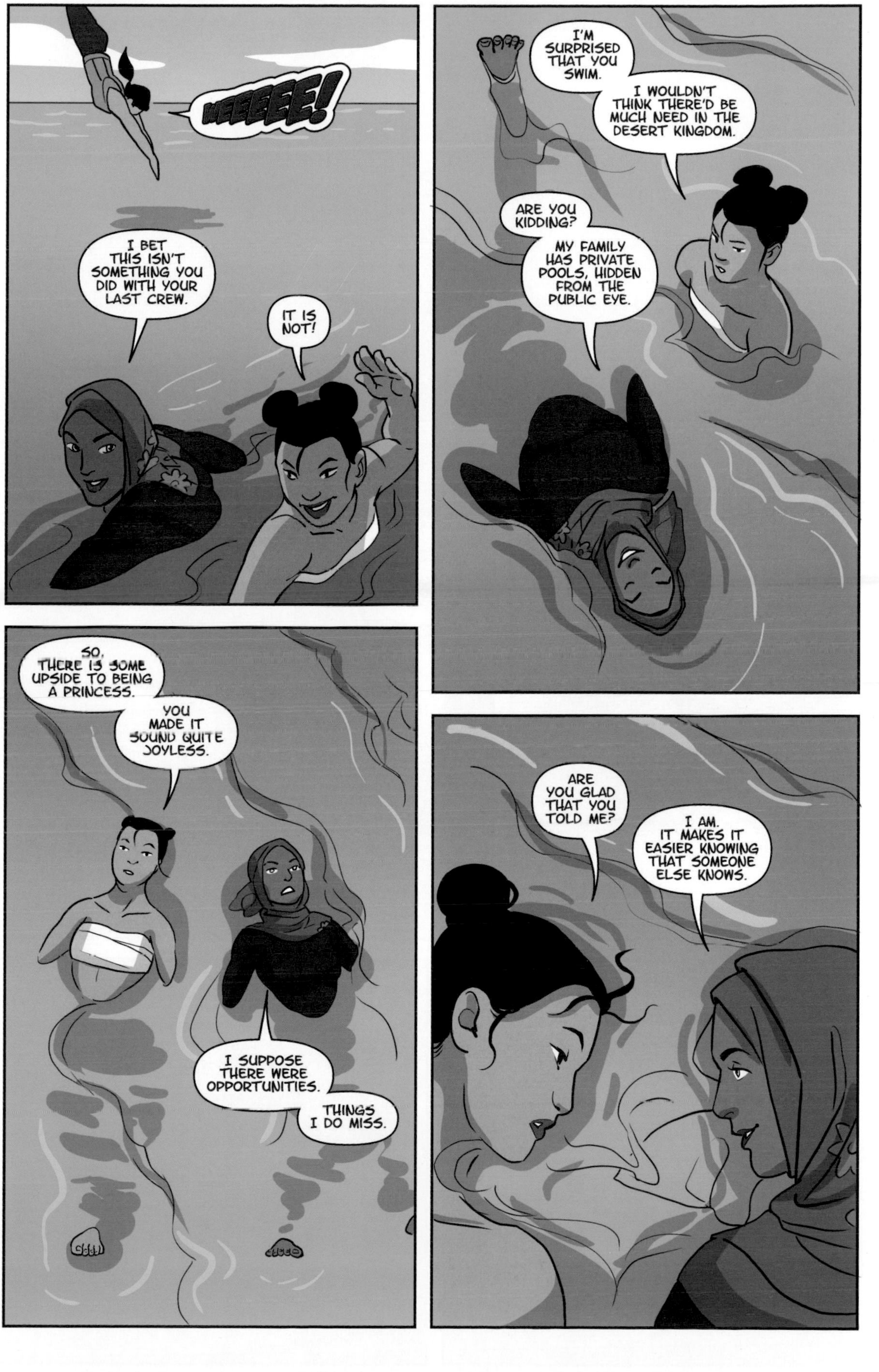
WEEEEE!
I BET THIS ISN'T SOMETHING YOU DID WITH YOUR LAST CREW.
IT IS NOT!
I'M SURPRISED THAT YOU SWIM.
I WOULDN'T THINK THERE'D BE MUCH NEED IN THE DESERT KINGDOM.
ARE YOU KIDDING?
MY FAMILY HAS PRIVATE POOLS, HIDDEN FROM THE PUBLIC EYE.
SO, THERE IS SOME UPSIDE TO BEING A PRINCESS.
YOU MADE IT SOUND QUITE JOYLESS.
I SUPPOSE THERE WERE OPPORTUNITIES.
THINGS I DO MISS.
ARE YOU GLAD THAT YOU TOLD ME?
I AM. IT MAKES IT EASIER KNOWING THAT SOMEONE ELSE KNOWS.

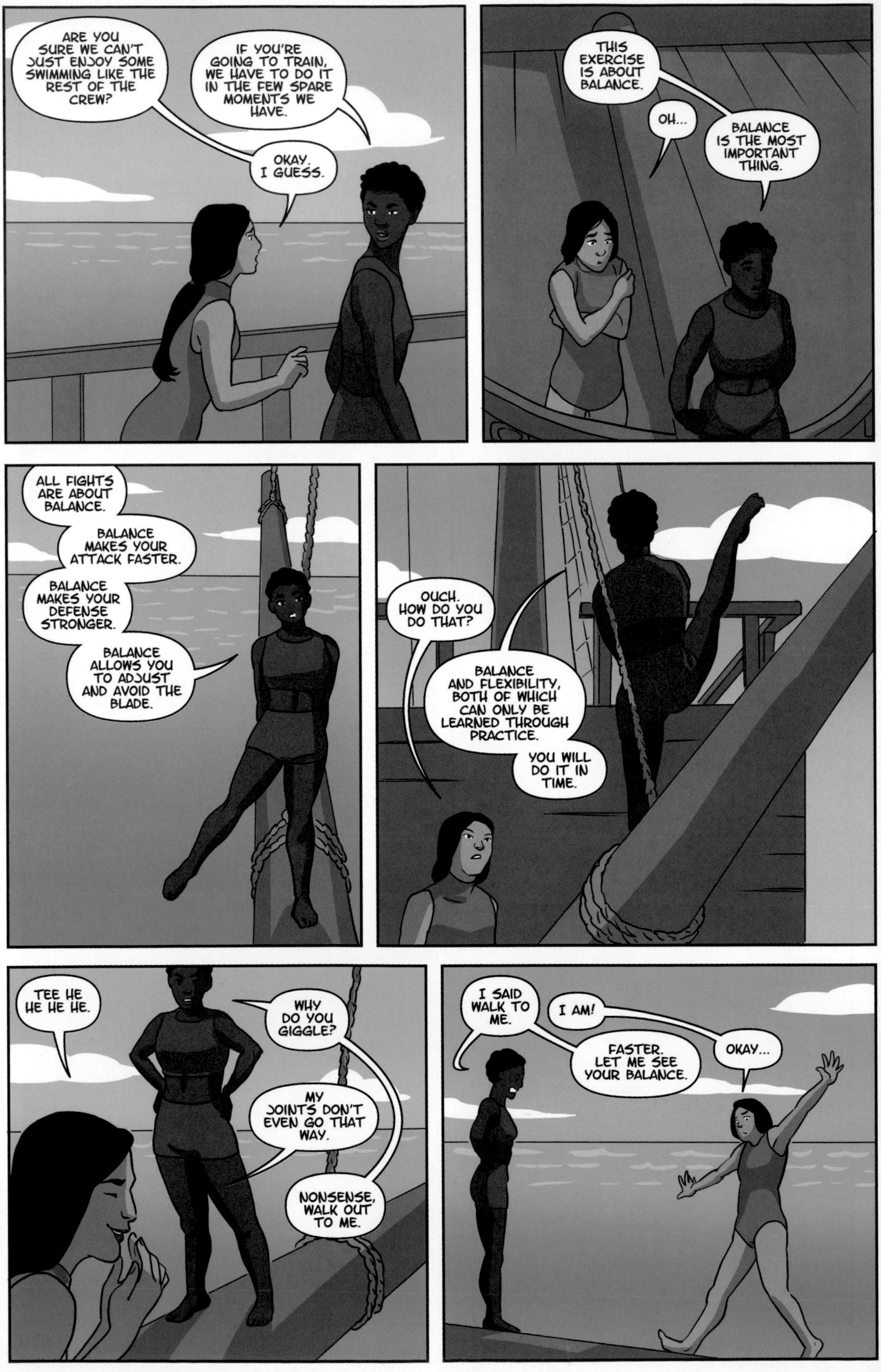
ARE YOU SURE WE CAN'T JUST ENJOY SOME SWIMMING LIKE THE REST OF THE CREW?
IF YOU'RE GOING TO TRAIN, WE HAVE TO DO IT IN THE FEW SPARE MOMENTS WE HAVE.
OKAY. I GUESS.
THIS EXERCISE IS ABOUT BALANCE.
OH...
BALANCE IS THE MOST IMPORTANT THING.
ALL FIGHTS ARE ABOUT BALANCE.
BALANCE MAKES YOUR ATTACK FASTER.
BALANCE MAKES YOUR DEFENSE STRONGER.
BALANCE ALLOWS YOU TO ADJUST AND AVOID THE BLADE.
OUCH. HOW DO YOU DO THAT?
BALANCE AND FLEXIBILITY, BOTH OF WHICH CAN ONLY BE LEARNED THROUGH PRACTICE.
YOU WILL DO IT IN TIME.
TEE HE HE HE HE.
WHY DO YOU GIGGLE?
MY JOINTS DON'T EVEN GO THAT WAY.
NONSENSE, WALK OUT TO ME.
I SAID WALK TO ME.
I AM!
FASTER. LET ME SEE YOUR BALANCE.
OKAY...

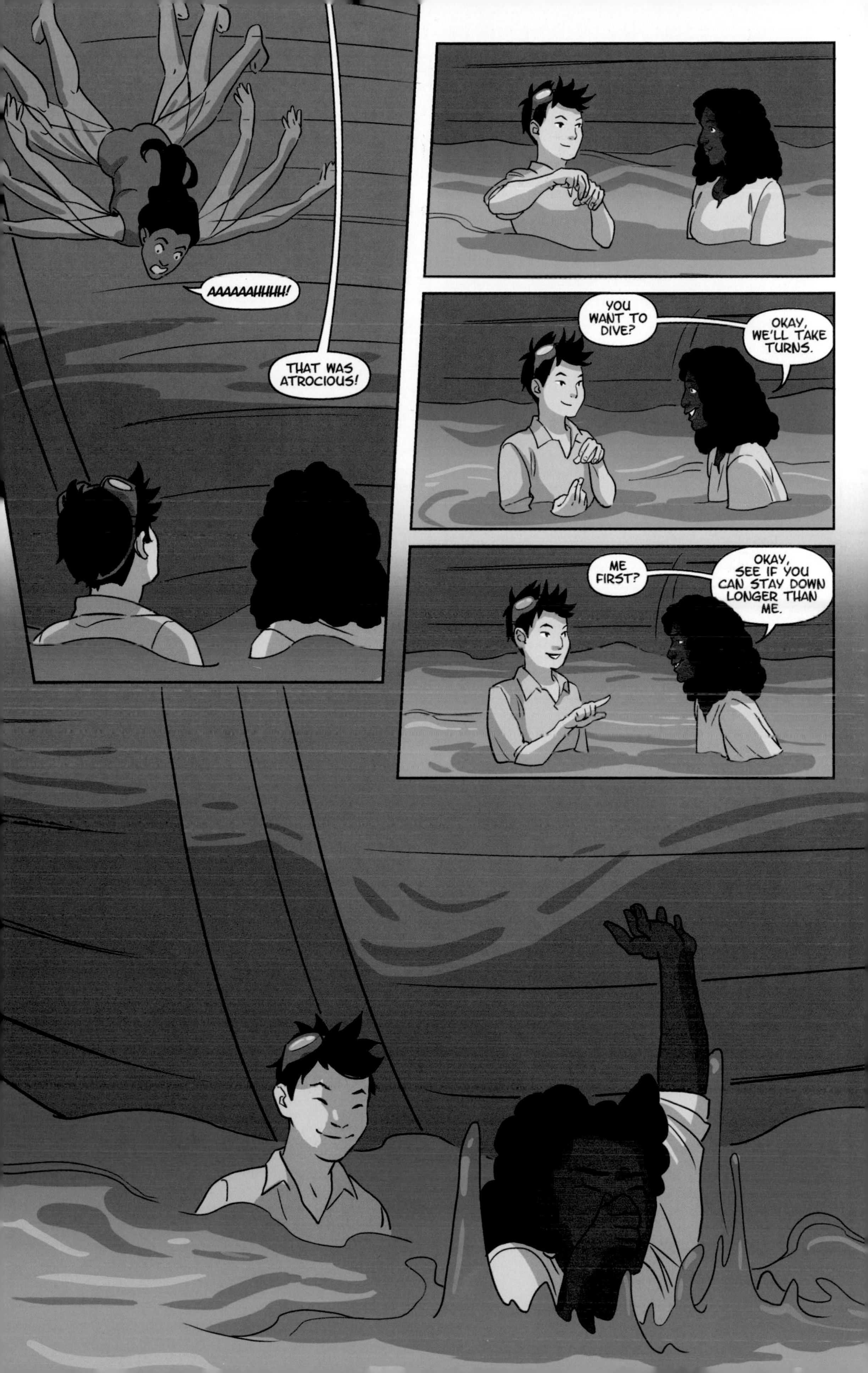
AAAAAAHHHH!
THAT WAS ATROCIOUS!
YOU WANT TO DIVE?
OKAY, WE'LL TAKE TURNS.
ME FIRST?
OKAY, SEE IF YOU CAN STAY DOWN LONGER THAN ME.

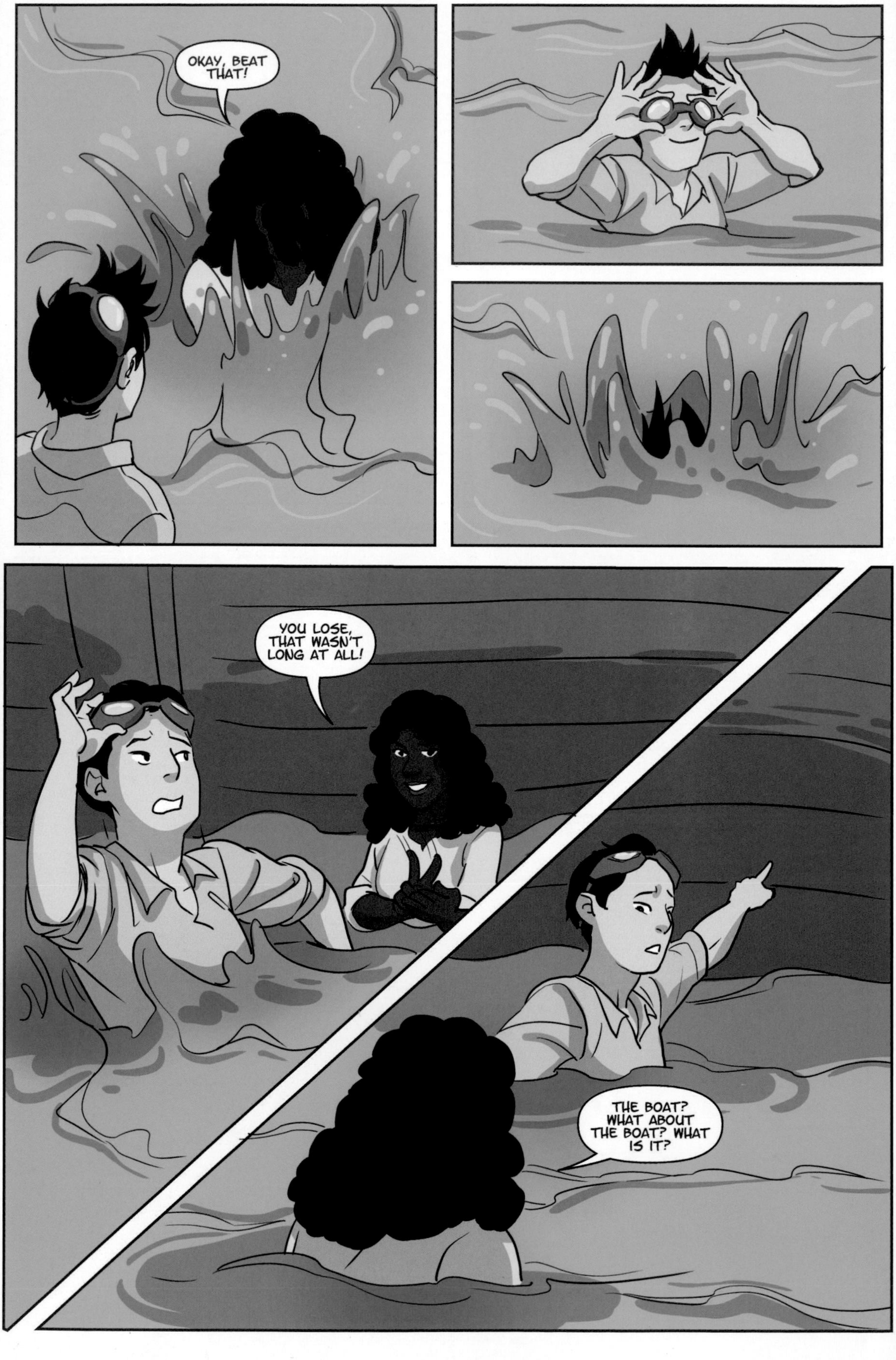
OKAY, BEAT THAT!
YOU LOSE, THAT WASN'T LONG AT ALL!
THE BOAT? WHAT ABOUT THE BOAT? WHAT IS IT?

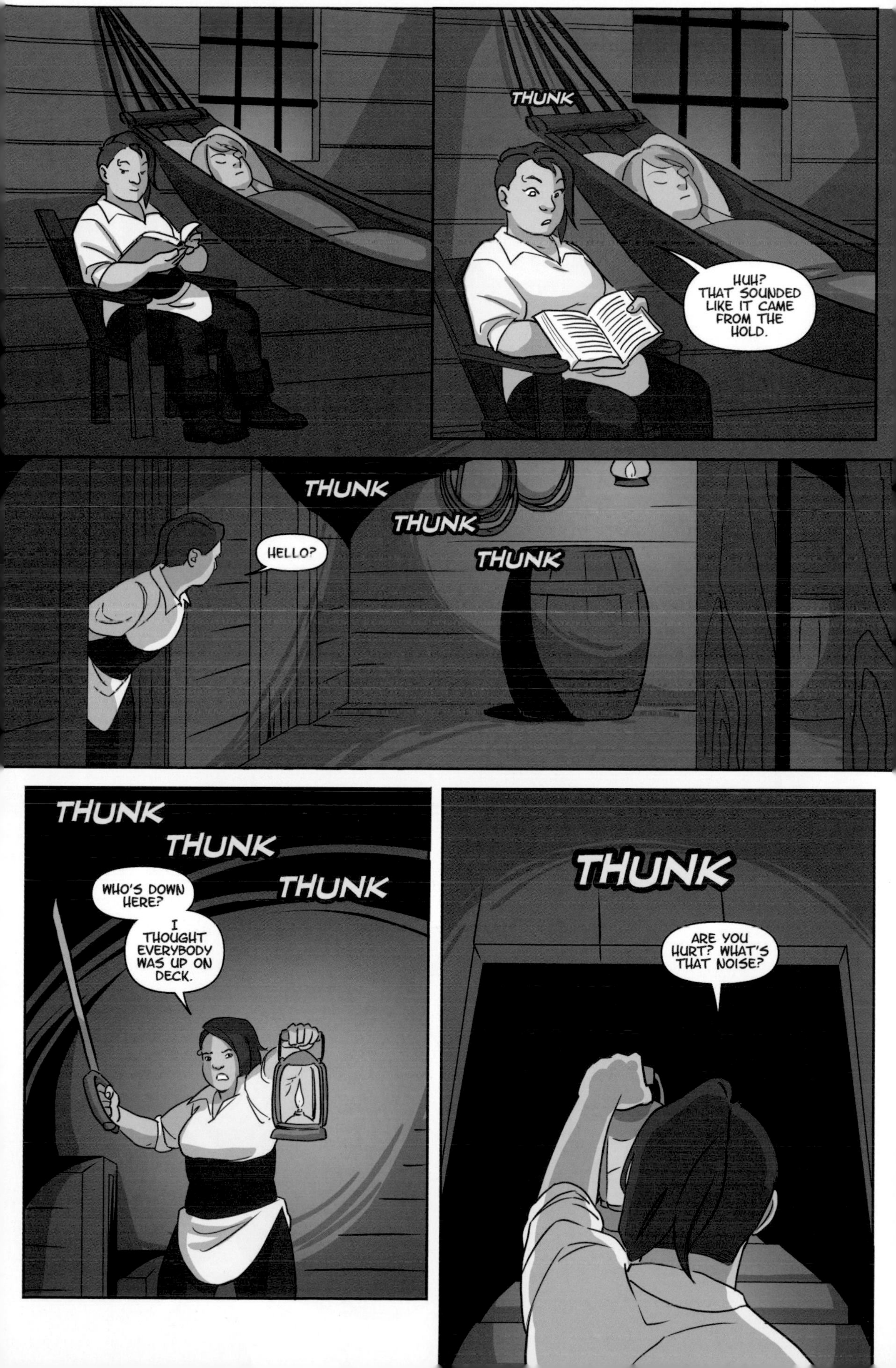
THUNK
HUH? THAT SOUNDED LIKE IT CAME FROM THE HOLD.
THUNK
THUNK
THUNK
HELLO?
THUNK
THUNK
THUNK
WHO'S DOWN HERE?
I THOUGHT EVERYBODY WAS UP ON DECK.
THUNK
ARE YOU HURT? WHAT'S THAT NOISE?

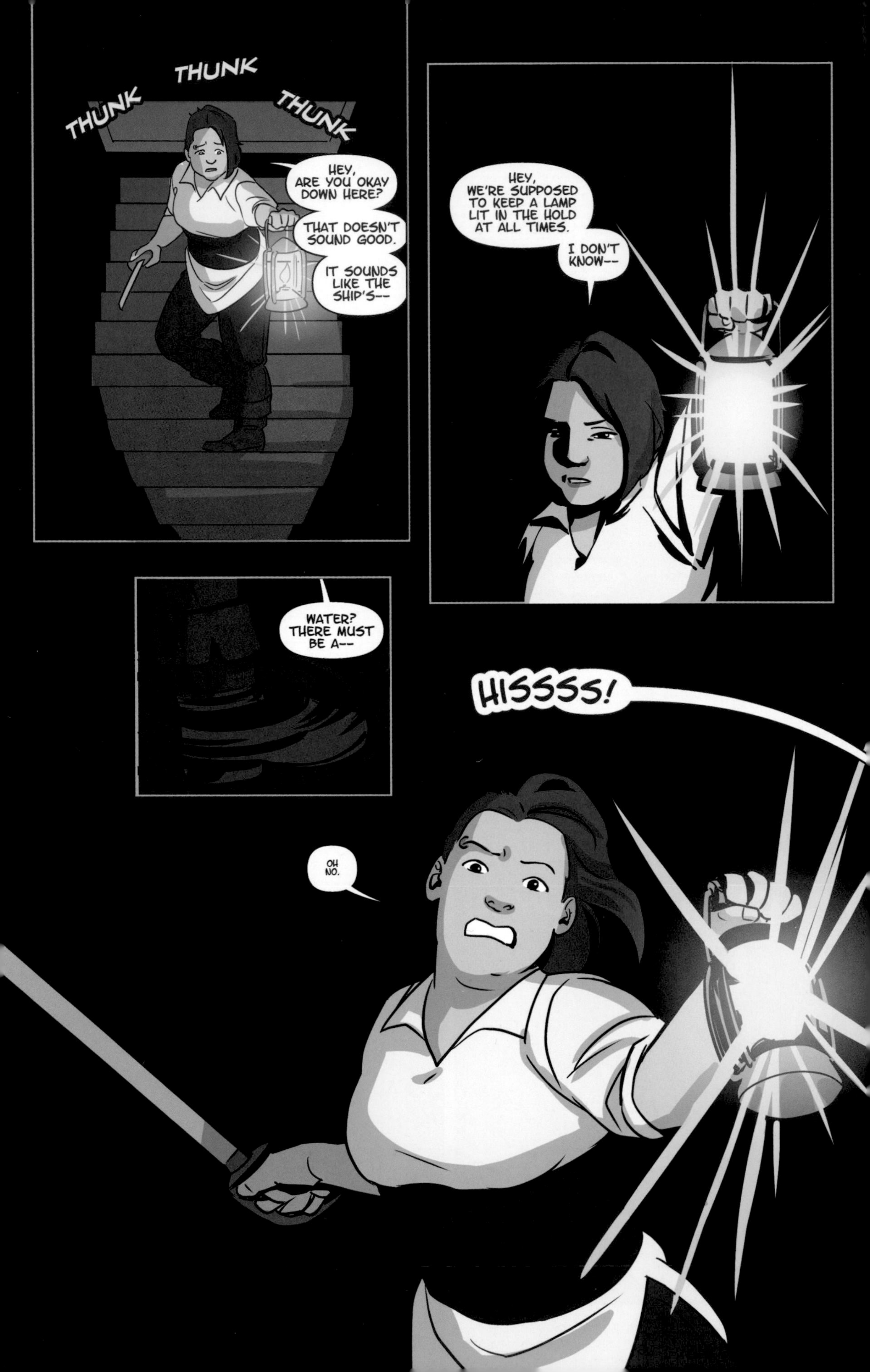
THUNK
THUNK
THUNK
HEY, ARE YOU OKAY DOWN HERE?
THAT DOESN'T SOUND GOOD.
IT SOUNDS LIKE THE SHIP'S--
HEY, WE'RE SUPPOSED TO KEEP A LAMP LIT IN THE HOLD AT ALL TIMES.
I DON'T KNOW--
WATER? THERE MUST BE A--
HISSSS!
OH NO.

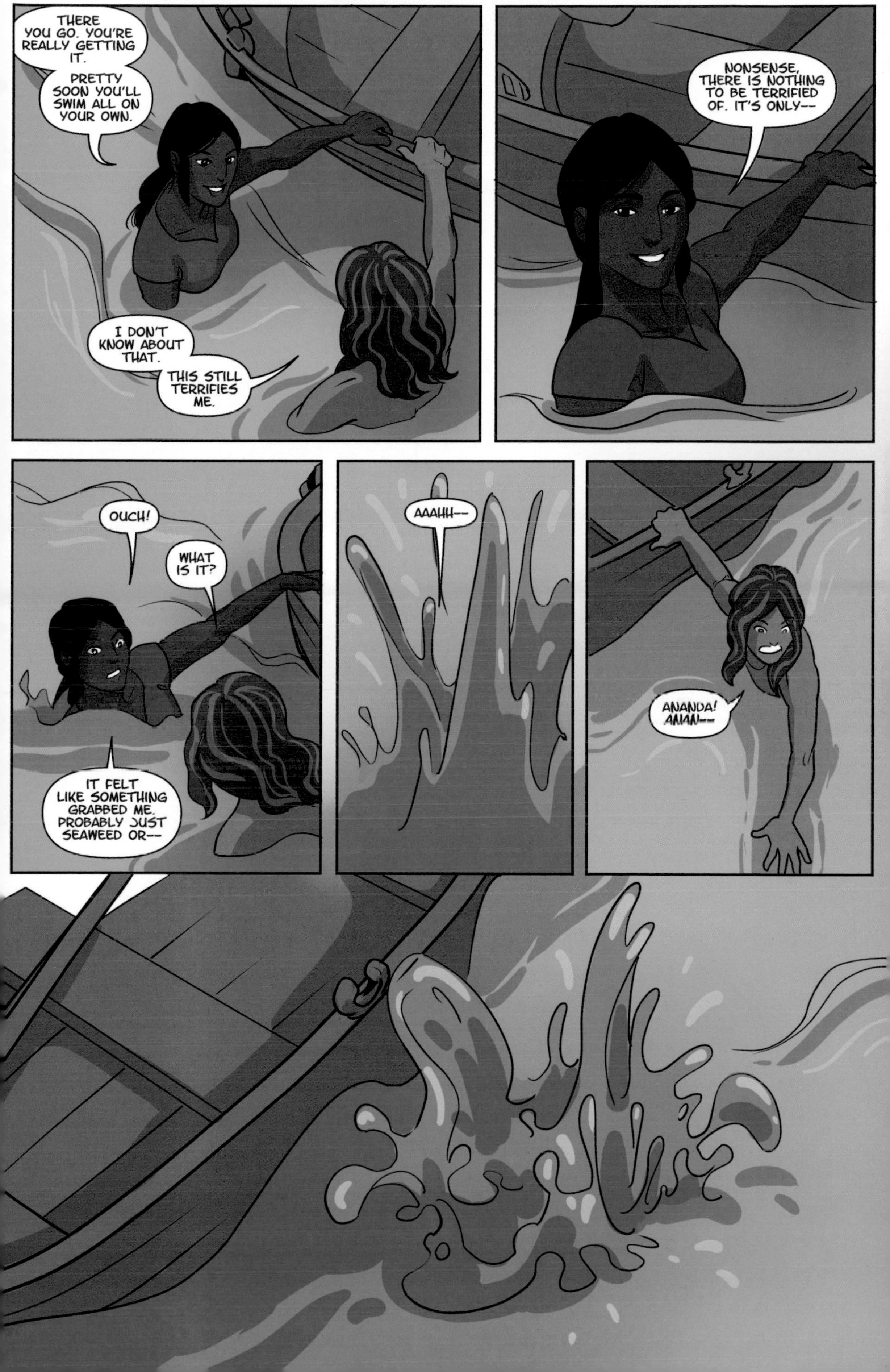
THERE YOU GO. YOU'RE REALLY GETTING IT.
PRETTY SOON YOU'LL SWIM ALL ON YOUR OWN.
I DON'T KNOW ABOUT THAT.
THIS STILL TERRIFIES ME.
NONSENSE, THERE IS NOTHING TO BE TERRIFIED OF. IT'S ONLY--
OUCH!
WHAT IS IT?
IT FELT LIKE SOMETHING GRABBED ME. PROBABLY JUST SEAWEED OR--
AAAHH--
ANANDA! ANAN--

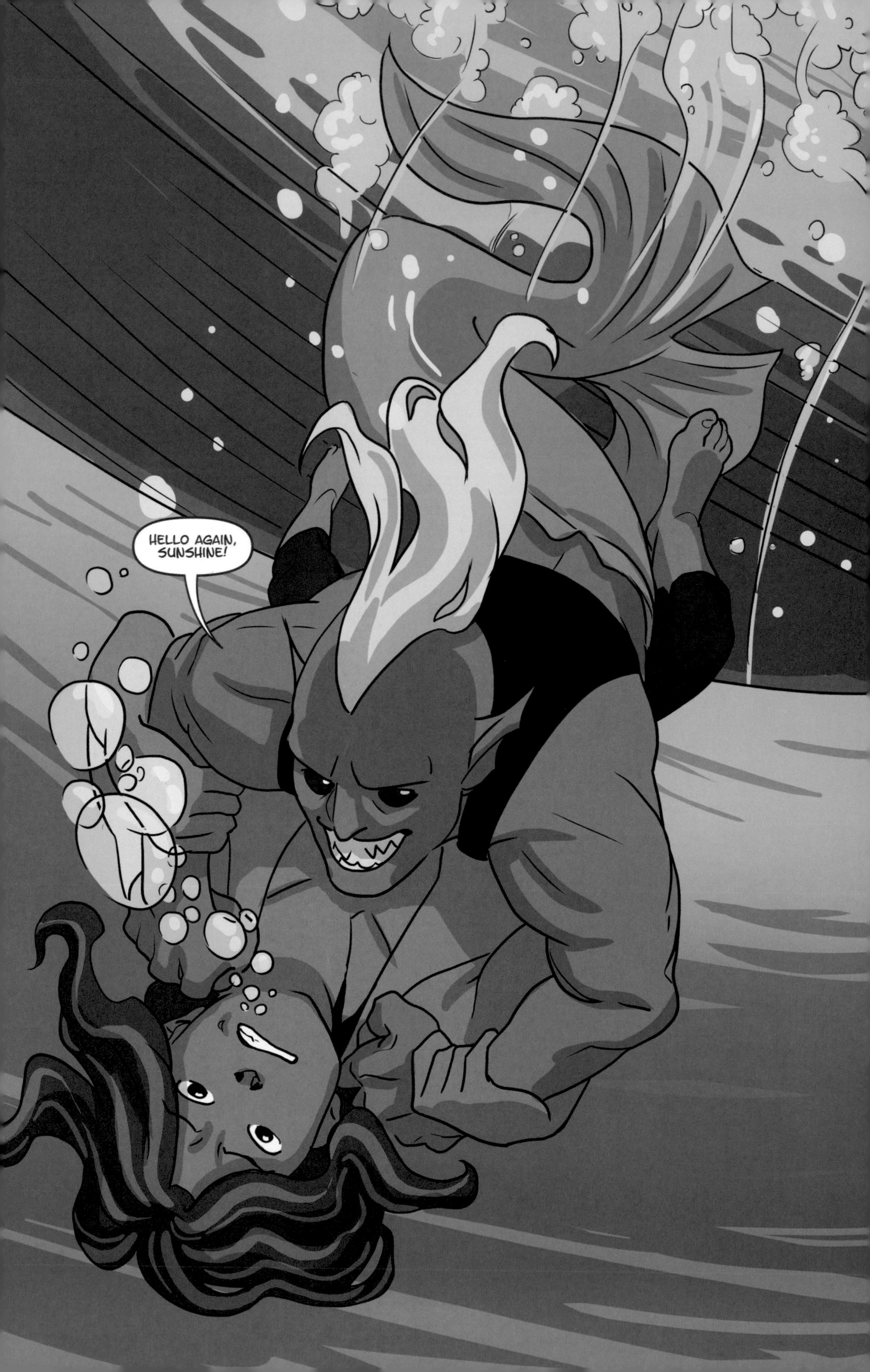
HELLO AGAIN, SUNSHINE!

Princeless

Raven

THE PIRATE PRINCESS

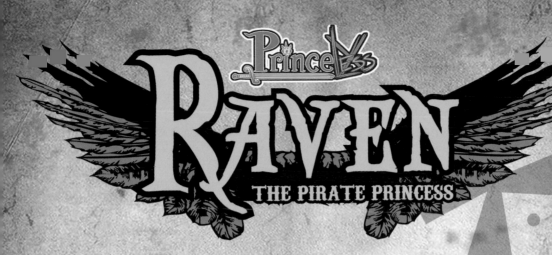

Year Three: Monsters of the Deep

Chapter Six: Deep Breath

Written By: Jeremy Whitley

Pencils By: Telênia Albuquerque

Inks By: Pocket Owl

Colors By: Lexillo

Lettered By: Alex Scherkenbach

Edited By: Nicole D'Andria

Cover By: Telênia Albuquerque

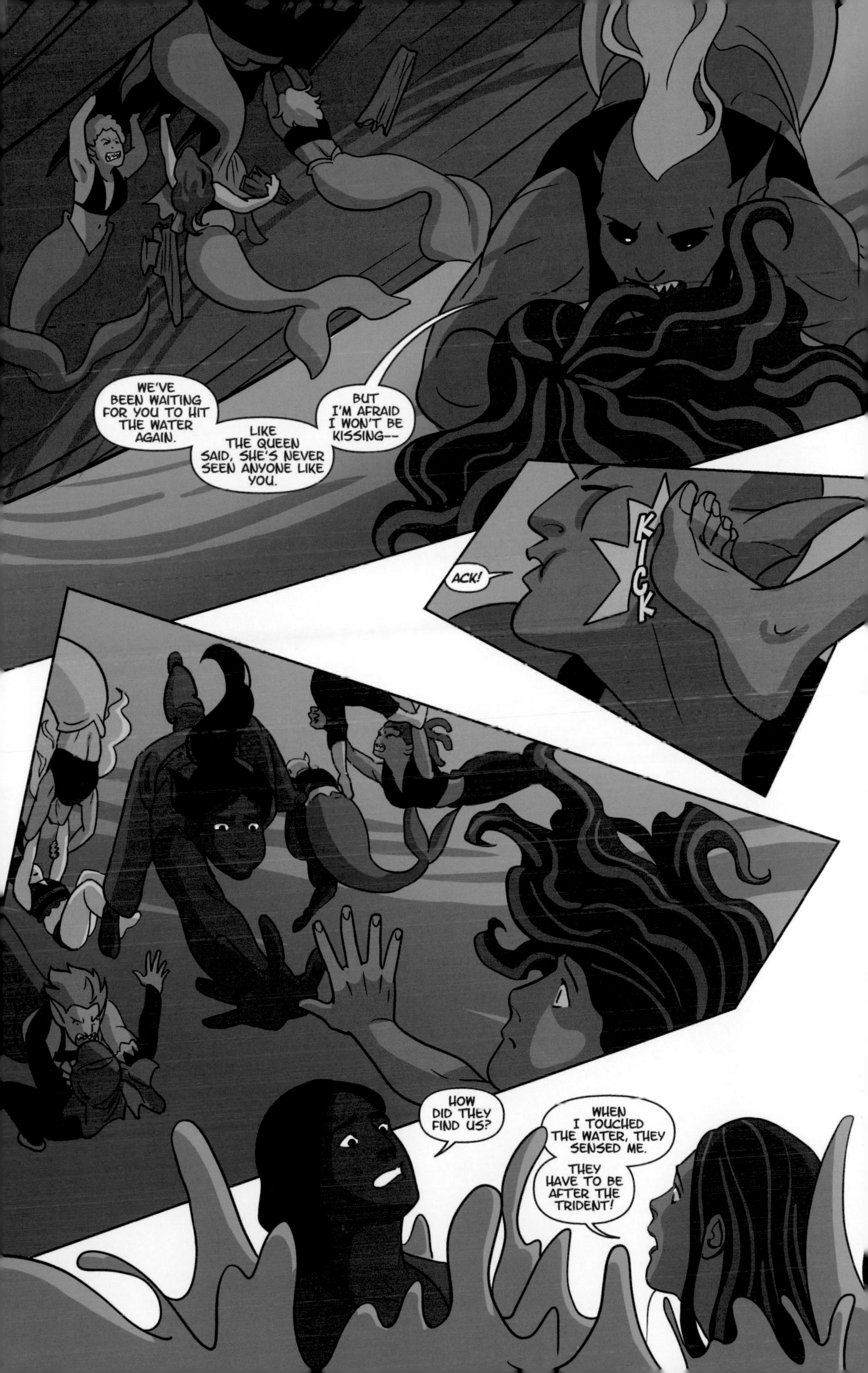
WE'VE BEEN WAITING FOR YOU TO HIT THE WATER AGAIN.
LIKE THE QUEEN SAID, SHE'S NEVER SEEN ANYONE LIKE YOU.
BUT I'M AFRAID I WON'T BE KISSING--
KICK
ACK!
HOW DID THEY FIND US?
WHEN I TOUCHED THE WATER, THEY SENSED ME.
THEY HAVE TO BE AFTER THE TRIDENT!

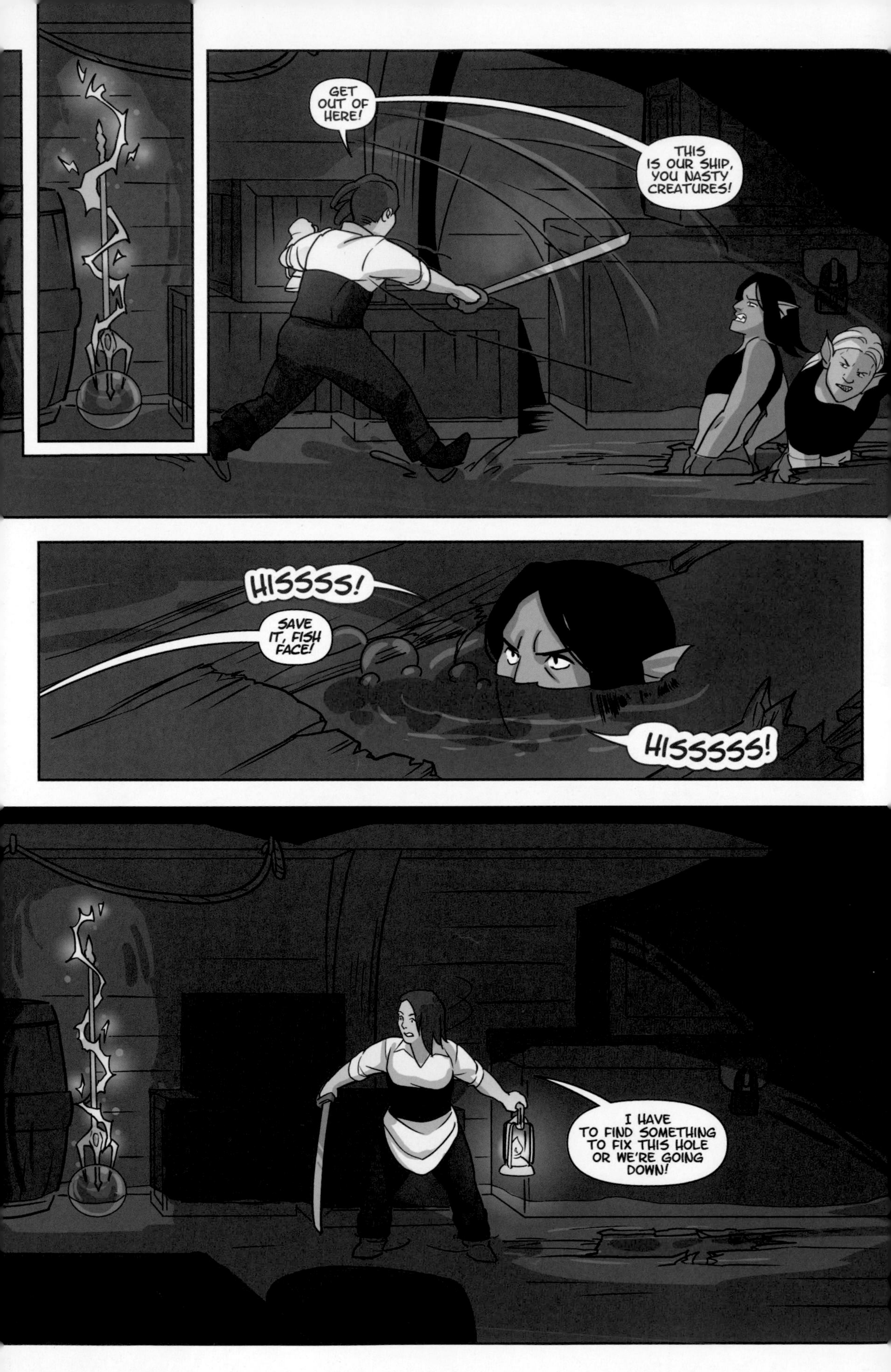
GET OUT OF HERE!
THIS IS OUR SHIP, YOU NASTY CREATURES!
HISSSS!
SAVE IT, FISH FACE!
HISSSSS!
I HAVE TO FIND SOMETHING TO FIX THIS HOLE OR WE'RE GOING DOWN!

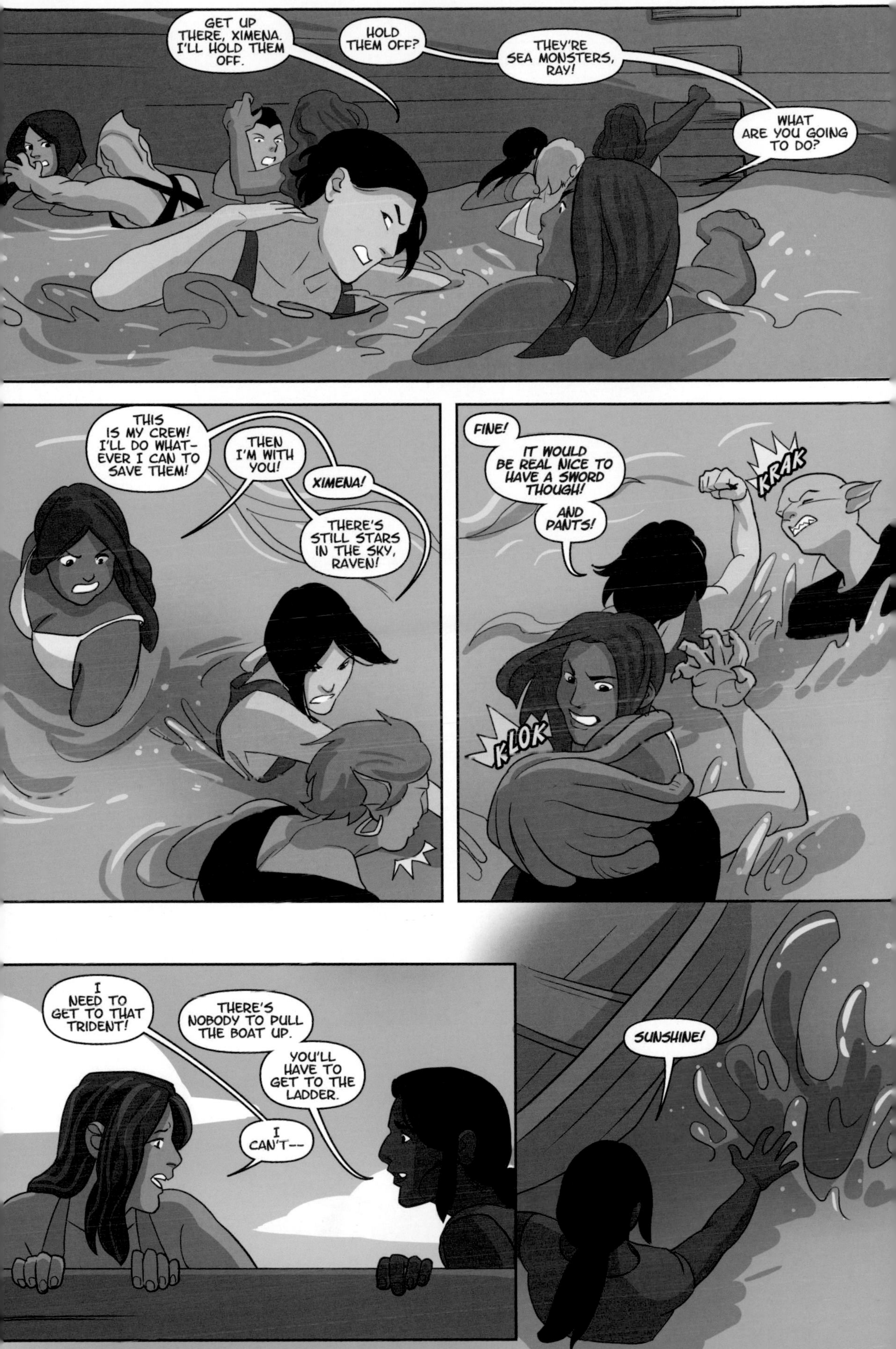
GET UP THERE, XIMENA. I'LL HOLD THEM OFF.
HOLD THEM OFF?
THEY'RE SEA MONSTERS, RAY!
WHAT ARE YOU GOING TO DO?
THIS IS MY CREW! I'LL DO WHATEVER I CAN TO SAVE THEM!
THEN I'M WITH YOU!
XIMENA!
THERE'S STILL STARS IN THE SKY, RAVEN!
FINE!
IT WOULD BE REAL NICE TO HAVE A SWORD THOUGH!
AND PANTS!
KRAK
KLOK
I NEED TO GET TO THAT TRIDENT!
THERE'S NOBODY TO PULL THE BOAT UP.
YOU'LL HAVE TO GET TO THE LADDER.
I CAN'T--
SUNSHINE!

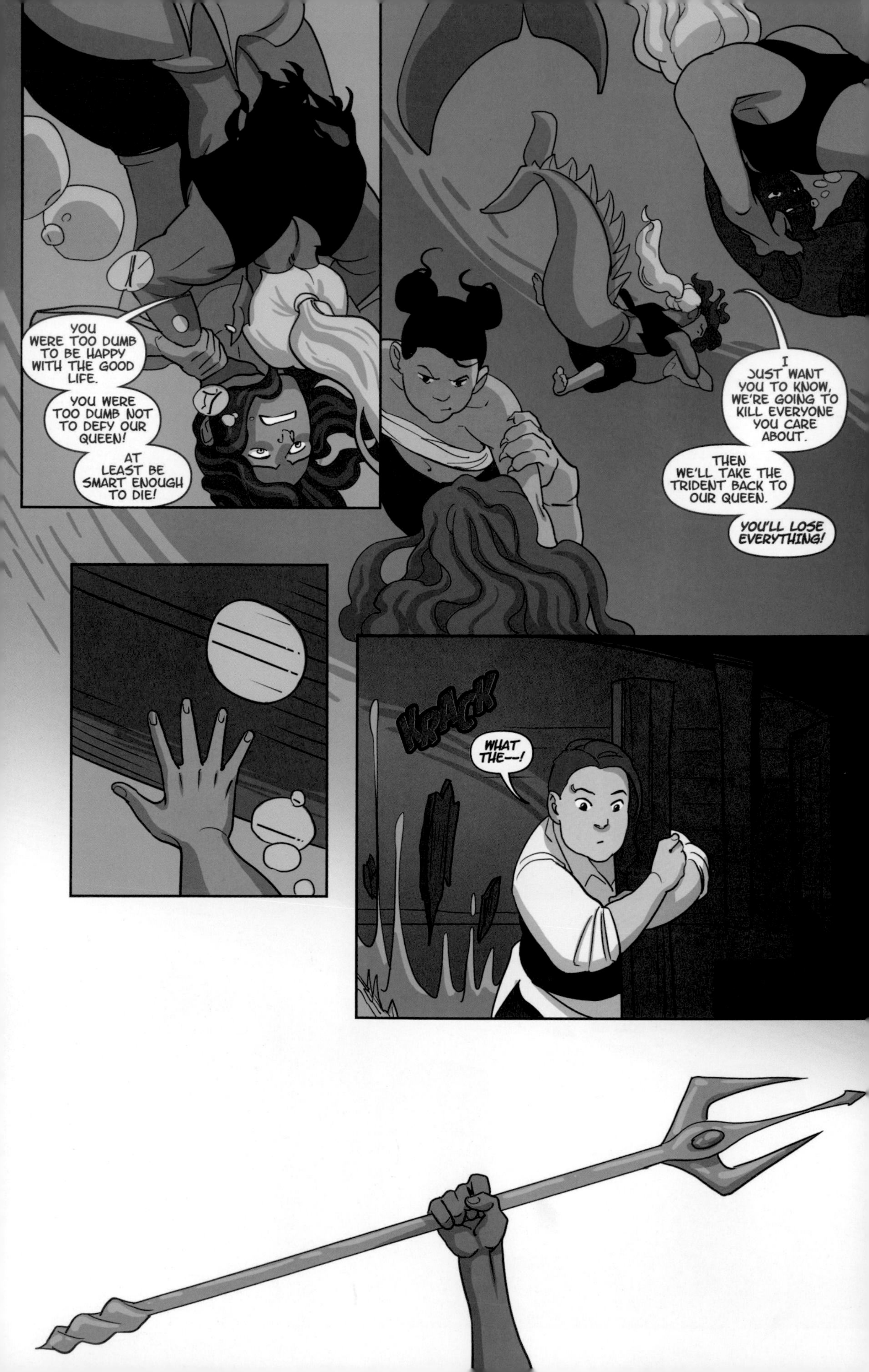
YOU WERE TOO DUMB TO BE HAPPY WITH THE GOOD LIFE.
YOU WERE TOO DUMB NOT TO DEFY OUR QUEEN!
AT LEAST BE SMART ENOUGH TO DIE!
I JUST WANT YOU TO KNOW, WE'RE GOING TO KILL EVERYONE YOU CARE ABOUT.
THEN WE'LL TAKE THE TRIDENT BACK TO OUR QUEEN.
YOU'LL LOSE EVERYTHING!
KRACK
WHAT THE--!

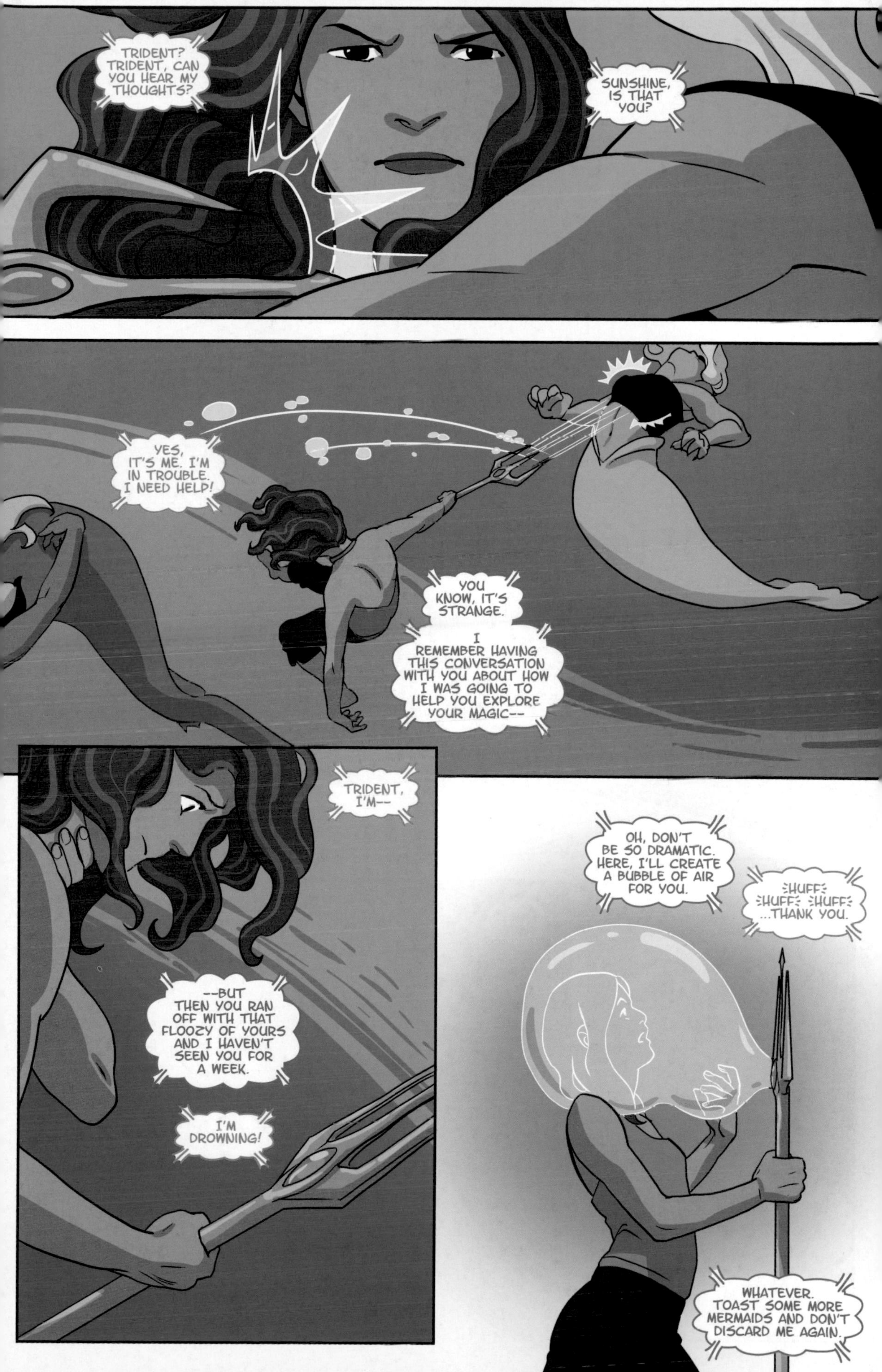
TRIDENT? TRIDENT, CAN YOU HEAR MY THOUGHTS?
SUNSHINE, IS THAT YOU?
YES, IT'S ME. I'M IN TROUBLE. I NEED HELP!
YOU KNOW, IT'S STRANGE.
I REMEMBER HAVING THIS CONVERSATION WITH YOU ABOUT HOW I WAS GOING TO HELP YOU EXPLORE YOUR MAGIC--
TRIDENT, I'M--
--BUT THEN YOU RAN OFF WITH THAT FLOOZY OF YOURS AND I HAVEN'T SEEN YOU FOR A WEEK.
I'M DROWNING!
OH, DON'T BE SO DRAMATIC. HERE, I'LL CREATE A BUBBLE OF AIR FOR YOU.
HUFF HUFF HUFF ...THANK YOU.
WHATEVER. TOAST SOME MORE MERMAIDS AND DON'T DISCARD ME AGAIN.

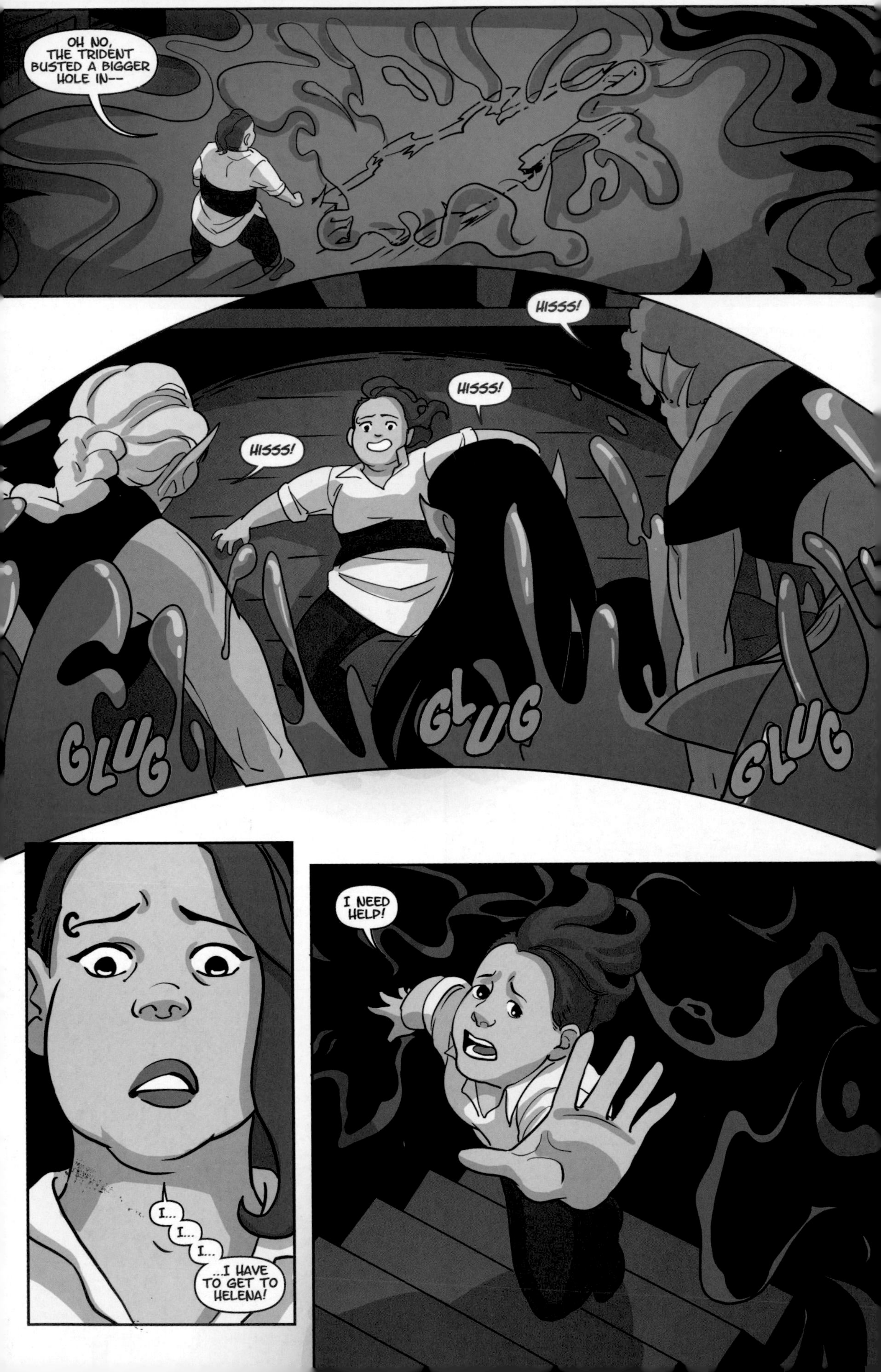
OH NO, THE TRIDENT BUSTED A BIGGER HOLE IN--
HISSS!
HISSS!
HISSS!
GLUG
GLUG
GLUG
I...
I...
I...
...I HAVE TO GET TO HELENA!
I NEED HELP!

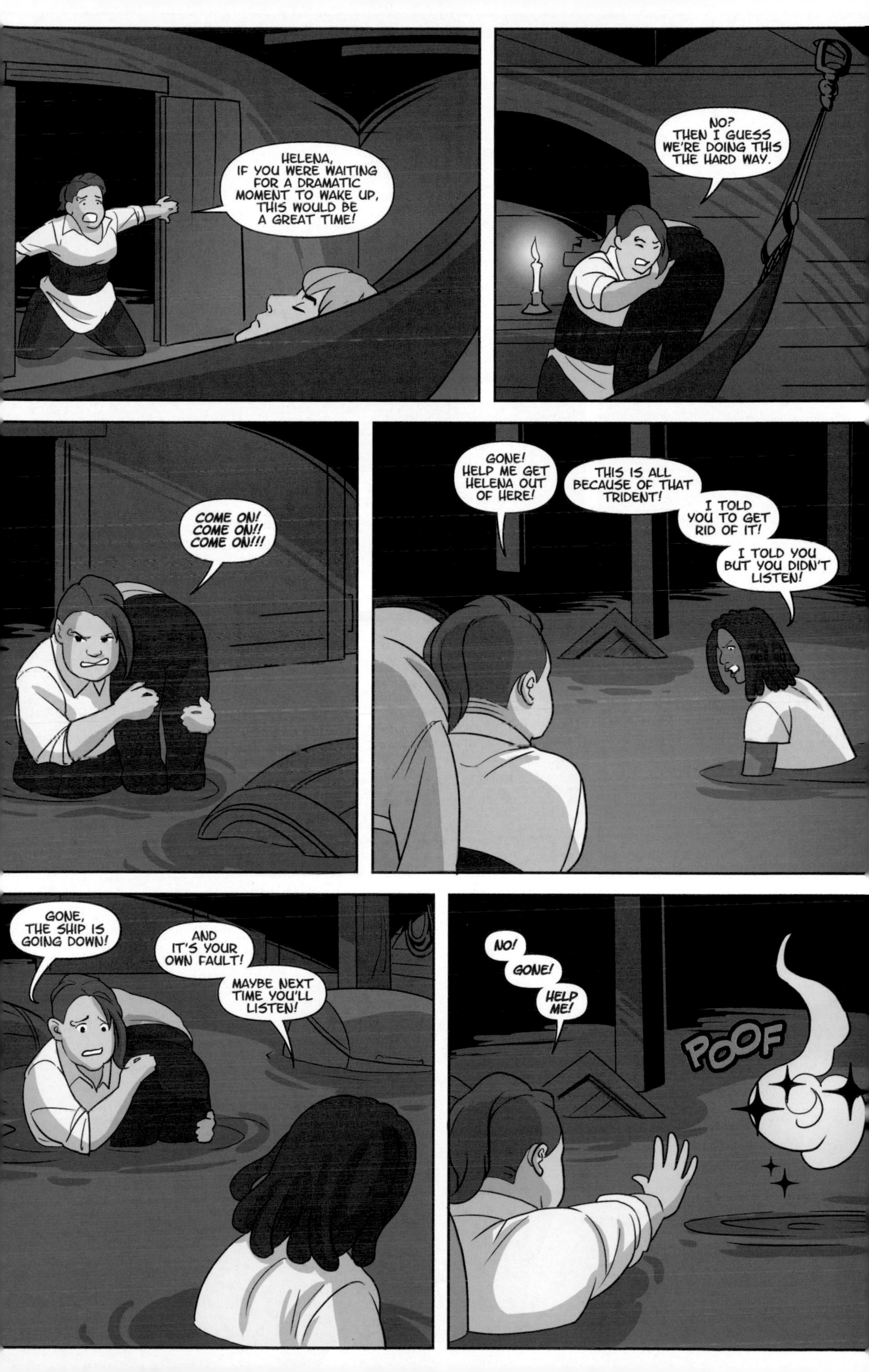
HELENA, IF YOU WERE WAITING FOR A DRAMATIC MOMENT TO WAKE UP, THIS WOULD BE A GREAT TIME!
NO? THEN I GUESS WE'RE DOING THIS THE HARD WAY.
COME ON! COME ON!! COME ON!!!
GONE! HELP ME GET HELENA OUT OF HERE!
THIS IS ALL BECAUSE OF THAT TRIDENT!
I TOLD YOU TO GET RID OF IT!
I TOLD YOU BUT YOU DIDN'T LISTEN!
GONE, THE SHIP IS GOING DOWN!
AND IT'S YOUR OWN FAULT!
MAYBE NEXT TIME YOU'LL LISTEN!
NO!
GONE!
HELP ME!
POOF

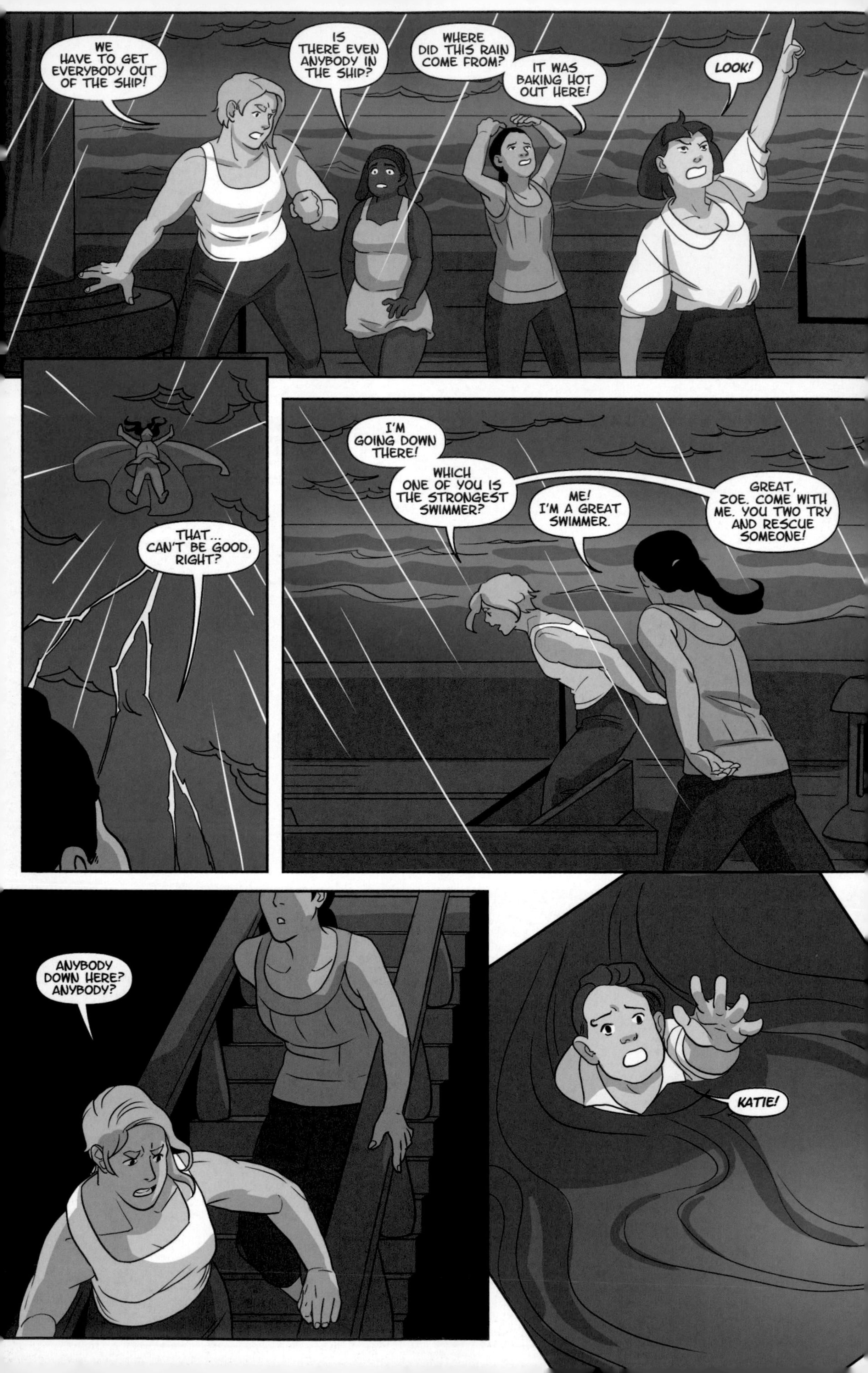
WE HAVE TO GET EVERYBODY OUT OF THE SHIP!
IS THERE EVEN ANYBODY IN THE SHIP?
WHERE DID THIS RAIN COME FROM?
IT WAS BAKING HOT OUT HERE!
LOOK!
THAT... CAN'T BE GOOD, RIGHT?
I'M GOING DOWN THERE!
WHICH ONE OF YOU IS THE STRONGEST SWIMMER?
ME! I'M A GREAT SWIMMER.
GREAT, ZOE. COME WITH ME. YOU TWO TRY AND RESCUE SOMEONE!
ANYBODY DOWN HERE? ANYBODY?
KATIE!

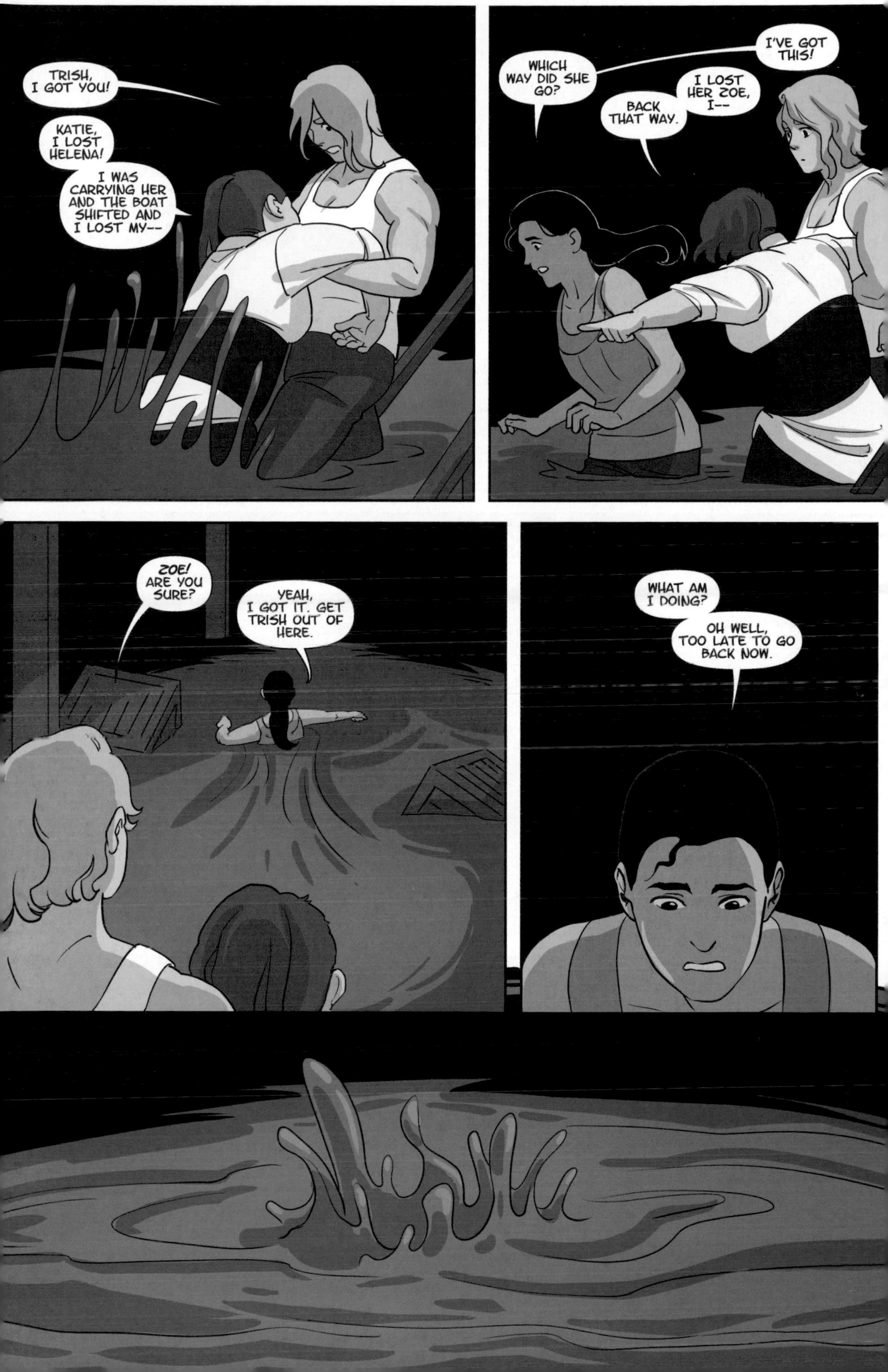
TRISH, I GOT YOU!
KATIE, I LOST HELENA!
I WAS CARRYING HER AND THE BOAT SHIFTED AND I LOST MY--
WHICH WAY DID SHE GO?
I'VE GOT THIS!
I LOST HER ZOE, I--
BACK THAT WAY.
ZOE! ARE YOU SURE?
YEAH, I GOT IT. GET TRISH OUT OF HERE.
WHAT AM I DOING?
OH WELL, TOO LATE TO GO BACK NOW.

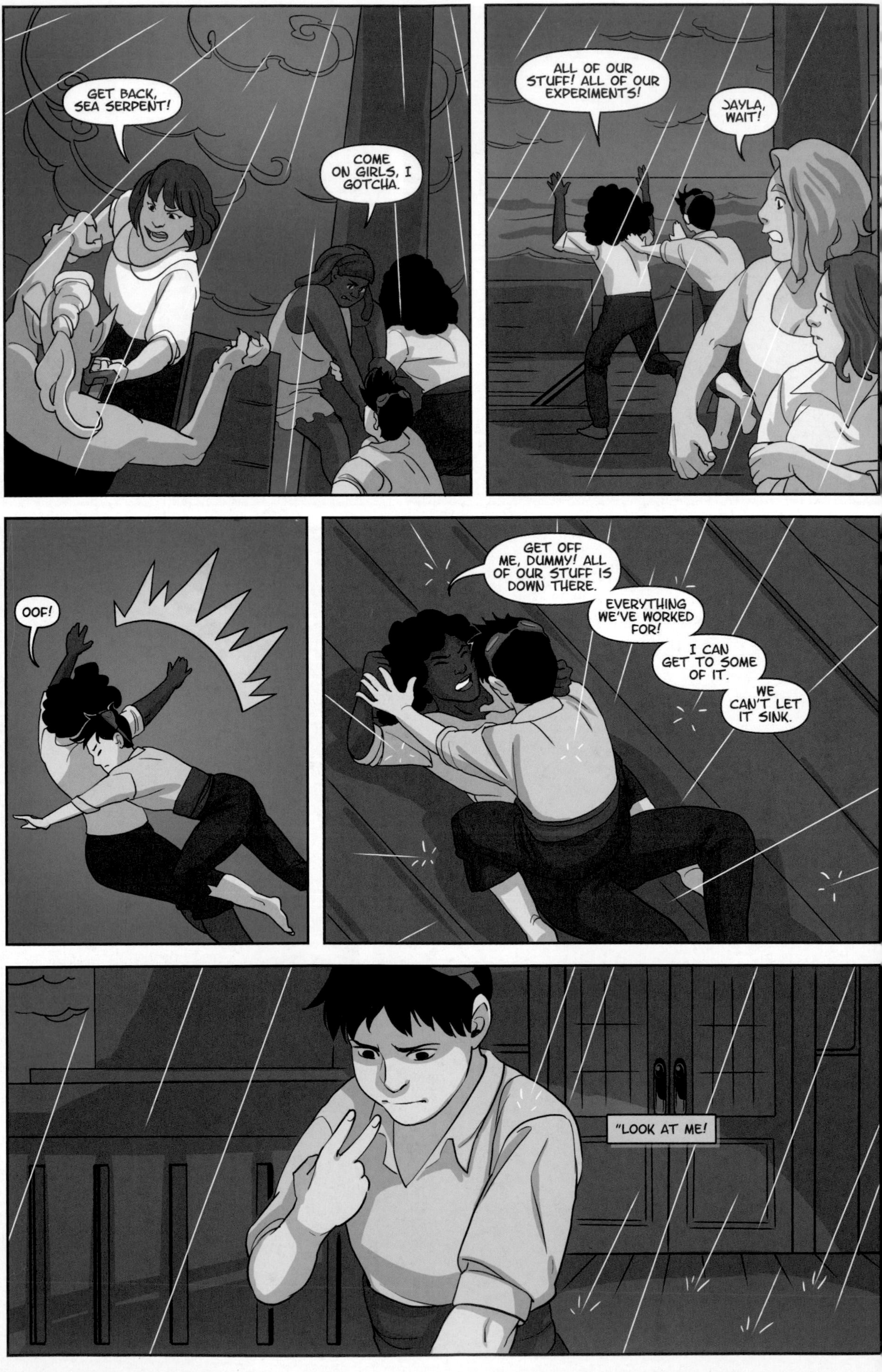
GET BACK, SEA SERPENT!
COME ON GIRLS, I GOTCHA.
ALL OF OUR STUFF! ALL OF OUR EXPERIMENTS!
JAYLA, WAIT!
OOF!
GET OFF ME, DUMMY! ALL OF OUR STUFF IS DOWN THERE.
EVERYTHING WE'VE WORKED FOR!
I CAN GET TO SOME OF IT.
WE CAN'T LET IT SINK.
"LOOK AT ME!

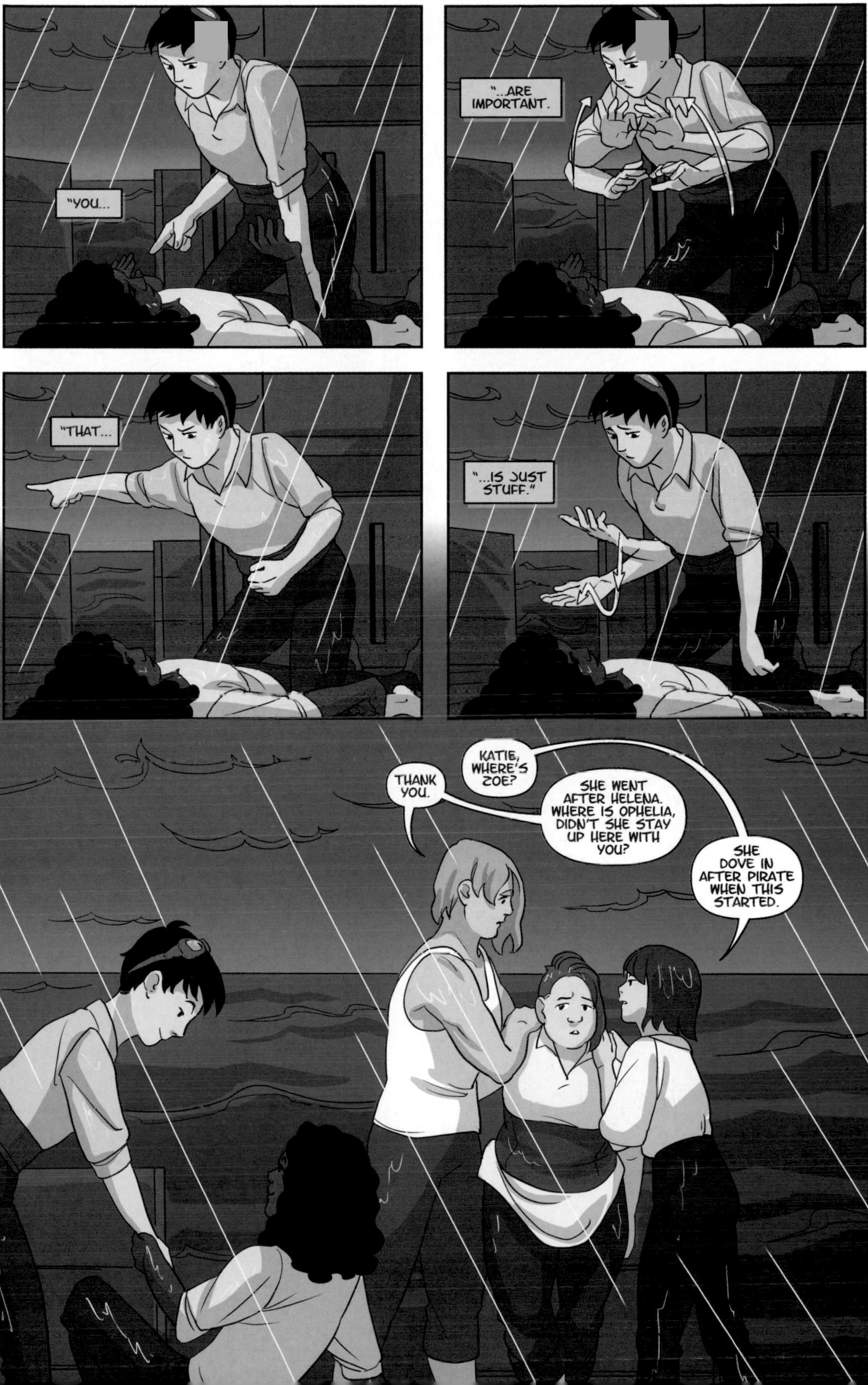
"YOU...
"...ARE IMPORTANT.
"THAT...
"...IS JUST STUFF."
THANK YOU.
KATIE, WHERE'S ZOE?
SHE WENT AFTER HELENA. WHERE IS OPHELIA, DIDN'T SHE STAY UP HERE WITH YOU?
SHE DOVE IN AFTER PIRATE WHEN THIS STARTED.

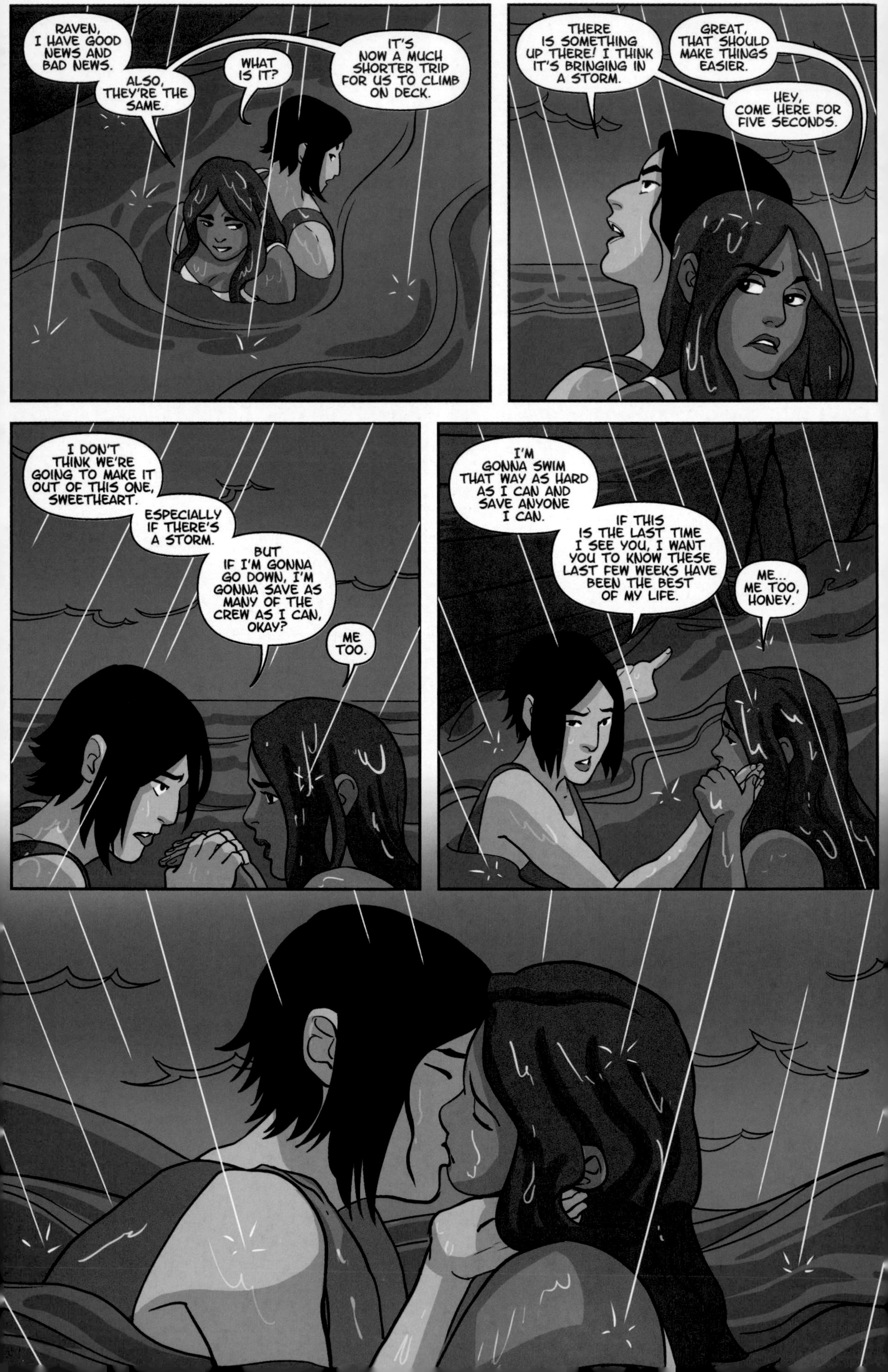
RAVEN, I HAVE GOOD NEWS AND BAD NEWS.
ALSO, THEY'RE THE SAME.
WHAT IS IT?
IT'S NOW A MUCH SHORTER TRIP FOR US TO CLIMB ON DECK.
THERE IS SOMETHING UP THERE! I THINK IT'S BRINGING IN A STORM.
GREAT, THAT SHOULD MAKE THINGS EASIER.
HEY, COME HERE FOR FIVE SECONDS.
I DON'T THINK WE'RE GOING TO MAKE IT OUT OF THIS ONE, SWEETHEART.
ESPECIALLY IF THERE'S A STORM.
BUT IF I'M GONNA GO DOWN, I'M GONNA SAVE AS MANY OF THE CREW AS I CAN, OKAY?
ME TOO.
I'M GONNA SWIM THAT WAY AS HARD AS I CAN AND SAVE ANYONE I CAN.
IF THIS IS THE LAST TIME I SEE YOU, I WANT YOU TO KNOW THESE LAST FEW WEEKS HAVE BEEN THE BEST OF MY LIFE.
ME... ME TOO, HONEY.

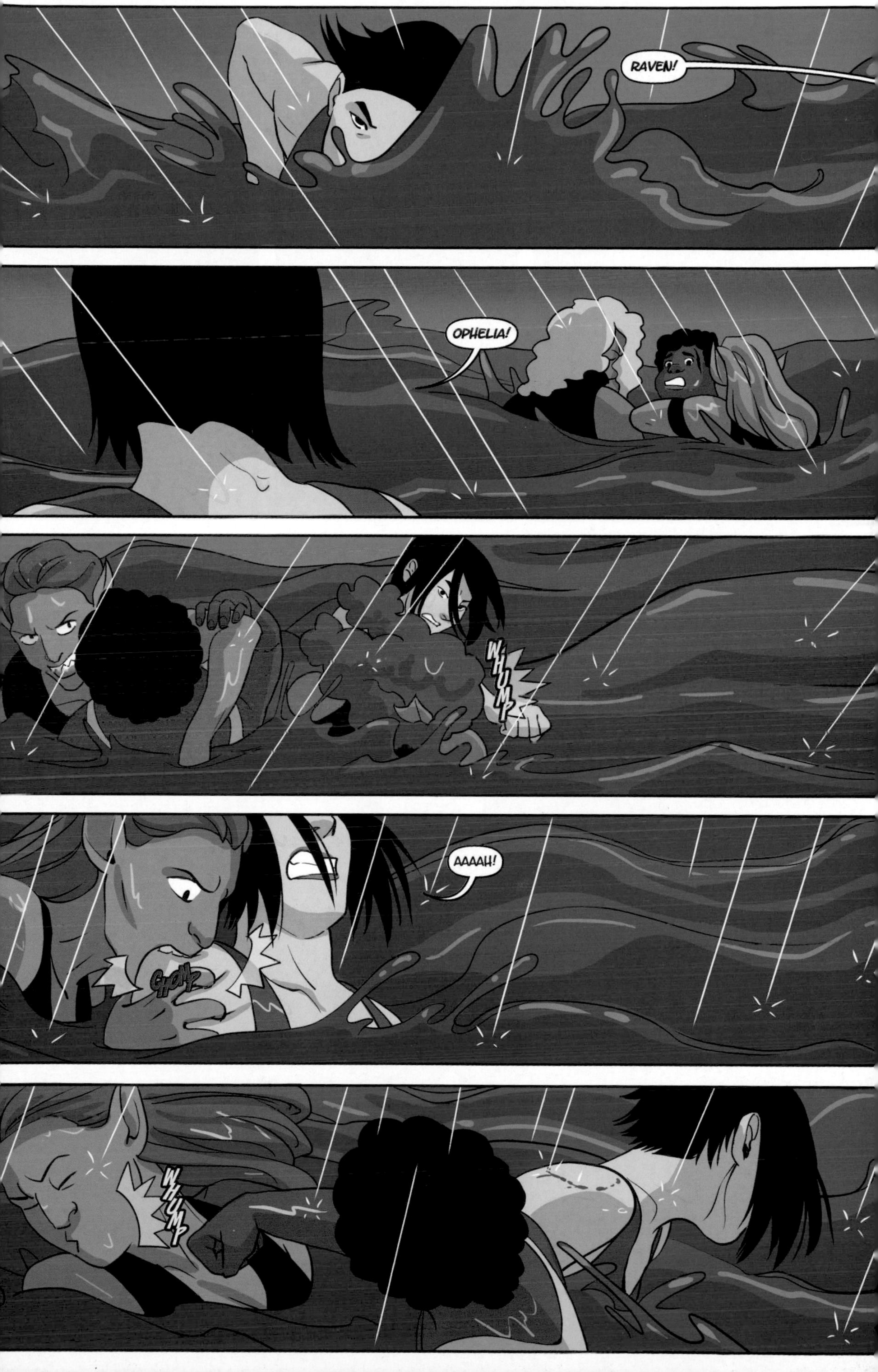
RAVEN!
OPHELIA!
WHUMP
AAAAH!
CHOMP
WHUMP

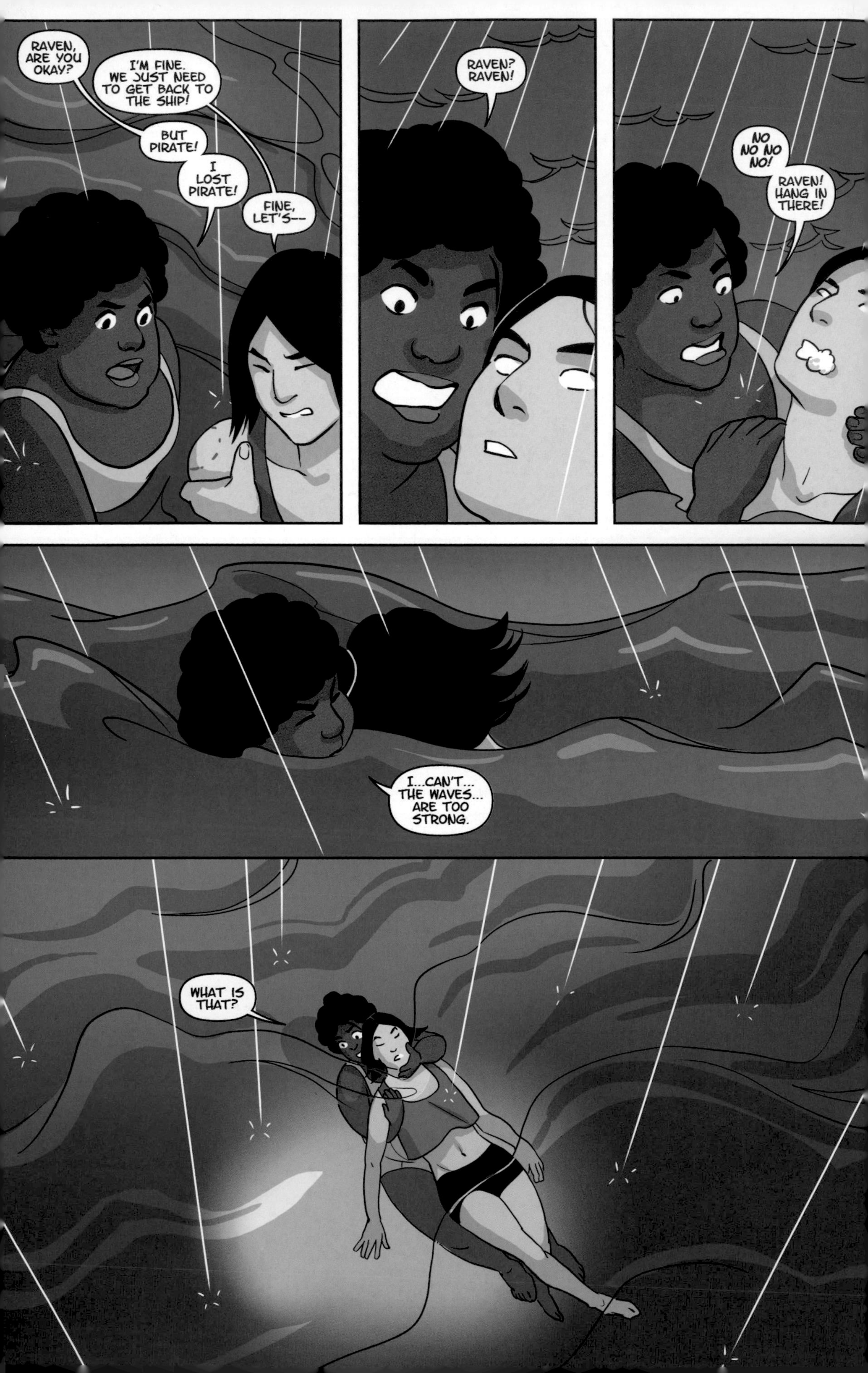
RAVEN, ARE YOU OKAY?
I'M FINE. WE JUST NEED TO GET BACK TO THE SHIP!
BUT PIRATE!
I LOST PIRATE!
FINE, LET'S--
RAVEN? RAVEN!
NO NO NO NO!
RAVEN! HANG IN THERE!
I...CAN'T... THE WAVES... ARE TOO STRONG.
WHAT IS THAT?

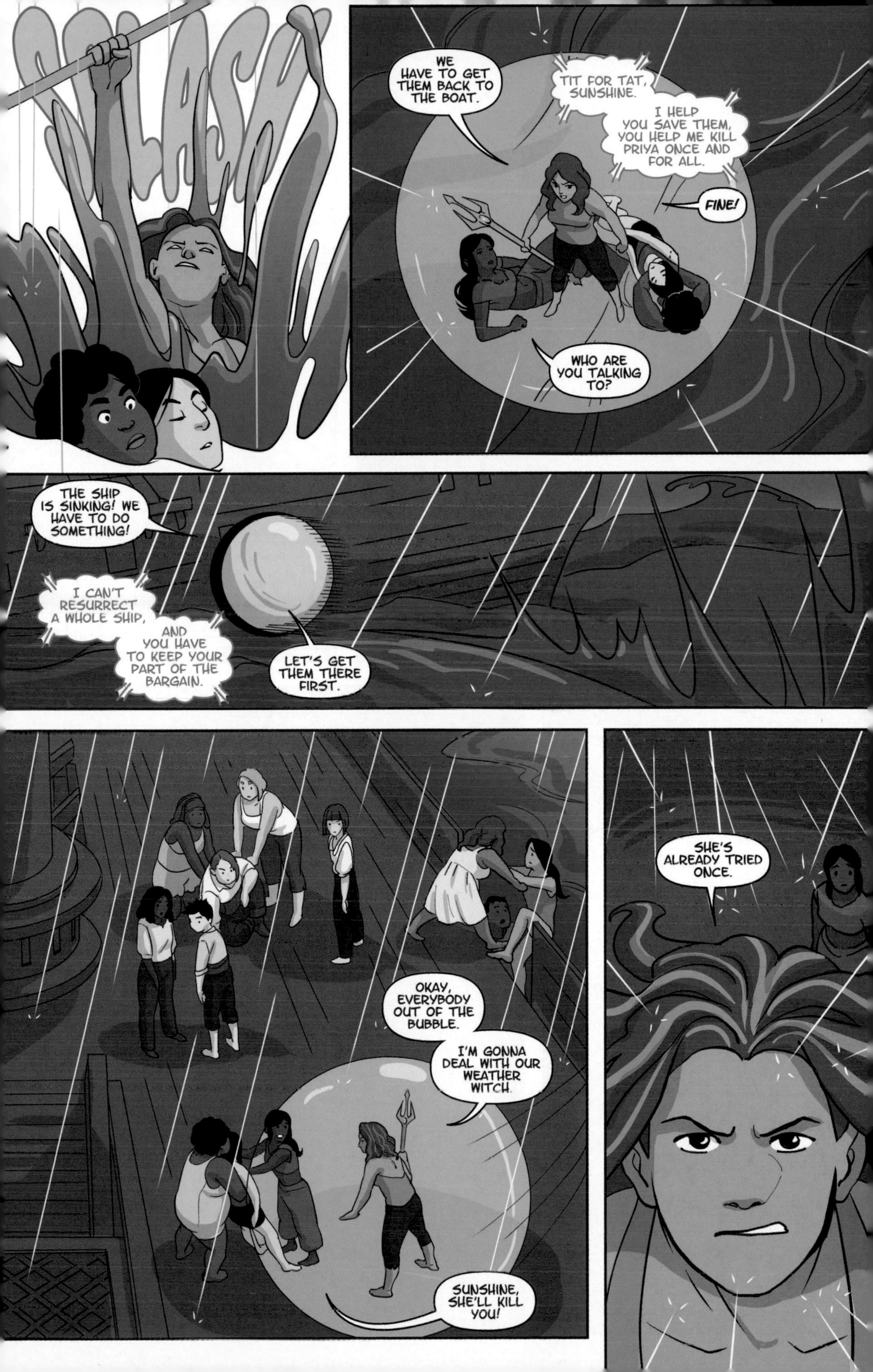
SPLASH
WE HAVE TO GET THEM BACK TO THE BOAT.
TIT FOR TAT, SUNSHINE.
I HELP YOU SAVE THEM, YOU HELP ME KILL PRIYA ONCE AND FOR ALL.
FINE!
WHO ARE YOU TALKING TO?
THE SHIP IS SINKING! WE HAVE TO DO SOMETHING!
I CAN'T RESURRECT A WHOLE SHIP,
AND YOU HAVE TO KEEP YOUR PART OF THE BARGAIN.
LET'S GET THEM THERE FIRST.
OKAY, EVERYBODY OUT OF THE BUBBLE.
I'M GONNA DEAL WITH OUR WEATHER WITCH.
SUNSHINE, SHE'LL KILL YOU!
SHE'S ALREADY TRIED ONCE.

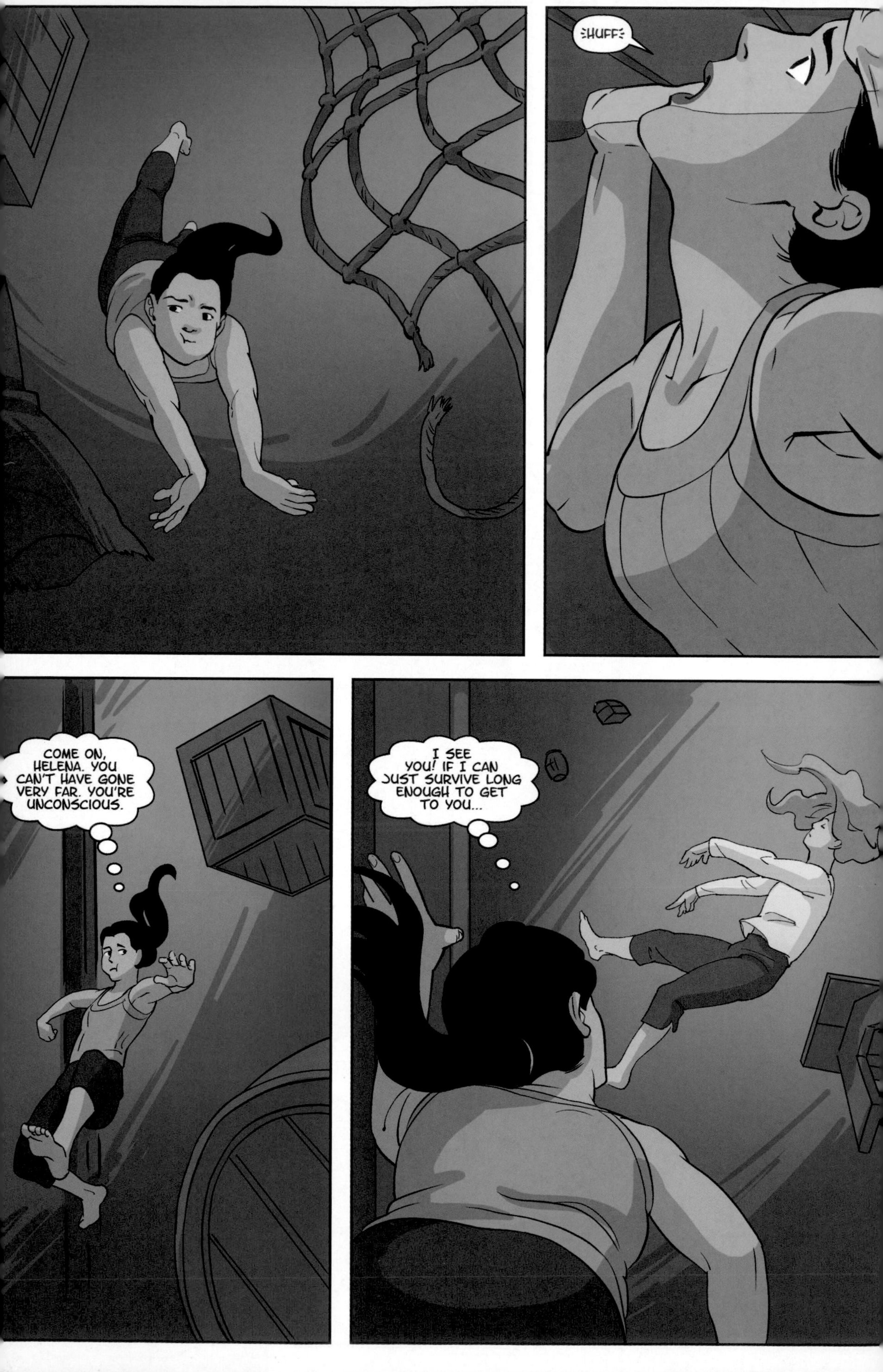
HUFF
COME ON, HELENA. YOU CAN'T HAVE GONE VERY FAR. YOU'RE UNCONSCIOUS.
I SEE YOU! IF I CAN JUST SURVIVE LONG ENOUGH TO GET TO YOU...

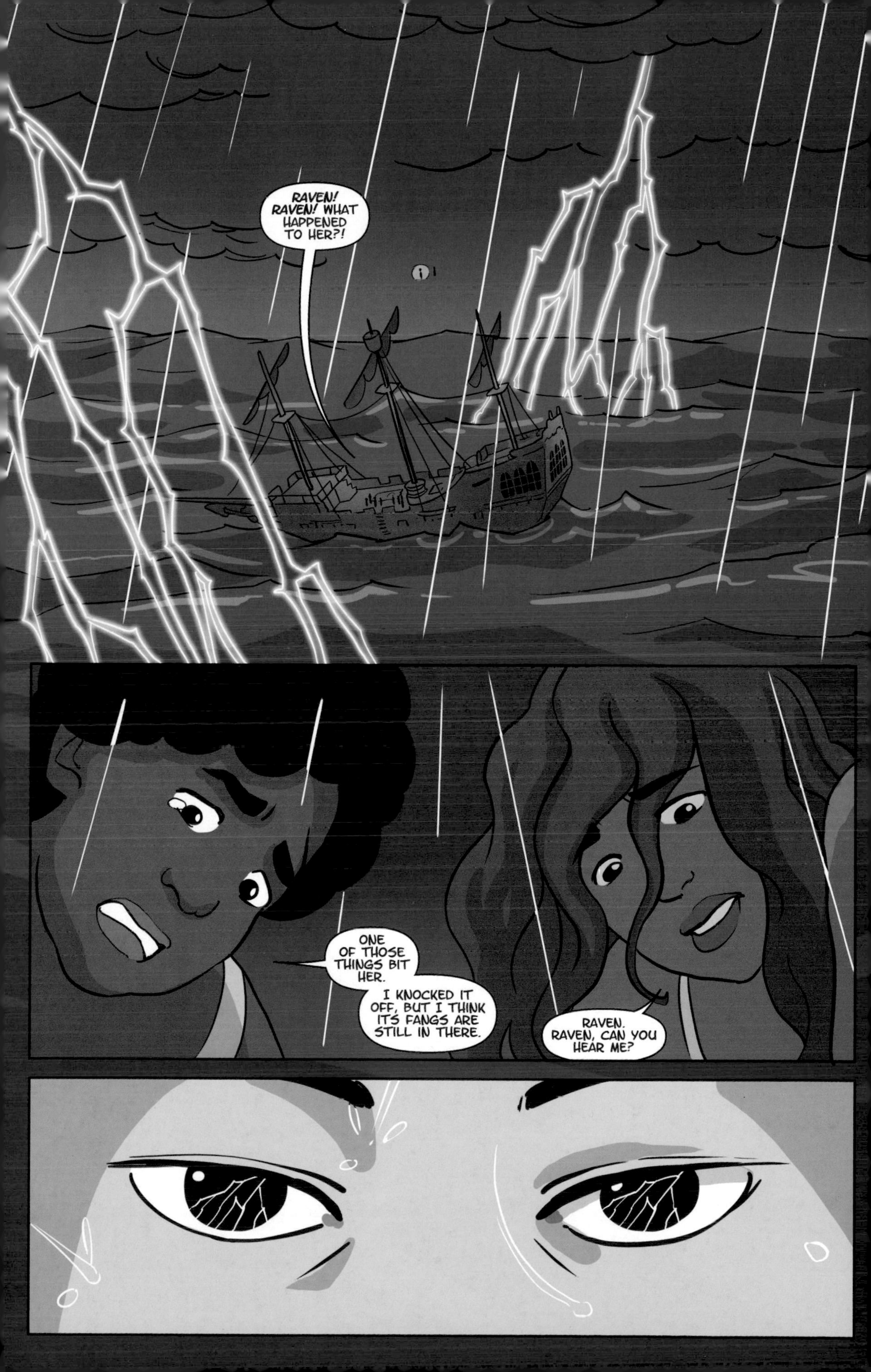
RAVEN! RAVEN! WHAT HAPPENED TO HER?!
ONE OF THOSE THINGS BIT HER.
I KNOCKED IT OFF, BUT I THINK ITS FANGS ARE STILL IN THERE.
RAVEN. RAVEN, CAN YOU HEAR ME?

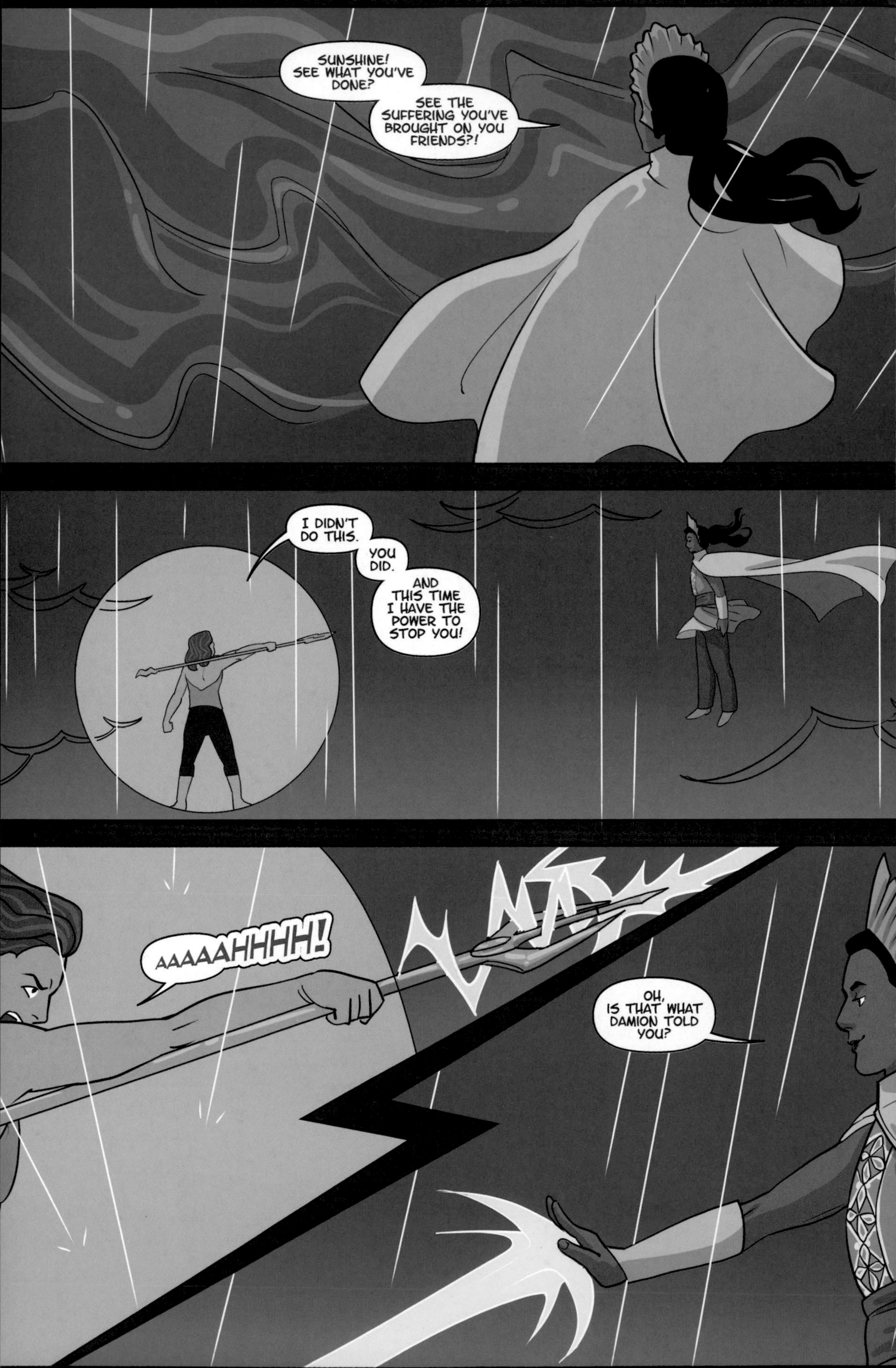
SUNSHINE! SEE WHAT YOU'VE DONE?
SEE THE SUFFERING YOU'VE BROUGHT ON YOU FRIENDS?!
I DIDN'T DO THIS.
YOU DID.
AND THIS TIME I HAVE THE POWER TO STOP YOU!
AAAAAHHHH!
OH, IS THAT WHAT DAMION TOLD YOU?

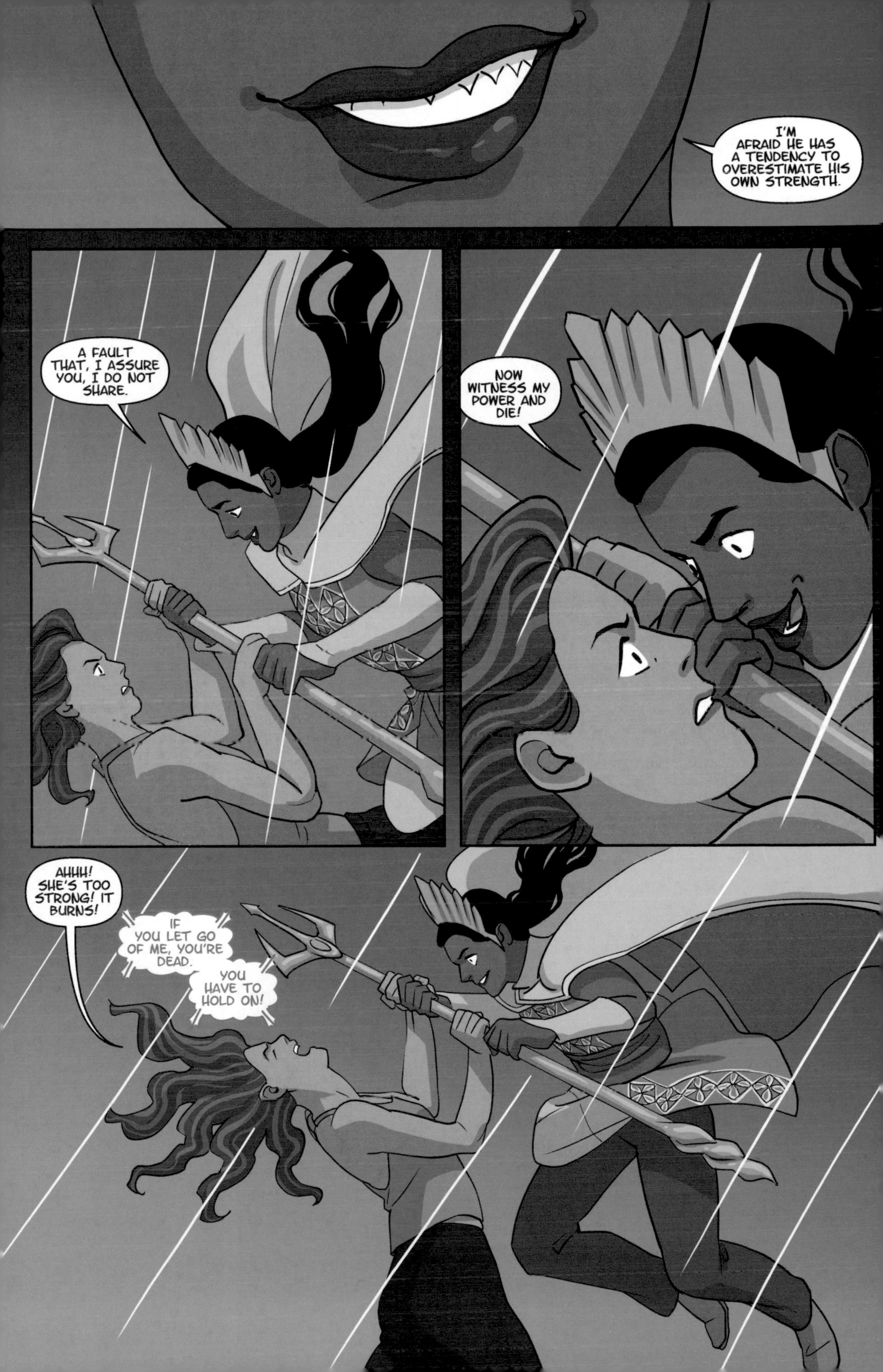
I'M AFRAID HE HAS A TENDENCY TO OVERESTIMATE HIS OWN STRENGTH.
A FAULT THAT, I ASSURE YOU, I DO NOT SHARE.
NOW WITNESS MY POWER AND DIE!
AHHH! SHE'S TOO STRONG! IT BURNS!
IF YOU LET GO OF ME, YOU'RE DEAD.
YOU HAVE TO HOLD ON!

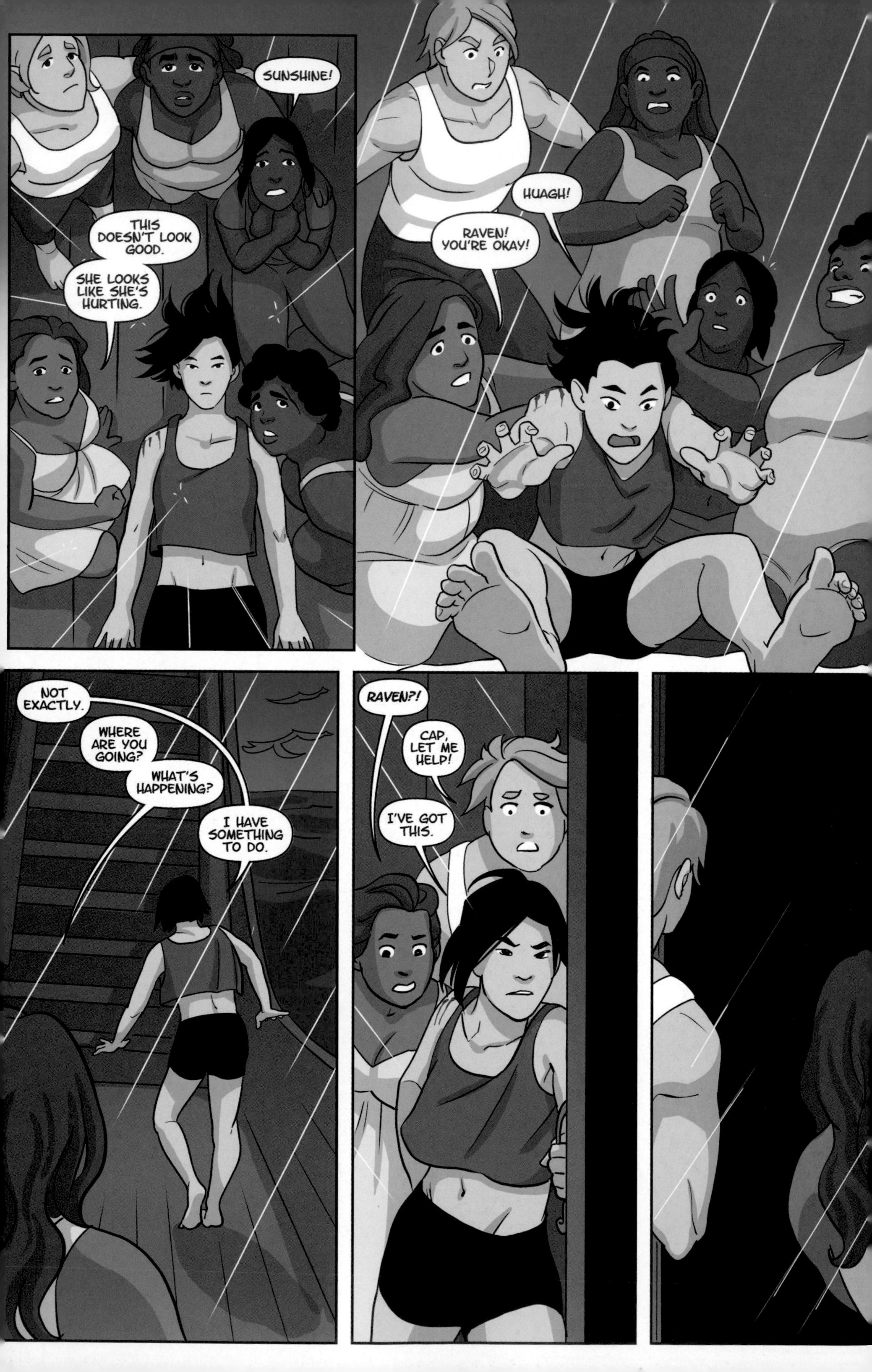
SUNSHINE!
THIS DOESN'T LOOK GOOD.
SHE LOOKS LIKE SHE'S HURTING.
HUAGH!
RAVEN! YOU'RE OKAY!
NOT EXACTLY.
WHERE ARE YOU GOING?
WHAT'S HAPPENING?
I HAVE SOMETHING TO DO.
RAVEN?!
CAP, LET ME HELP!
I'VE GOT THIS.

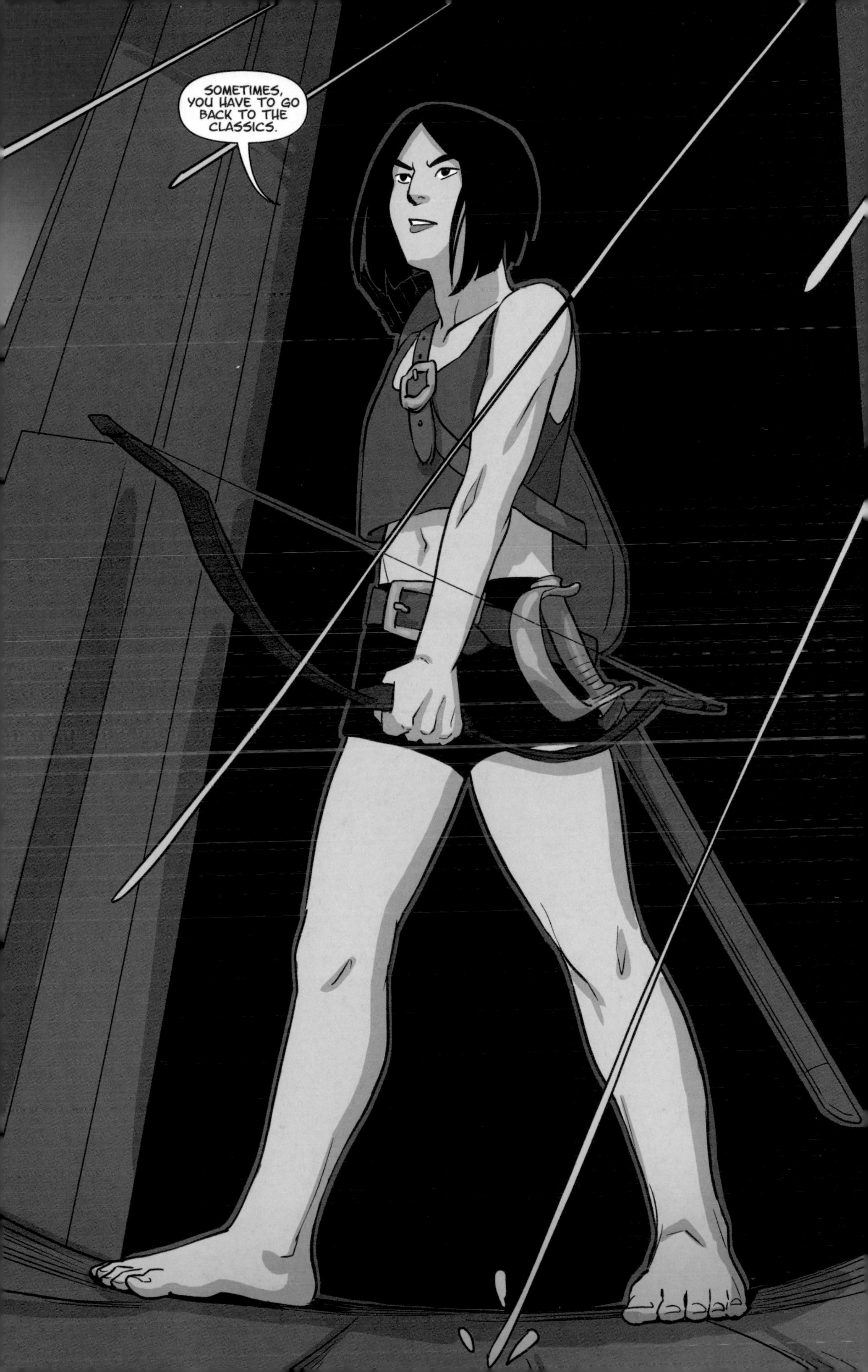
SOMETIMES, YOU HAVE TO GO BACK TO THE CLASSICS.

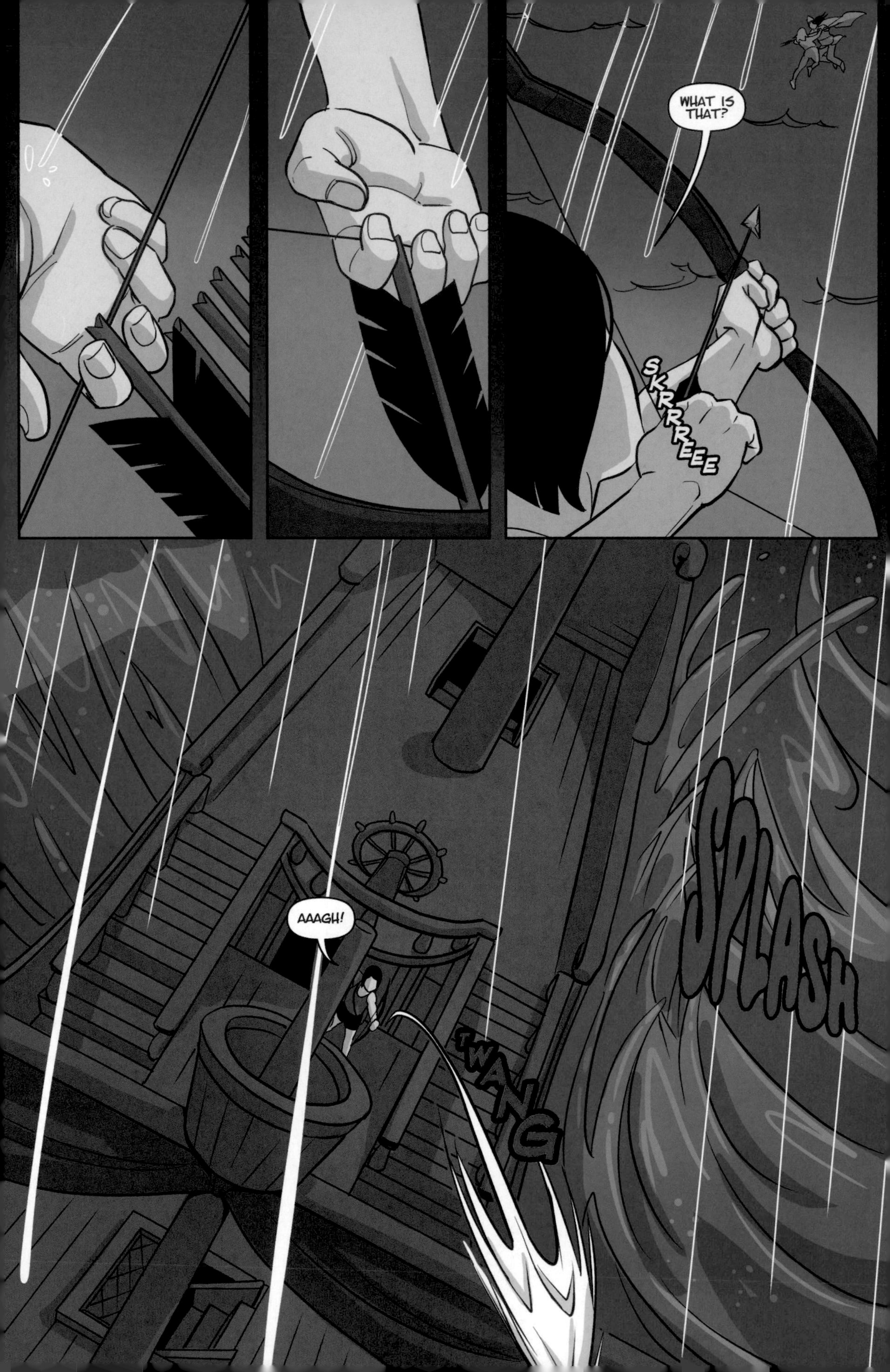
WHAT IS THAT?
SKRRREEE
AAAGH!
SPLASH
TWANG

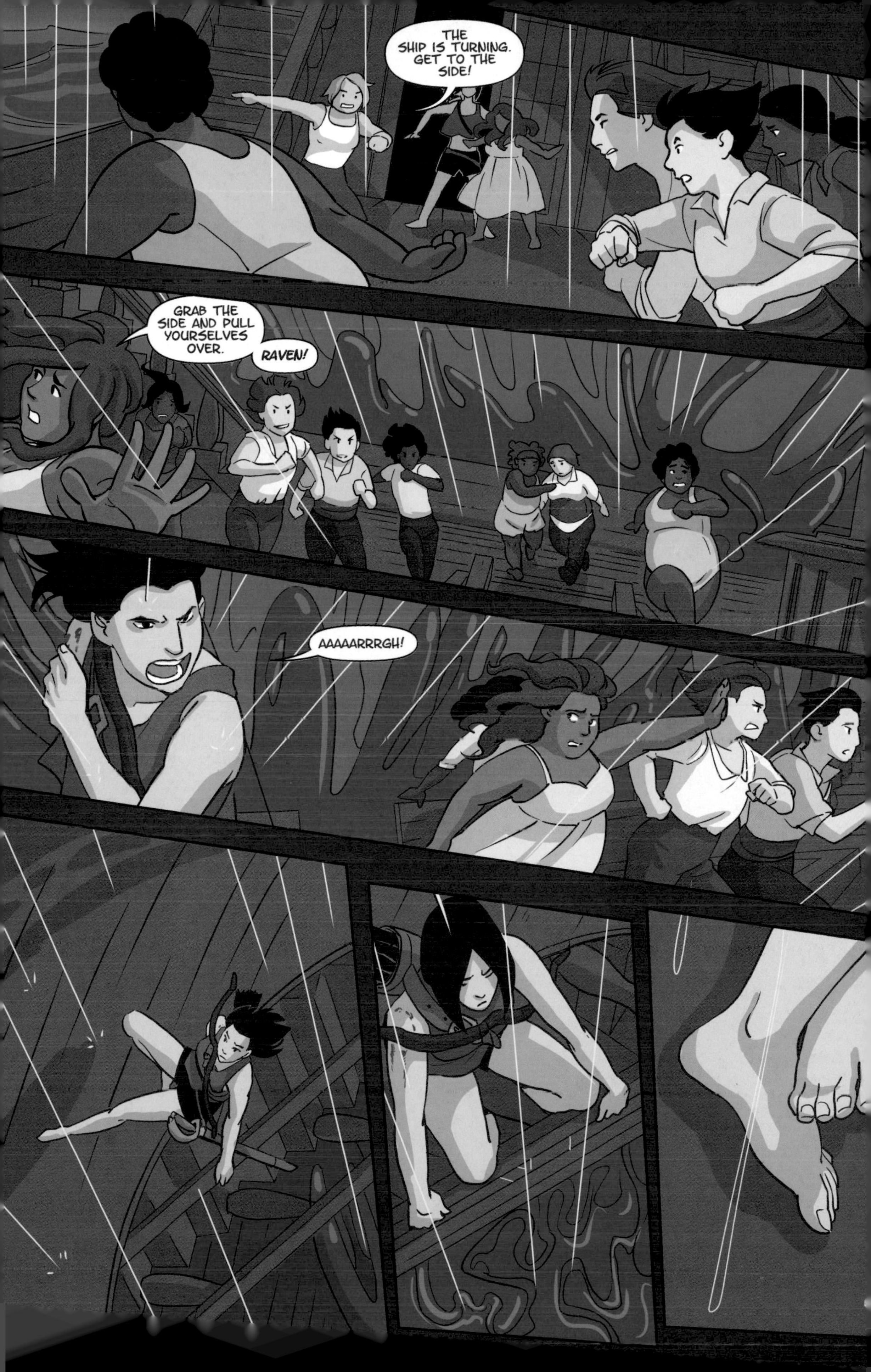
THE SHIP IS TURNING. GET TO THE SIDE!
GRAB THE SIDE AND PULL YOURSELVES OVER.
RAVEN!
AAAAARRRGH!

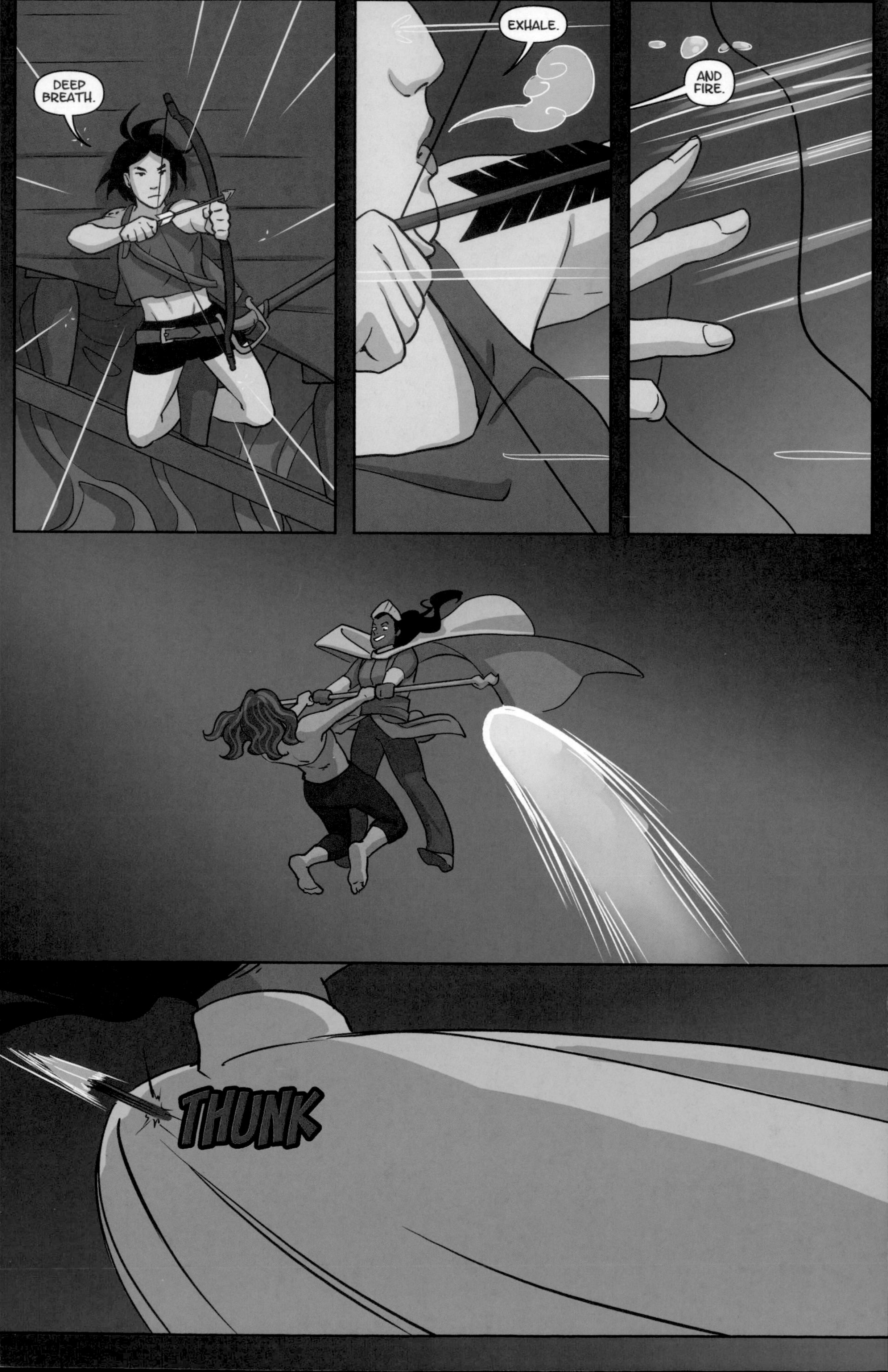

DEEP BREATH.
EXHALE.
AND FIRE.
THUNK

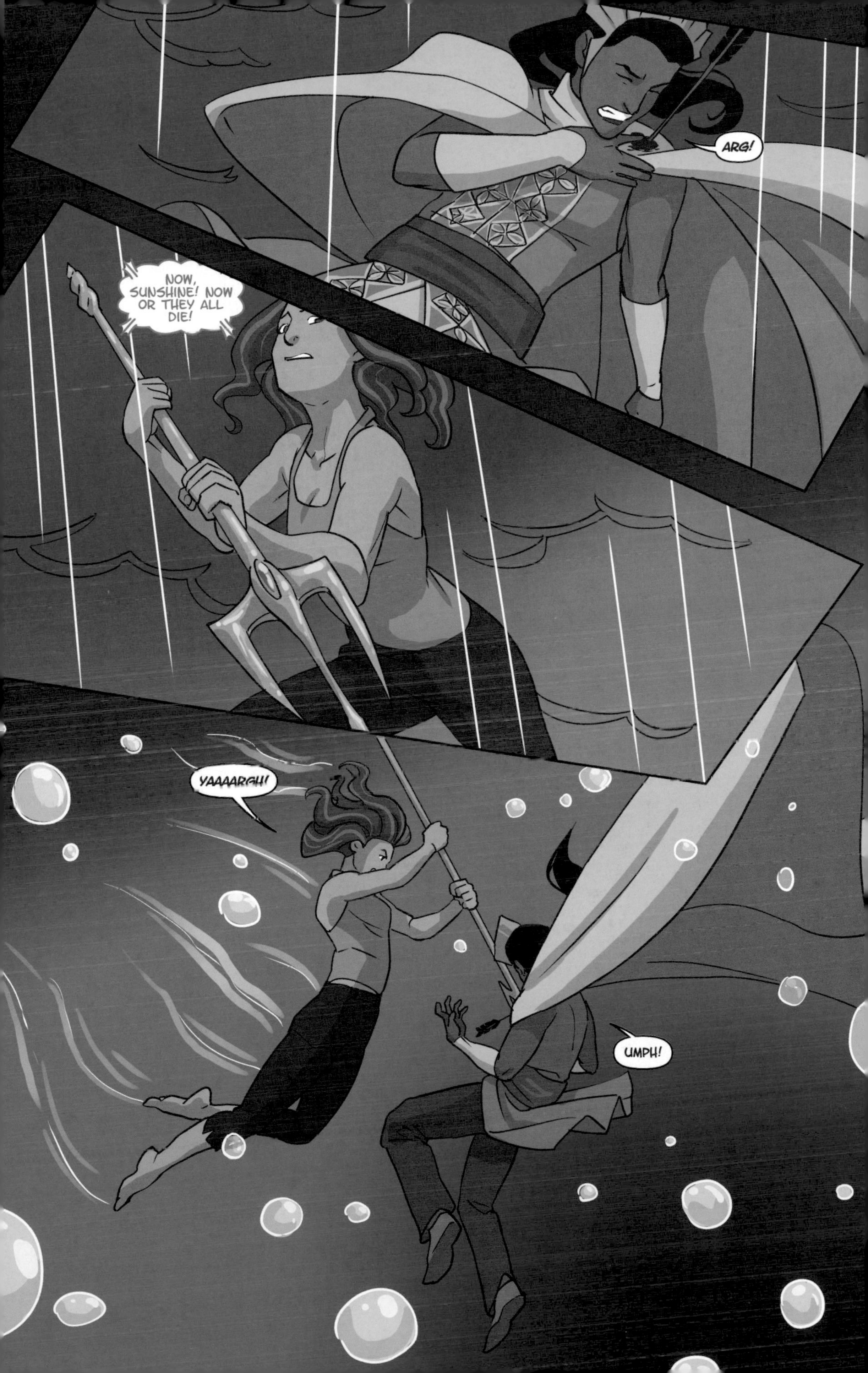
ARG!
NOW, SUNSHINE! NOW OR THEY ALL DIE!
YAAAARGH!
UMPH!

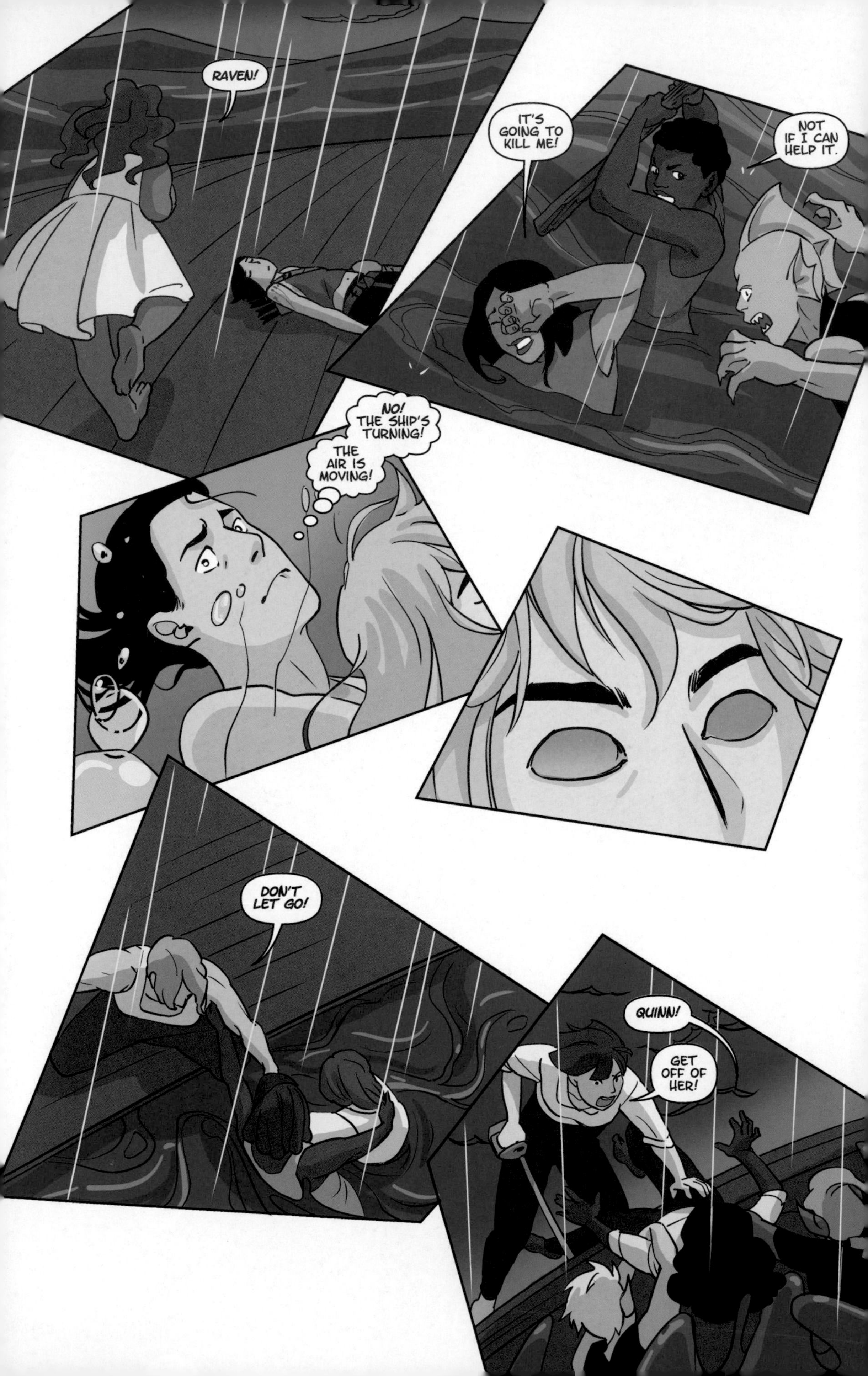
RAVEN!
IT'S GOING TO KILL ME!
NOT IF I CAN HELP IT.
NO! THE SHIP'S TURNING!
THE AIR IS MOVING!
DON'T LET GO!
QUINN!
GET OFF OF HER!

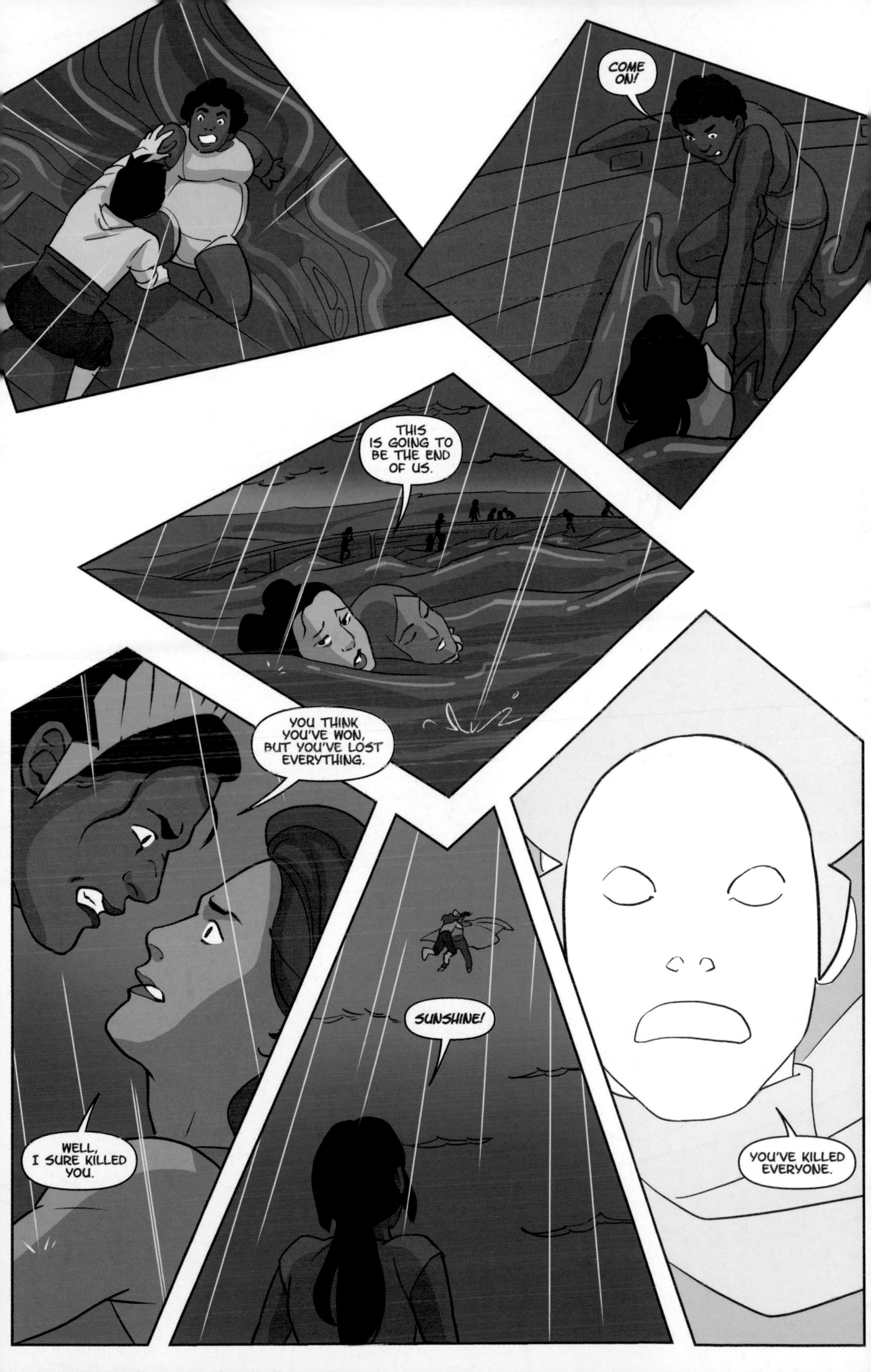
COME ON!
THIS IS GOING TO BE THE END OF US.
YOU THINK YOU'VE WON, BUT YOU'VE LOST EVERYTHING.
WELL, I SURE KILLED YOU.
SUNSHINE!
YOU'VE KILLED EVERYONE.

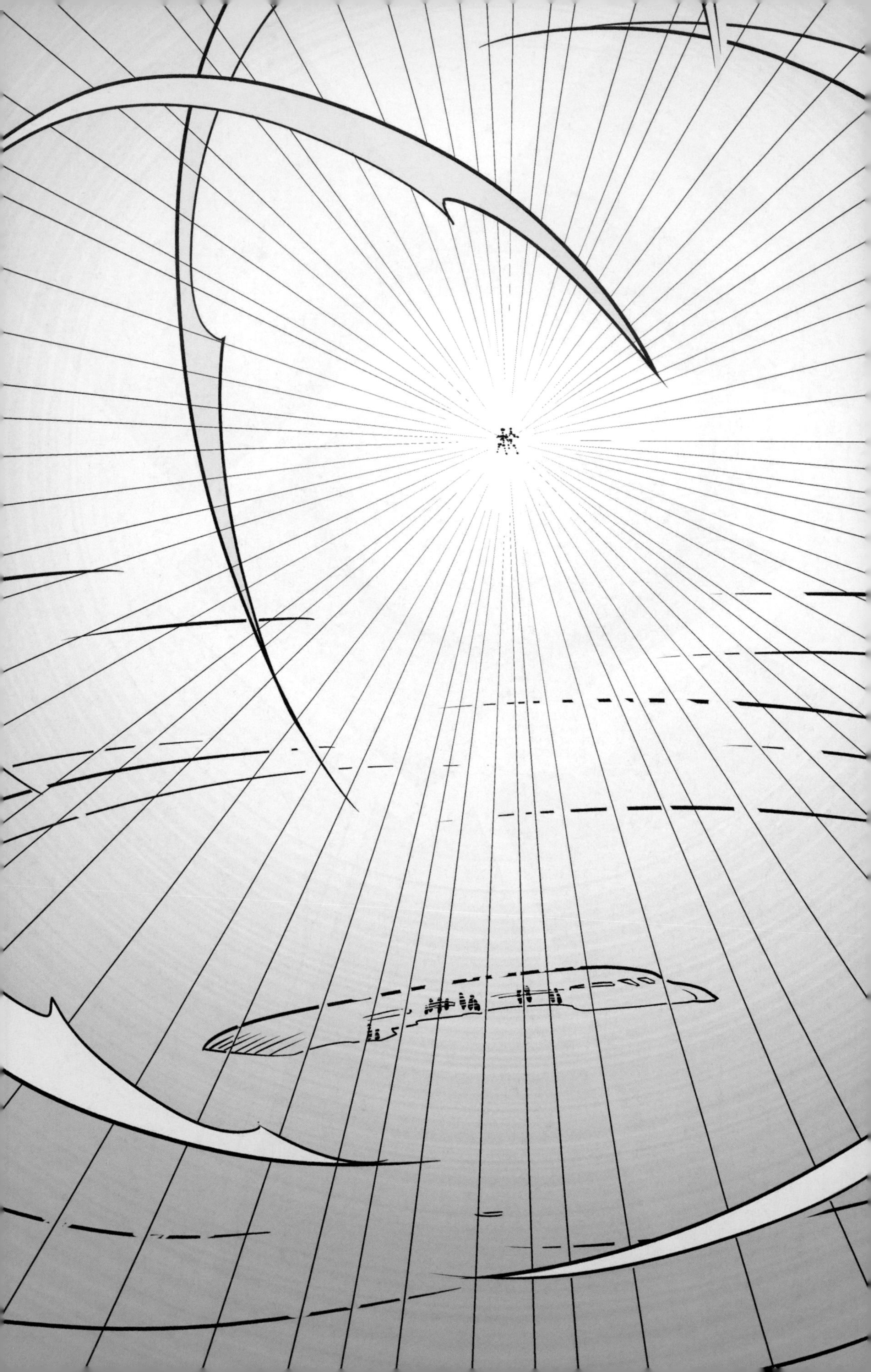

Princeless

RAVEN

THE PIRATE PRINCESS

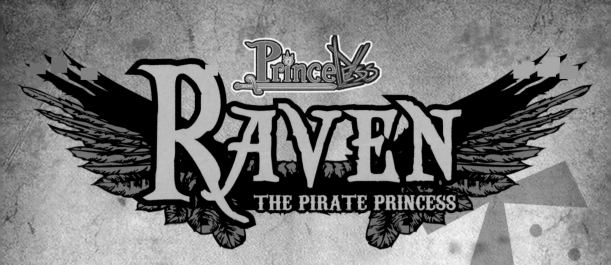

Year Three: Monsters of the Deep

Chapter Seven: What We Have To Do

Written By: Jeremy Whitley

Pencils By:
(Pages 1-15) Xenia Pamfil
(Pages 16-26) Telenîa Albuquerque

Inks By:
(Pages 1-15) JB Fuller
(Pages 16-26) Pocket Owl

Colors By:
(Pages 1-15) Lexillo
(Pages 16-26) Valentina Pinto

Lettered By: Alex Scherkenbach
Edited By: Nicole D'Andria

Cover By: Telênia Albuquerque

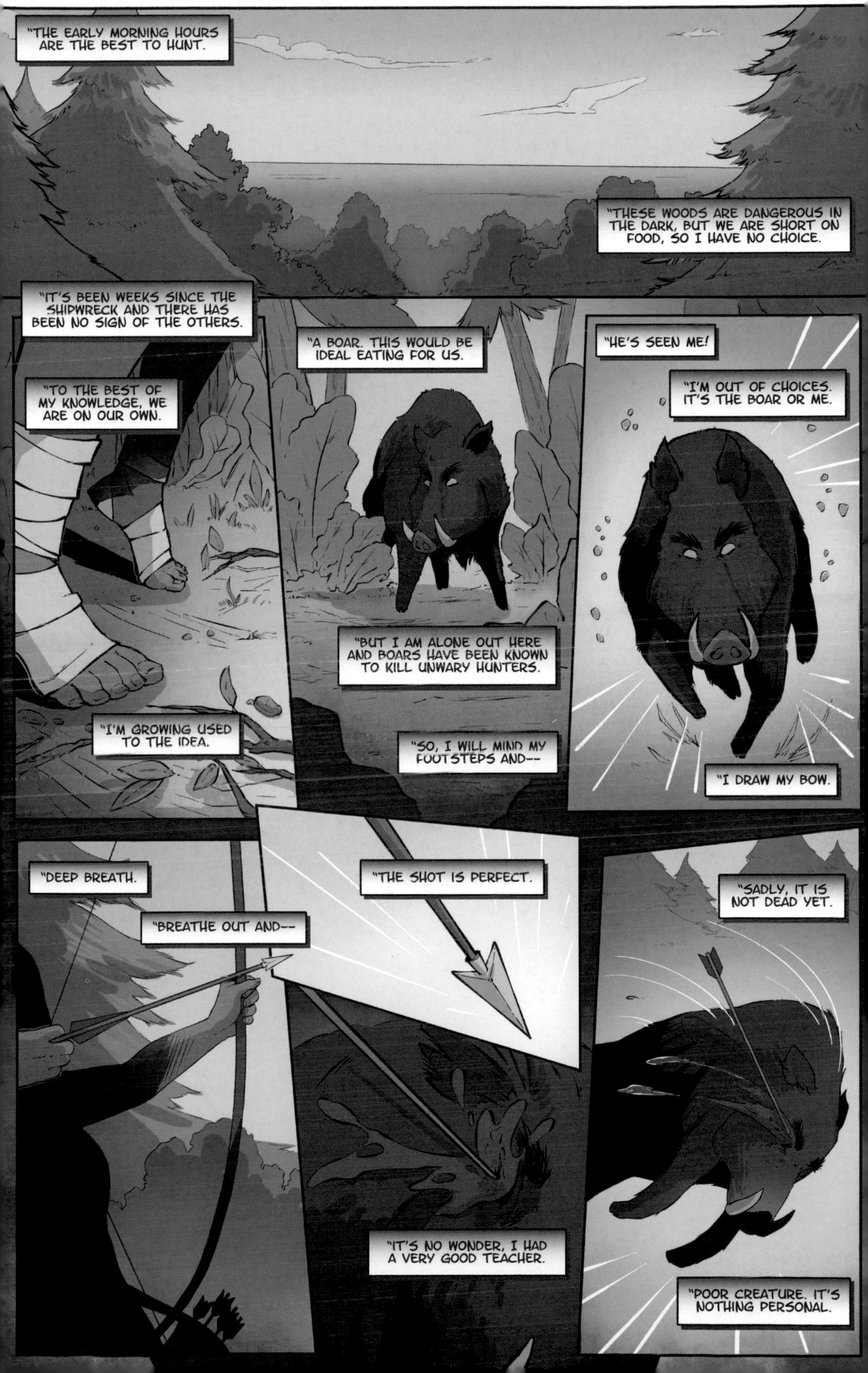
"THE EARLY MORNING HOURS ARE THE BEST TO HUNT.
"THESE WOODS ARE DANGEROUS IN THE DARK, BUT WE ARE SHORT ON FOOD, SO I HAVE NO CHOICE.
"IT'S BEEN WEEKS SINCE THE SHIPWRECK AND THERE HAS BEEN NO SIGN OF THE OTHERS.
"TO THE BEST OF MY KNOWLEDGE, WE ARE ON OUR OWN.
"I'M GROWING USED TO THE IDEA.
"A BOAR. THIS WOULD BE IDEAL EATING FOR US.
"BUT I AM ALONE OUT HERE AND BOARS HAVE BEEN KNOWN TO KILL UNWARY HUNTERS.
"SO, I WILL MIND MY FOOTSTEPS AND--
"HE'S SEEN ME!
"I'M OUT OF CHOICES. IT'S THE BOAR OR ME.
"I DRAW MY BOW.
"DEEP BREATH.
"BREATHE OUT AND--
"THE SHOT IS PERFECT.
"IT'S NO WONDER, I HAD A VERY GOOD TEACHER.
"SADLY, IT IS NOT DEAD YET.
"POOR CREATURE. IT'S NOTHING PERSONAL.

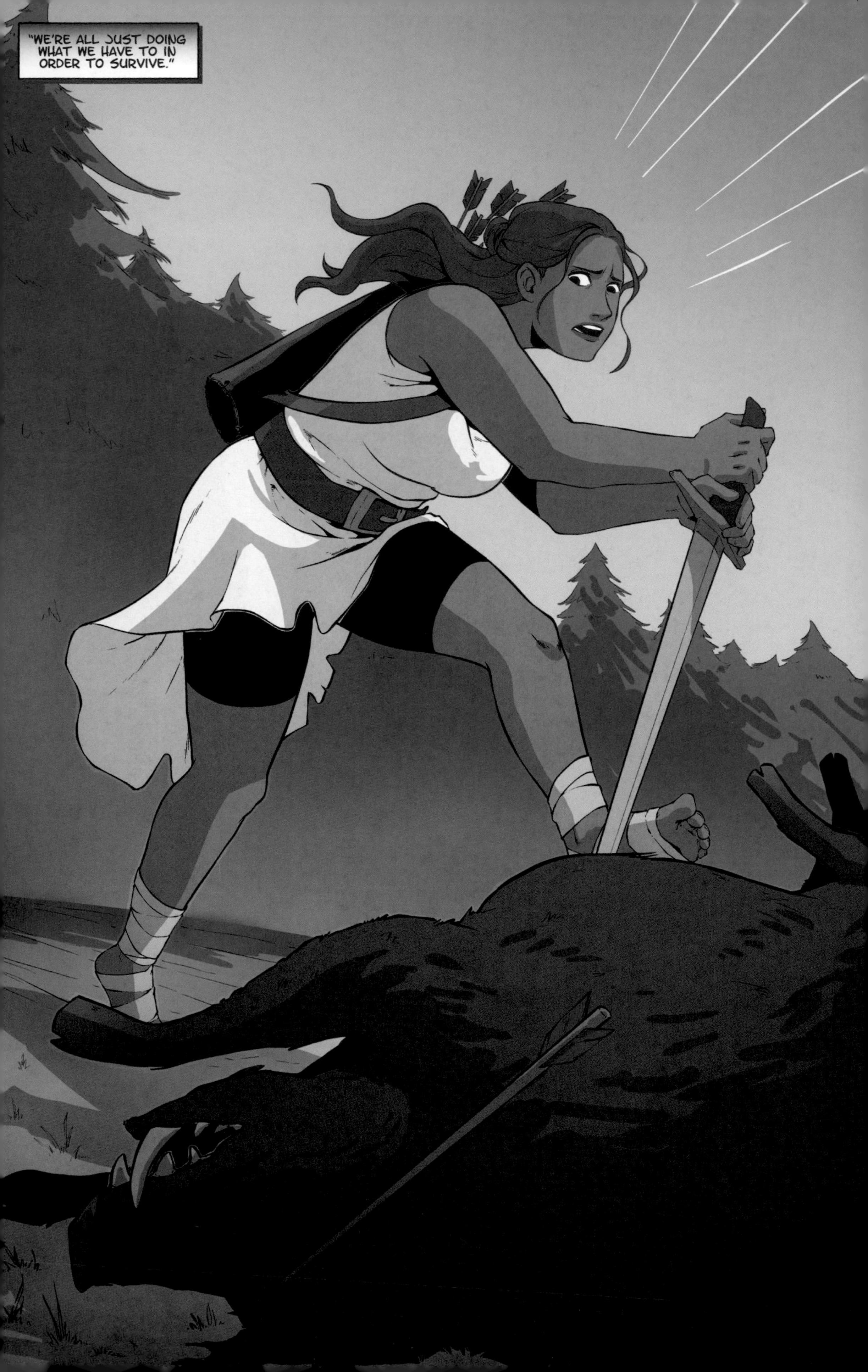
"WE'RE ALL JUST DOING WHAT WE HAVE TO IN ORDER TO SURVIVE."

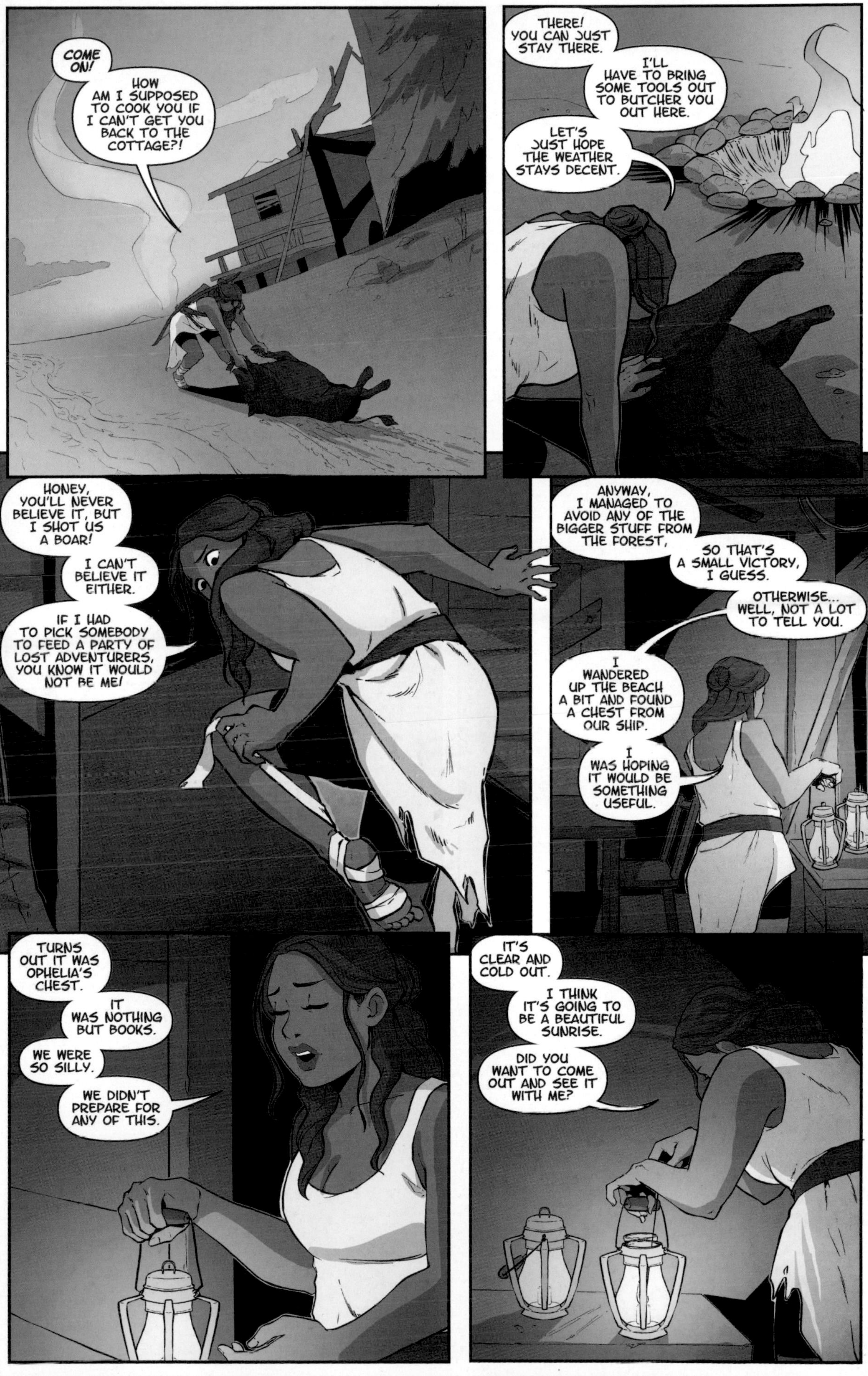
COME ON!
HOW AM I SUPPOSED TO COOK YOU IF I CAN'T GET YOU BACK TO THE COTTAGE?!
THERE! YOU CAN JUST STAY THERE.
I'LL HAVE TO BRING SOME TOOLS OUT TO BUTCHER YOU OUT HERE.
LET'S JUST HOPE THE WEATHER STAYS DECENT.
HONEY, YOU'LL NEVER BELIEVE IT, BUT I SHOT US A BOAR!
I CAN'T BELIEVE IT EITHER.
IF I HAD TO PICK SOMEBODY TO FEED A PARTY OF LOST ADVENTURERS, YOU KNOW IT WOULD NOT BE ME!
ANYWAY, I MANAGED TO AVOID ANY OF THE BIGGER STUFF FROM THE FOREST,
SO THAT'S A SMALL VICTORY, I GUESS.
OTHERWISE... WELL, NOT A LOT TO TELL YOU.
I WANDERED UP THE BEACH A BIT AND FOUND A CHEST FROM OUR SHIP.
I WAS HOPING IT WOULD BE SOMETHING USEFUL.
TURNS OUT IT WAS OPHELIA'S CHEST.
IT WAS NOTHING BUT BOOKS.
WE WERE SO SILLY.
WE DIDN'T PREPARE FOR ANY OF THIS.
IT'S CLEAR AND COLD OUT.
I THINK IT'S GOING TO BE A BEAUTIFUL SUNRISE.
DID YOU WANT TO COME OUT AND SEE IT WITH ME?

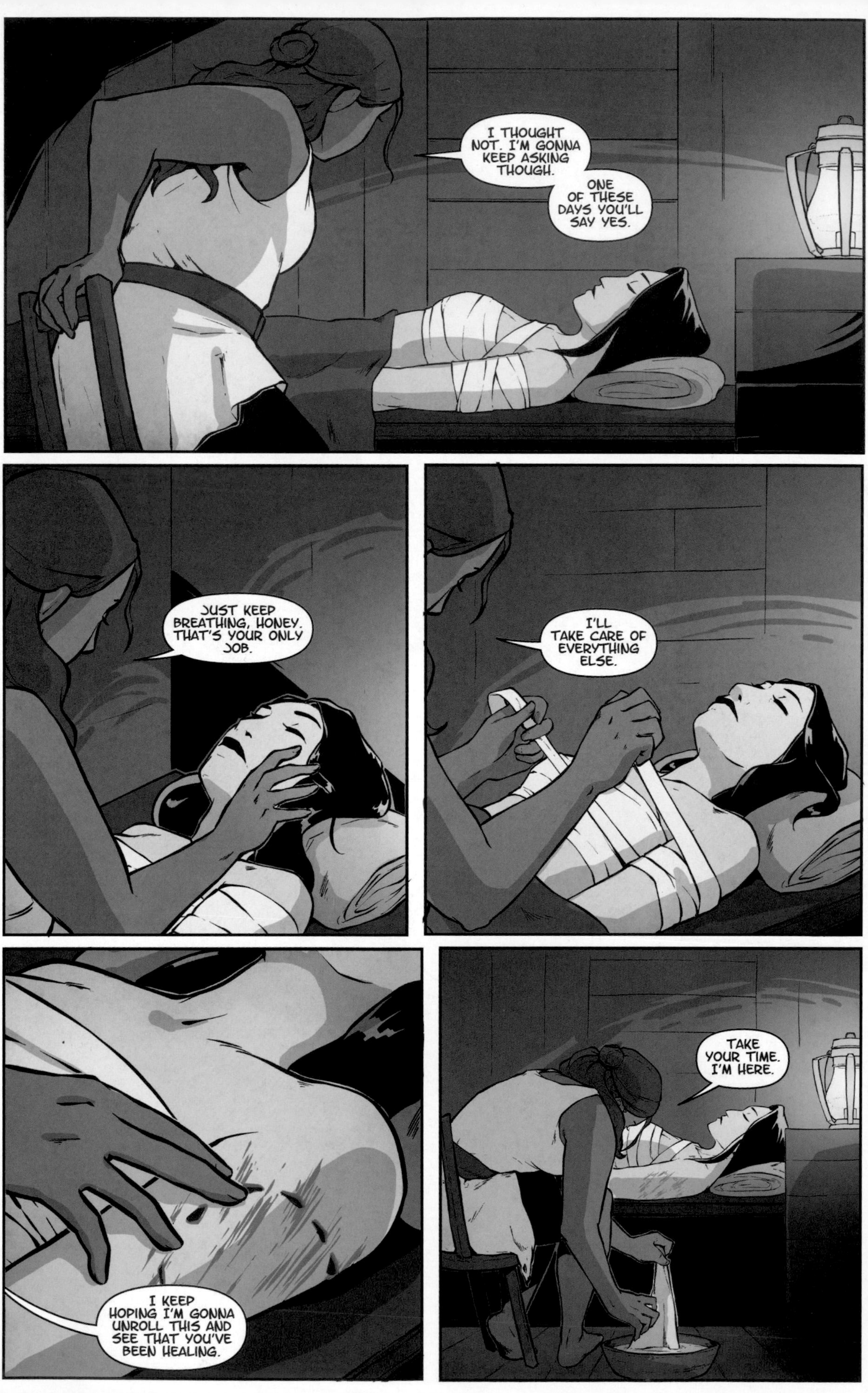
I THOUGHT NOT. I'M GONNA KEEP ASKING THOUGH.
ONE OF THESE DAYS YOU'LL SAY YES.
JUST KEEP BREATHING, HONEY. THAT'S YOUR ONLY JOB.
I'LL TAKE CARE OF EVERYTHING ELSE.
I KEEP HOPING I'M GONNA UNROLL THIS AND SEE THAT YOU'VE BEEN HEALING.
TAKE YOUR TIME. I'M HERE.

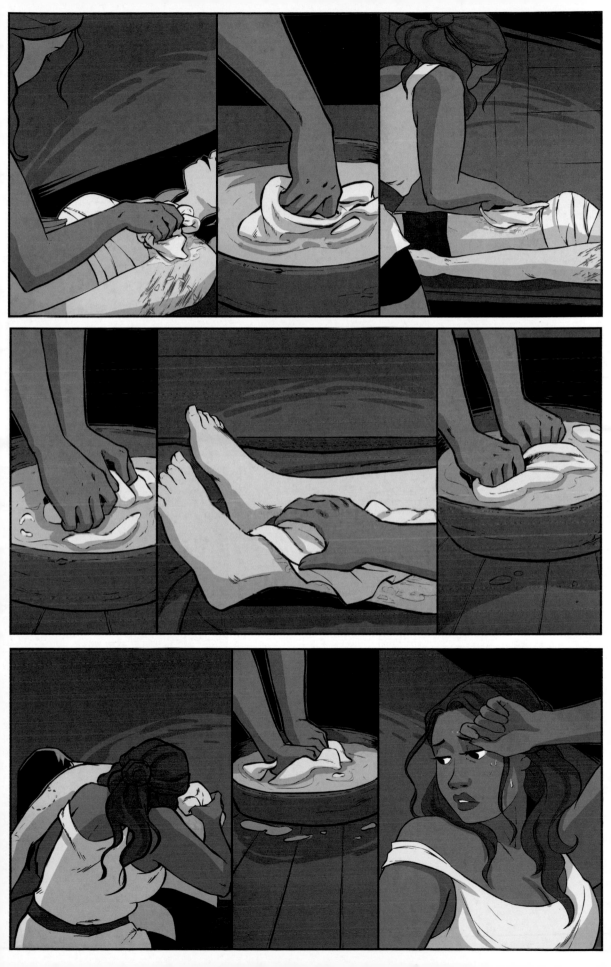

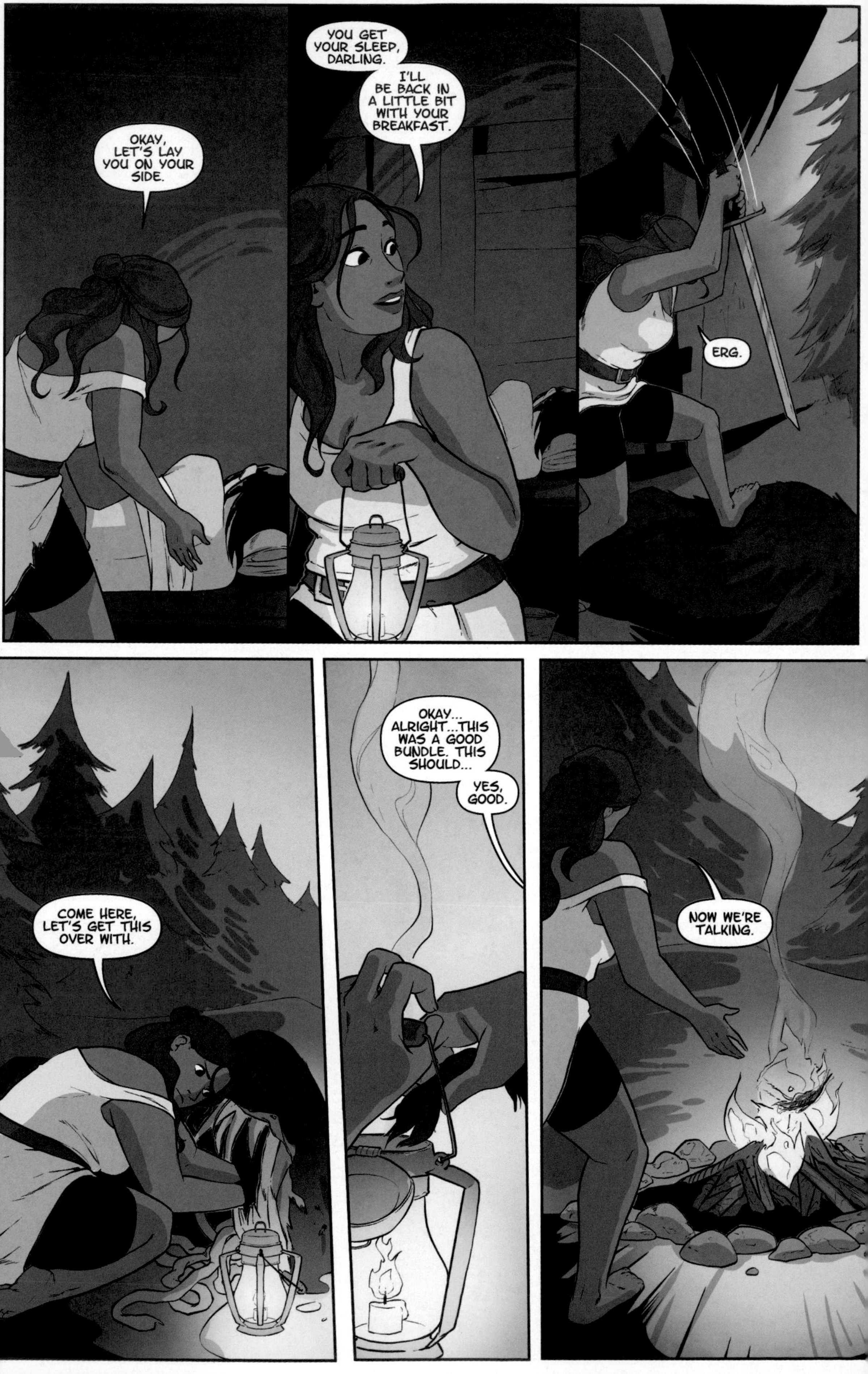
OKAY, LET'S LAY YOU ON YOUR SIDE.
YOU GET YOUR SLEEP, DARLING.
I'LL BE BACK IN A LITTLE BIT WITH YOUR BREAKFAST.
ERG.
COME HERE, LET'S GET THIS OVER WITH.
OKAY... ALRIGHT...THIS WAS A GOOD BUNDLE. THIS SHOULD...
YES, GOOD.
NOW WE'RE TALKING.

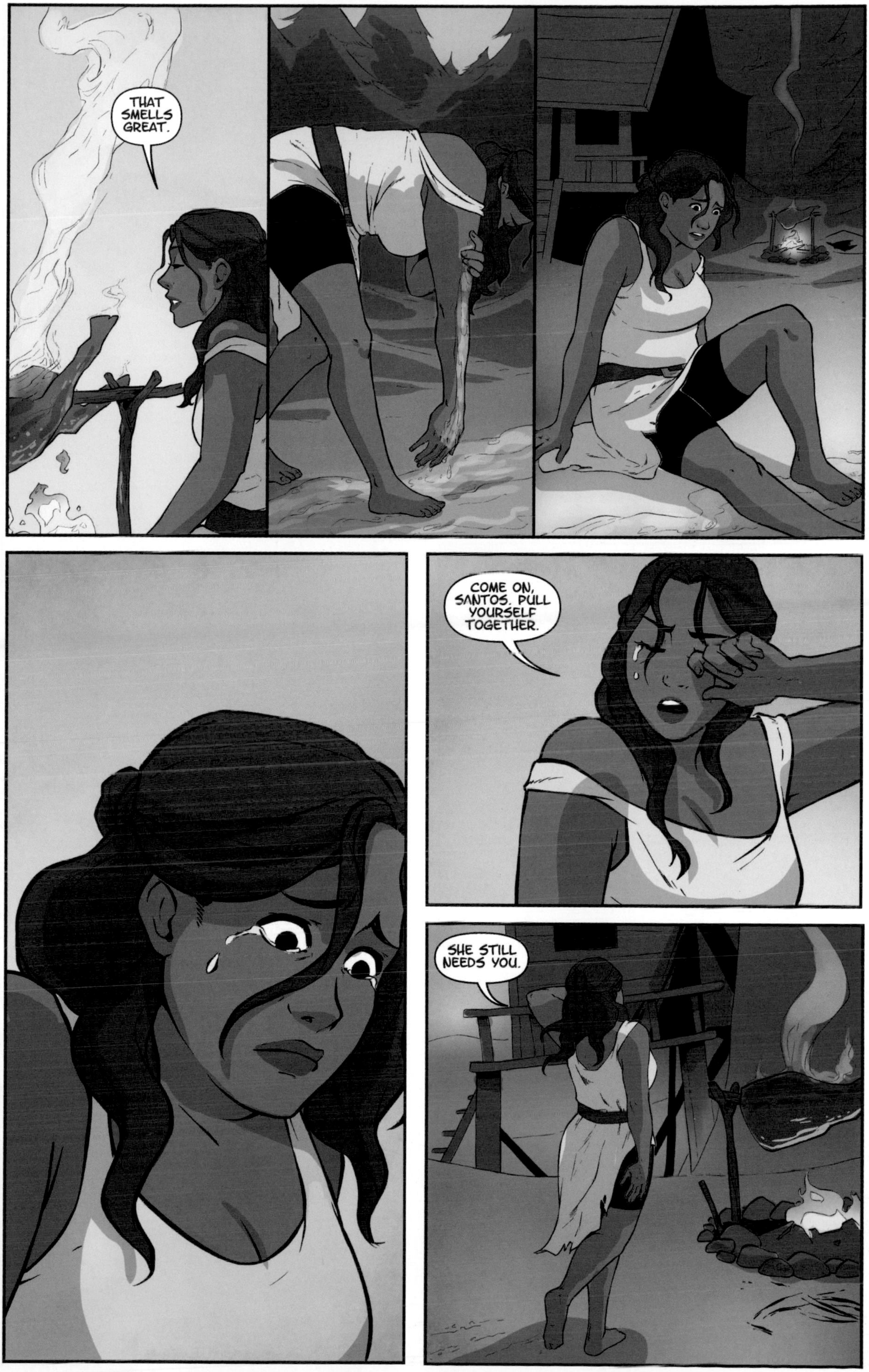
THAT SMELLS GREAT.
COME ON, SANTOS. PULL YOURSELF TOGETHER.
SHE STILL NEEDS YOU.

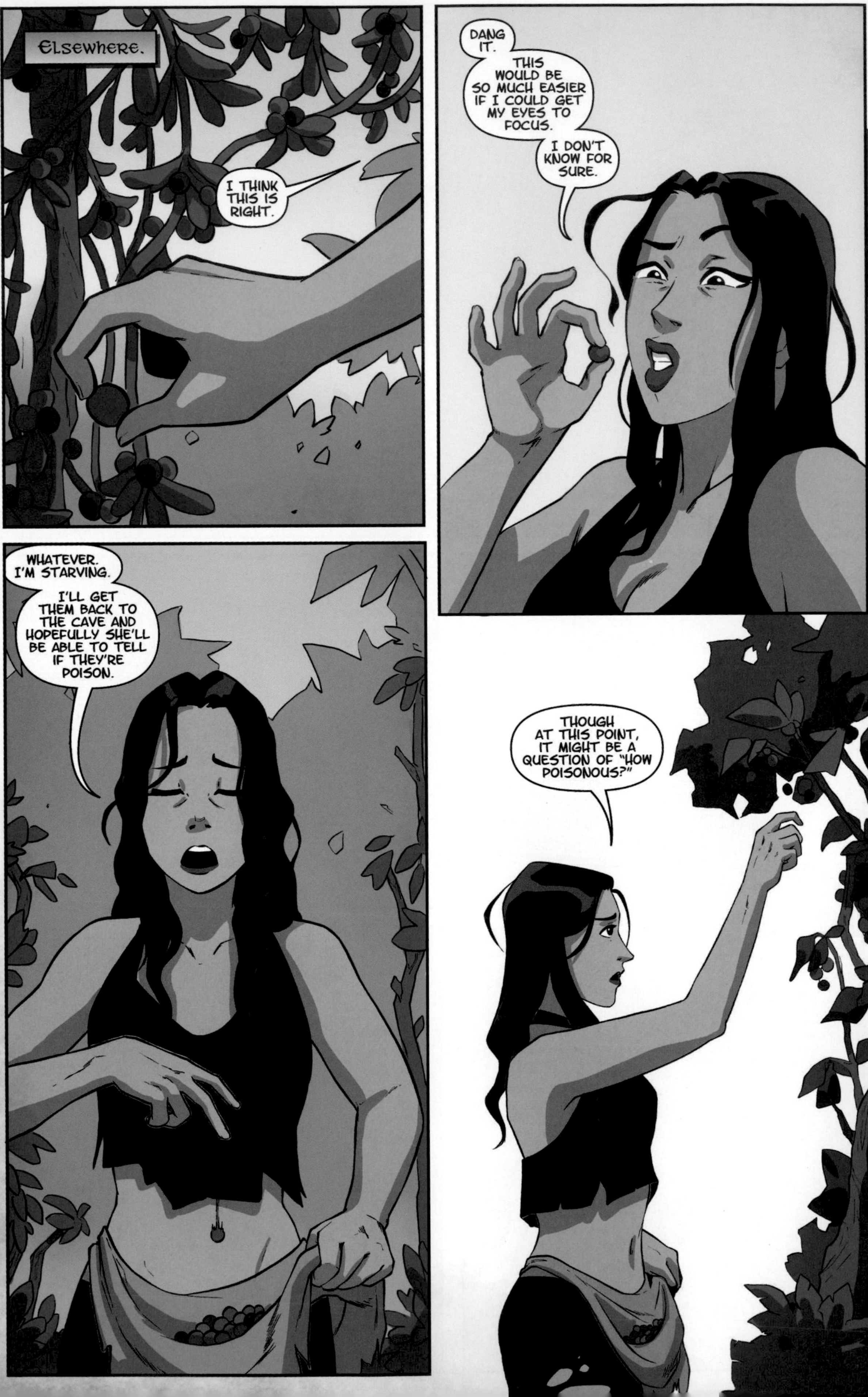
Elsewhere.
I THINK THIS IS RIGHT.
DANG IT.
THIS WOULD BE SO MUCH EASIER IF I COULD GET MY EYES TO FOCUS.
I DON'T KNOW FOR SURE.
WHATEVER. I'M STARVING.
I'LL GET THEM BACK TO THE CAVE AND HOPEFULLY SHE'LL BE ABLE TO TELL IF THEY'RE POISON.
THOUGH AT THIS POINT, IT MIGHT BE A QUESTION OF "HOW POISONOUS?"

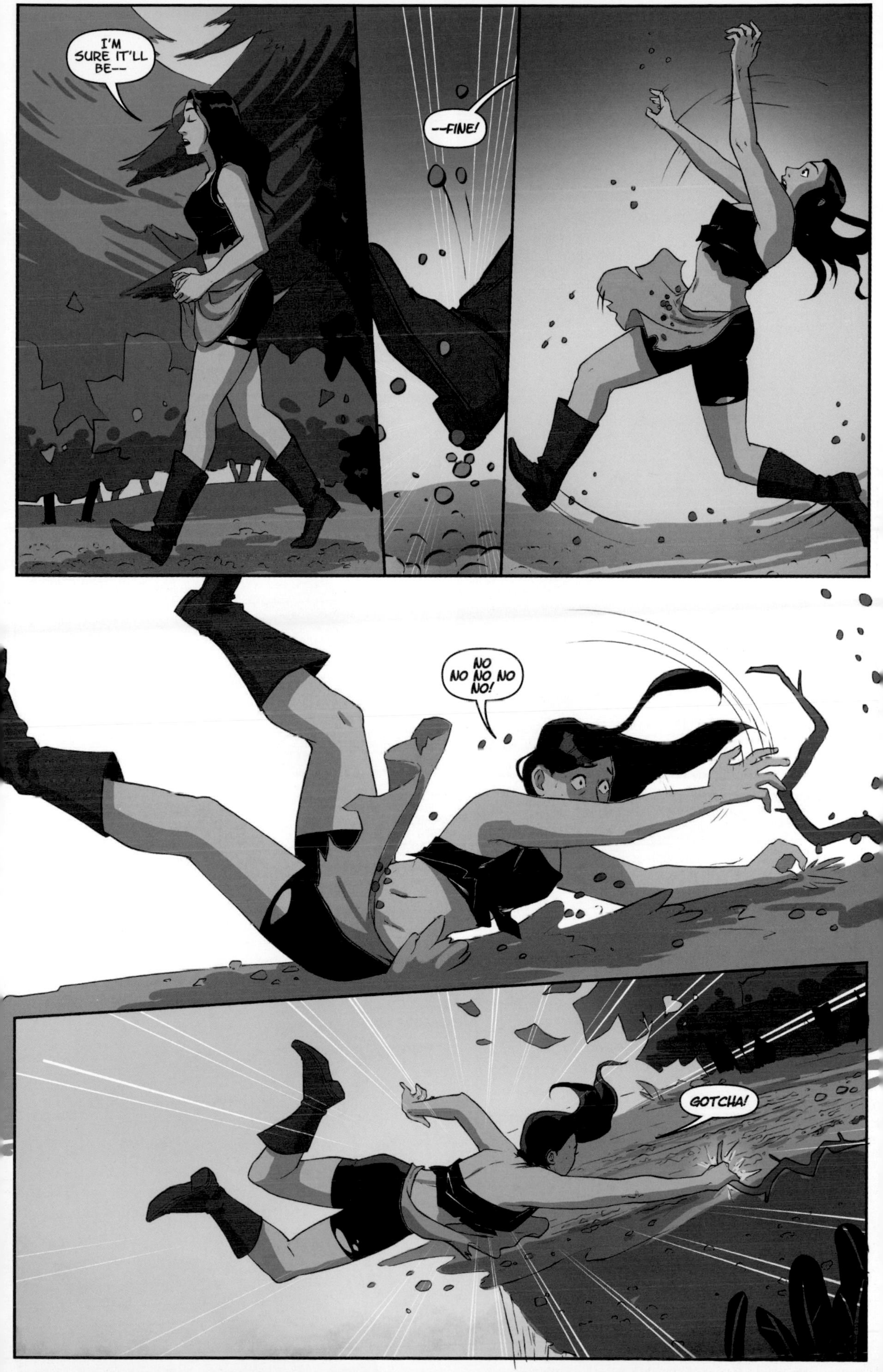
I'M SURE IT'LL BE--
--FINE!
NO NO NO NO NO!
GOTCHA!

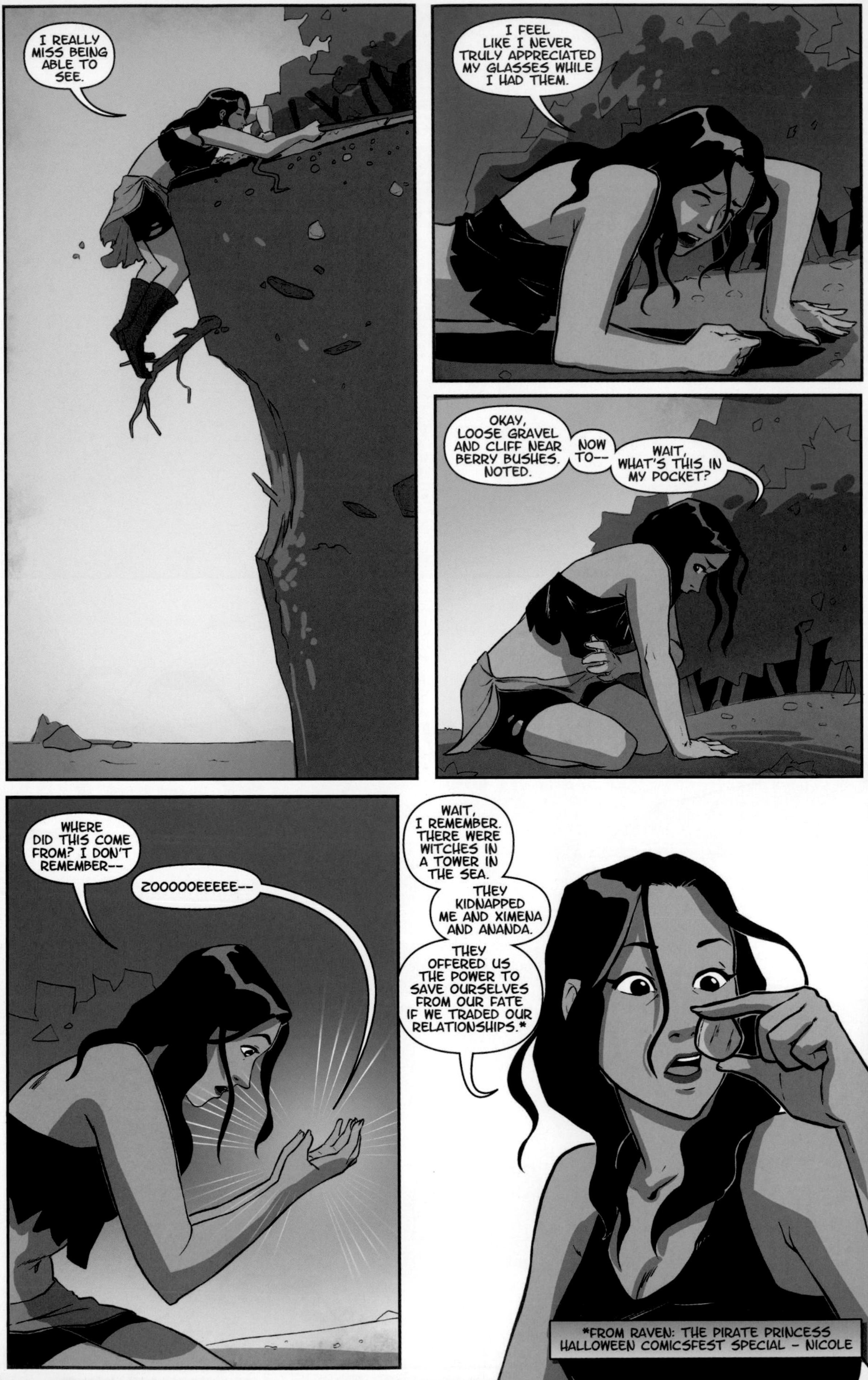
I REALLY MISS BEING ABLE TO SEE.
I FEEL LIKE I NEVER TRULY APPRECIATED MY GLASSES WHILE I HAD THEM.
OKAY, LOOSE GRAVEL AND CLIFF NEAR BERRY BUSHES. NOTED.
NOW TO--
WAIT, WHAT'S THIS IN MY POCKET?
WHERE DID THIS COME FROM? I DON'T REMEMBER--
ZOOOOOEEEEE--
WAIT, I REMEMBER. THERE WERE WITCHES IN A TOWER IN THE SEA.
THEY KIDNAPPED ME AND XIMENA AND ANANDA.
THEY OFFERED US THE POWER TO SAVE OURSELVES FROM OUR FATE IF WE TRADED OUR RELATIONSHIPS.*
*FROM RAVEN: THE PIRATE PRINCESS HALLOWEEN COMICSFEST SPECIAL - NICOLE

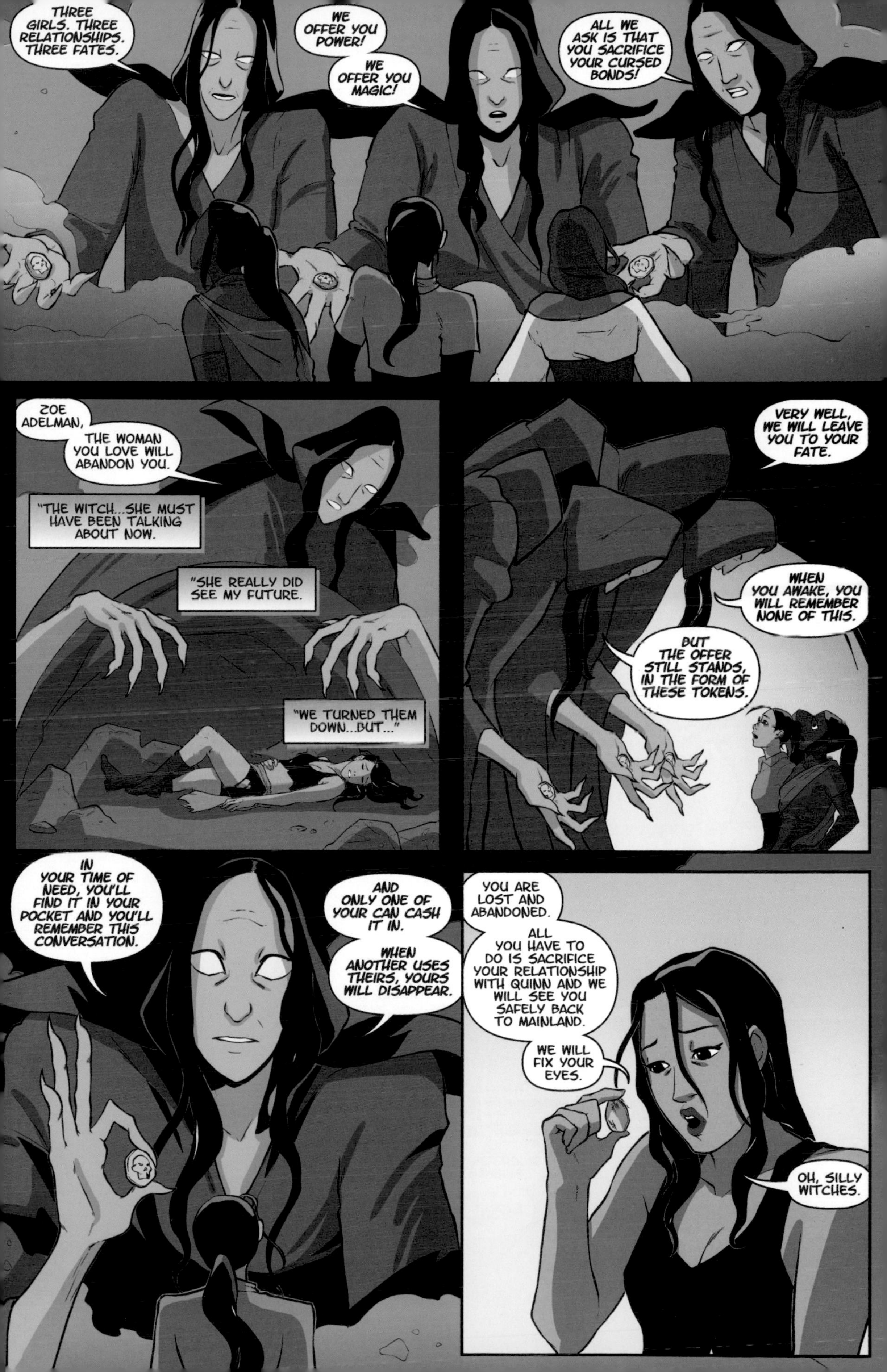

THREE GIRLS. THREE RELATIONSHIPS. THREE FATES.
WE OFFER YOU POWER!
WE OFFER YOU MAGIC!
ALL WE ASK IS THAT YOU SACRIFICE YOUR CURSED BONDS!
ZOE ADELMAN,
THE WOMAN YOU LOVE WILL ABANDON YOU.
"THE WITCH...SHE MUST HAVE BEEN TALKING ABOUT NOW.
"SHE REALLY DID SEE MY FUTURE.
"WE TURNED THEM DOWN...BUT..."
VERY WELL, WE WILL LEAVE YOU TO YOUR FATE.
WHEN YOU AWAKE, YOU WILL REMEMBER NONE OF THIS.
BUT THE OFFER STILL STANDS, IN THE FORM OF THESE TOKENS.
IN YOUR TIME OF NEED, YOU'LL FIND IT IN YOUR POCKET AND YOU'LL REMEMBER THIS CONVERSATION.
AND ONLY ONE OF YOUR CAN CASH IT IN.
WHEN ANOTHER USES THEIRS, YOURS WILL DISAPPEAR.
YOU ARE LOST AND ABANDONED.
ALL YOU HAVE TO DO IS SACRIFICE YOUR RELATIONSHIP WITH QUINN AND WE WILL SEE YOU SAFELY BACK TO MAINLAND.
WE WILL FIX YOUR EYES.
OH, SILLY WITCHES.

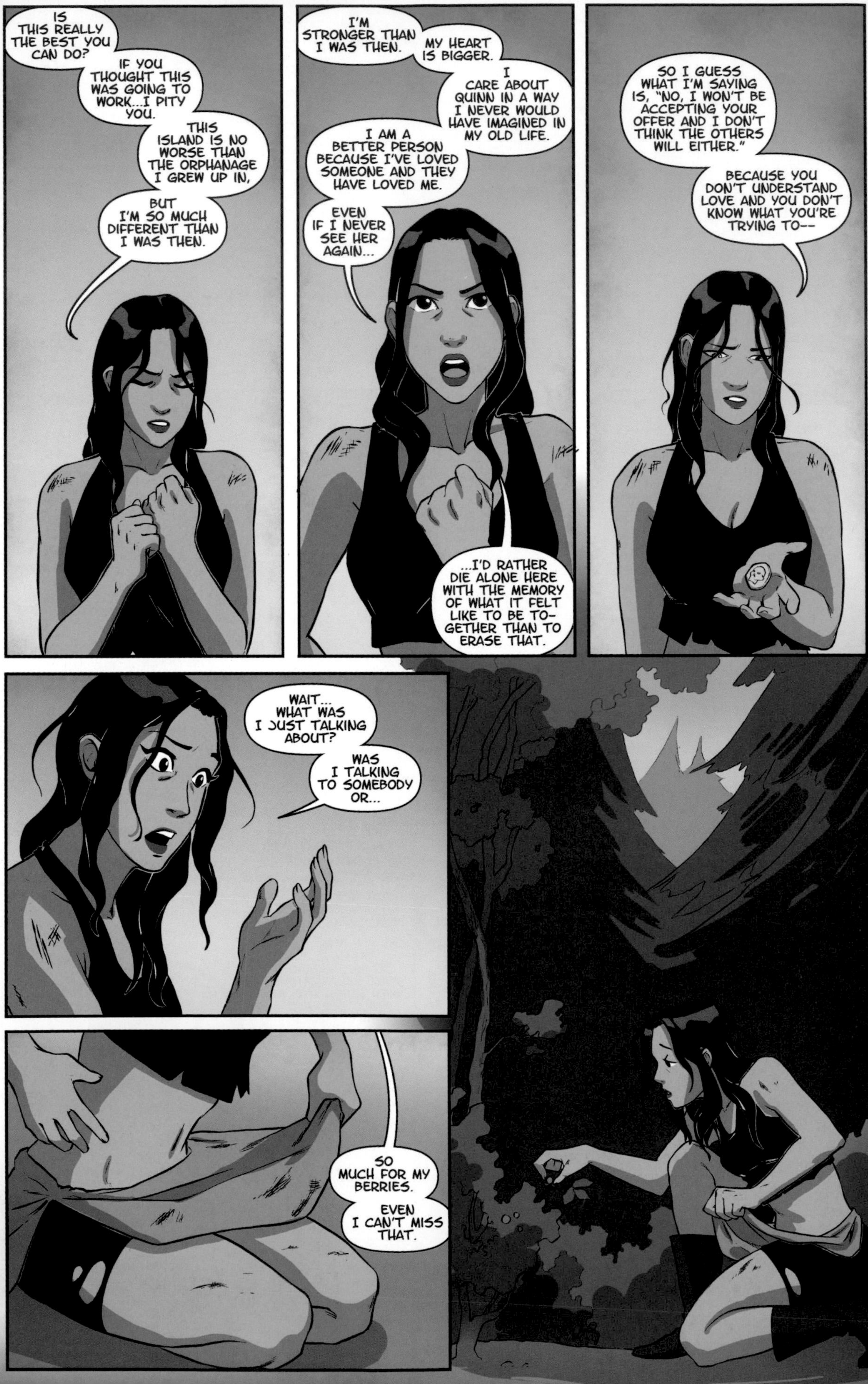
IS THIS REALLY THE BEST YOU CAN DO?
IF YOU THOUGHT THIS WAS GOING TO WORK...I PITY YOU.
THIS ISLAND IS NO WORSE THAN THE ORPHANAGE I GREW UP IN,
BUT I'M SO MUCH DIFFERENT THAN I WAS THEN.
I'M STRONGER THAN I WAS THEN.
MY HEART IS BIGGER.
I CARE ABOUT QUINN IN A WAY I NEVER WOULD HAVE IMAGINED IN MY OLD LIFE.
I AM A BETTER PERSON BECAUSE I'VE LOVED SOMEONE AND THEY HAVE LOVED ME.
EVEN IF I NEVER SEE HER AGAIN...
...I'D RATHER DIE ALONE HERE WITH THE MEMORY OF WHAT IT FELT LIKE TO BE TO-GETHER THAN TO ERASE THAT.
SO I GUESS WHAT I'M SAYING IS, "NO, I WON'T BE ACCEPTING YOUR OFFER AND I DON'T THINK THE OTHERS WILL EITHER."
BECAUSE YOU DON'T UNDERSTAND LOVE AND YOU DON'T KNOW WHAT YOU'RE TRYING TO--
WAIT... WHAT WAS I JUST TALKING ABOUT?
WAS I TALKING TO SOMEBODY OR...
SO MUCH FOR MY BERRIES.
EVEN I CAN'T MISS THAT.

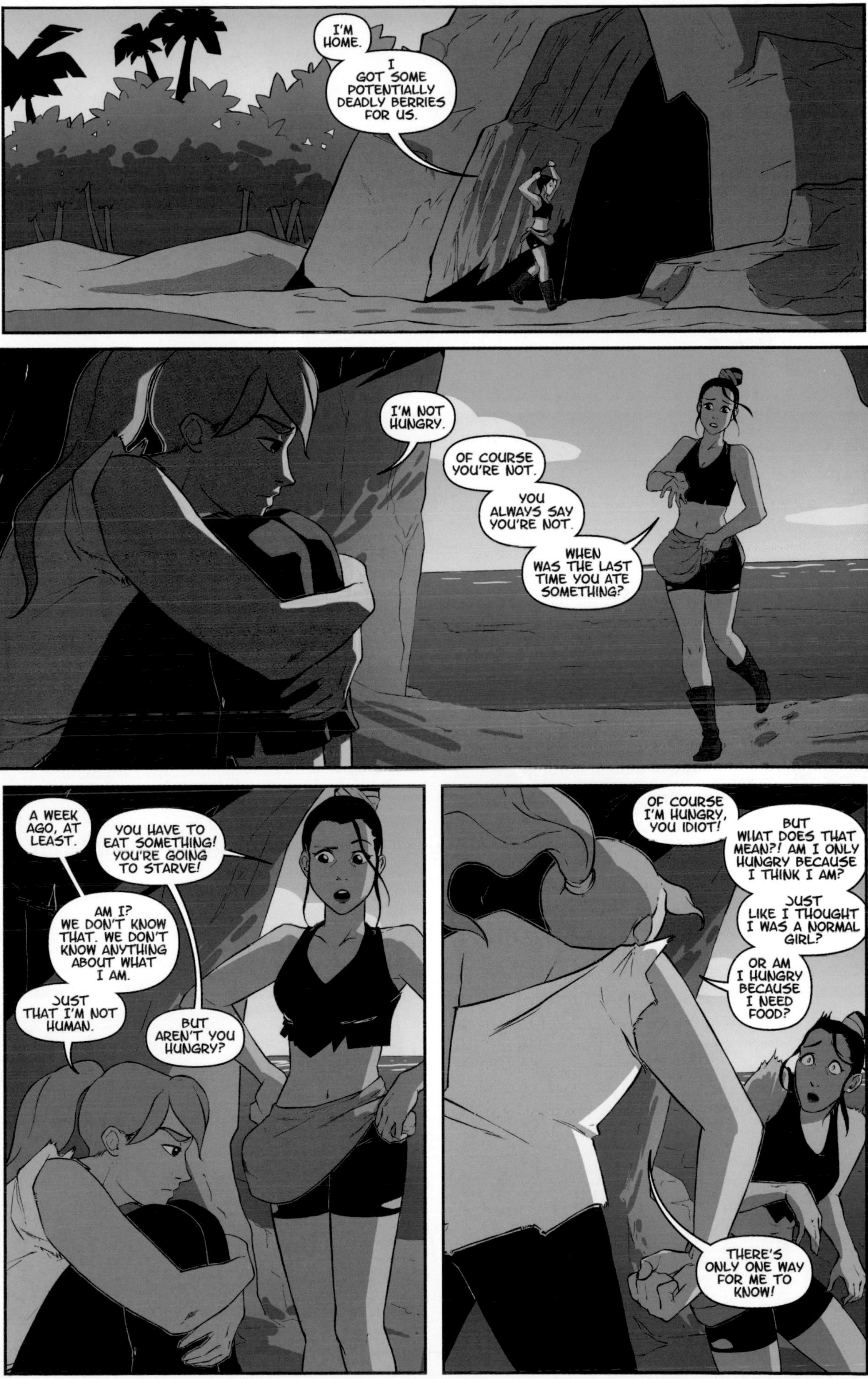
I'M HOME.
I GOT SOME POTENTIALLY DEADLY BERRIES FOR US.
I'M NOT HUNGRY.
OF COURSE YOU'RE NOT.
YOU ALWAYS SAY YOU'RE NOT.
WHEN WAS THE LAST TIME YOU ATE SOMETHING?
A WEEK AGO, AT LEAST.
YOU HAVE TO EAT SOMETHING! YOU'RE GOING TO STARVE!
AM I? WE DON'T KNOW THAT. WE DON'T KNOW ANYTHING ABOUT WHAT I AM.
JUST THAT I'M NOT HUMAN.
BUT AREN'T YOU HUNGRY?
OF COURSE I'M HUNGRY, YOU IDIOT!
BUT WHAT DOES THAT MEAN?! AM I ONLY HUNGRY BECAUSE I THINK I AM?
JUST LIKE I THOUGHT I WAS A NORMAL GIRL?
OR AM I HUNGRY BECAUSE I NEED FOOD?
THERE'S ONLY ONE WAY FOR ME TO KNOW!

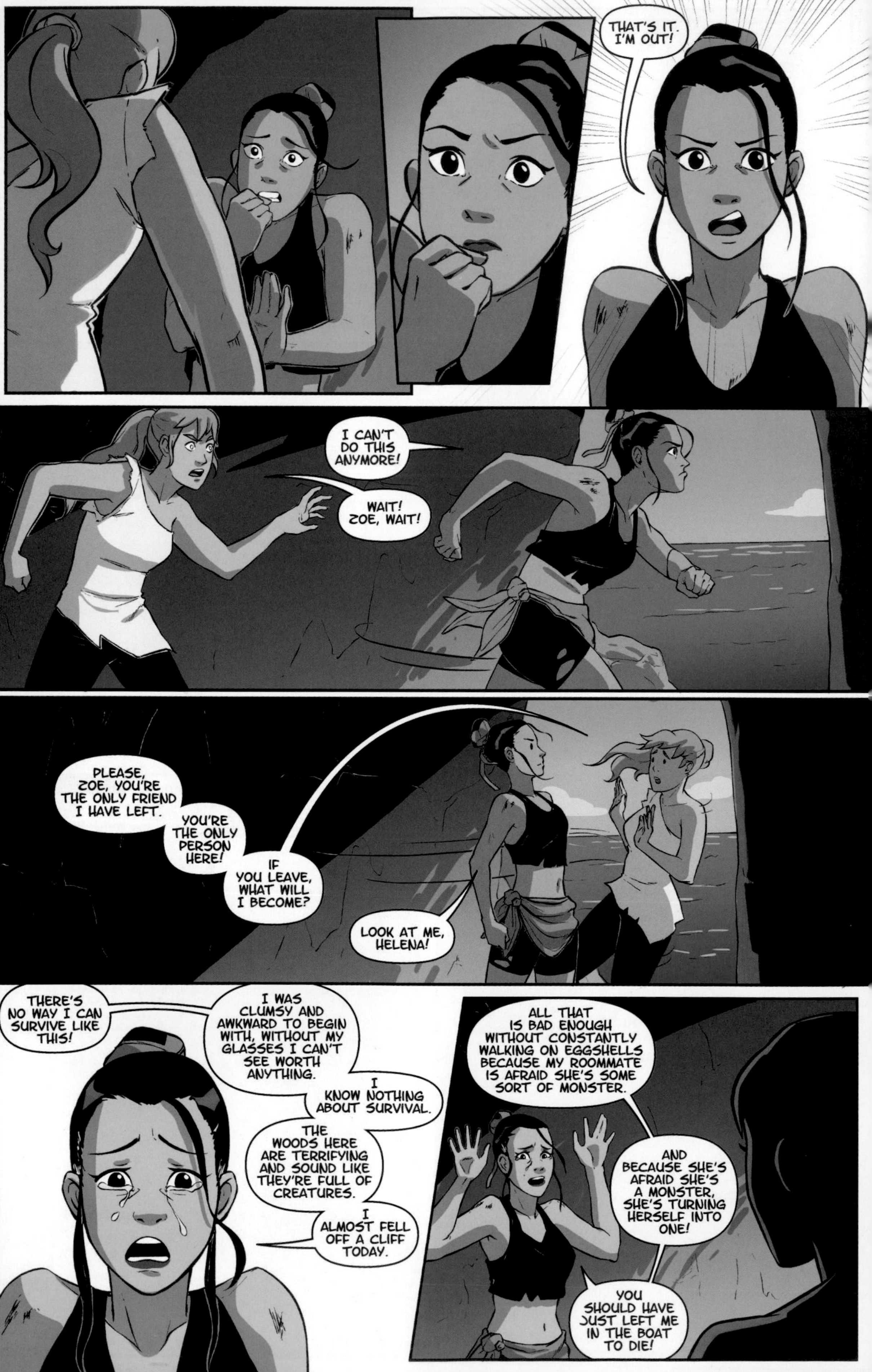
THAT'S IT. I'M OUT!
I CAN'T DO THIS ANYMORE!
WAIT! ZOE, WAIT!
PLEASE, ZOE, YOU'RE THE ONLY FRIEND I HAVE LEFT.
YOU'RE THE ONLY PERSON HERE!
IF YOU LEAVE, WHAT WILL I BECOME?
LOOK AT ME, HELENA!
THERE'S NO WAY I CAN SURVIVE LIKE THIS!
I WAS CLUMSY AND AWKWARD TO BEGIN WITH, WITHOUT MY GLASSES I CAN'T SEE WORTH ANYTHING.
I KNOW NOTHING ABOUT SURVIVAL.
THE WOODS HERE ARE TERRIFYING AND SOUND LIKE THEY'RE FULL OF CREATURES.
I ALMOST FELL OFF A CLIFF TODAY.
ALL THAT IS BAD ENOUGH WITHOUT CONSTANTLY WALKING ON EGGSHELLS BECAUSE MY ROOMMATE IS AFRAID SHE'S SOME SORT OF MONSTER.
AND BECAUSE SHE'S AFRAID SHE'S A MONSTER, SHE'S TURNING HERSELF INTO ONE!
YOU SHOULD HAVE JUST LEFT ME IN THE BOAT TO DIE!

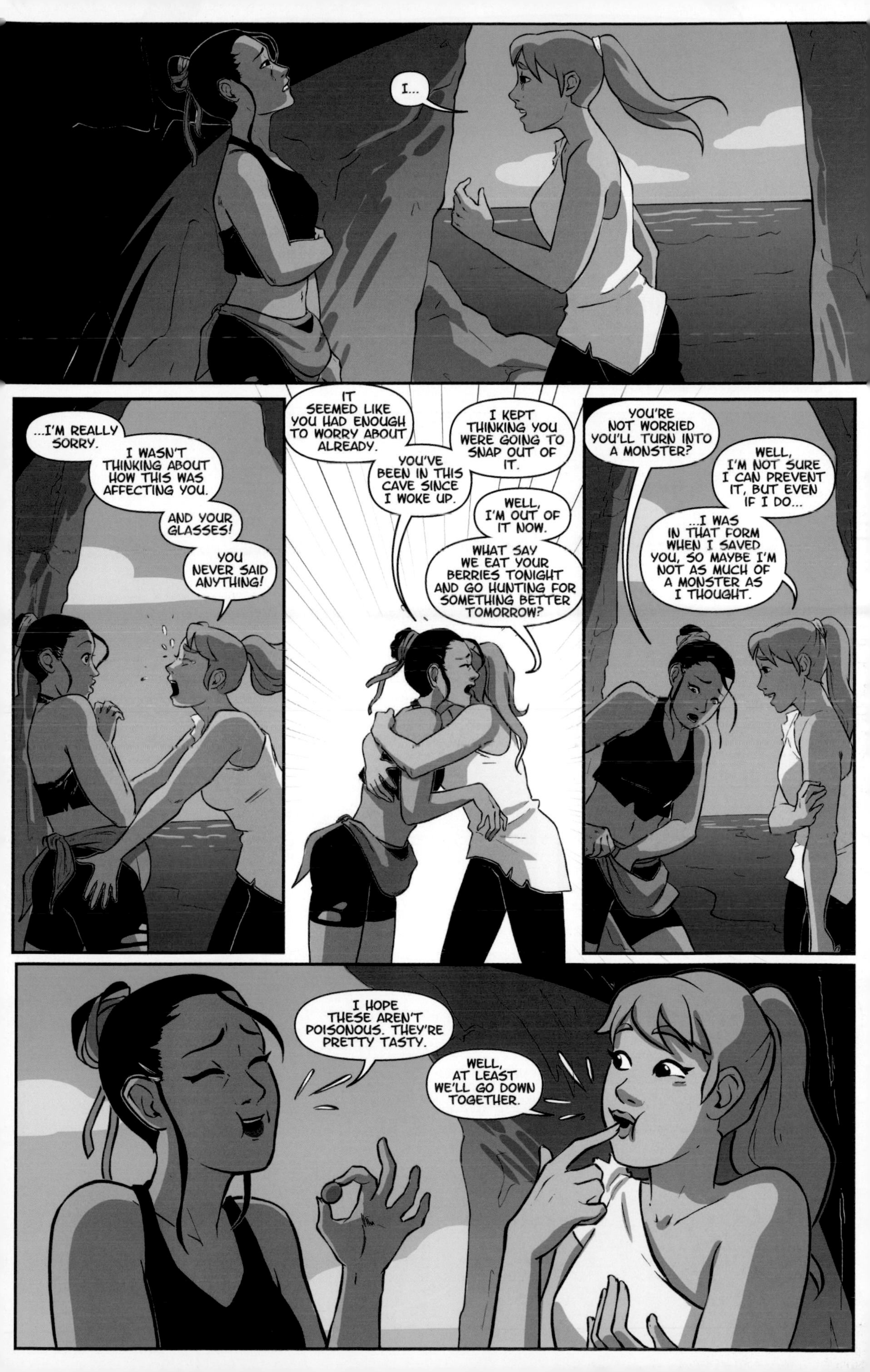
I...
...I'M REALLY SORRY.
I WASN'T THINKING ABOUT HOW THIS WAS AFFECTING YOU.
AND YOUR GLASSES!
YOU NEVER SAID ANYTHING!
IT SEEMED LIKE YOU HAD ENOUGH TO WORRY ABOUT ALREADY.
YOU'VE BEEN IN THIS CAVE SINCE I WOKE UP.
I KEPT THINKING YOU WERE GOING TO SNAP OUT OF IT.
WELL, I'M OUT OF IT NOW.
WHAT SAY WE EAT YOUR BERRIES TONIGHT AND GO HUNTING FOR SOMETHING BETTER TOMORROW?
YOU'RE NOT WORRIED YOU'LL TURN INTO A MONSTER?
WELL, I'M NOT SURE I CAN PREVENT IT, BUT EVEN IF I DO...
...I WAS IN THAT FORM WHEN I SAVED YOU, SO MAYBE I'M NOT AS MUCH OF A MONSTER AS I THOUGHT.
I HOPE THESE AREN'T POISONOUS. THEY'RE PRETTY TASTY.
WELL, AT LEAST WE'LL GO DOWN TOGETHER.

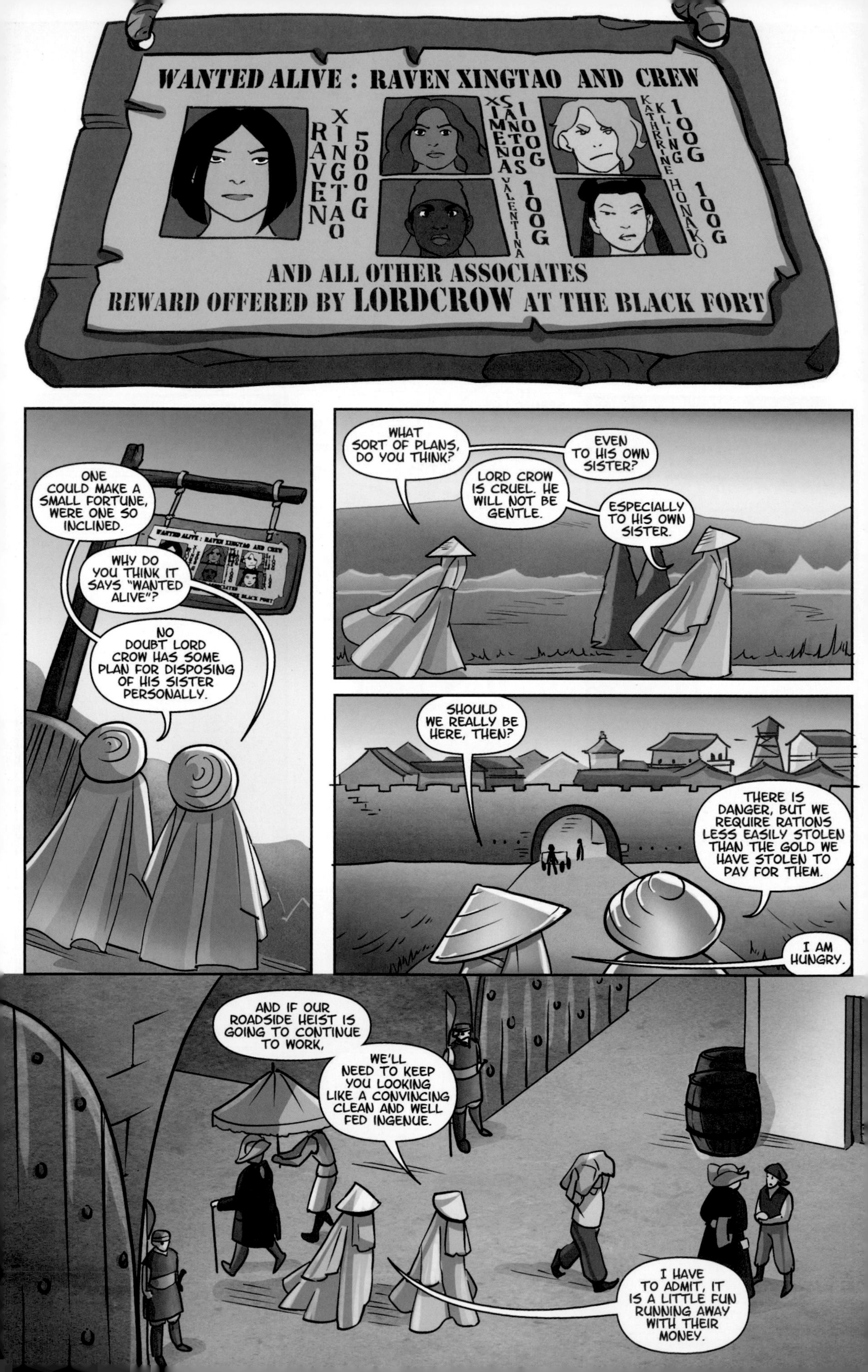
WANTED ALIVE : RAVEN XINGTAO AND CREW
RAVEN XINGTAO 500G
XIMENA SANTOS 100G
KATHRINE KLING 100G
VALENTINA 100G
HONAKO 100G
AND ALL OTHER ASSOCIATES
REWARD OFFERED BY LORDCROW AT THE BLACK FORT
ONE COULD MAKE A SMALL FORTUNE, WERE ONE SO INCLINED.
WHY DO YOU THINK IT SAYS "WANTED ALIVE"?
NO DOUBT LORD CROW HAS SOME PLAN FOR DISPOSING OF HIS SISTER PERSONALLY.
WHAT SORT OF PLANS, DO YOU THINK?
EVEN TO HIS OWN SISTER?
LORD CROW IS CRUEL. HE WILL NOT BE GENTLE.
ESPECIALLY TO HIS OWN SISTER.
SHOULD WE REALLY BE HERE, THEN?
THERE IS DANGER, BUT WE REQUIRE RATIONS LESS EASILY STOLEN THAN THE GOLD WE HAVE STOLEN TO PAY FOR THEM.
I AM HUNGRY.
AND IF OUR ROADSIDE HEIST IS GOING TO CONTINUE TO WORK,
WE'LL NEED TO KEEP YOU LOOKING LIKE A CONVINCING CLEAN AND WELL FED INGENUE.
I HAVE TO ADMIT, IT IS A LITTLE FUN RUNNING AWAY WITH THEIR MONEY.

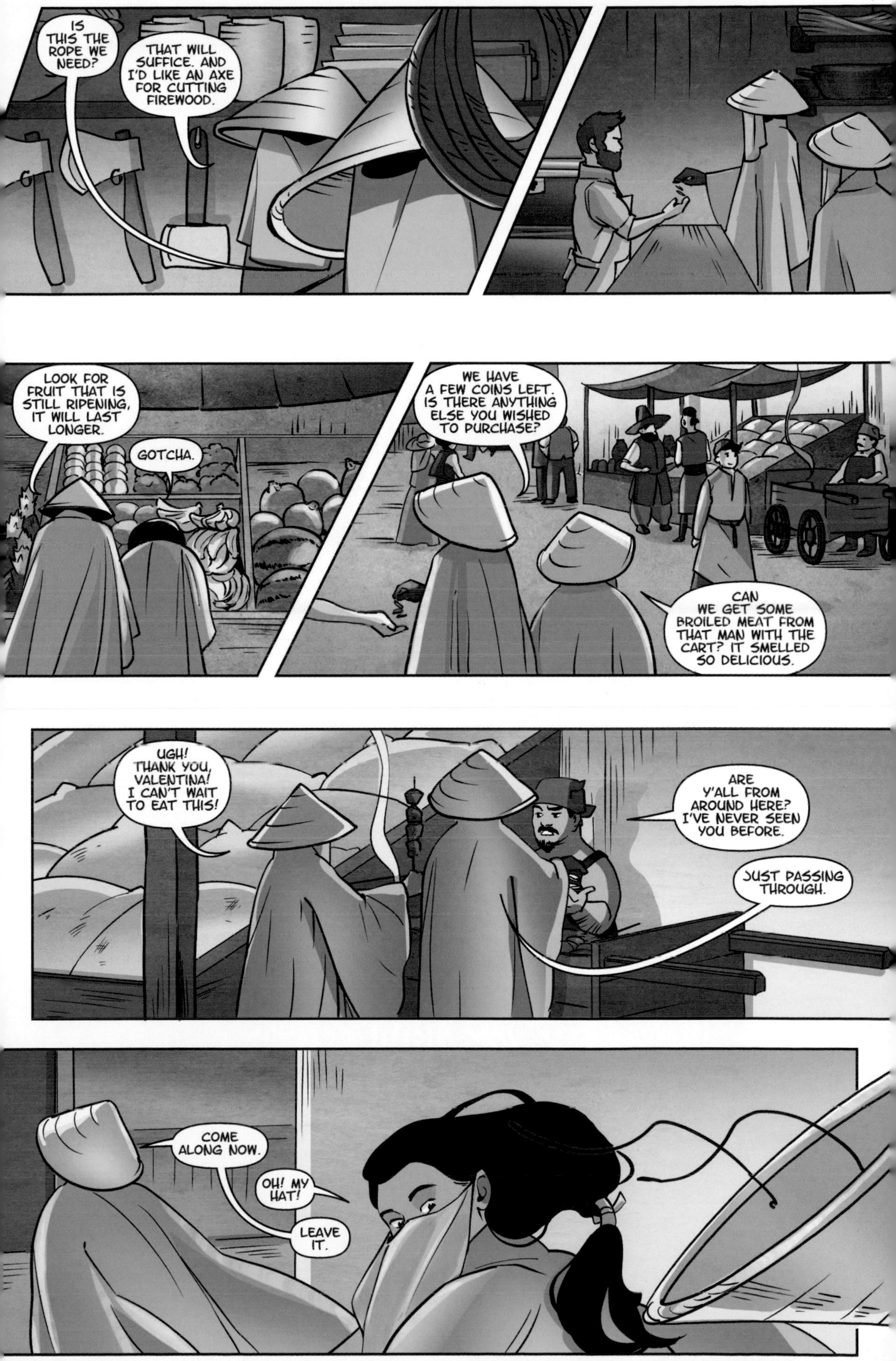
IS THIS THE ROPE WE NEED?
THAT WILL SUFFICE. AND I'D LIKE AN AXE FOR CUTTING FIREWOOD.
LOOK FOR FRUIT THAT IS STILL RIPENING, IT WILL LAST LONGER.
GOTCHA.
WE HAVE A FEW COINS LEFT. IS THERE ANYTHING ELSE YOU WISHED TO PURCHASE?
CAN WE GET SOME BROILED MEAT FROM THAT MAN WITH THE CART? IT SMELLED SO DELICIOUS.
UGH! THANK YOU, VALENTINA! I CAN'T WAIT TO EAT THIS!
ARE Y'ALL FROM AROUND HERE? I'VE NEVER SEEN YOU BEFORE.
JUST PASSING THROUGH.
COME ALONG NOW.
OH! MY HAT!
LEAVE IT.

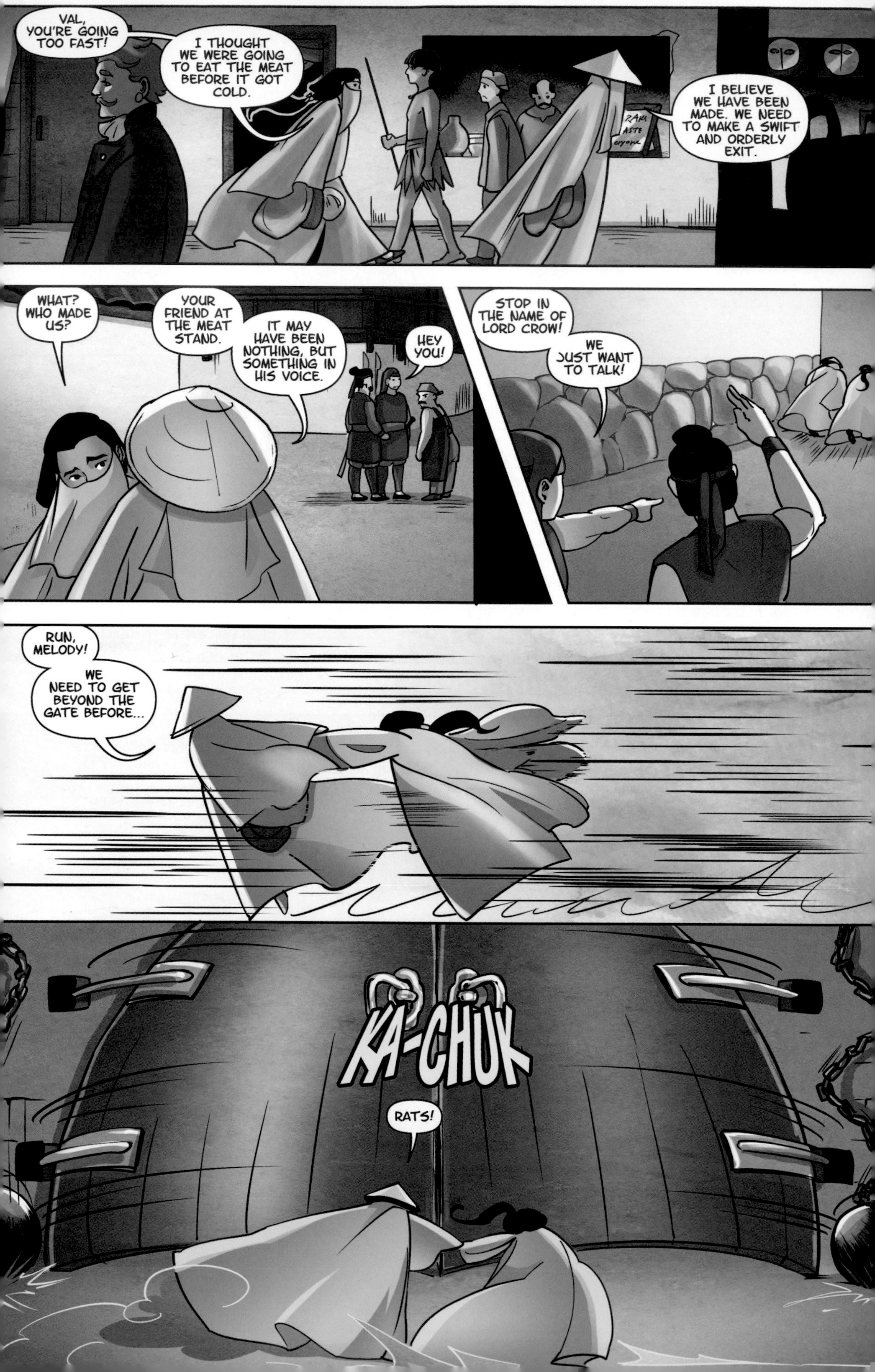
VAL, YOU'RE GOING TOO FAST!
I THOUGHT WE WERE GOING TO EAT THE MEAT BEFORE IT GOT COLD.
I BELIEVE WE HAVE BEEN MADE. WE NEED TO MAKE A SWIFT AND ORDERLY EXIT.
WHAT? WHO MADE US?
YOUR FRIEND AT THE MEAT STAND.
IT MAY HAVE BEEN NOTHING, BUT SOMETHING IN HIS VOICE.
HEY YOU!
STOP IN THE NAME OF LORD CROW!
WE JUST WANT TO TALK!
RUN, MELODY!
WE NEED TO GET BEYOND THE GATE BEFORE...
KA-CHUK
RATS!

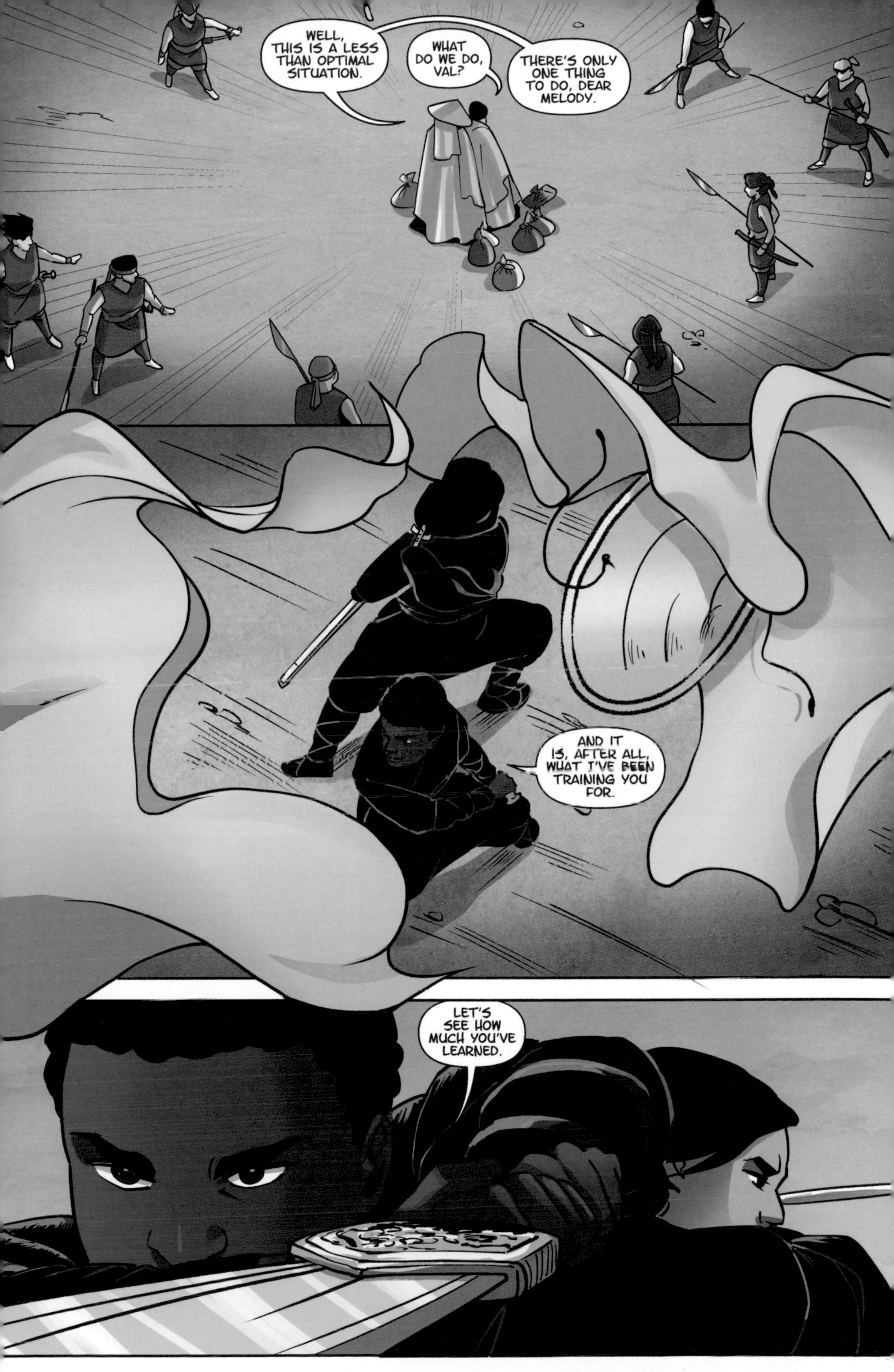
WELL, THIS IS A LESS THAN OPTIMAL SITUATION.
WHAT DO WE DO, VAL?
THERE'S ONLY ONE THING TO DO, DEAR MELODY.
AND IT IS, AFTER ALL, WHAT I'VE BEEN TRAINING YOU FOR.
LET'S SEE HOW MUCH YOU'VE LEARNED.

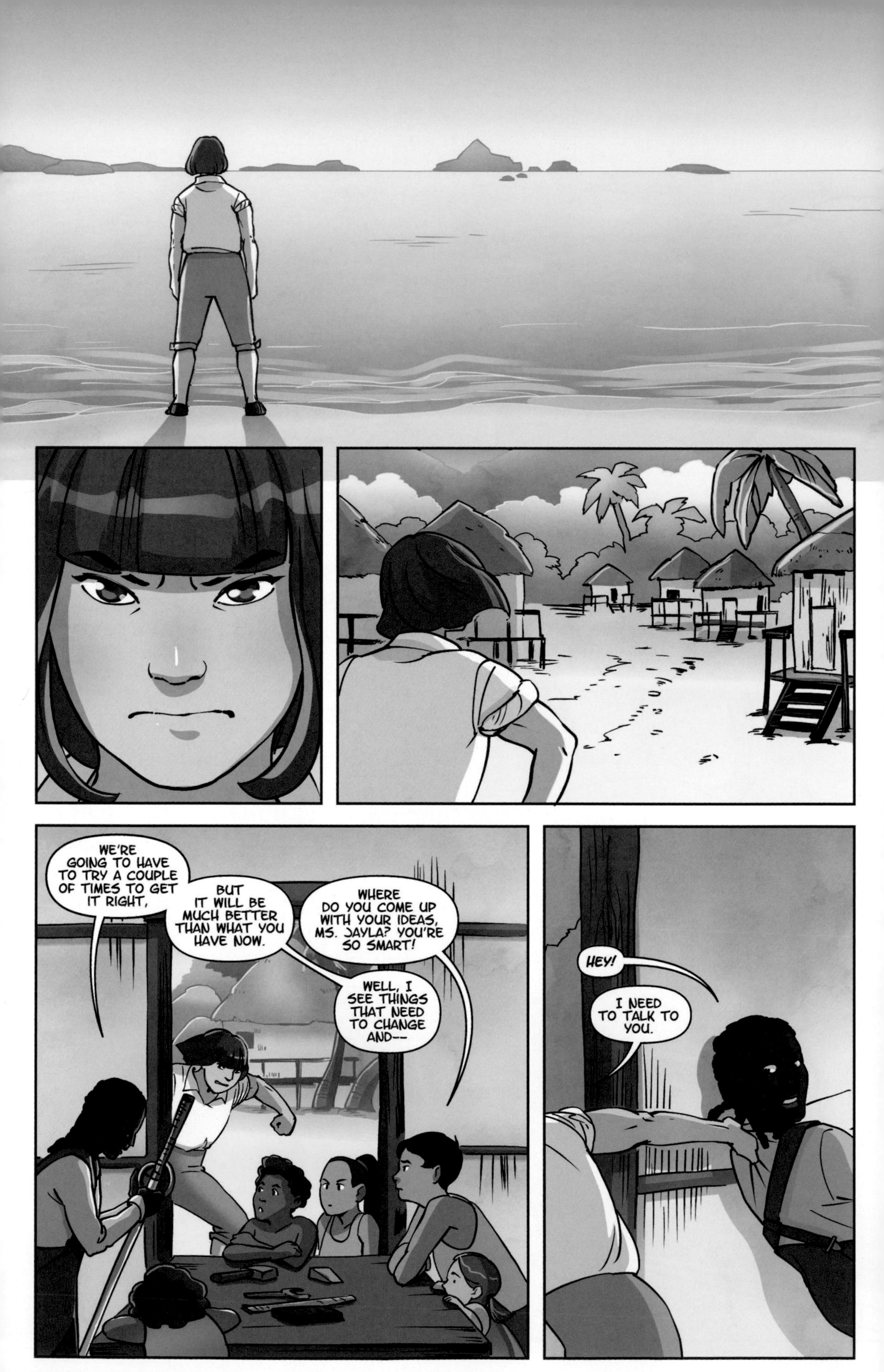
WE'RE GOING TO HAVE TO TRY A COUPLE OF TIMES TO GET IT RIGHT,
BUT IT WILL BE MUCH BETTER THAN WHAT YOU HAVE NOW.
WHERE DO YOU COME UP WITH YOUR IDEAS, MS. JAYLA? YOU'RE SO SMART!
WELL, I SEE THINGS THAT NEED TO CHANGE AND--
HEY!
I NEED TO TALK TO YOU.

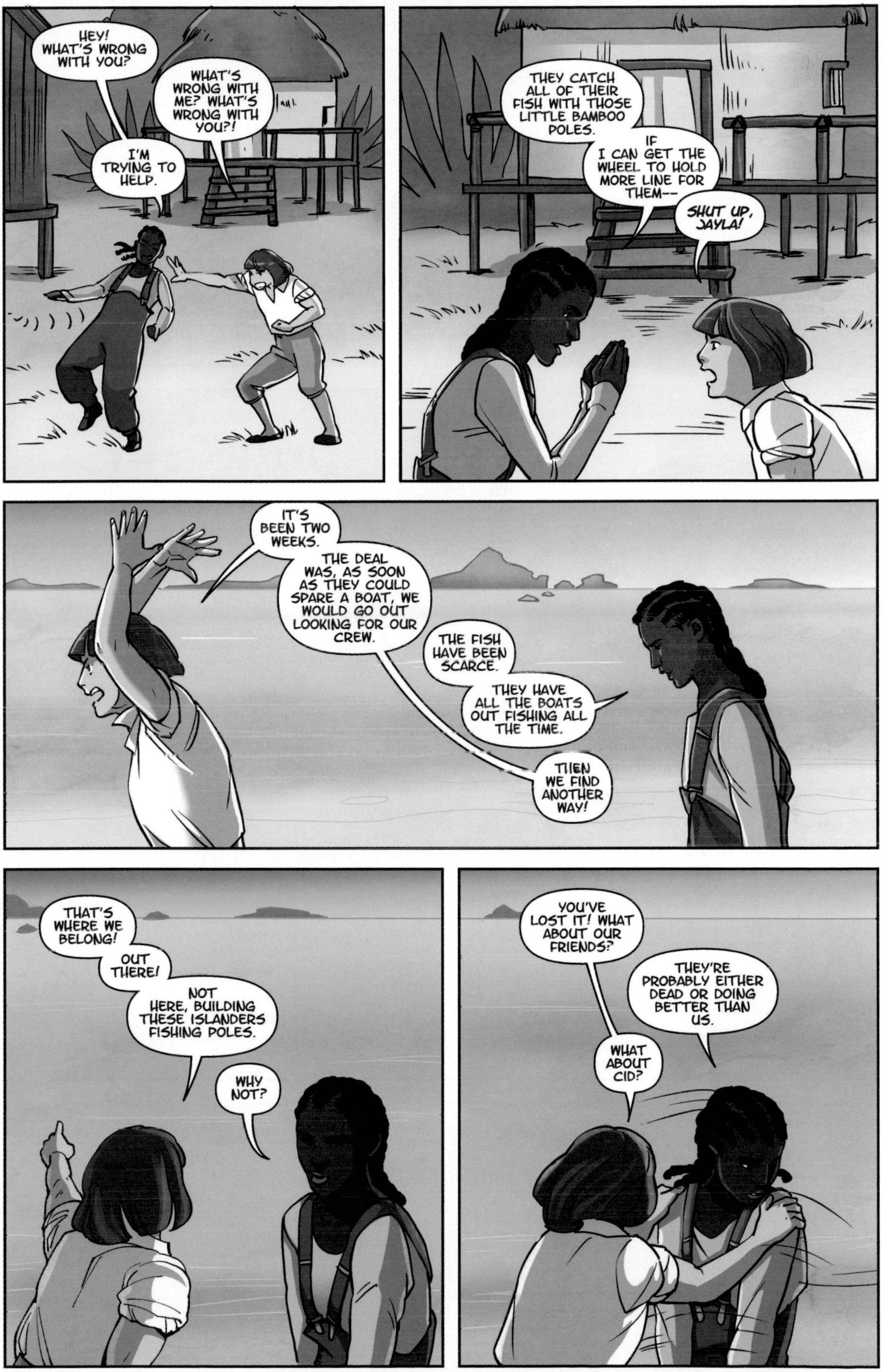
HEY! WHAT'S WRONG WITH YOU?
WHAT'S WRONG WITH ME? WHAT'S WRONG WITH YOU?!
I'M TRYING TO HELP.
THEY CATCH ALL OF THEIR FISH WITH THOSE LITTLE BAMBOO POLES.
IF I CAN GET THE WHEEL TO HOLD MORE LINE FOR THEM--
SHUT UP, JAYLA!
IT'S BEEN TWO WEEKS.
THE DEAL WAS, AS SOON AS THEY COULD SPARE A BOAT, WE WOULD GO OUT LOOKING FOR OUR CREW.
THE FISH HAVE BEEN SCARCE.
THEY HAVE ALL THE BOATS OUT FISHING ALL THE TIME.
THEN WE FIND ANOTHER WAY!
THAT'S WHERE WE BELONG!
OUT THERE!
NOT HERE, BUILDING THESE ISLANDERS FISHING POLES.
WHY NOT?
YOU'VE LOST IT! WHAT ABOUT OUR FRIENDS?
THEY'RE PROBABLY EITHER DEAD OR DOING BETTER THAN US.
WHAT ABOUT CID?

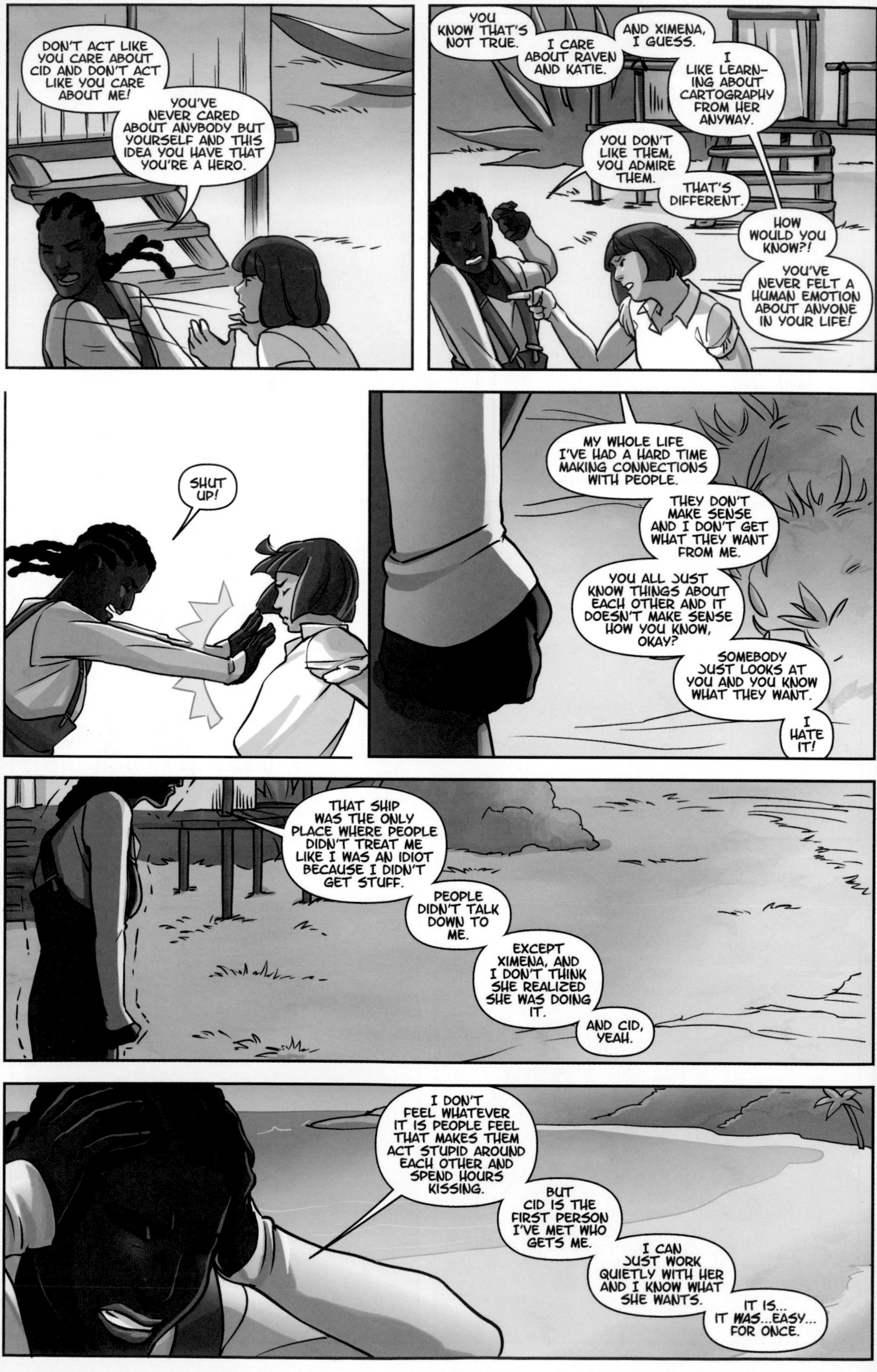
DON'T ACT LIKE YOU CARE ABOUT CID AND DON'T ACT LIKE YOU CARE ABOUT ME!
YOU'VE NEVER CARED ABOUT ANYBODY BUT YOURSELF AND THIS IDEA YOU HAVE THAT YOU'RE A HERO.
YOU KNOW THAT'S NOT TRUE.
I CARE ABOUT RAVEN AND KATIE.
AND XIMENA, I GUESS.
I LIKE LEARNING ABOUT CARTOGRAPHY FROM HER ANYWAY.
YOU DON'T LIKE THEM, YOU ADMIRE THEM.
THAT'S DIFFERENT.
HOW WOULD YOU KNOW?!
YOU'VE NEVER FELT A HUMAN EMOTION ABOUT ANYONE IN YOUR LIFE!
SHUT UP!
MY WHOLE LIFE I'VE HAD A HARD TIME MAKING CONNECTIONS WITH PEOPLE.
THEY DON'T MAKE SENSE AND I DON'T GET WHAT THEY WANT FROM ME.
YOU ALL JUST KNOW THINGS ABOUT EACH OTHER AND IT DOESN'T MAKE SENSE HOW YOU KNOW, OKAY?
SOMEBODY JUST LOOKS AT YOU AND YOU KNOW WHAT THEY WANT.
I HATE IT!
THAT SHIP WAS THE ONLY PLACE WHERE PEOPLE DIDN'T TREAT ME LIKE I WAS AN IDIOT BECAUSE I DIDN'T GET STUFF.
PEOPLE DIDN'T TALK DOWN TO ME.
EXCEPT XIMENA, AND I DON'T THINK SHE REALIZED SHE WAS DOING IT.
AND CID, YEAH.
I DON'T FEEL WHATEVER IT IS PEOPLE FEEL THAT MAKES THEM ACT STUPID AROUND EACH OTHER AND SPEND HOURS KISSING.
BUT CID IS THE FIRST PERSON I'VE MET WHO GETS ME.
I CAN JUST WORK QUIETLY WITH HER AND I KNOW WHAT SHE WANTS.
IT IS... IT WAS...EASY... FOR ONCE.

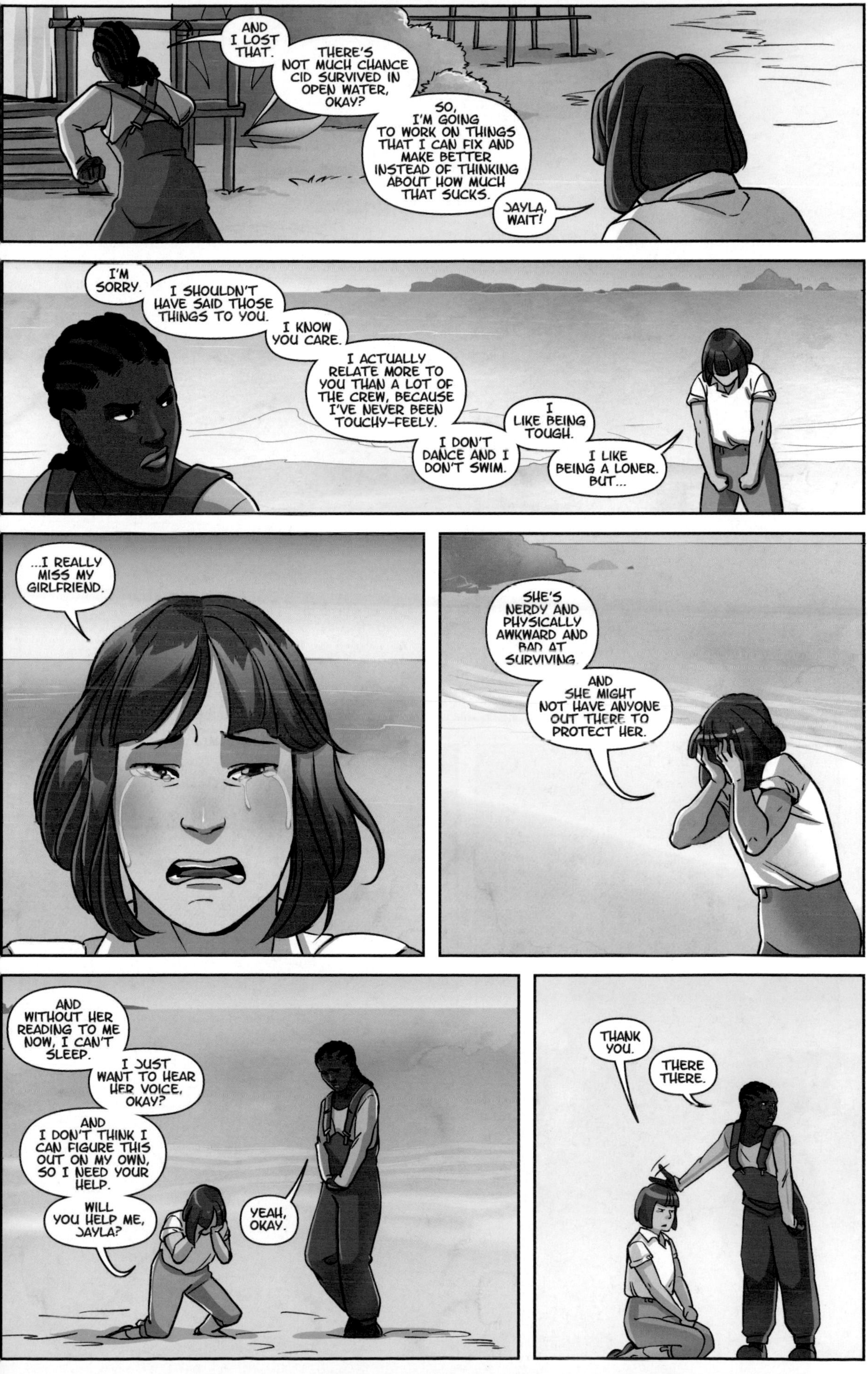
AND I LOST THAT.
THERE'S NOT MUCH CHANCE CID SURVIVED IN OPEN WATER, OKAY?
SO, I'M GOING TO WORK ON THINGS THAT I CAN FIX AND MAKE BETTER INSTEAD OF THINKING ABOUT HOW MUCH THAT SUCKS.
JAYLA, WAIT!
I'M SORRY.
I SHOULDN'T HAVE SAID THOSE THINGS TO YOU.
I KNOW YOU CARE.
I ACTUALLY RELATE MORE TO YOU THAN A LOT OF THE CREW, BECAUSE I'VE NEVER BEEN TOUCHY-FEELY.
I DON'T DANCE AND I DON'T SWIM.
I LIKE BEING TOUGH.
I LIKE BEING A LONER. BUT...
...I REALLY MISS MY GIRLFRIEND.
SHE'S NERDY AND PHYSICALLY AWKWARD AND BAD AT SURVIVING.
AND SHE MIGHT NOT HAVE ANYONE OUT THERE TO PROTECT HER.
AND WITHOUT HER READING TO ME NOW, I CAN'T SLEEP.
I JUST WANT TO HEAR HER VOICE, OKAY?
AND I DON'T THINK I CAN FIGURE THIS OUT ON MY OWN, SO I NEED YOUR HELP.
WILL YOU HELP ME, JAYLA?
YEAH, OKAY.
THANK YOU.
THERE THERE.

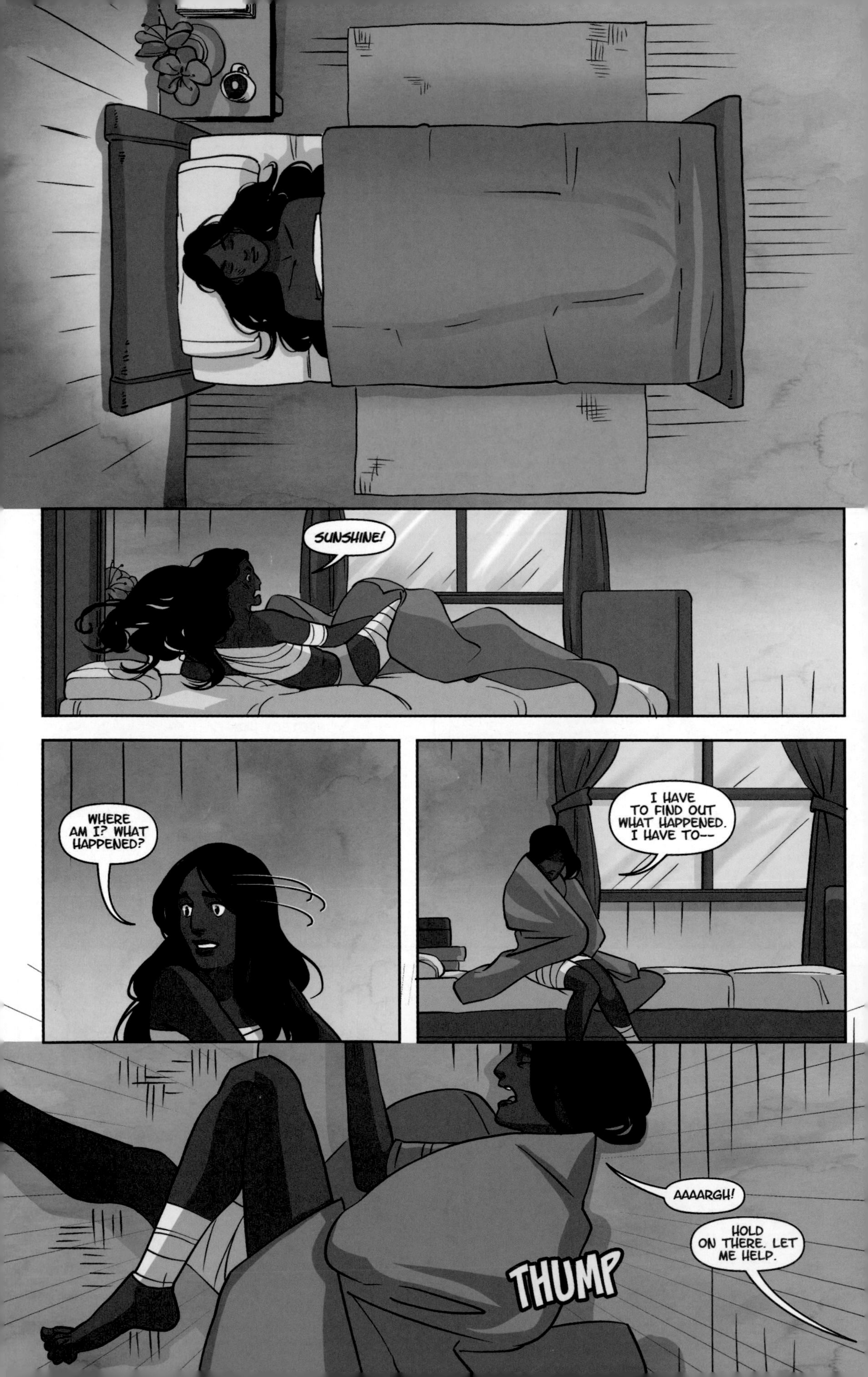
SUNSHINE!
WHERE AM I? WHAT HAPPENED?
I HAVE TO FIND OUT WHAT HAPPENED. I HAVE TO--
AAAARGH!
THUMP
HOLD ON THERE. LET ME HELP.

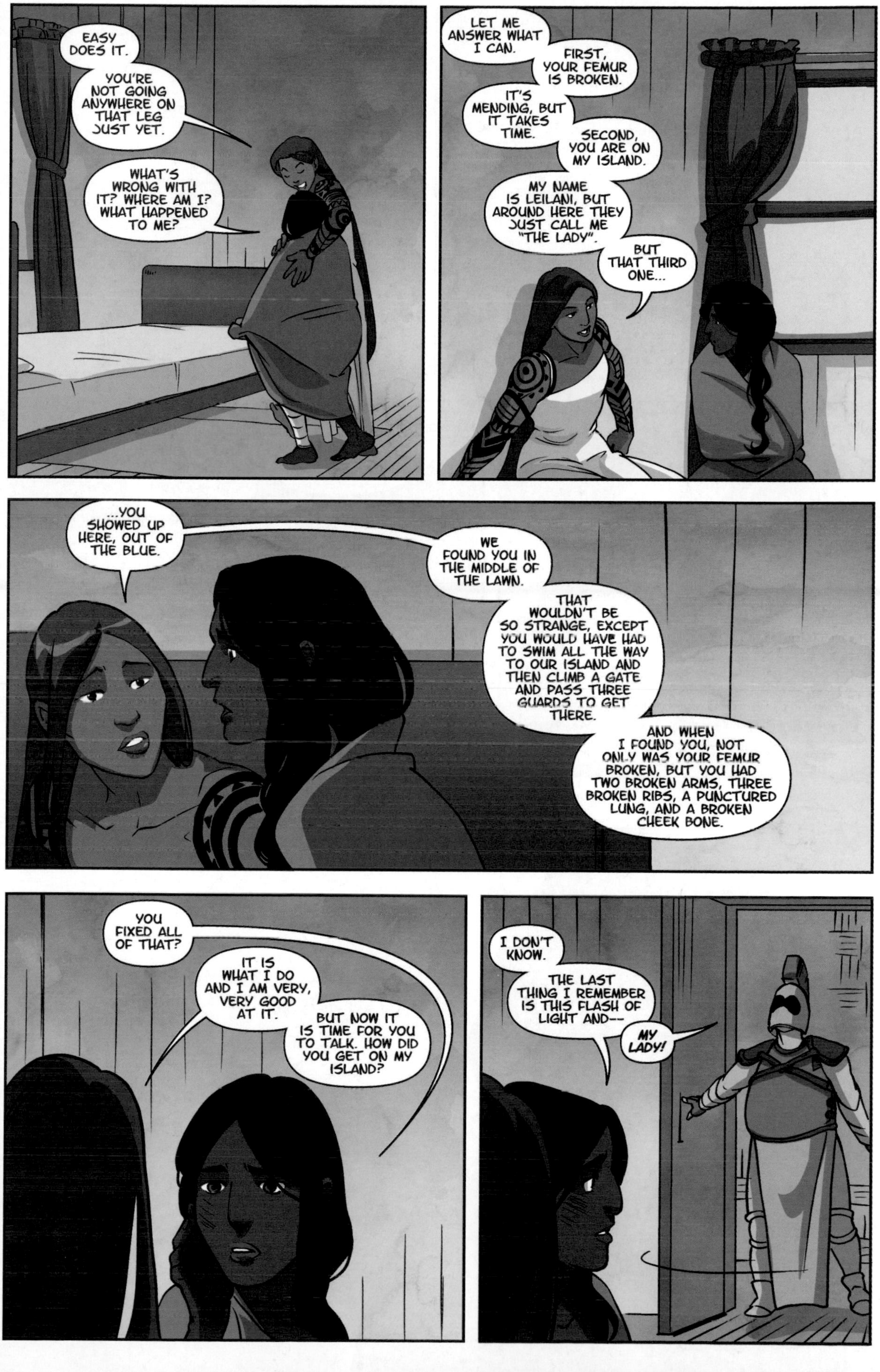
EASY DOES IT.
YOU'RE NOT GOING ANYWHERE ON THAT LEG JUST YET.
WHAT'S WRONG WITH IT? WHERE AM I? WHAT HAPPENED TO ME?
LET ME ANSWER WHAT I CAN.
FIRST, YOUR FEMUR IS BROKEN.
IT'S MENDING, BUT IT TAKES TIME.
SECOND, YOU ARE ON MY ISLAND.
MY NAME IS LEILANI, BUT AROUND HERE THEY JUST CALL ME "THE LADY".
BUT THAT THIRD ONE...
...YOU SHOWED UP HERE, OUT OF THE BLUE.
WE FOUND YOU IN THE MIDDLE OF THE LAWN.
THAT WOULDN'T BE SO STRANGE, EXCEPT YOU WOULD HAVE HAD TO SWIM ALL THE WAY TO OUR ISLAND AND THEN CLIMB A GATE AND PASS THREE GUARDS TO GET THERE.
AND WHEN I FOUND YOU, NOT ONLY WAS YOUR FEMUR BROKEN, BUT YOU HAD TWO BROKEN ARMS, THREE BROKEN RIBS, A PUNCTURED LUNG, AND A BROKEN CHEEK BONE.
YOU FIXED ALL OF THAT?
IT IS WHAT I DO AND I AM VERY, VERY GOOD AT IT.
BUT NOW IT IS TIME FOR YOU TO TALK. HOW DID YOU GET ON MY ISLAND?
I DON'T KNOW.
THE LAST THING I REMEMBER IS THIS FLASH OF LIGHT AND--
MY LADY!

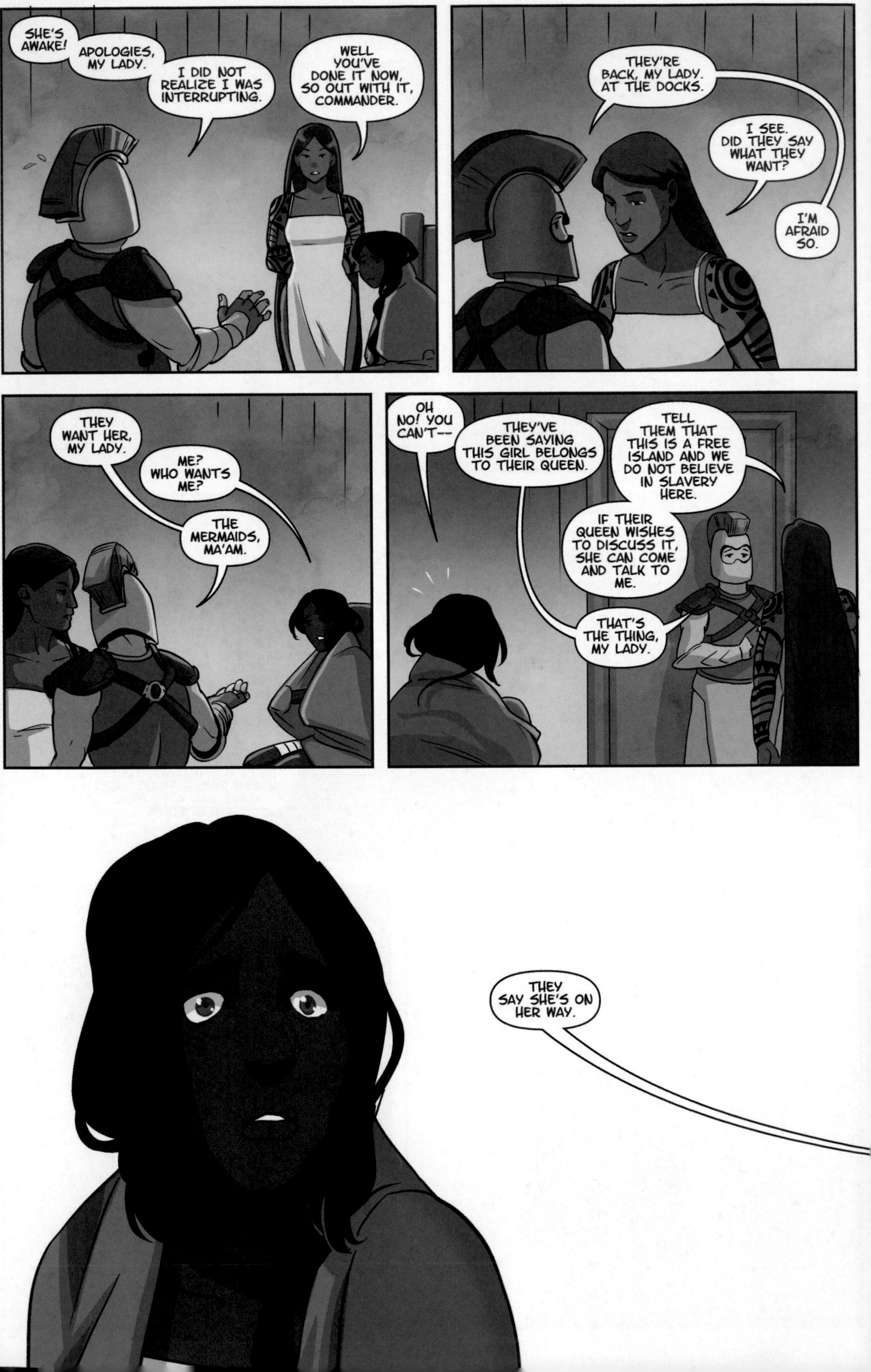
SHE'S AWAKE!
APOLOGIES, MY LADY.
I DID NOT REALIZE I WAS INTERRUPTING.
WELL YOU'VE DONE IT NOW, SO OUT WITH IT, COMMANDER.
THEY'RE BACK, MY LADY. AT THE DOCKS.
I SEE. DID THEY SAY WHAT THEY WANT?
I'M AFRAID SO.
THEY WANT HER, MY LADY.
ME? WHO WANTS ME?
THE MERMAIDS, MA'AM.
OH NO! YOU CAN'T--
THEY'VE BEEN SAYING THIS GIRL BELONGS TO THEIR QUEEN.
TELL THEM THAT THIS IS A FREE ISLAND AND WE DO NOT BELIEVE IN SLAVERY HERE.
IF THEIR QUEEN WISHES TO DISCUSS IT, SHE CAN COME AND TALK TO ME.
THAT'S THE THING, MY LADY.
THEY SAY SHE'S ON HER WAY.

Princeless Raven: The Pirate Princess

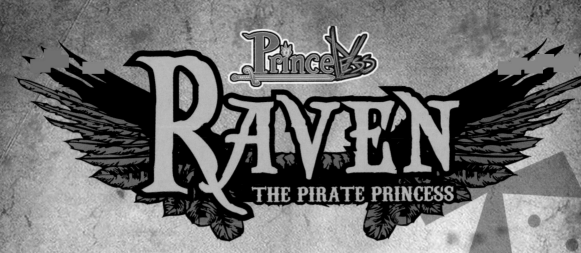

Year Three: Monsters of the Deep

Chapter Eight: Return of the Queen

Written By: Jeremy Whitley

Pencils By:

(Pages 3-5, 13-20) Xenia Pamfil

(Pages 1-2, 6-12, 21-24) Telenia Albuquerque

Inks By:

(Pages 3-5, 13-20) JB Fuller

(Pages 1-2, 6-12, 21-24) Pocket Owl

Colors By:

(Pages 3-5, 13-20) Lexillo

(Pages 1-2, 6-12, 21-24) Valentina Pinto

Lettered By: Alex Scherkenbach
Edited By: Nicole D'Andria

Cover By: Telênia Albuquerque

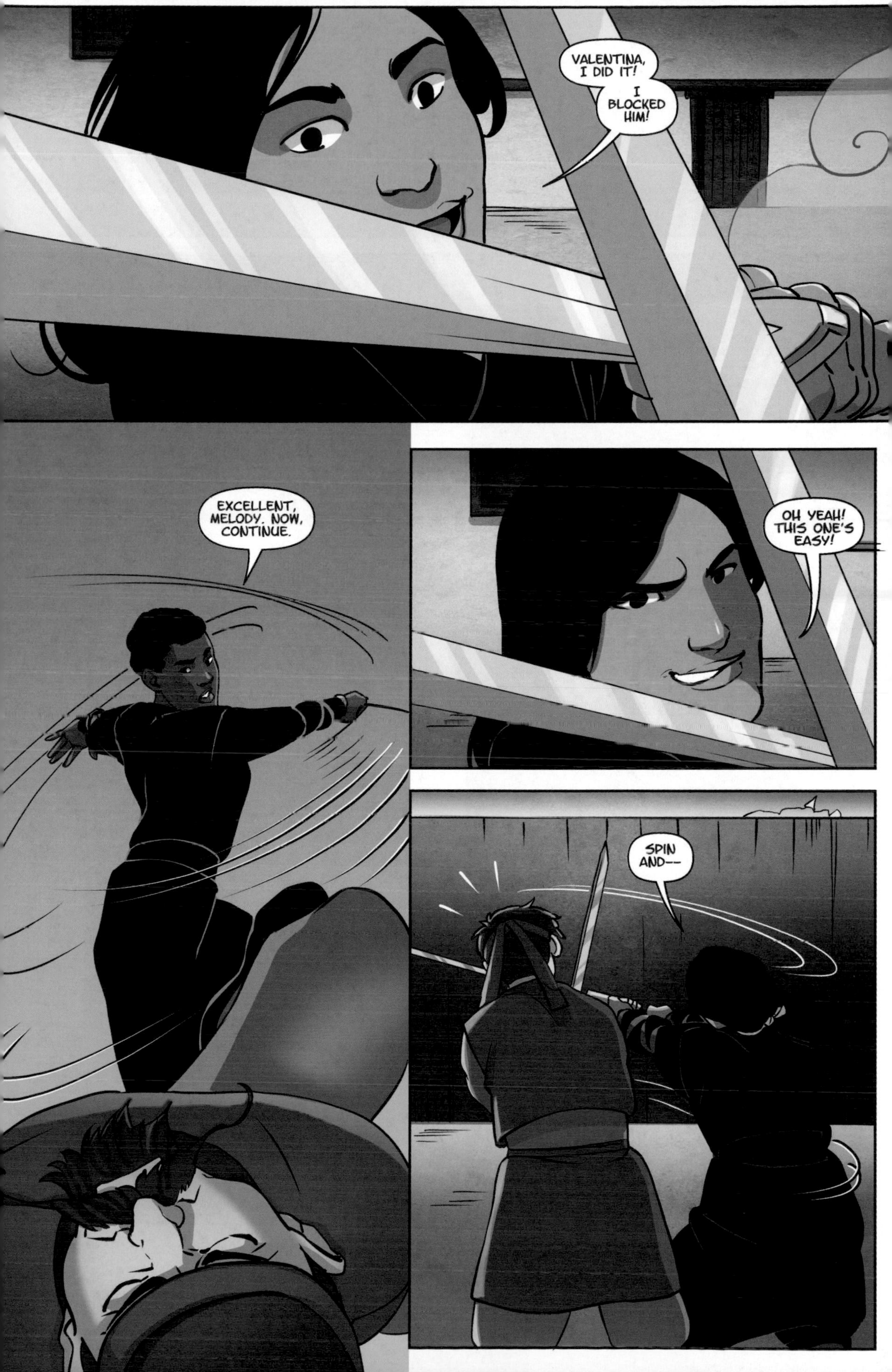
VALENTINA, I DID IT!
I BLOCKED HIM!
EXCELLENT, MELODY. NOW, CONTINUE.
OH YEAH! THIS ONE'S EASY!
SPIN AND--

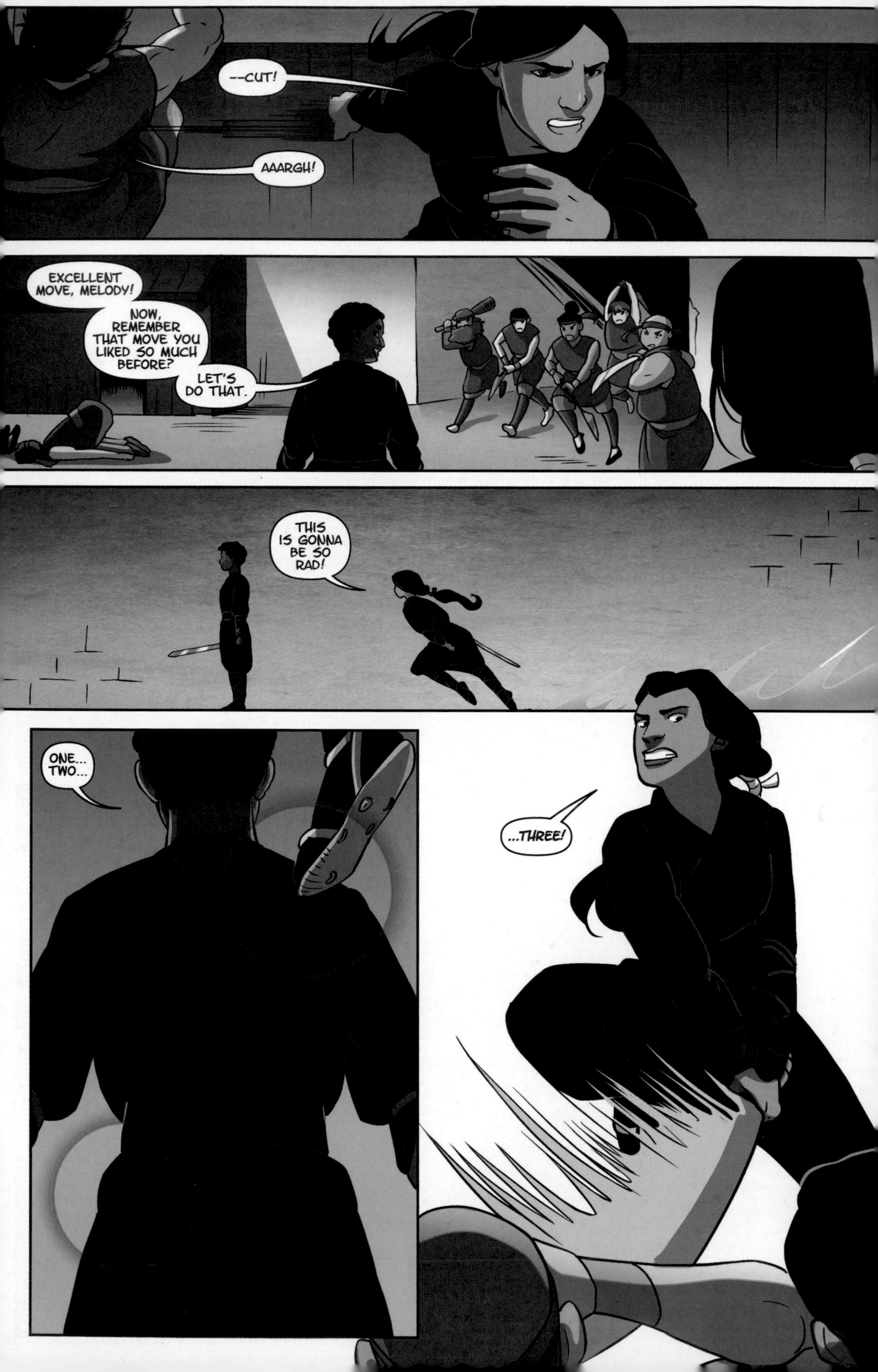
--CUT!
AAARGH!
EXCELLENT MOVE, MELODY!
NOW, REMEMBER THAT MOVE YOU LIKED SO MUCH BEFORE?
LET'S DO THAT.
THIS IS GONNA BE SO RAD!
ONE... TWO...
...THREE!

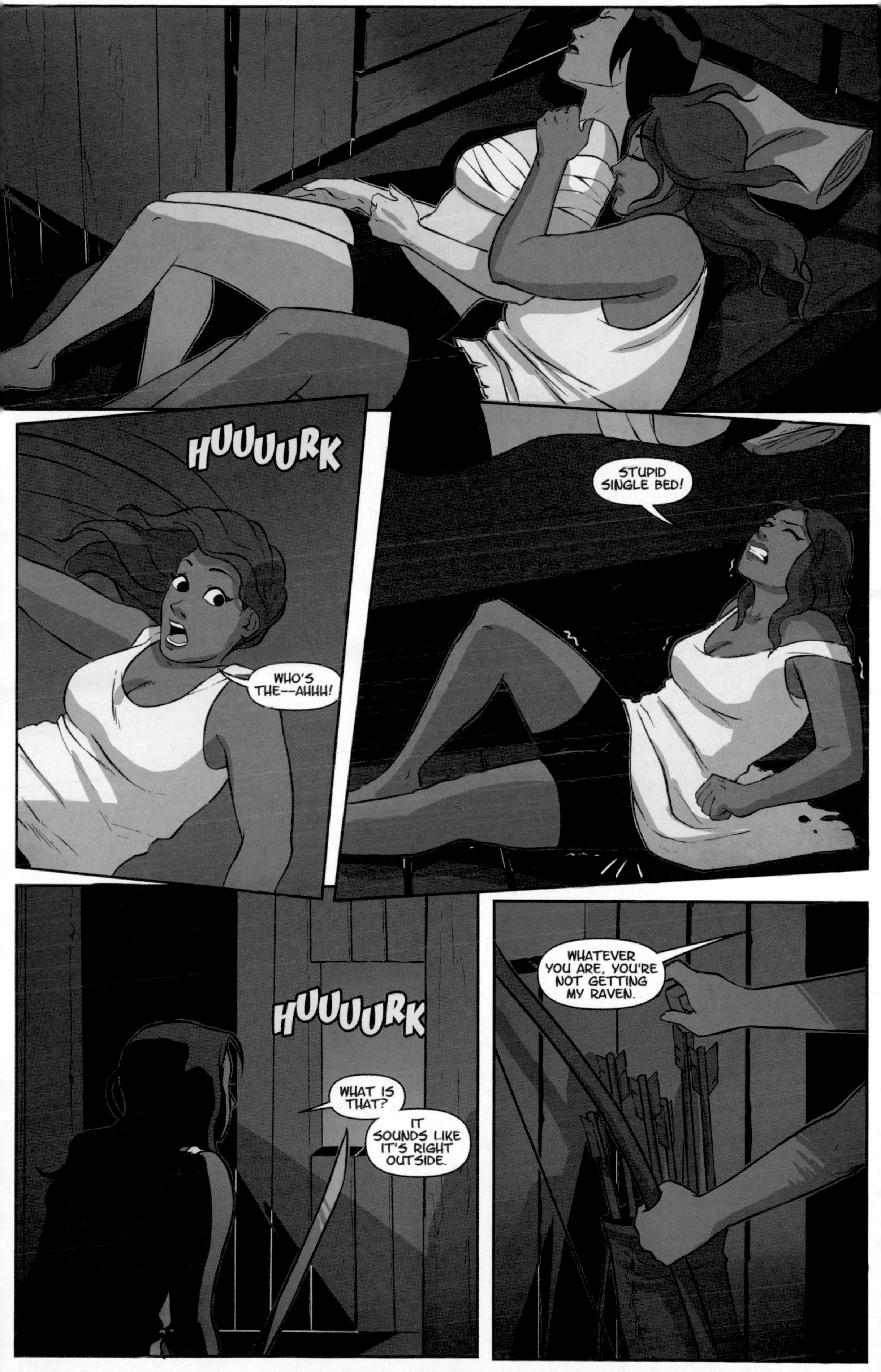
HUUUURK
WHO'S THE--AHHH!
STUPID SINGLE BED!
HUUUURK
WHAT IS THAT?
IT SOUNDS LIKE IT'S RIGHT OUTSIDE.
WHATEVER YOU ARE, YOU'RE NOT GETTING MY RAVEN.

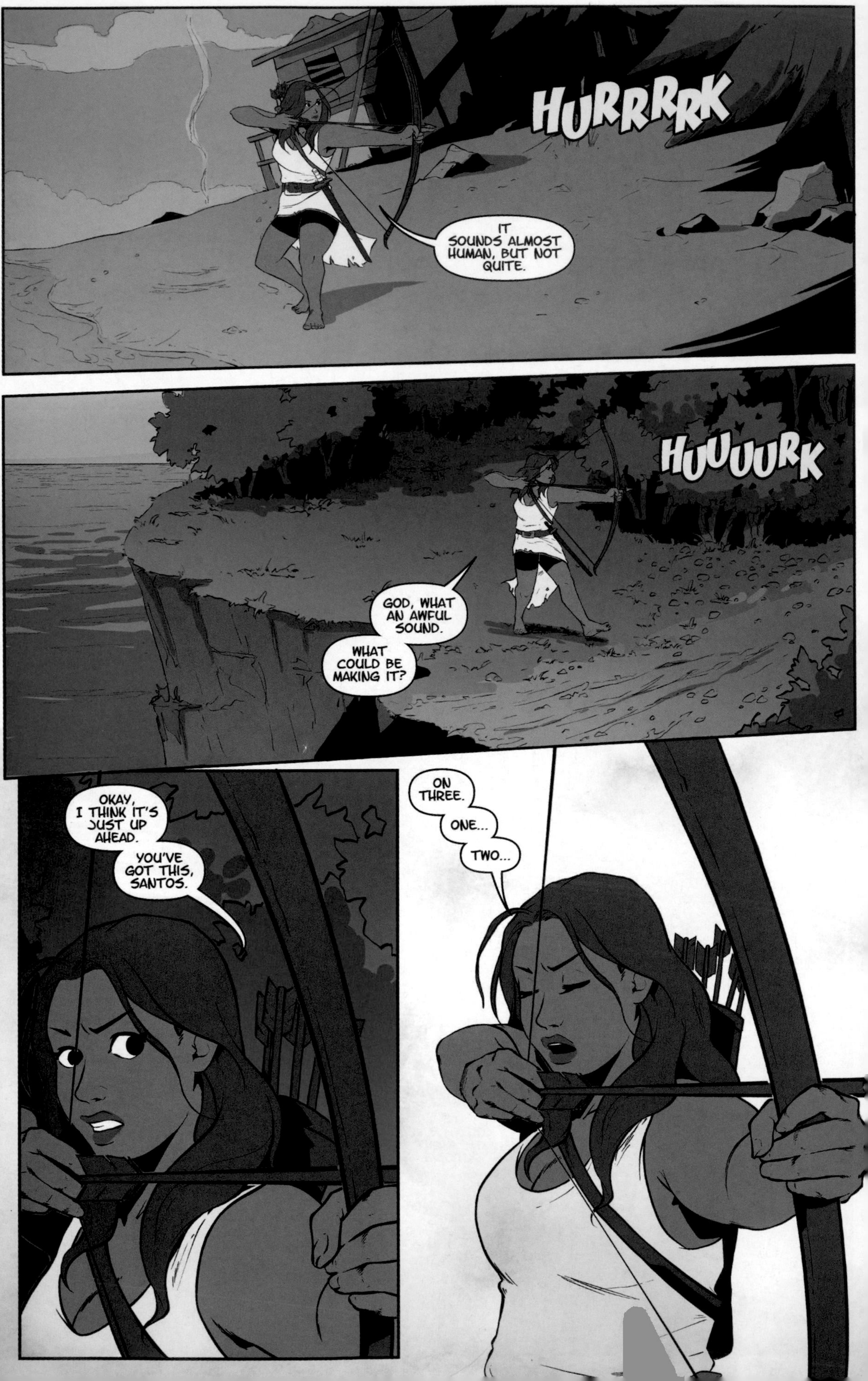
HURRRRK
IT SOUNDS ALMOST HUMAN, BUT NOT QUITE.
HUUUURK
GOD, WHAT AN AWFUL SOUND.
WHAT COULD BE MAKING IT?
OKAY, I THINK IT'S JUST UP AHEAD.
YOU'VE GOT THIS, SANTOS.
ON THREE.
ONE...
TWO...

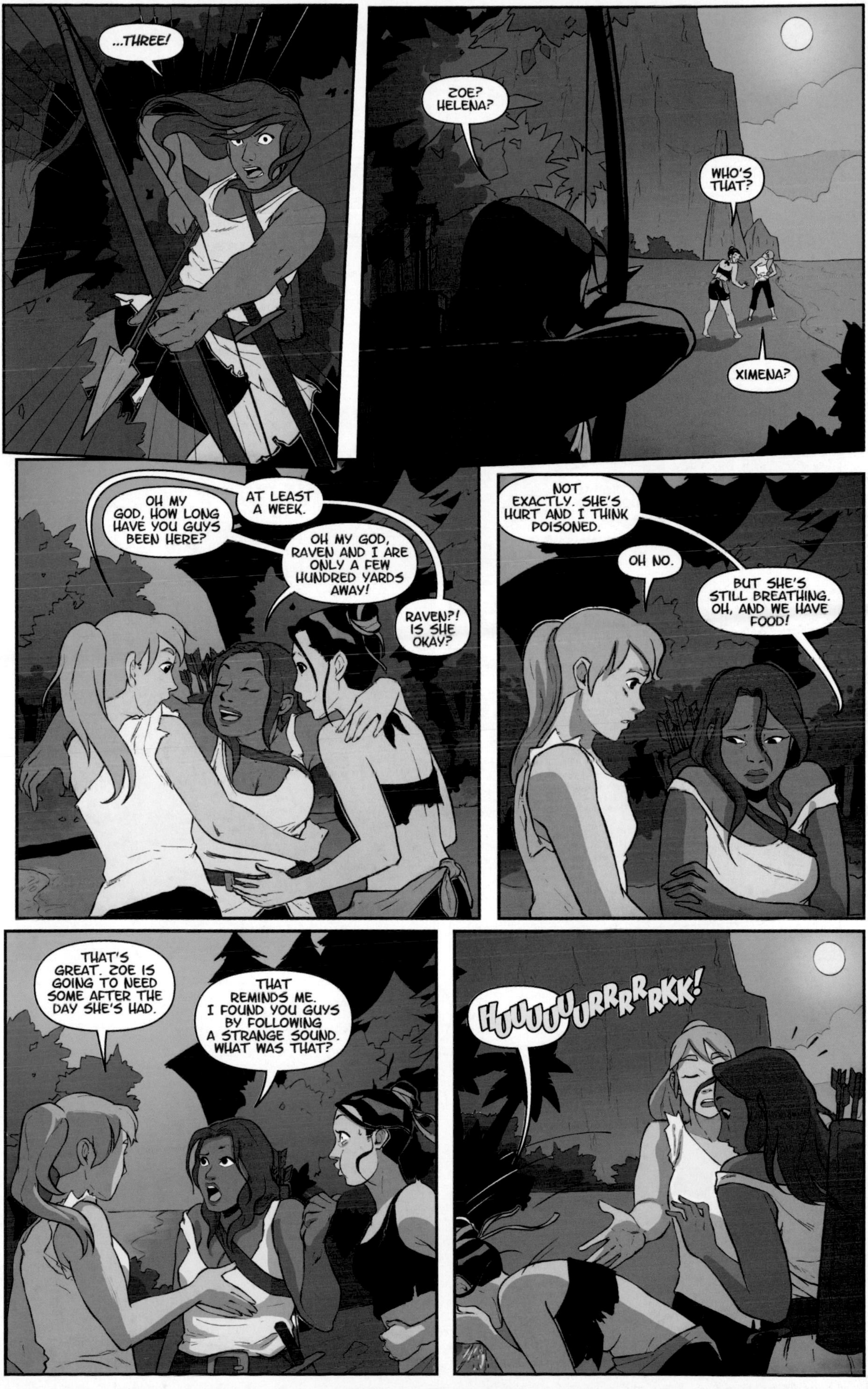

...THREE!
ZOE? HELENA?
WHO'S THAT?
XIMENA?
OH MY GOD, HOW LONG HAVE YOU GUYS BEEN HERE?
AT LEAST A WEEK.
OH MY GOD, RAVEN AND I ARE ONLY A FEW HUNDRED YARDS AWAY!
RAVEN?! IS SHE OKAY?
NOT EXACTLY. SHE'S HURT AND I THINK POISONED.
OH NO.
BUT SHE'S STILL BREATHING. OH, AND WE HAVE FOOD!
THAT'S GREAT. ZOE IS GOING TO NEED SOME AFTER THE DAY SHE'S HAD.
THAT REMINDS ME. I FOUND YOU GUYS BY FOLLOWING A STRANGE SOUND. WHAT WAS THAT?
HUUUUUURRRRRKK!

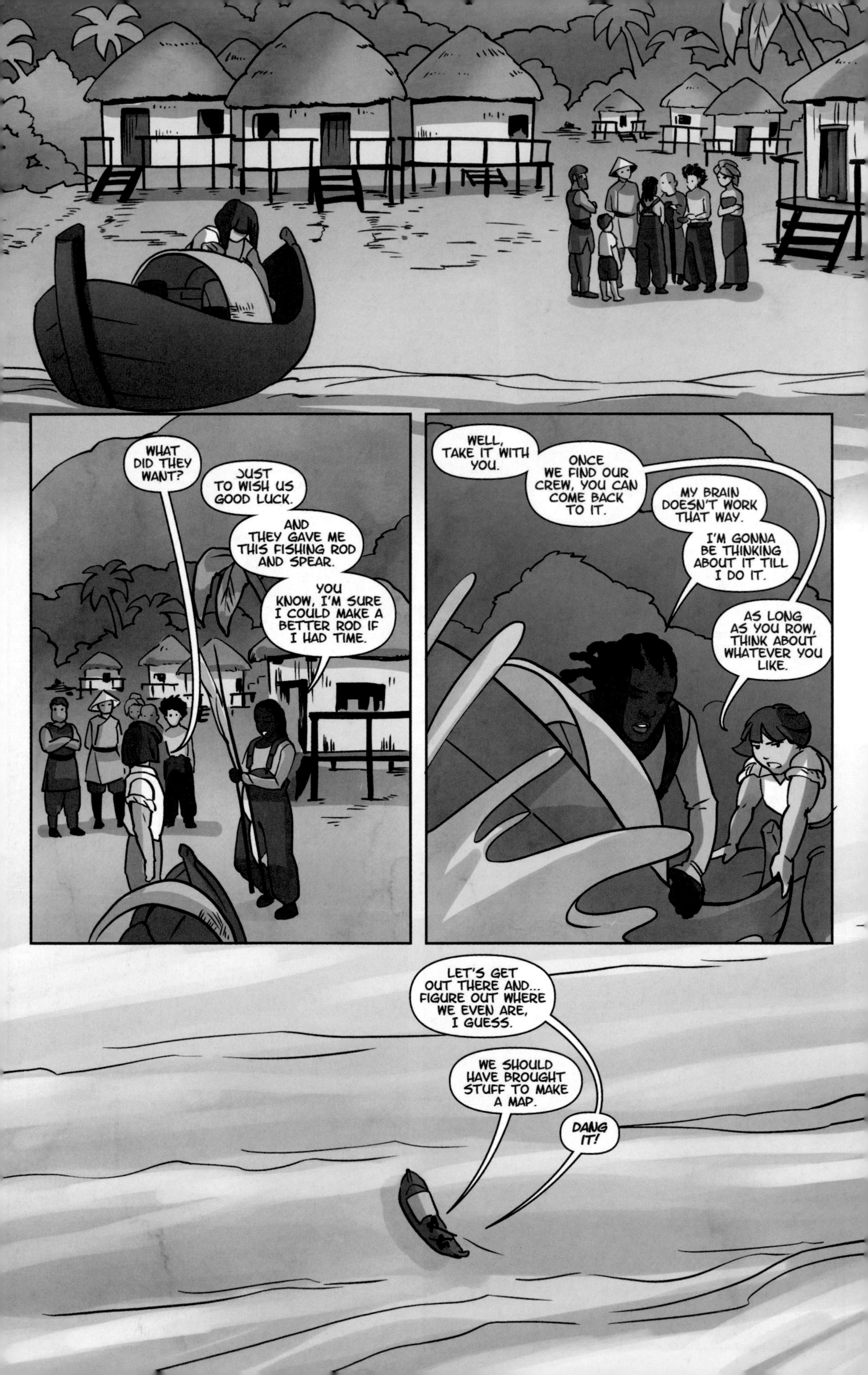
WHAT DID THEY WANT?
JUST TO WISH US GOOD LUCK.
AND THEY GAVE ME THIS FISHING ROD AND SPEAR.
YOU KNOW, I'M SURE I COULD MAKE A BETTER ROD IF I HAD TIME.
WELL, TAKE IT WITH YOU.
ONCE WE FIND OUR CREW, YOU CAN COME BACK TO IT.
MY BRAIN DOESN'T WORK THAT WAY.
I'M GONNA BE THINKING ABOUT IT TILL I DO IT.
AS LONG AS YOU ROW, THINK ABOUT WHATEVER YOU LIKE.
LET'S GET OUT THERE AND... FIGURE OUT WHERE WE EVEN ARE, I GUESS.
WE SHOULD HAVE BROUGHT STUFF TO MAKE A MAP.
DANG IT!

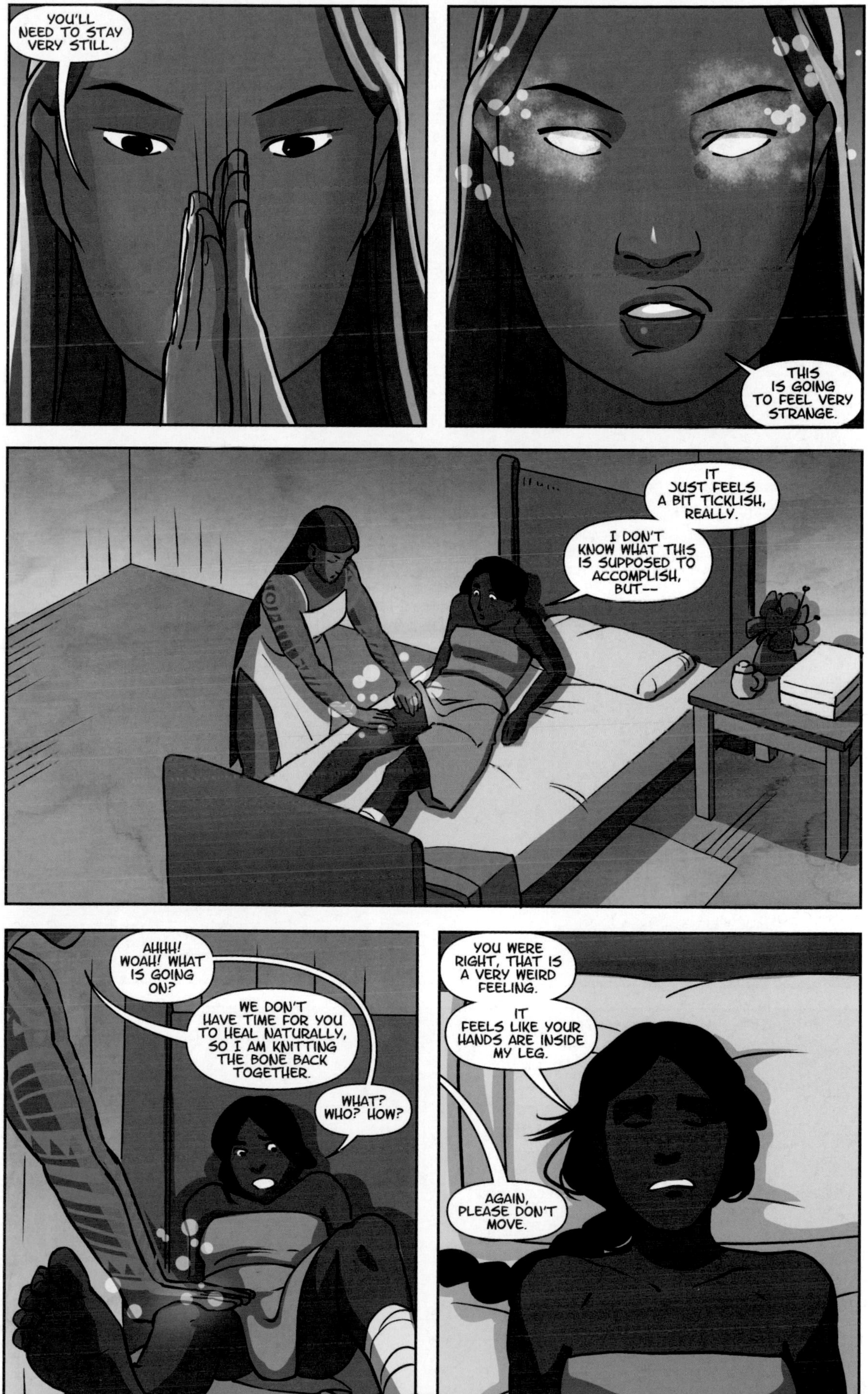
YOU'LL NEED TO STAY VERY STILL.
THIS IS GOING TO FEEL VERY STRANGE.
IT JUST FEELS A BIT TICKLISH, REALLY.
I DON'T KNOW WHAT THIS IS SUPPOSED TO ACCOMPLISH, BUT--
AHHH! WOAH! WHAT IS GOING ON?
WE DON'T HAVE TIME FOR YOU TO HEAL NATURALLY, SO I AM KNITTING THE BONE BACK TOGETHER.
WHAT? WHO? HOW?
YOU WERE RIGHT, THAT IS A VERY WEIRD FEELING.
IT FEELS LIKE YOUR HANDS ARE INSIDE MY LEG.
AGAIN, PLEASE DON'T MOVE.

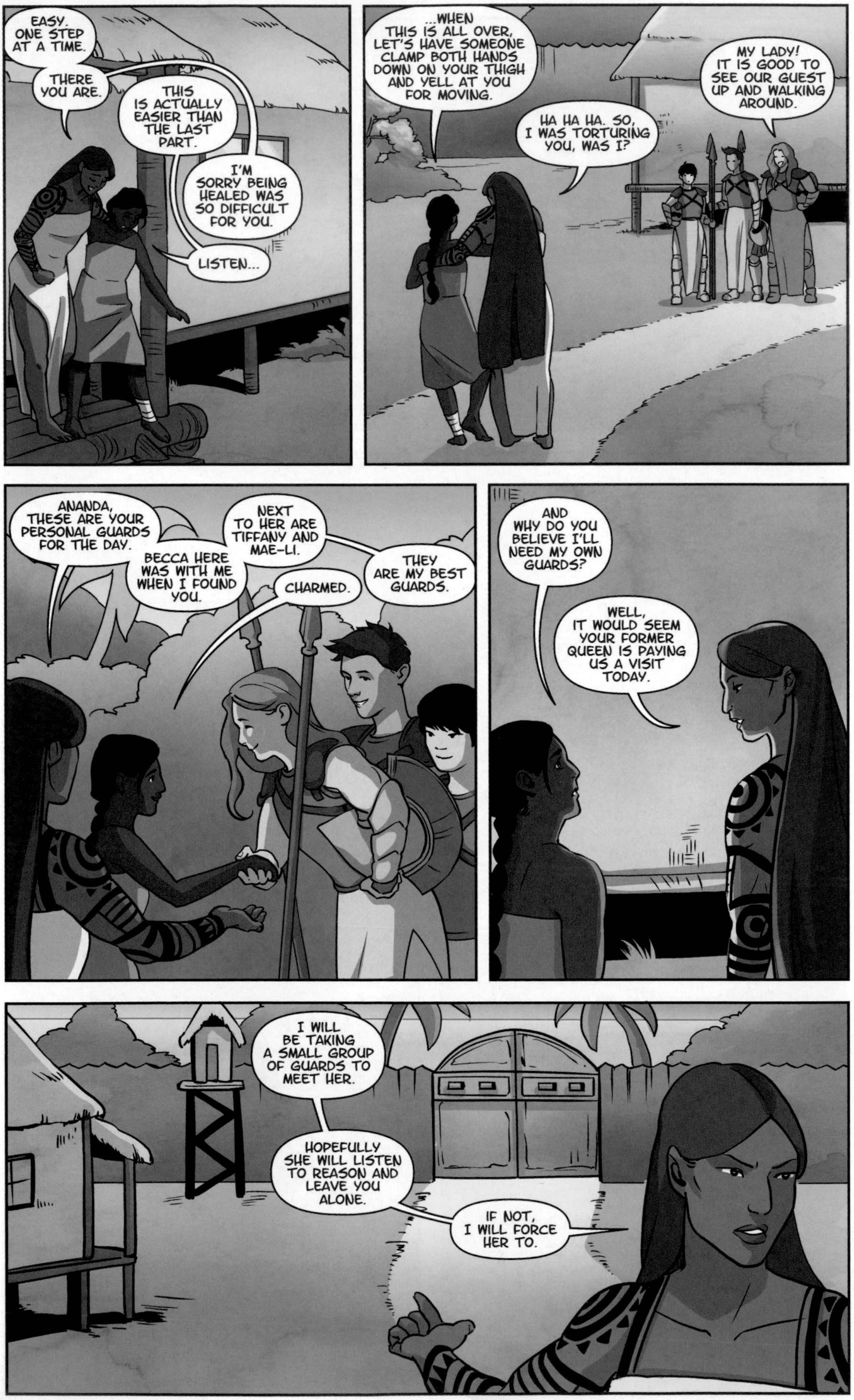
EASY. ONE STEP AT A TIME.
THERE YOU ARE.
THIS IS ACTUALLY EASIER THAN THE LAST PART.
I'M SORRY BEING HEALED WAS SO DIFFICULT FOR YOU.
LISTEN...
...WHEN THIS IS ALL OVER, LET'S HAVE SOMEONE CLAMP BOTH HANDS DOWN ON YOUR THIGH AND YELL AT YOU FOR MOVING.
HA HA HA. SO, I WAS TORTURING YOU, WAS I?
MY LADY! IT IS GOOD TO SEE OUR GUEST UP AND WALKING AROUND.
ANANDA, THESE ARE YOUR PERSONAL GUARDS FOR THE DAY.
BECCA HERE WAS WITH ME WHEN I FOUND YOU.
NEXT TO HER ARE TIFFANY AND MAE-LI.
THEY ARE MY BEST GUARDS.
CHARMED.
AND WHY DO YOU BELIEVE I'LL NEED MY OWN GUARDS?
WELL, IT WOULD SEEM YOUR FORMER QUEEN IS PAYING US A VISIT TODAY.
I WILL BE TAKING A SMALL GROUP OF GUARDS TO MEET HER.
HOPEFULLY SHE WILL LISTEN TO REASON AND LEAVE YOU ALONE.
IF NOT, I WILL FORCE HER TO.

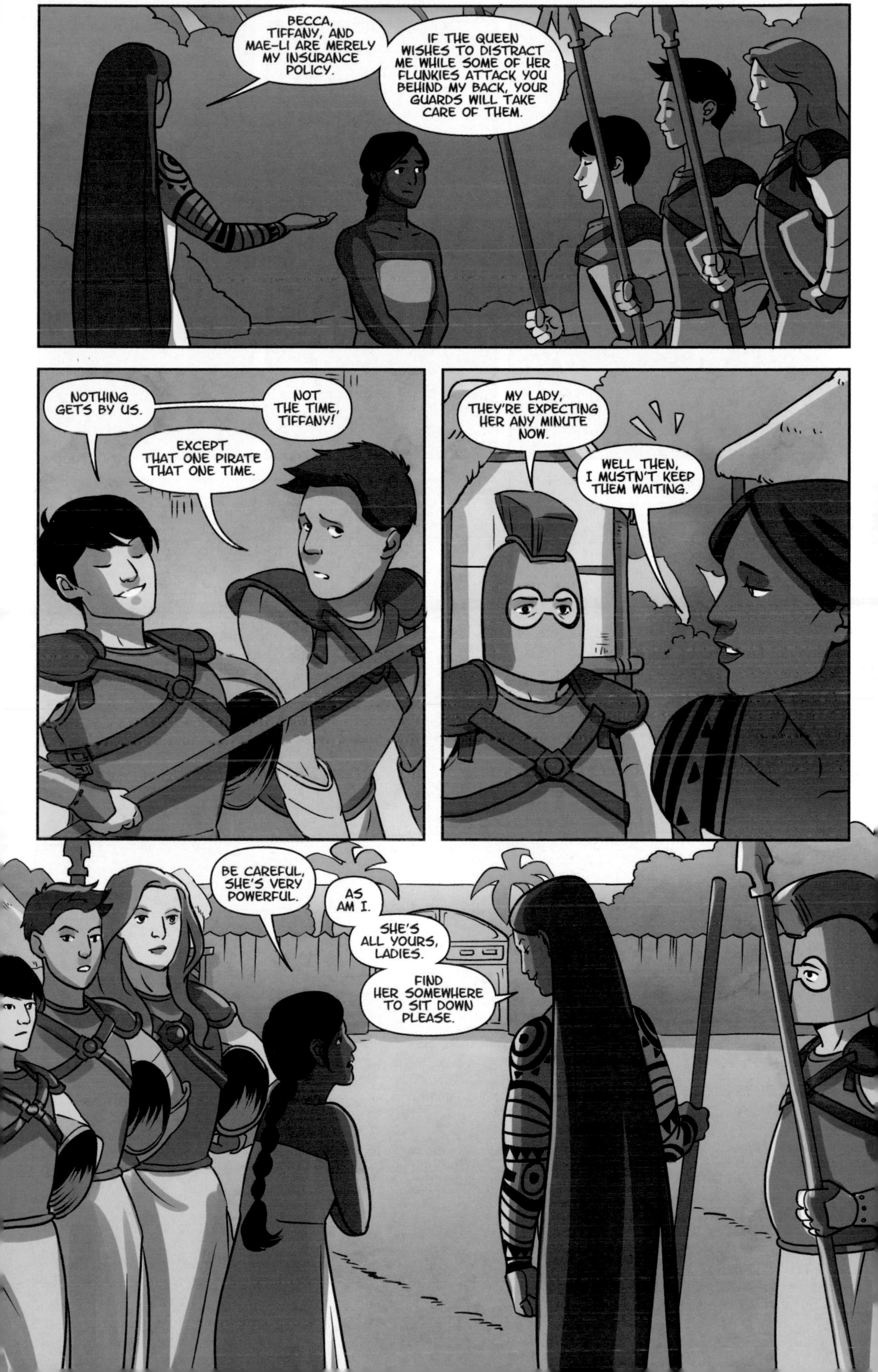
BECCA, TIFFANY, AND MAE-LI ARE MERELY MY INSURANCE POLICY.
IF THE QUEEN WISHES TO DISTRACT ME WHILE SOME OF HER FLUNKIES ATTACK YOU BEHIND MY BACK, YOUR GUARDS WILL TAKE CARE OF THEM.
NOTHING GETS BY US.
NOT THE TIME, TIFFANY!
EXCEPT THAT ONE PIRATE THAT ONE TIME.
MY LADY, THEY'RE EXPECTING HER ANY MINUTE NOW.
WELL THEN, I MUSTN'T KEEP THEM WAITING.
BE CAREFUL, SHE'S VERY POWERFUL.
AS AM I.
SHE'S ALL YOURS, LADIES.
FIND HER SOMEWHERE TO SIT DOWN PLEASE.

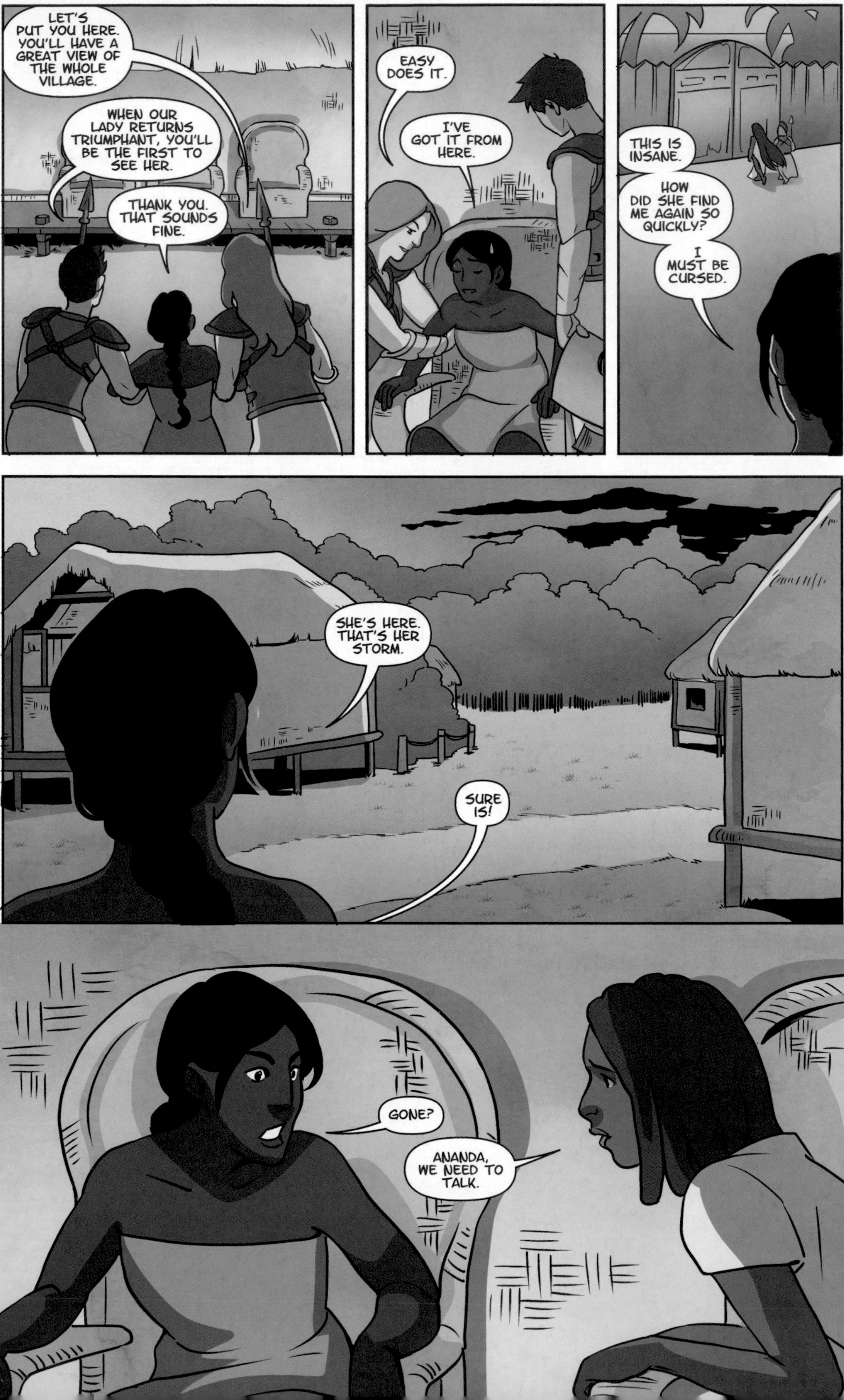
LET'S PUT YOU HERE. YOU'LL HAVE A GREAT VIEW OF THE WHOLE VILLAGE.
WHEN OUR LADY RETURNS TRIUMPHANT, YOU'LL BE THE FIRST TO SEE HER.
THANK YOU. THAT SOUNDS FINE.
EASY DOES IT.
I'VE GOT IT FROM HERE.
THIS IS INSANE.
HOW DID SHE FIND ME AGAIN SO QUICKLY?
I MUST BE CURSED.
SHE'S HERE. THAT'S HER STORM.
SURE IS!
GONE?
ANANDA, WE NEED TO TALK.

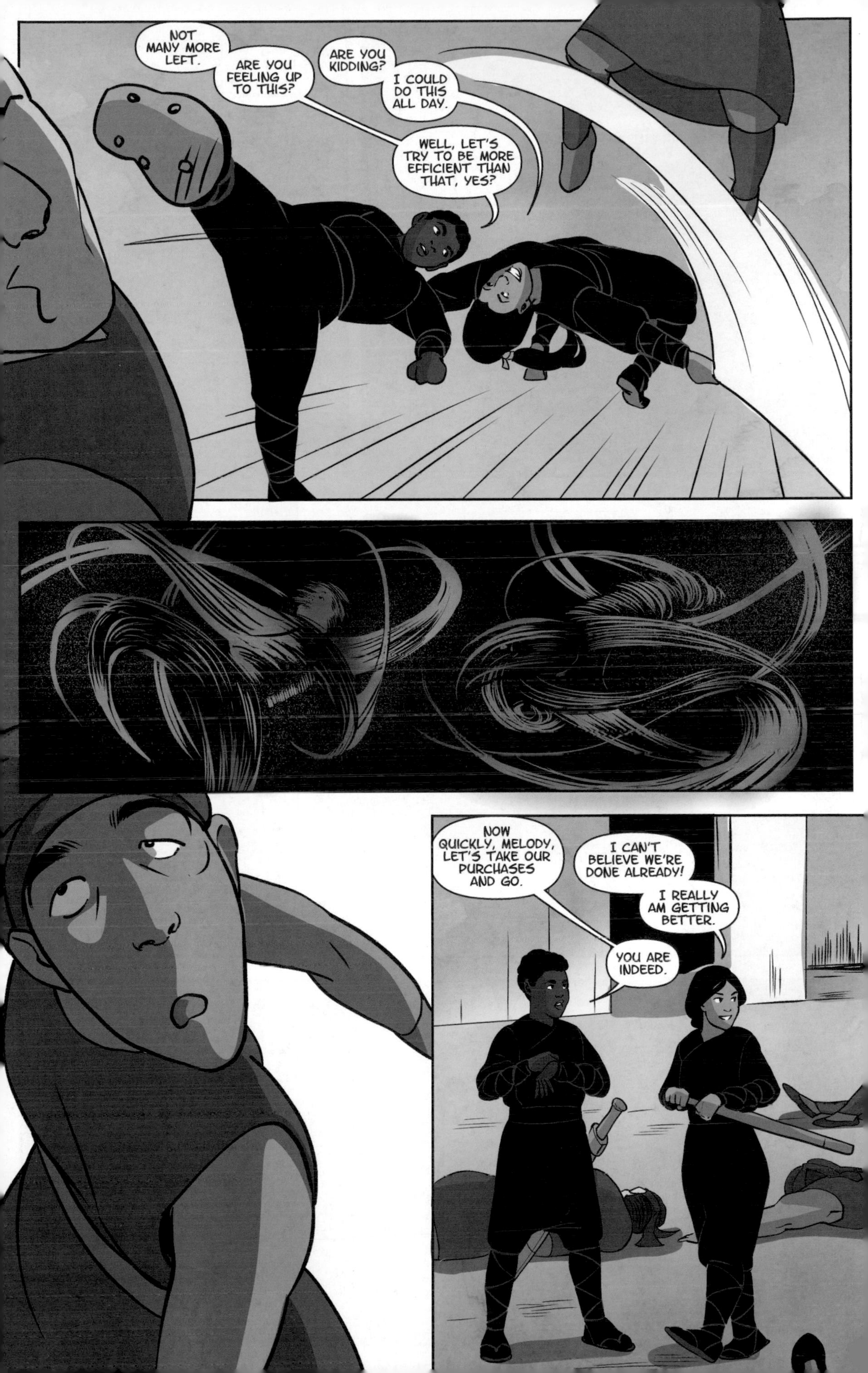
NOT MANY MORE LEFT.
ARE YOU FEELING UP TO THIS?
ARE YOU KIDDING?
I COULD DO THIS ALL DAY.
WELL, LET'S TRY TO BE MORE EFFICIENT THAN THAT, YES?
NOW QUICKLY, MELODY, LET'S TAKE OUR PURCHASES AND GO.
I CAN'T BELIEVE WE'RE DONE ALREADY!
I REALLY AM GETTING BETTER.
YOU ARE INDEED.

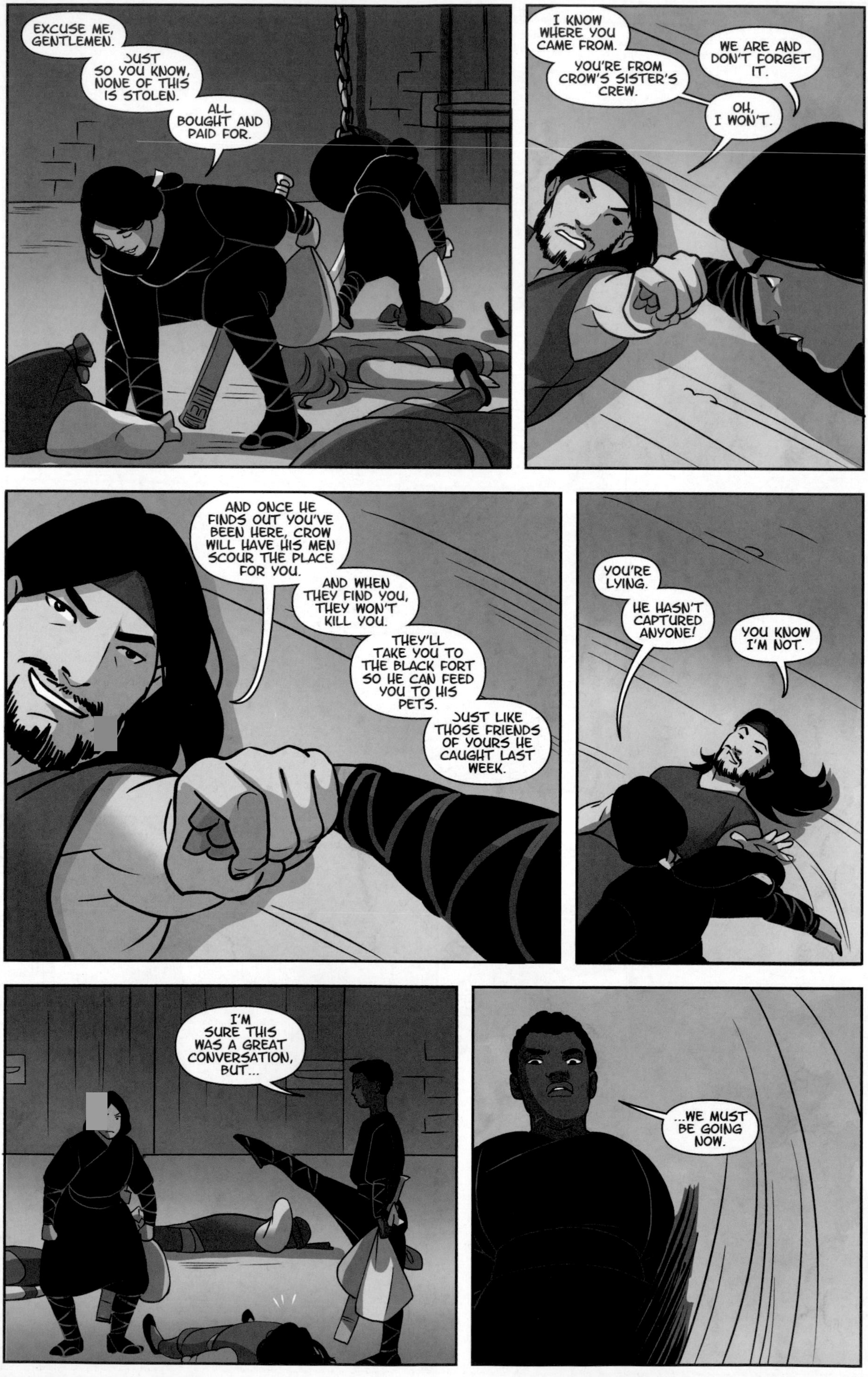
EXCUSE ME, GENTLEMEN.
JUST SO YOU KNOW, NONE OF THIS IS STOLEN.
ALL BOUGHT AND PAID FOR.
I KNOW WHERE YOU CAME FROM.
YOU'RE FROM CROW'S SISTER'S CREW.
WE ARE AND DON'T FORGET IT.
OH, I WON'T.
AND ONCE HE FINDS OUT YOU'VE BEEN HERE, CROW WILL HAVE HIS MEN SCOUR THE PLACE FOR YOU.
AND WHEN THEY FIND YOU, THEY WON'T KILL YOU.
THEY'LL TAKE YOU TO THE BLACK FORT SO HE CAN FEED YOU TO HIS PETS.
JUST LIKE THOSE FRIENDS OF YOURS HE CAUGHT LAST WEEK.
YOU'RE LYING.
HE HASN'T CAPTURED ANYONE!
YOU KNOW I'M NOT.
I'M SURE THIS WAS A GREAT CONVERSATION, BUT...
...WE MUST BE GOING NOW.

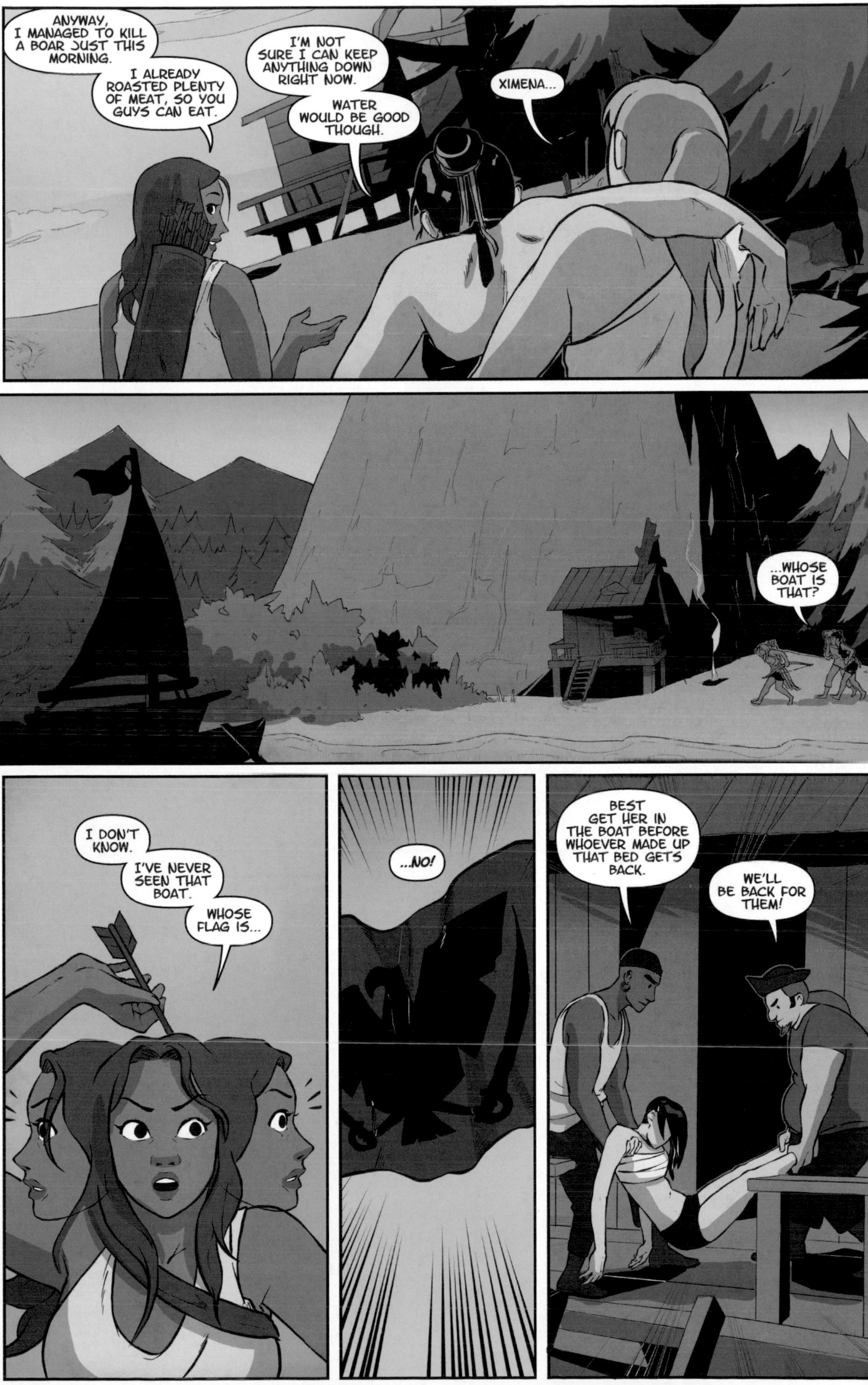

ANYWAY, I MANAGED TO KILL A BOAR JUST THIS MORNING.
I ALREADY ROASTED PLENTY OF MEAT, SO YOU GUYS CAN EAT.
I'M NOT SURE I CAN KEEP ANYTHING DOWN RIGHT NOW.
WATER WOULD BE GOOD THOUGH.
XIMENA...
...WHOSE BOAT IS THAT?
I DON'T KNOW.
I'VE NEVER SEEN THAT BOAT.
WHOSE FLAG IS...
...NO!
BEST GET HER IN THE BOAT BEFORE WHOEVER MADE UP THAT BED GETS BACK.
WE'LL BE BACK FOR THEM!

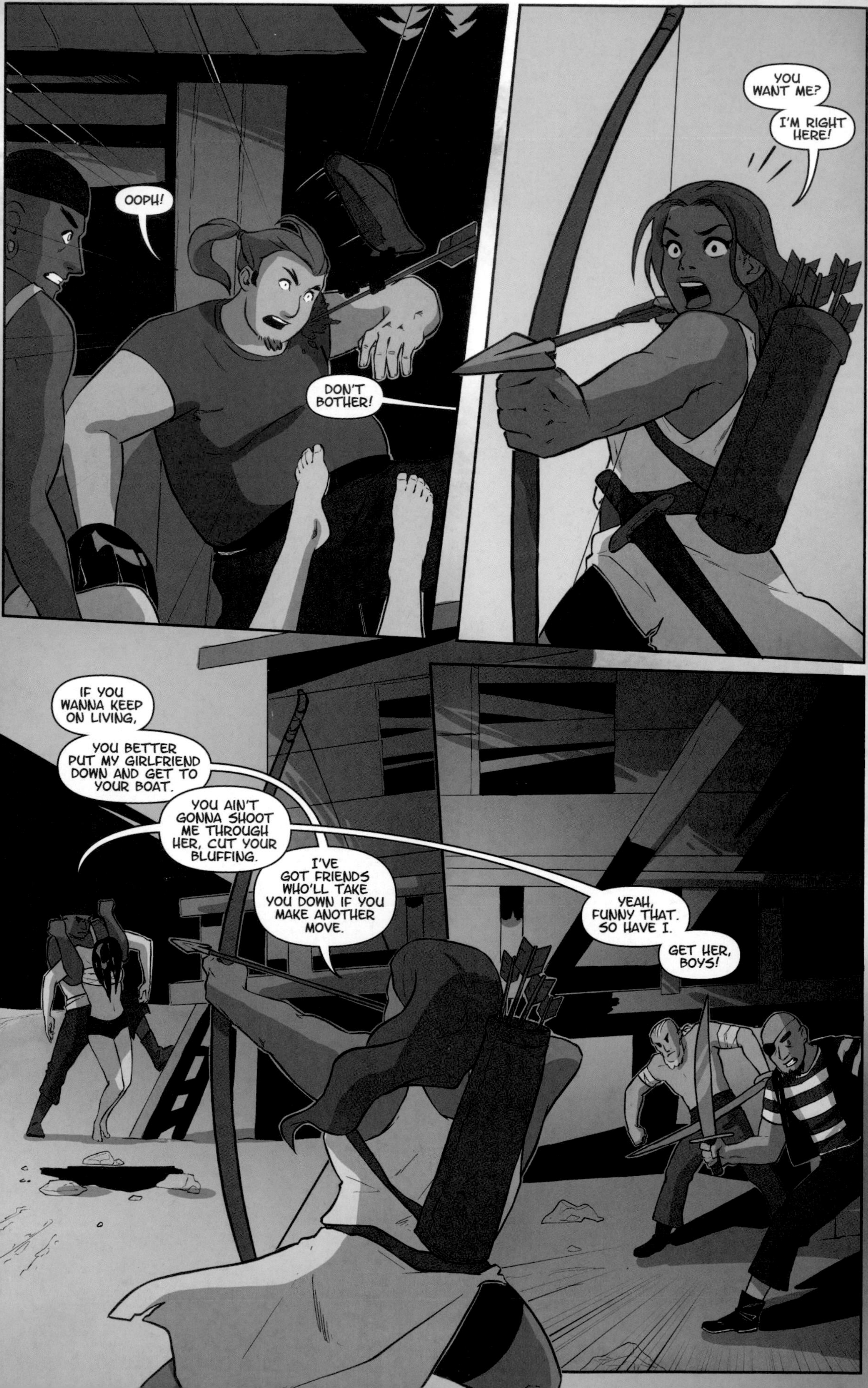
OOPH!
DON'T BOTHER!
YOU WANT ME?
I'M RIGHT HERE!
IF YOU WANNA KEEP ON LIVING,
YOU BETTER PUT MY GIRLFRIEND DOWN AND GET TO YOUR BOAT.
YOU AIN'T GONNA SHOOT ME THROUGH HER, CUT YOUR BLUFFING.
I'VE GOT FRIENDS WHO'LL TAKE YOU DOWN IF YOU MAKE ANOTHER MOVE.
YEAH, FUNNY THAT. SO HAVE I.
GET HER, BOYS!

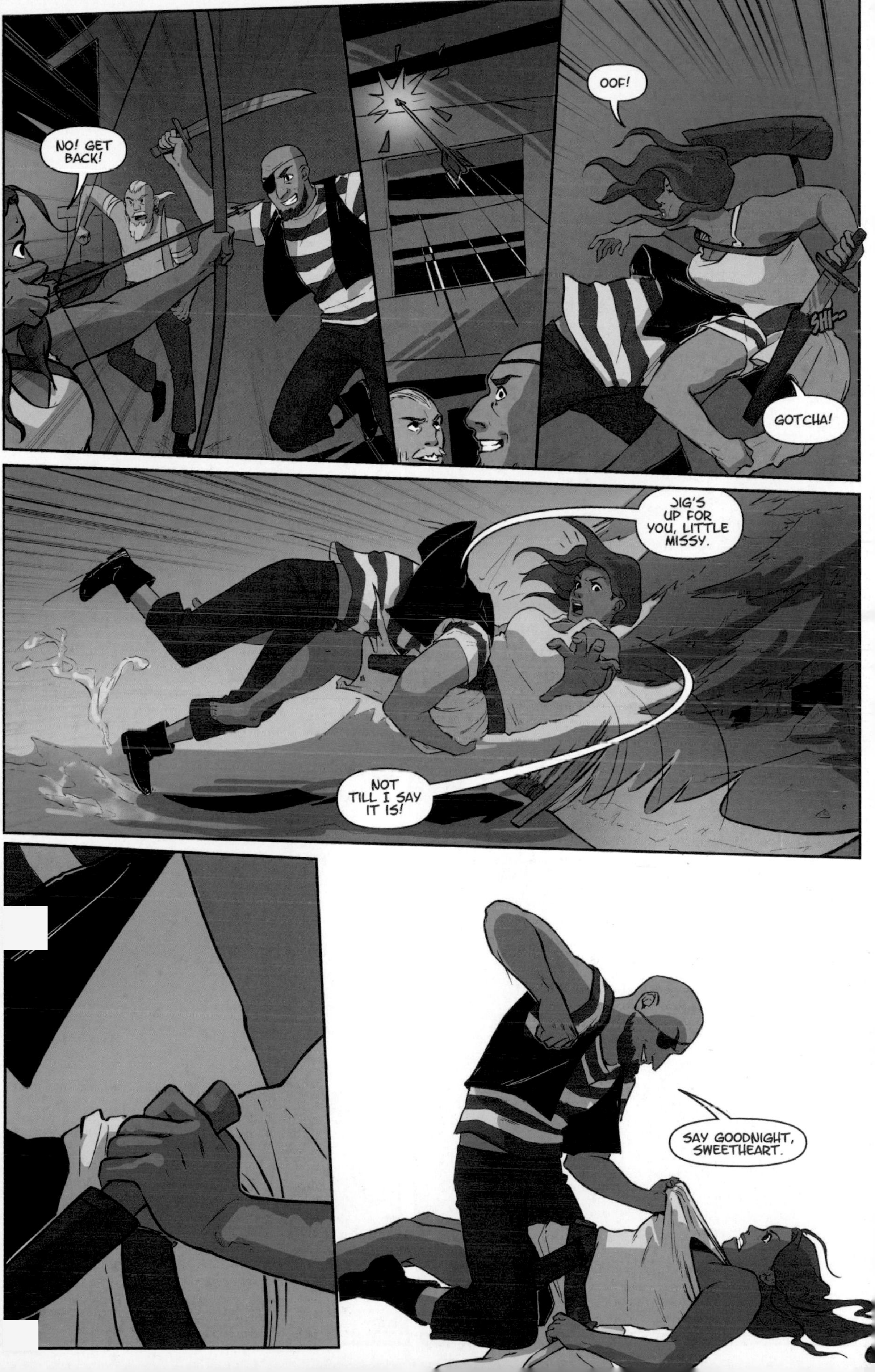
NO! GET BACK!
OOF!
SHH--
GOTCHA!
JIG'S UP FOR YOU, LITTLE MISSY.
NOT TILL I SAY IT IS!
SAY GOODNIGHT, SWEETHEART.

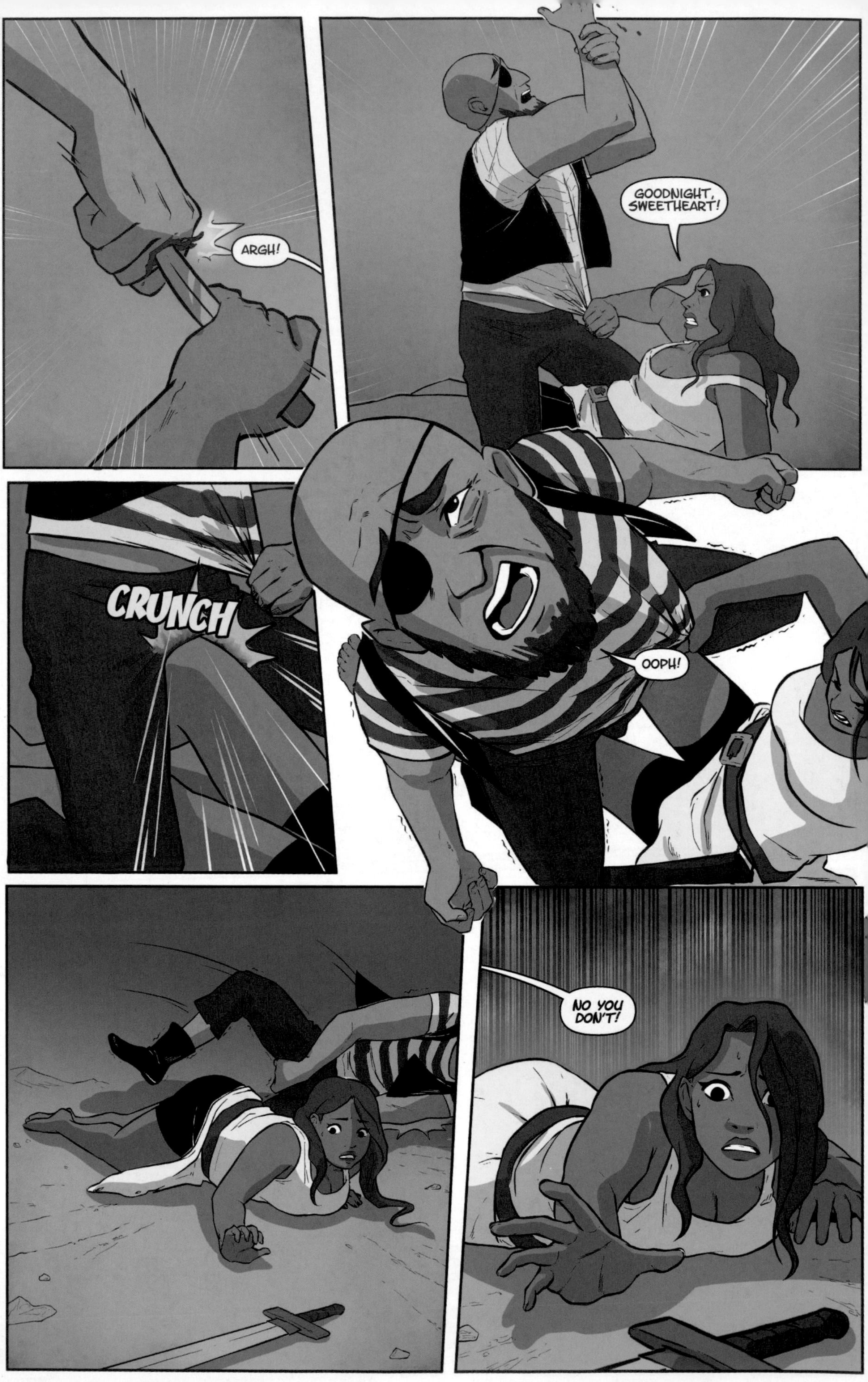
ARGH!
GOODNIGHT, SWEETHEART!
CRUNCH
OOPH!
NO YOU DON'T!

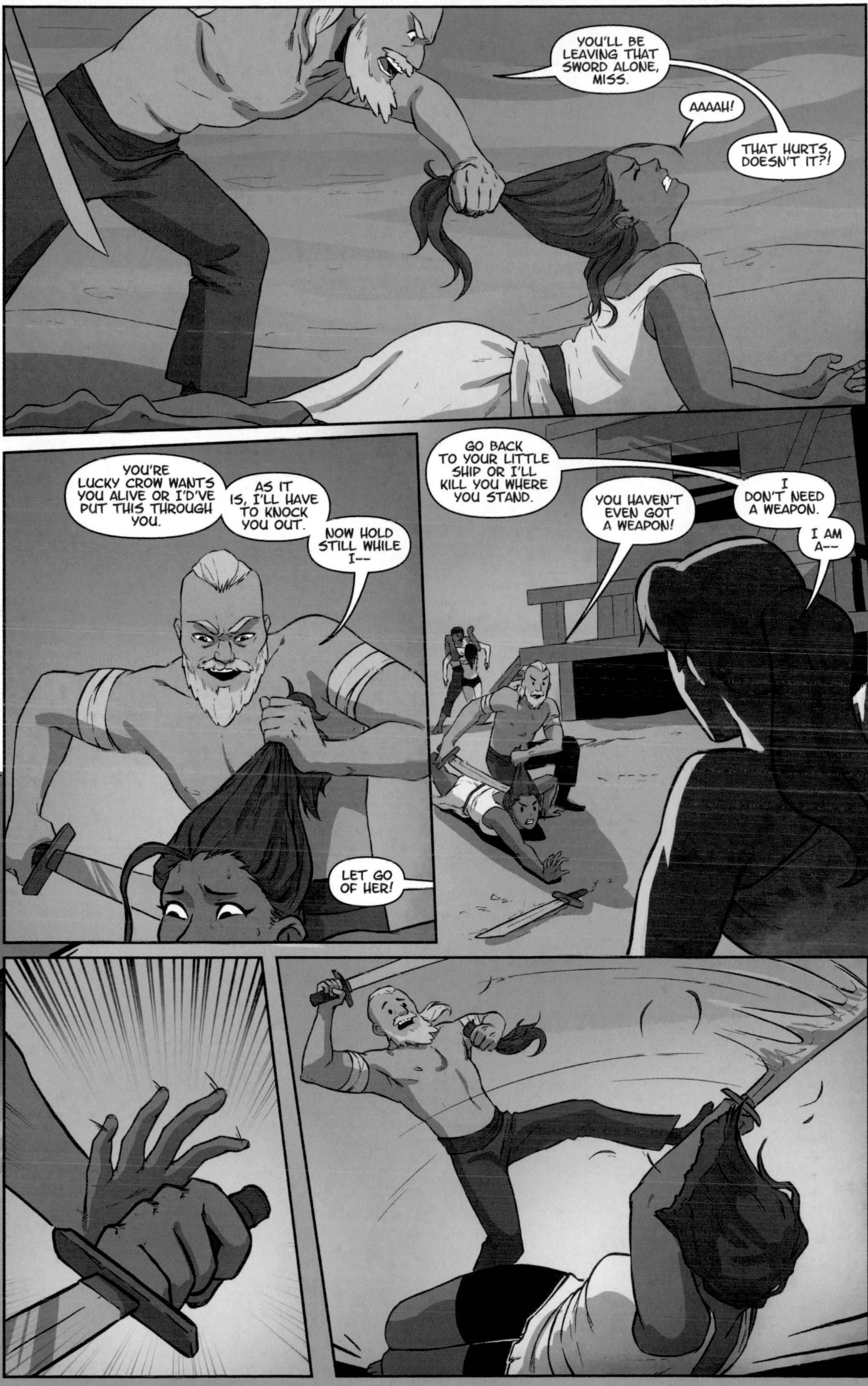
YOU'LL BE LEAVING THAT SWORD ALONE, MISS.
AAAAH!
THAT HURTS, DOESN'T IT?!
YOU'RE LUCKY CROW WANTS YOU ALIVE OR I'D'VE PUT THIS THROUGH YOU.
AS IT IS, I'LL HAVE TO KNOCK YOU OUT.
NOW HOLD STILL WHILE I--
LET GO OF HER!
GO BACK TO YOUR LITTLE SHIP OR I'LL KILL YOU WHERE YOU STAND.
YOU HAVEN'T EVEN GOT A WEAPON!
I DON'T NEED A WEAPON.
I AM A--

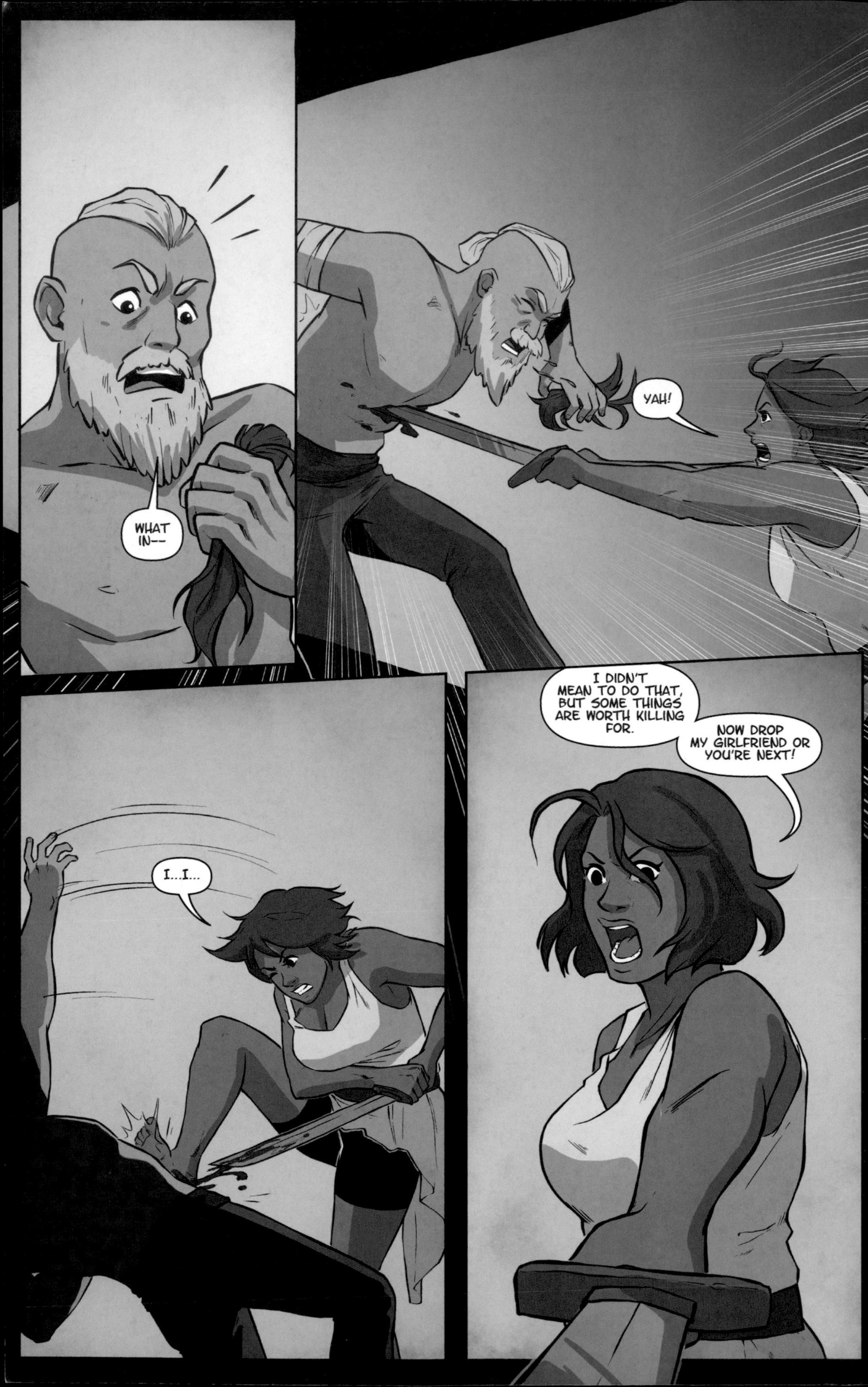
WHAT IN--
YAH!
I...I...
I DIDN'T MEAN TO DO THAT, BUT SOME THINGS ARE WORTH KILLING FOR.
NOW DROP MY GIRLFRIEND OR YOU'RE NEXT!

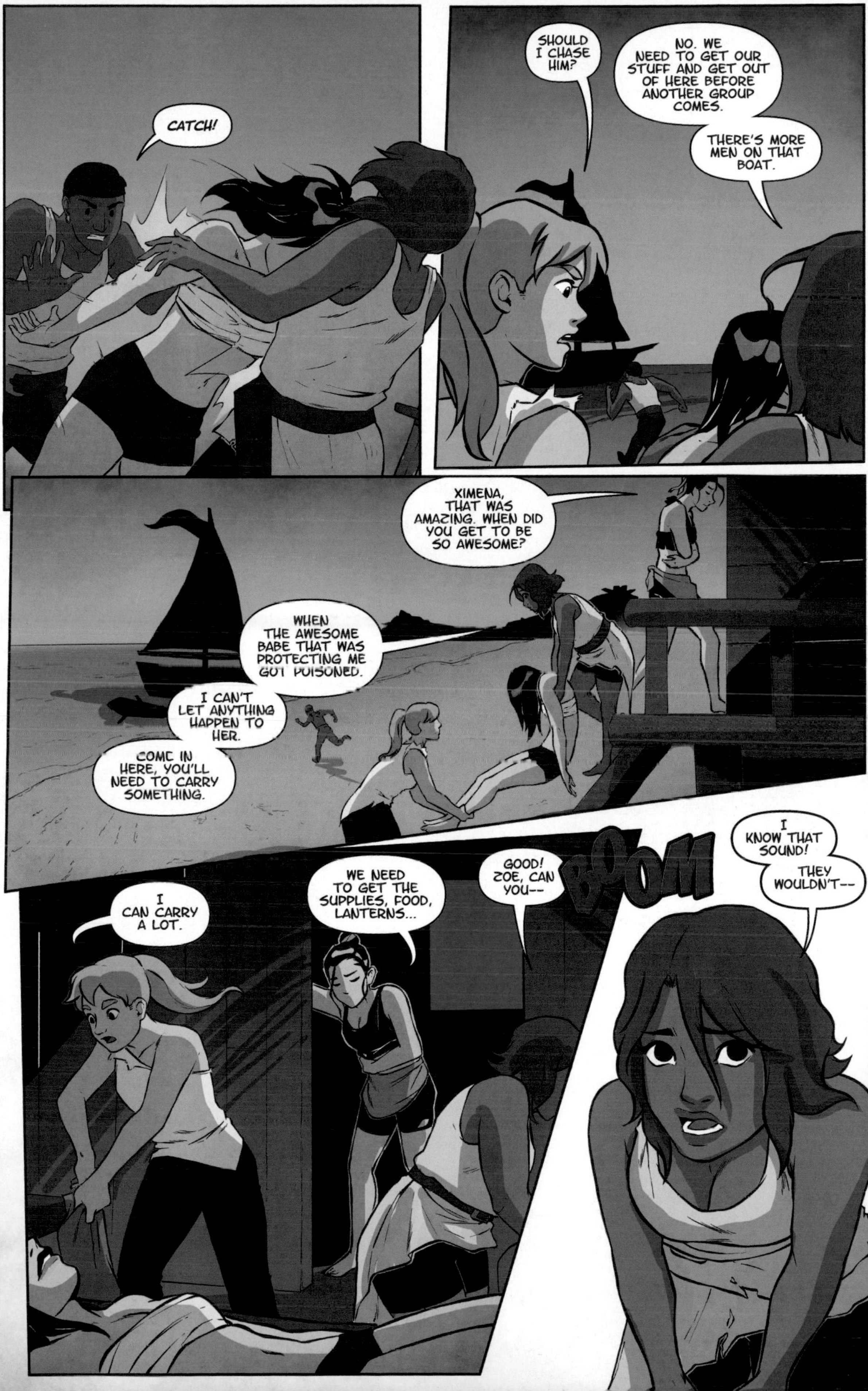
CATCH!
SHOULD I CHASE HIM?
NO. WE NEED TO GET OUR STUFF AND GET OUT OF HERE BEFORE ANOTHER GROUP COMES.
THERE'S MORE MEN ON THAT BOAT.
XIMENA, THAT WAS AMAZING. WHEN DID YOU GET TO BE SO AWESOME?
WHEN THE AWESOME BABE THAT WAS PROTECTING ME GOT POISONED.
I CAN'T LET ANYTHING HAPPEN TO HER.
COME IN HERE, YOU'LL NEED TO CARRY SOMETHING.
I CAN CARRY A LOT.
WE NEED TO GET THE SUPPLIES, FOOD, LANTERNS...
GOOD! ZOE, CAN YOU--
BOOM
I KNOW THAT SOUND!
THEY WOULDN'T--

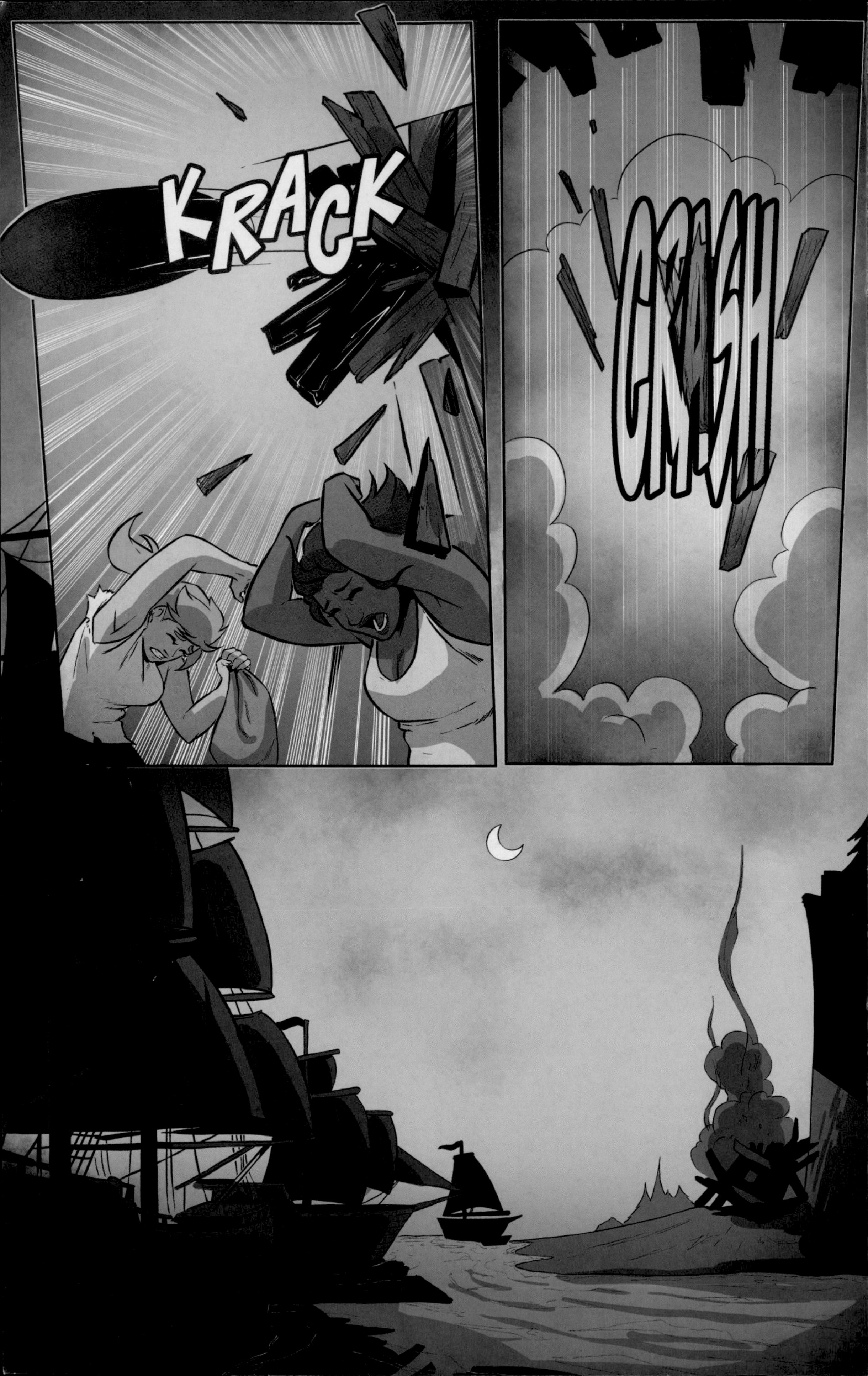
KRACK
CRASH

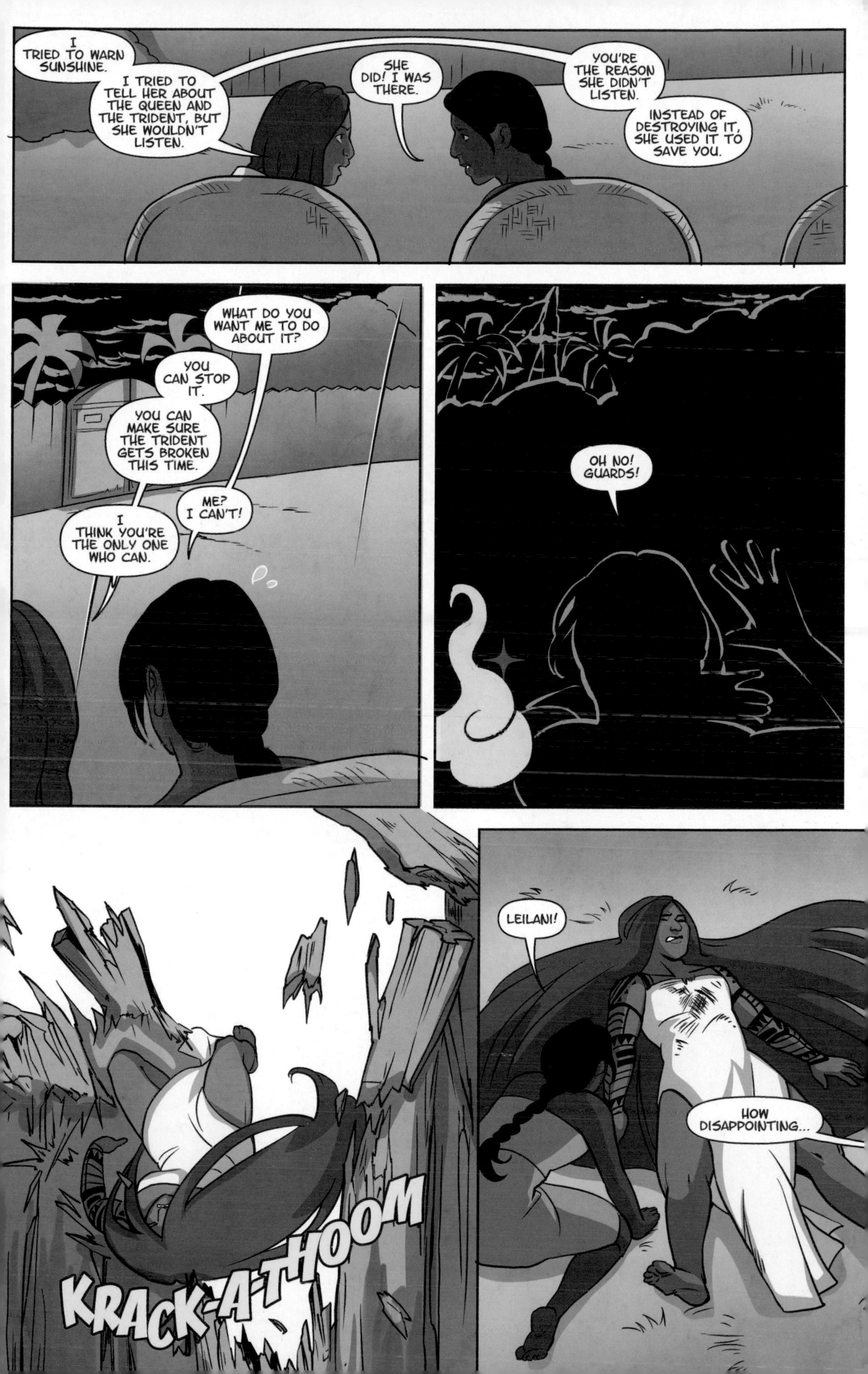
I TRIED TO WARN SUNSHINE.
I TRIED TO TELL HER ABOUT THE QUEEN AND THE TRIDENT, BUT SHE WOULDN'T LISTEN.
SHE DID! I WAS THERE.
YOU'RE THE REASON SHE DIDN'T LISTEN.
INSTEAD OF DESTROYING IT, SHE USED IT TO SAVE YOU.
WHAT DO YOU WANT ME TO DO ABOUT IT?
YOU CAN STOP IT.
YOU CAN MAKE SURE THE TRIDENT GETS BROKEN THIS TIME.
ME? I CAN'T!
I THINK YOU'RE THE ONLY ONE WHO CAN.
OH NO! GUARDS!
KRACK-A-THOOM
LEILANI!
HOW DISAPPOINTING...

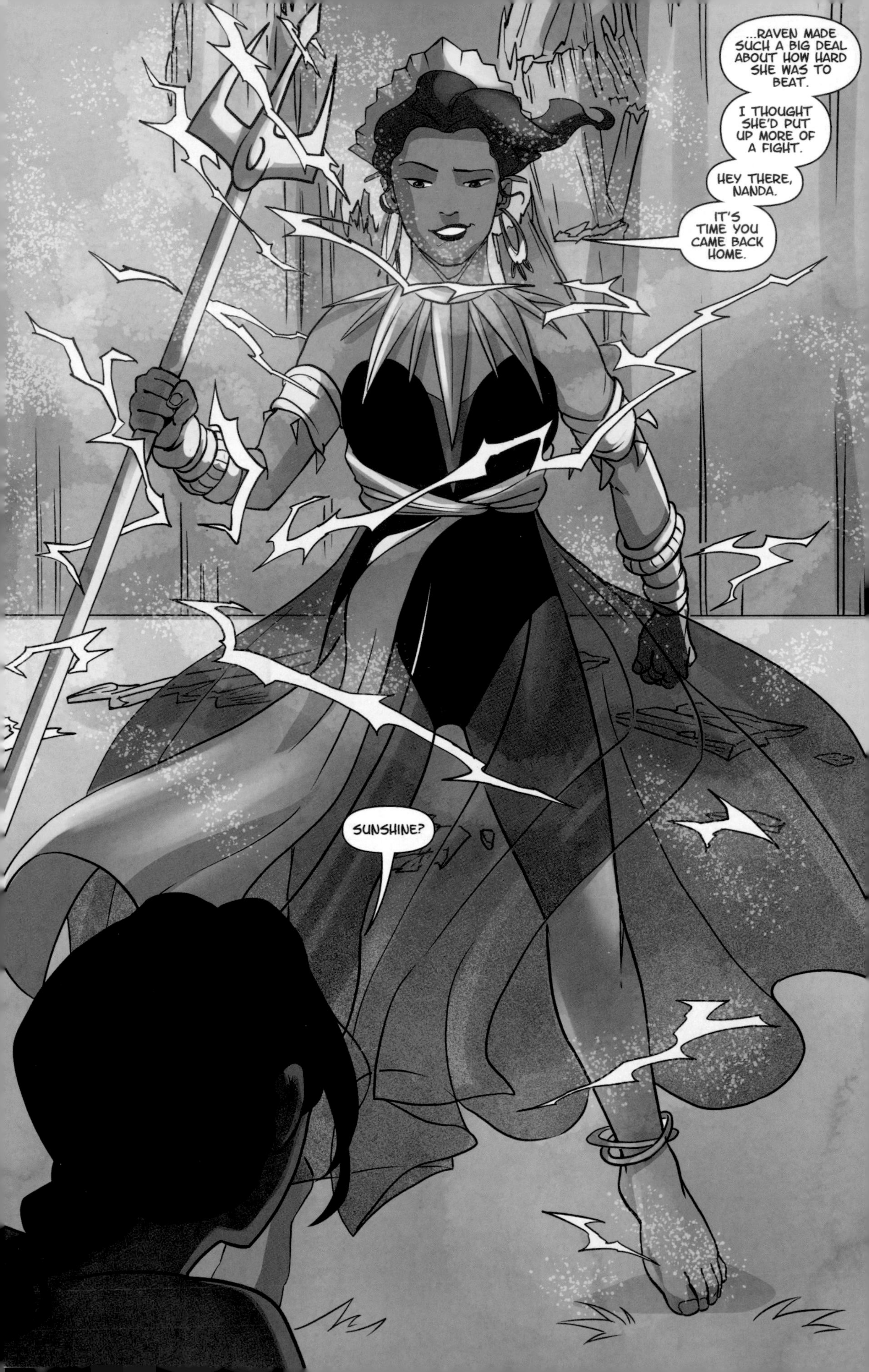
...RAVEN MADE SUCH A BIG DEAL ABOUT HOW HARD SHE WAS TO BEAT.
I THOUGHT SHE'D PUT UP MORE OF A FIGHT.
HEY THERE, NANDA.
IT'S TIME YOU CAME BACK HOME.
SUNSHINE?

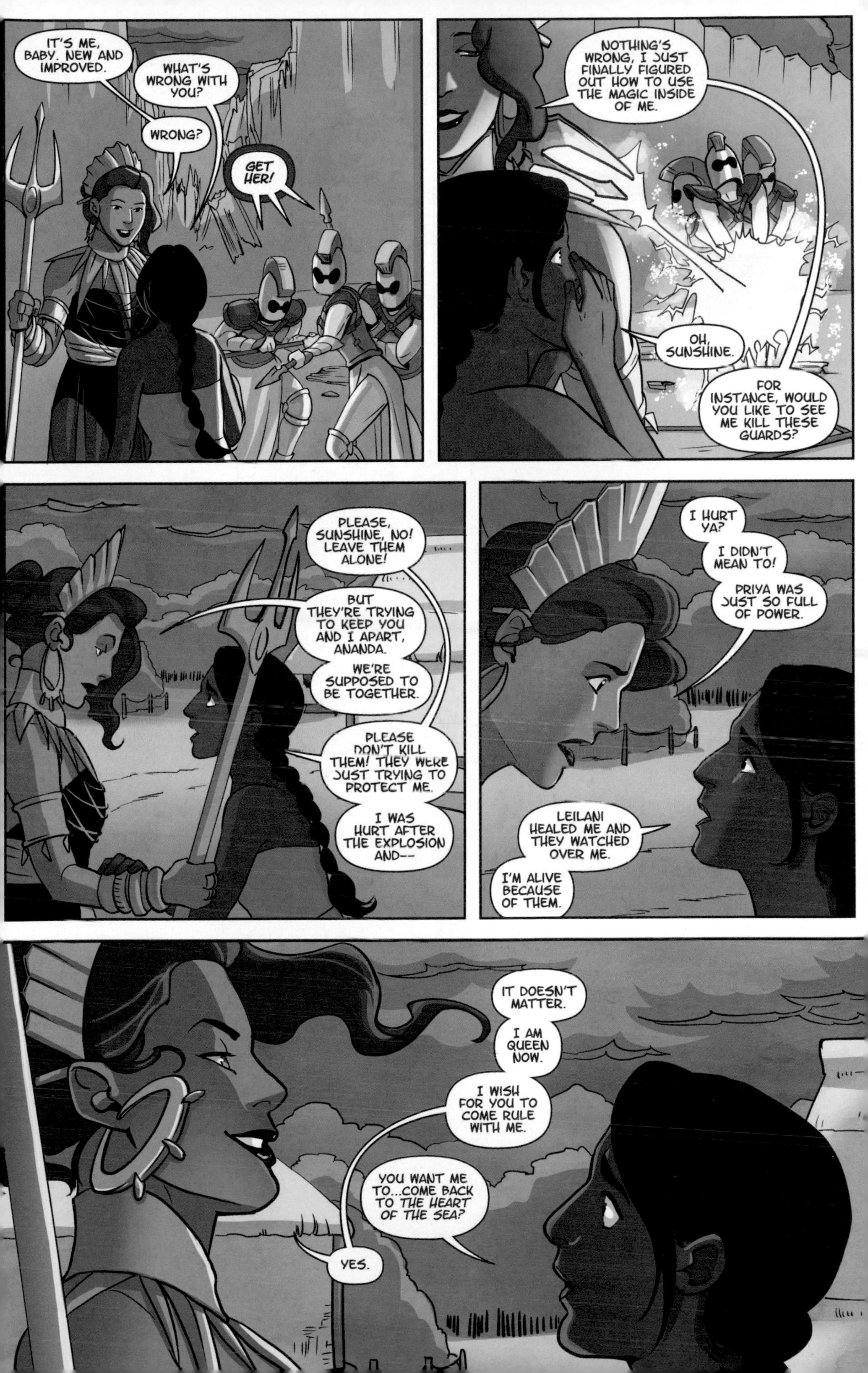
IT'S ME, BABY. NEW AND IMPROVED.
WHAT'S WRONG WITH YOU?
WRONG?
GET HER!
NOTHING'S WRONG, I JUST FINALLY FIGURED OUT HOW TO USE THE MAGIC INSIDE OF ME.
OH, SUNSHINE.
FOR INSTANCE, WOULD YOU LIKE TO SEE ME KILL THESE GUARDS?
PLEASE, SUNSHINE, NO! LEAVE THEM ALONE!
BUT THEY'RE TRYING TO KEEP YOU AND I APART, ANANDA.
WE'RE SUPPOSED TO BE TOGETHER.
PLEASE DON'T KILL THEM! THEY WERE JUST TRYING TO PROTECT ME.
I WAS HURT AFTER THE EXPLOSION AND--
I HURT YA?
I DIDN'T MEAN TO!
PRIYA WAS JUST SO FULL OF POWER.
LEILANI HEALED ME AND THEY WATCHED OVER ME.
I'M ALIVE BECAUSE OF THEM.
IT DOESN'T MATTER.
I AM QUEEN NOW.
I WISH FOR YOU TO COME RULE WITH ME.
YOU WANT ME TO...COME BACK TO THE HEART OF THE SEA?
YES.

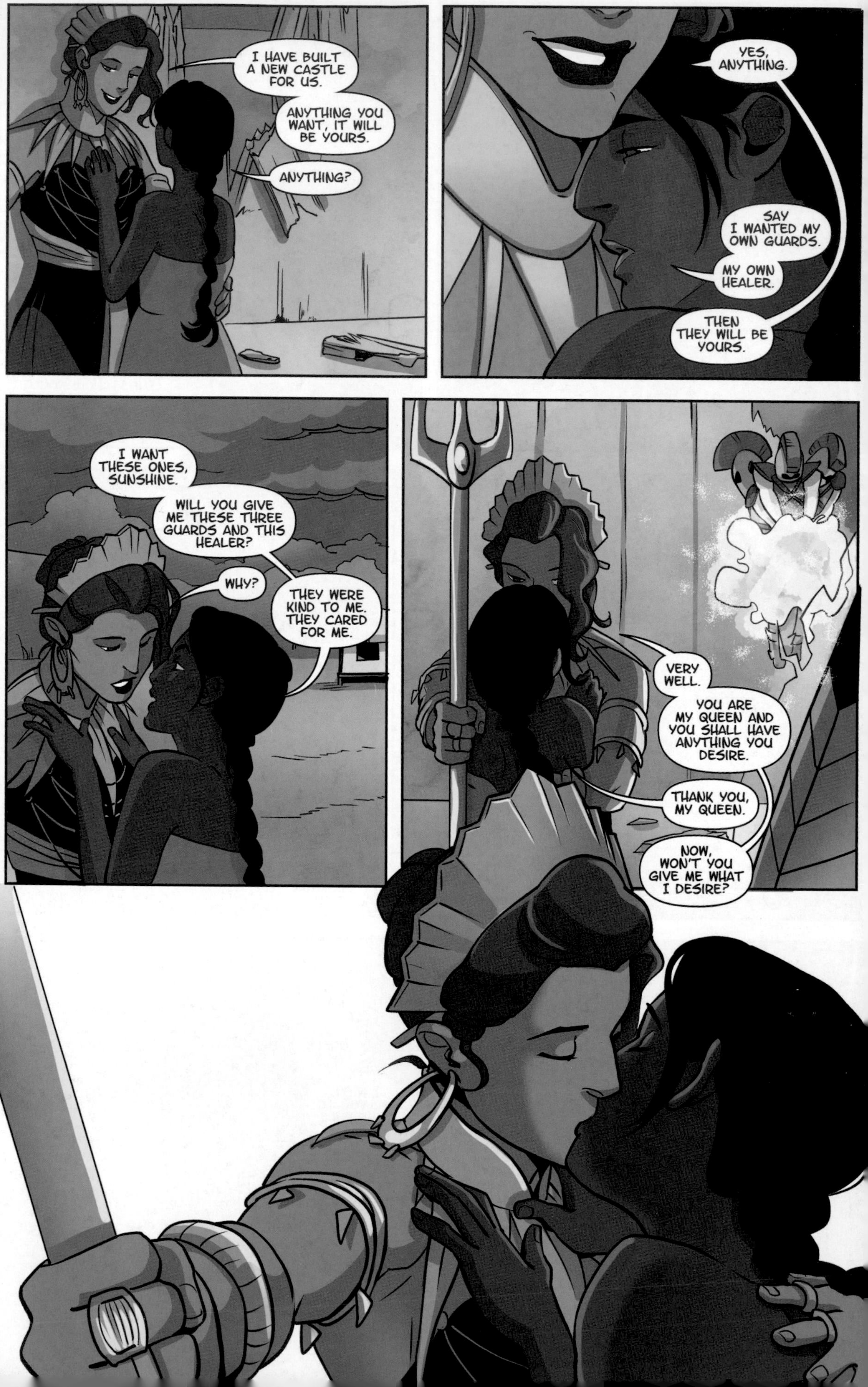
I HAVE BUILT A NEW CASTLE FOR US.
ANYTHING YOU WANT, IT WILL BE YOURS.
ANYTHING?
YES, ANYTHING.
SAY I WANTED MY OWN GUARDS.
MY OWN HEALER.
THEN THEY WILL BE YOURS.
I WANT THESE ONES, SUNSHINE.
WILL YOU GIVE ME THESE THREE GUARDS AND THIS HEALER?
WHY?
THEY WERE KIND TO ME. THEY CARED FOR ME.
VERY WELL.
YOU ARE MY QUEEN AND YOU SHALL HAVE ANYTHING YOU DESIRE.
THANK YOU, MY QUEEN.
NOW, WON'T YOU GIVE ME WHAT I DESIRE?

Issue 8
Page 17 Progression

Page 17:

Panel 1: The backup pirate has ahold of Ximena by her hair, pulling her back away from the sword.

BACK UP PIRATE
You'll be leaving that sword alone, miss.

XIMENA
Aaaah!

BACK UP PIRATE
That hurts, doesn't it?!

Panel 2: The backup pirate is pulling out his own sword with his free hand as he yanks Ximena's hair with the other.

BACK UP PIRATE
You're lucky Crow wants you alive or I'dve put this through you. As it is, I'll have to knock you out.

BACK UP PIRATE
Now hold still while I—

HELENA (OFF PANEL)
Let go of her!

Panel 3: Helena stands on her own. She left Zoe back down the beach. She doesn't have a weapon. She just glares at them.

HELENA
Go back to your little ship or I'll kill you where you stand.

SHIELDED PIRATE
You haven't even got a weapon!

HELENA
I don't need a weapon. I am a—

Panel 4: Ximena's hand grabs the sword.

Panel 5: Ximena spins on the ground, swinging her sword wildly.

Page 17 Final Inks

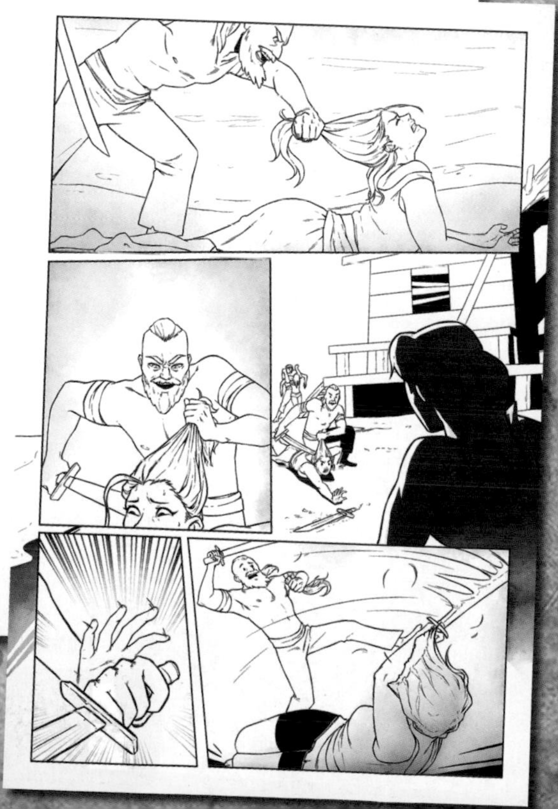

Page 17 Pencils

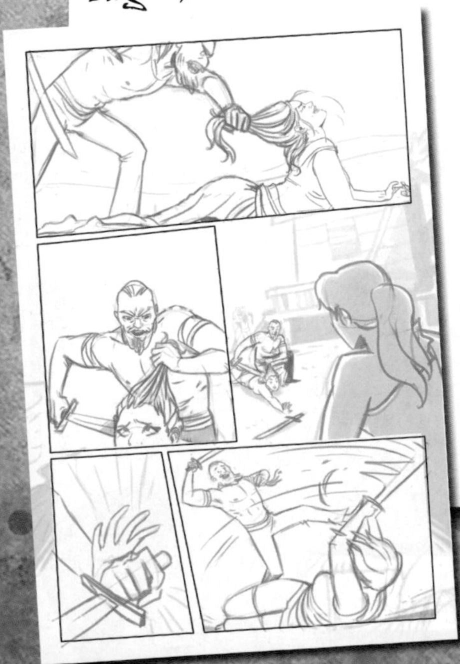

Issue 8
Page 24 Progression

Page 24:

Panel 1: Sunshine holds Ananda close to her.

SUNSHINE
I have built a new castle for us.

SUNSHINE
Anything you want, it will be yours.

ANANDA
Anything?

Panel 2: Sunshine smiles. Ananda cuddles up to her.

SUNSHINE
Yes, anything.

ANANDA
Say I wanted my own guards. My own healer.

SUNSHINE
Then they will be yours.

Panel 3: Ananda gets within kissing distance of Sunshine.

ANANDA
I want these ones, Sunshine. Will you give me these three guards and this healer?

SUNSHINE
Why?

ANANDA
They were kind to me. They cared for me.

Panel 4: Sunshine waves her trident. The guards and Leilani begin to float.

SUNSHINE
Very well. You are my Queen and you shall have anything you desire.

ANANDA
Thank you, my queen.

SUNSHINE
Now, won't you give me what I desire?

Panel 5: Sunshine and Ananda kiss.

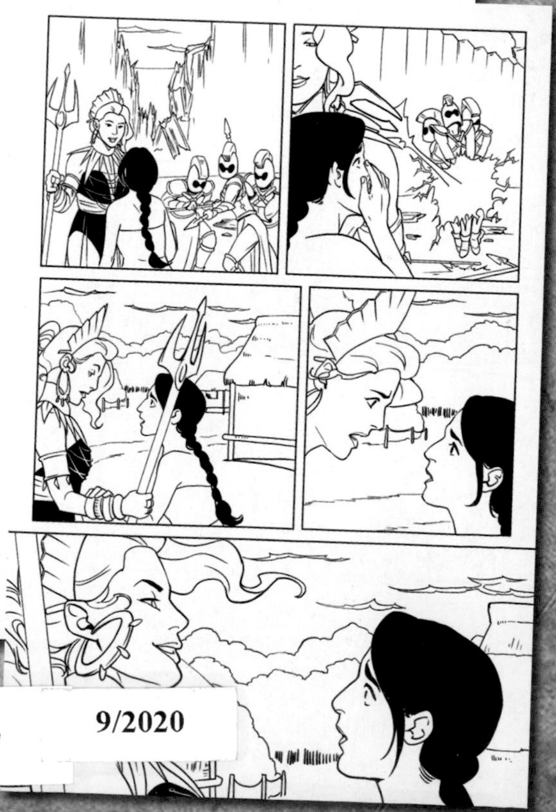
Page 24 Final Inks

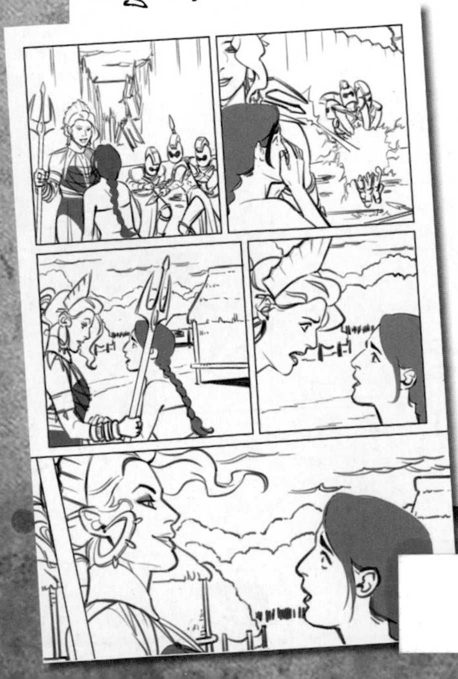
Page 24 Pencils